A Scot Is Not Enough

"You tempt me in the best and worst of ways, Miss MacDonald."

Of all the women to crave, he'd chosen her—a seductive Jacobite with a worthy heart.

"The fireworks," she whispered. "Their light is fading."

He consumed the shadow between her small breasts. Asking to see them wouldn't do, not with the considerable respect his soul was building for this woman. But he wanted—needed—something to sate his carnal nature.

His gaze ascended to her silken collarbone and the pale skin covering it.

"Your shoulder," he demanded gruffly. "I want to see it."

Knowing glittered in hazel eyes.

"Ask for it."

Jagged air left his lungs. Power was hers and he ceded all of it.

"Would you . . . please . . . uncover your shoulder?"

The corners of her mouth curled up.

"Uncover it yourself."

Also by Gina Conkle

A Scot Is Not Enough

A SCOTTISH TREASURES NOVEL

GINA CONKLE

AVONBOOKS

An Imprint of HarperCollinsPublishers

A SCOT IS NOT ENOUGH. Copyright © 2022 by Gina Conkle. All rights reserved. Printed in the United States of America. No part of this book may be used or reproduced in any manner whatsoever without written permission except in the case of brief quotations embodied in critical articles and reviews. For information, address HarperCollins Publishers, 195 Broadway, New York, NY 10007.

First Avon Books mass market printing: April 2022

Print Edition ISBN: 978-0-06-299900-9
Digital Edition ISBN: 978-0-06-299896-5

Cover design by Patricia Barrow
Cover illustration by Gene Mollica Studio, LLC

Avon, Avon & logo, and Avon Books & logo are registered trademarks of HarperCollins Publishers in the United States of America and other countries.

HarperCollins is a registered trademark of HarperCollins Publishers in the United States of America and other countries.

FIRST EDITION

Printed in Lithuania

22 23 24 25 26 SB 10 9 8 7 6 5 4 3 2 1

*This book is dedicated to two women with huge
hearts who have supported historical romance:
Monique Daoust and Kimberly Rocha.*

*Monique is no longer with us, but she left
an indelible impression on many authors'
lives. This, I hope, honors her memory.*

*Kimberly, you are a vibrant presence in the romance
world. Thank you for what you do for historical
romance. Keep your flame burning bright!*

A Scot Is Not Enough

Chapter One

September 1753

$\mathcal{L}$aw and disorder collided brilliantly at Bow Street, an entertainment of human nature, drawing merchants and matrons alike. They crammed the gallery, chewing gossip like candy, the courtroom their circus, the victims and the accused their performers. A motley mix of humanity, all of them.

Except for her. The clever blonde.

She graced the gallery, a wash of silk and sex. A woman unescorted with lips painted an ungovernable shade of red. Her subtle smirk was fine art and her intelligence a sonata. She caught every one of the magistrate's witticisms, if one accepted her musical laugh as evidence. Mr. Fielding was, at heart, a writer. What else were they good for except crafting quips? Though one had to be quick to catch them. Courtroom observers sometimes scratched their heads at Fielding's brisk commentaries. Not the blonde. She took notes, an interesting habit. And he,

Alexander Sloane, Undersecretary to the Undersecretary of the Duke of Newcastle (a mouthful, that!), took note of her.

The elegant woman made his assignment—tracking Bow Street's sudden influx of money—less dreary.

Fielding considered him a nuisance; the thief takers considered him a spy.

He was both.

Not a popular position to be in.

He slipped away as the courtroom proceedings ended, intent on taking himself to his room at the White Hart on King Street to work on his other assignment—studying a mysterious Jacobite ledger. Dinner and a pint while he deciphered smudged columns and coded entries would be his entertainment. Both tasks spanned a month or two, depending on the duke's whim. The pressure was immense. Reporting directly to His Grace allowed no margin for error.

Walking through Bow Street's hallways, he fed on the challenge. Precision ran in his veins. The natural world was a messy place, but numbers were truth in its purest form and corralling them a joy.

Before he'd departed for Bow Street, the duke had handed over the Jacobite ledger. *"Unravel this, Mr. Sloane, and we can talk about your appointment."*

Court of the Exchequer. To be a judge in the financial courts, and he, Baron Sloane.

The position wouldn't make him a peer, but the centuries-old honorific quickened his step through a private doorway to a realm of leather and tallow candles. Fielding's office. The Bow Street ledger waited by a puddle of wax on the magistrate's desk, a folded copy of *The Covent-Garden Journal* on top of it.

He slid the book off the desk, strode to the private entrance, and reached for the door.

"Mr. Sloane. Just the man I was looking for."

Hand falling to his side, Alexander turned and waited, rigid as a duke's man should. Calculation sparked in the magistrate's eyes. Fielding closed the main door, shutting off public noise splashing into the room.

The quiet . . . there was dread in it.

Fielding never met with him privately.

"How may I be of assistance?"

The magistrate limped by on gout-riddled feet. "I have a task for you."

"More expenditures to tally?"

"No. I need you to follow a woman."

"A woman?"

"Yes, the petticoated variety. Two arms, two legs, two breasts. Commonly considered the gentler sex."

"I am aware," he said aridly.

The magistrate landed in his chair, his black robes billowing. "It's a simple job. Keep your distance, take notes on her day-to-day whereabouts, and report your findings directly to me." Fielding's gaze knifed him. "But no one else can know."

Not even the duke was the warning, hanging as sharp as a gleaming sword over Alexander's head. A cold "damned if you do, damned if you don't" chill came with it.

He tucked the ledger tightly under his arm. "I gather the woman in question is not the average London criminal."

"Neither average nor a criminal. She is, however, a known Jacobite sympathizer."

"A scurrilous lot."

The Jacobite ledger with its fanciful code names came to mind. Lady Pink was one, Lord Blue another. The Uprising of '45 had ended seven years ago. Any rebels who'd survived the war had been shot, hanged, or fled. Only the most brazen—or foolish— would spawn trouble in London. In either case, he was ill-equipped to track them.

"I appreciate the vote of confidence, sir, but I am not a thief taker."

"Which makes you perfect for the job." Fielding rummaged through ledgers. "Miss MacDonald knows them all . . . probably better than their mothers," he muttered in a voice cracking from ill health.

The magistrate was an aging crow of a man. Cold creatures, crows, as canny as they were destructive. They collected shiny things, as much to mark their territory as to distract. Could be why Fielding didn't want him underfoot. A veneer of corruption smeared Bow Street, which was the other reason he was here. The latest claim was the magistrate wrote under a pseudonym, instigating the Paper War between *The Covent-Garden Journal* and Grub Street newspapers all in the name of selling his books.

Not illegal, but far from upstanding.

"Sir, my purpose here is to oversee your use of the crown's funds."

"For law and order, Mr. Sloane." Fielding's voice rose with righteous fervor. "And there is no better way to see justice done than to be part of it."

He marched to the desk. "I must vigorously object. I serve—"

"Object to your heart's content, but imagine how pleased His Grace will be when I tell him the fine work you've done on behalf of the crown." Fielding opened a ledger and thumbed through its pages. "Might hasten the path to your next position."

Baron of the Exchequer. Anger kindled, from the tight spot he was in and from the black-robed crow who pinned him there.

"That's extortion."

"It's following a woman. How hard can that be?"

"I don't care for your methods."

Fielding was unmoved, his eyes and his robes wrinkled. Probably his soul too. His desk was a hodgepodge of account books, records of known criminals and suspected criminals. Alexander chafed at the taint placed on the latter cohort. Mere hearsay landed a person in the books. Once in, the entries became ruthless and detailed, assuming guilt. Ledgers crammed the shelves, all with hasty sketches next to lists of habits, unique attributes, and known associates. Fielding slid one of those ledgers forward.

"Report her activities to me once a week, and when the time comes, I shall report your excellent work to the duke."

Alexander met the magistrate's cold stare. "What are you looking for? If the woman is not a criminal, why is she in your books?"

"Ah, yes, my ledgers." Fielding reached for a quill. "We both know you don't agree with my methods. If my assumptions about this woman are incorrect, this is your chance to prove me wrong."

A trap neatly set.

Fingers drumming the account book under his arm, Alexander looked down. Fine-boned features smirked from the page. The clever blonde. Her name was Miss Cecelia MacDonald. The artist paid fair tribute. An arrow-straight nose with delicate nostrils and eyes sparkling and mischievous. She was texture in a gray city, adventure waiting to happen. Farther down was her small-bosomed cleavage. His gaze clung to that fascinating indent, imagining what the artist couldn't capture.

"I wouldn't know what to do with this woman." Alexander groaned. Good Lord, his wits had fled him. "Correction. I know what to do with a woman. But this"—he waved a hand over the page—"is a delicate matter."

"Miss MacDonald is hardly delicate. She is a demirep."

"A demirep?"

"A woman who, I collect, intrigues every man she likes, under the name and appearance of virtue, yet is what everybody knows her to be but what nobody calls her."

"There is no law against uncertain virtue."

"Order is the foundation of any good society, and ambiguity the devil's device." Fielding dipped his quill in the inkwell with a decisive *clink*. "You would do well to remember that."

Alexander touched the scurrilous sketch, a haze seeping into his bones. In London, a thin stratum of the fair sex lived free of propriety's constraints. Women uncontained by families. Women who left more questions than answers in their wake, which made them provocative, and Bow Street counted Miss MacDonald in their number.

A woman of certain freedoms.

Beyond the magistrate's window, bright bonnets and staid tricorns bobbed. Coats were clasped against crisp September air, smiling faces above them. Some would seek home and hearth, while others would seek Covent Garden's lush entertainments. A driven man, Alexander had achieved much in his twenty-nine years; he would achieve a great deal more before he left Bow Street. He allowed no time for rampant pleasures.

"There she is," Fielding said. "Your quarry."

Duty didn't draw Alexander forward. Temptation did.

Cool air leeched, glass to skin. The window was a thin barrier to the play of life on the street. Miss MacDonald glittered, a diamond among the drab. Her incandescent smile was a gift bestowed on two men dancing attendance, tradesmen by the look of their shoes and coats. What an interesting world she inhabited. Prettiness and charm stamped her calling card.

What harm was there in following her?

Behind him, the window reflected a watery version of Fielding, his bewigged head bent, his hand gripping a quill that scratched paper with furious speed.

"Mr. Sloane . . ."

"Yes?"

"Do not show your face in my chambers until Wednesday next." More quill scratches. "And when you do, you'd better have something interesting to report."

Alexander's grim smile showed in the glass. Fielding had him neatly cornered. There'd be no refusing the magistrate, but if he played his cards right, this could end well. *Very well.*

Outside Miss MacDonald laughed, the faint notes calling him.

A week investigating her. A chase, as it were.

Hair on his arms pricked. This was . . . primal. He, the hunter, and she his prey.

"Leave the ledger," Fielding droned. "You won't need it."

Alexander's eyes were on the world outside, the account book somehow finding the desk. His lovely quarry raised her hood, a gentle dismissal for her male audience.

Excitement caught fire in his veins. His hunt had begun.

Chapter Two

Fletcher's House of Corsets and Stays was a temple of feminine wantonness. Red-and-white-striped walls, white shelves delicately chipped, and reverent shoppers searching for sublime undergarments in a cloud of rosewater perfume. Women of modest means flocked daily to the shop, handing over hard-earned silver to buy Fletcher House creations.

Cecelia twirled a pretty pink ribbon lacing jet-black stays.

A breath of femininity, that ribbon. Transformative.

Drab linen stays were *de rigueur*, the uniform of maids, matrons, grocers' and drapers' wives, housekeepers, and the like. A travesty the Fletcher sisters, Mary and Margaret, had set out to change.

Harlots wore bright stays and ladies of the highest social circles wore colorful corsets—what did *that* mean?

Cecelia smirked. *A question to be answered another time.*

She staked a spot at the window. On one side of the display shelf, stays fanned in a rainbow of color, and matched stockings fanned on the other. She picked up vermillion stays.

"Cecelia." Mary Fletcher approached, arms out to hug her.

"Don't." She dipped a formal curtsey.

Brow puzzling, Mary did the same. "Why are we curtseying?"

"Because I'm being followed."

Quick knowledge washed Mary. A graceful beauty of twenty-nine years, her intelligent gray eyes adjusted to subterfuge the way cats' eyes adjusted to the dark. Hands folding primly, she played the attentive shopkeeper. Not for a second did she remove her gaze from Cecelia and check the street outside her window.

"The man across the street," Mary said.

"How ever did you guess?"

"Because no man is that interested in a chandler shop."

Cecelia giggled while studying a seam. "Rather intent, isn't he? One might think he's hunting for the Holy Grail in that window."

"Except he's hunting you."

Her stomach quivered. Mary's warning was uttered in a genteel Edinburgh accent with a back-of-the-mouth treatment of each word. Her accent was smooth as whisky while Cecelia tried hard to scrub away hers. Edinburgh accents didn't strike the same chord as a Western Isles accent. More rebels came from the Western Isles than Edinburgh. Mary was of a different mind. She had supported the rebellion, and in the years since the surrender, the woman chased duty and hard work the way others chased wine and debauchery. But she had a point. This was serious. Cecelia had lost awareness, her thoughts drifting aimlessly, the entire hack ride from Bow Street. She hadn't known where she was until the driver stopped outside Mary's shop on White Cross Street.

The stays flopped in her hands. "I am a little off today."

"You have been since Anne departed for Scotland."

Anne, Anne, Anne. The woman had been strength and reason, the shepherdess of their fledgling league, and her dearest friend. In the fortnight since Anne's departure, she had become the league's *de facto* leader, which cramped her like an ill-fitting shoe. Despite being a social creature, she often marched to her own drum, all the better to blaze an unforgettable path.

"I have something to put the bloom back in your cheeks," Mary said. "News of the *sgian-dubh*."

She snapped to attention. "What news?"

The *sgian-dubh*, Clanranald MacDonald's ancient ceremonial dagger, had gone missing after Cumberland's men ransacked the clan chief's home in Arisaig, after the surrender in spring of '46. Lore claimed the knife had been a gift from the Romans to a MacDonald warrior. For centuries, Clanranald chiefs used it at annual clan meetings. More relic than weapon, it was a symbol of pride. Finding the *sgian-dubh* had, in fact, been her primary mission in London.

Mary fussed with the window display. "Its location is explained in a document I have for you—"

"A document?" she hissed. "What are you thinking?"

The shop's doorbell jingled. A matron entered, her eyes rounding with delight at the brilliant display. "Good afternoon, Miss Fletcher. Such gorgeous colors. I saw them from across the street and just had to come see them up close."

"Thank you, Mrs. Rimsby."

Mrs. Rimsby wedged herself between Mary and Cecelia. "Open for another hour, are you?"

"For you, Mrs. Rimsby," Mary said, "my shop is open as long as you need."

Cecelia glared at the woman's back.

The matron petted the stays with fleshy fingers. "Such extravagant colors. And quite affordable."

Cecelia scooped them up. "Why don't you go to the fitting room and try them on?"

"But those are samples," Mrs. Rimsby sputtered.

"Then hold them up to your skin and see what color you think Mr. Rimsby would like." Cecelia folded them into Mrs. Rimsby's arms and winked. "Better yet, find what color strikes your fancy. Because nothing sparks the marital fires like a happy woman."

And nothing sent proper matrons fleeing like hinting at sexual congress.

Mrs. Rimsby gaped as Mary herded her across the shop with a soothing, "Ask my sister to take you to the fitting room. She'll hold the looking glass and you can decide what colors suit you."

Cecelia seethed. *A document!*

They had all agreed—no incriminating papers, nothing to create a trail which might lead to them. Not after stealing Jacobite gold from the Countess of Denton last month. Cecelia's league of Scotswomen had formed after the surrender of '46 to quietly hunt down and take back the gold and the *sgian-dubh*, which had been taken from their clan.

The Countess of Denton, however, viewed the matter differently.

The spiteful woman couldn't report the crime; the crown also wanted the lost Jacobite treasure.

But that didn't stop her from ordering her men to ransack Anne's house (which had been empty) and burn Anne's warehouse (which had not been empty). Most of the league had fled London by the skin of their teeth mere hours before those events. With the women returned to the City, they had to exercise the utmost caution.

And today, a man was following Cecelia.

Though a man following her could be for any number of reasons.

She reached for emerald green stockings and held them to the window's light. He was still there, shadowed by the chandler's awning, his tricorn pulled low. The front of his cocked hat was long—a hunter's hat. How appropriate. Her hunter wore a bottle green frock coat with brass buttons and plain wide cuffs. His square-toed leather shoes weren't noteworthy. Those polished buttons were. Her follower had money.

Which put him in an uncertain category. Nothing about him cried criminal.

Nothing cried admirer either. Quite a conundrum, the gentleman in green.

She set down emerald stockings in favor of a butter yellow pair. When she unspooled them, the hat across the street tipped a fraction higher.

"Like pale colors, do you?"

"Talking to yourself?" Mary slipped in beside her and began reorganizing the display.

"I'm baiting my hook."

"The man following you is not a fish."

"With delicious calves like that, I hope not." She dropped the yellow stockings.

"You are incorrigible." Mary's *r*'s trilled.

"And you, dear, are going to help me figure out what shade my friend across the street favors"—she petted decadent pink stockings—"while you tell me about the *sgian-dubh* and the documents that should not be in your shop."

"Documents we had no choice but to accept if we want to accomplish our mission." Mary was steely voiced, plucking white stockings from the pile. "Try these."

She took them, but the tricorn tipped lower. Her mysterious hunter produced a pencil and a pocket journal from inside his coat and flipped it open. Lace cuffs danced at the back of long-fingered, masculine hands. Her gaze lingered on them.

Would his touch be soft? Or firm?

"No interest in the white," she said.

"Try the vermillion . . . though I should be flogged for encouraging you."

"Do they match my lips?" She smiled and set the stockings against her cheek.

"They do." Mary folded prim hands. "Your coquettish display has caught his attention."

Across the street, the pencil stopped. Her hunter's head nudged higher, but two hacks rolling by wrecked her view.

Cecelia slid her arm inside the stocking and checked the weave. "Tell me your news."

Mary was again fixing the display, her face a shop-keeper's solicitous mask. Since coming to the City, subterfuge had become an art form they'd perfected while living dual lives.

"One of Cumberland's men sold the *sgian-dubh* to Sir Hans Sloane," Mary said in a quiet voice.

"The collector physician who died last January?"

"The very same. Apparently, the *sgian-dubh* has been stored in his home at Bloomsbury Place. Kept in a crate all this time."

She huffed her disbelief. "That explains why no one knew its whereabouts."

"He willed everything to the crown for a public museum. It's been in the newspapers."

"And now Clanranald's *sgian-dubh* has been reduced to a curiosity to be gawked at."

"One of eighty thousand curiosities, I collect. Not even two houses joined together can display everything." Mary's voice pitched higher. "Can you imagine it?"

She yanked the stocking off her arm. "How am I going to find one dagger in that mess?"

Mary smiled coyly. "Sneak into the late doctor's house and search, one crate at a time?"

"Now who's being incorrigible?"

Mary picked up indigo stockings.

"Not those," Cecelia said. "The robin's egg blue, if you please."

Mary rummaged through the pile. "Margaret obtained inventory lists and notes from the last meeting of the museum trustees."

"Sweet Margaret bribing clerks?"

"Befriending them. No bribes necessary."

Shoppers strolled by the window. The Night Watchman was making his rounds along White Cross Street, lighting lamps. Her hunter had left the chandler's window and was leaning, arms crossed, against a lamppost while trading pleasantries with the watchman. His hat was still low and his face hidden.

A thrill bubbled inside her. He'd taken her bait and offered a taste of his own.

A full view of him. Tall, lean, confident. The cant of his body was a message: *I'm watching you watch me.*

She smiled. Her hunter knew how to tease.

How exhilarating—an intelligent adversary. Better than a beefy dockside ruffler who couldn't string coherent words together. But she'd have to see her hunter face-to-face to know his intent. Evil pooled in the eyes.

Mary was rolling up stockings beside her. "Read through them, will you?"

"Through what?"

"The meeting minutes and inventory lists." Mary's voice tinged with stern patience.

Cecelia reluctantly dragged her attention to the azure stockings thrusted at her. She took them, the wool cascading over her fingers.

"There were more than forty trustees present," Mary said. "All of them sharing a tome's worth of ideas on what to do with the doctor's bequest."

"An exhilarating read, I'm sure."

Her gaze wandered to green sleeves hugging contoured arms. It slid lower to firm thighs. A nice view, but London brimmed with well-formed men. Nothing new there, yet . . . his shadowed stare penetrated her. Quietly self-assured, her hunter. A man who understood the art of subtlety.

Feather-soft awareness teased her.

"Cecelia." Mary's voice cut through her haze.

Her focus crawled back, jarred this time by worry clouding Mary's face.

"One of the trustees is the Marquess of Swynford, the Countess of Denton's brother."

"A powerful family with their fingers in every pie. It doesn't mean anything."

"Or it could mean everything." Mary rerolled stockings in quick jerks. "Hopefully, you will give your full attention to the documents."

"Of course." Vague and obligatory, it was enough.

A little-known fact about rebellion: it required careful toil and not all of it fruitful. Anne would've delighted at poring over the documents to cultivate nuanced information. Cecelia, however, could think of a hundred other ways to spend her evening.

Skin around Mary's eyes softened. "I know this isn't easy without Anne, but we need you. Among the lot of us, you are the most knowledgeable of the City."

And therein was the problem. Knowledge of London came easy. Leadership's selflessness did not. It required a grander scope and consideration for others. But necessity was a stern taskmaster—an Anne-ism, which put a nostalgic smile on her lips.

"You're not worried about . . ." Mary let her words trail as she nudged her head at the man across the street.

"My hunter? No." Cecelia unspooled stockings the color of a robin's egg. "Or perhaps he's a fish who needs to be caught."

He shifted off the post, his black hat tipping higher.

Her lips parted, the narcotic effect of penetrating interest. She abandoned all pretense and stared openly. Shaded eyes were hard to see but easy to feel their heat and curiosity. A man who wanted to explore her up close. She took what she could—a view of the bottom tip of his nose, an even mouth, and late-day whiskers darkening his jaw.

Promising features.

She dropped the stockings and leaned over to pick

them up. Her barely-there cleavage reflected in the window. Tucked between her paltry breasts was a medallion. She touched the ribbon on which it hung, her finger tracing the black silk line from her neck to her bodice.

Her watcher's mouth twitched a half smile. Dust motes floated, enchantment to the day's end. Lulling, secretive. Across the street, her hunter's fine fingers rose slowly and touched the brim of his hat.

Her astonished gust fogged the window.

He saluted her cleavage!

"A gentleman flirt," she said under her breath.

How perfectly delicious.

Embers of delight cascaded her limbs. She slid her hand down her stomacher, silk liquid and sensual to touch—until a hack rolled in front of the shop. The same hack, which had delivered her to Fletcher's House of Corsets and Stays, had come to fetch her at twilight. The driver spied her in the window and tipped his hat.

She righted herself. "Mr. Munro is here. Time for me to go."

"Don't forget our meeting tomorrow morning, late."

"As if I could forget. I shall take these." She gave the robin's egg blue stockings to Mary and scooped up vermillion stockings. "These too. And stays to match. In silk, if you have them."

The shop's samples would fit her with ease.

"And the garters, do you want them in the same color?" Mary asked. "Or a contrasting hue?"

She batted the air. "Choose for me."

Mary's heels clicked her brisk retreat. She would return with a package, wrapped in brown paper and sealed with twine. No graceful boxes for White Cross

Street shoppers. But in between the stays and stockings of this purchase, Mary Fletcher would pass a stack of papers.

Cecelia adjusted her gloves and her mind. A night's worth of scouring inventory lists and meeting minutes lay ahead. From those documents, she would glean opportunities. Relentless detailed work was how they'd taken back some of the Jacobite gold. The same dogged methods would help to recover the *sgian-dubh*.

Their rebellion was not a vainglorious pursuit, rather a practical one. To restore what was left of their clan, to rebuild herds and homes, to resurrect Clanranald pride. Results sprouted from diligent labor, from bribing the right people in the right way, never brute force.

She shivered her distaste. Violence was the language of soldiers and dockside rufflers. But what about her mysterious hunter? Was he of that ilk?

Her gloves on, she peered around the waiting hack. The gentleman in green had vanished.

Chapter Three

Swan Lane was a blasted, cold place. Mist ghosted Miss MacDonald's stone house and her empty mews. The damp chill froze his stones and turned his breath into tiny nimbuses. He breathed into his icy hands for warmth, trying to make sense of his day.

Nothing added up. His latest journal entry was a litany of uninteresting notes.

Humble, well-kept homes. The cobbles clean. The ivy trimmed. No horse in the mews.

Miss MacDonald was home alone, save her maid-cum-servant named Jenny. He'd waited hours for the Scotswoman to depart and do something, anything, exciting. Criminals flirted best with darkness. Yet, Miss MacDonald stayed home with curtains half-drawn.

She was pacing an upper room, back and forth by her window.

He hugged his coat shut, missing his greatcoat and gloves. If he hadn't been so hasty in leaving Fielding's chamber, he would've been better prepared. Dinner was a lukewarm meat pie purchased from a street vendor while walking the considerable distance from White Cross Street to Swan Lane. He knew where she lived because it was a note in Fielding's ledger, the same as her servant's Christian name.

Earlier, he'd poked up and down Swan Lane and the narrow alley behind it, looking to add to those facts.

And . . . nothing.

What was he going to report?

Jacobite sympathizer incites rebellion with shopping.

This first day was not promising.

Fog carpeted Miss MacDonald's narrow courtyard. He stood at the edge of her mews, his eyes fixed on the vertical slash of light between her curtains. Three barrels behind him needed checking—his final task. He'd investigate them once he was certain Miss MacDonald was ensconced at home permanently for the night, which appeared to be the case.

A curtain wavered. Miss MacDonald paused at the window, dressed in frilly white night clothes, hair down, a feathered quill tapping her lips. He squinted at, yes, those were papers in her hand.

He grabbed his pencil and notebook and wrote *Miss MacDonald spent her night reading.*

The pencil's tip lingered on the page. Shame niggled him. "Dangerous minds, those readers," he murmured dryly.

He added *I am the worst gentleman for watching her* to the entry and jabbed a decisive period. But he wasn't done. His pencil became a forthright instrument to empty his mind.

Upon further study, Miss MacDonald
possesses a wide mouth, unremarkable lips,
and small breasts (as judged by her meager
bodice).

 And skinny arms. A blonde with lush
locks, her hair is all her own (as judged by
the quantity falling about her shoulders at
this late hour). The woman is a contradiction.
Attractive but not a beauty. She appears to
be innocent friendliness, though men flock
to her as if they know they'll find something
else. One could argue, they do her bidding.
The hack which delivered her to White Cross
Street today returned at twilight to take her
home. When did London's hack drivers start
doing that?

 Can Miss MacDonald bend the will of men?
 Evidence would prove that, yes, she can.
I am a perfect example (as judged by my
freezing stones while I stand in her mews
without my greatcoat). She is carnal invitation
in the flesh. Might be the sway of her hips.
I can only conclude that Miss MacDonald
ensorcells those around her.

He hesitated over one vexing fact, not listed in
Fielding's ledger.

Miss MacDonald has no known source of
income. How is she funded? This needs further
investigation.

The last sentence written, he was ready to put this
foolishness behind him. The magistrate had asked

him to report his findings. Didn't mean he had to read everything aloud. Nor did Fielding say how many hours a day must be devoted to this fruitless task.

He snapped his pocket journal shut. "There is nothing here."

Only those three barrels to check. If he worked fast, he'd have his head on the pillow well before midnight.

Scooting deeper into the mews, he let his eyes adjust to the dark. The small structure would fit a dog cart and one horse, but no animal had lived within the stone walls for some time. Dust-laden cobwebs dangled from rafters. Moldy straw bunched in one corner. Air reeked of river and ale, an aroma strongest by the waist-high barrels on the riverside wall. Quite a feat, their smell. Between the Thames and London Bridge's sagging structures, ale was sweet perfume.

Which begged the question: Why did the fashionable Miss MacDonald live in a simple house abutting the Thames? In boring Dowgate, no less?

He dropped to one knee and groped the middle barrel. A brand scarred its belly, *Mermaid Brewery*. The *M* and *B* curved fancifully and the *y* was a mermaid's tail underlining the words. Night hid the rest of the mythical woman from view, but his thumb brushed wavy lines that must be her hair. Hands running over coopered wood, he found no dust or cobwebs.

Clean barrels? In a dirty mews?

He checked the slash of light that was Miss MacDonald's window. Even if it took a lifetime, she'd not drink a barrel of ale this size, much less three.

Miss MacDonald sipped . . . Wine? Brandy? Champagne, when she gained entry to finer homes?

Irrelevant questions. What the woman poured into her pretty mouth made no difference.

He stood up, a sense of rightness swamping him. Of king and country and the sanctity of the union. Could be there was a crumb to follow here. He grabbed his notebook and pencil. At the heart of a blank page he wrote *Mermaid Brewery* and added a question mark—his second perplexing query about this woman.

Excitement jumping in his veins, he removed his coat, laid it on another barrel, and stuffed his notebook and pencil within the woolen folds. No need to dirty a new coat, though the night's damp air was brutal.

With careful hands, he removed the first lid and set it aside. Inside was black as pitch.

He swiped a hand through it. Empty.

Except ale mixed with a metallic odor reached his nose.

He jiggled the barrel, testing it. A raspy *clink* answered him.

Whatever Miss MacDonald was hiding rested at the bottom.

Tipping the barrel was out of the question—it'd make too much noise. He bent over, his body jostling coopered wood. Metal *clinked* again. He leaned in deeper, gripping the barrel's iron-banded rim with one hand, his hat falling off. He pushed up on his toes and reached for the bottom.

His fingertips grazed grainy metal.

"What the devil—"

"I was thinking the same thing," said an amused feminine voice.

He groaned, the barrel echoing his misery. Head down, arse up was not a defensible position.

"Are you in pain, sir?" the voice asked while a second one giggled.

"Only my pride."

He began to unfold himself.

"Don't. Move." A bone-chilling *click*. "If you do, I will shoot that fine arse of yours."

Cold sweat popped at his hairline. The *click* was a pistol cocked. Deucedly hard to know for certain with his head in a barrel, but he'd heard the sound often enough.

"Who are you, sir?"

A commanding feminine voice. Definitely the woman pointing a pistol at him.

"I am Mr. Alexander Sloane."

"Of . . . ?"

"London." A few minutes upside down and blood rushed his skull, pounding in his ears. "If you don't mind . . . the pressure in my head is increasing. I'd prefer to have this conversation standing up."

"You should have thought about that before you went arse up in my mews, Mr. Sloane."

Blood banged furiously behind his eyes while muffled feminine whispers ensued. *Wonderful.* A committee of two women was deciding what to do with him.

"Put your hands on the rim. Slowly, so I can see them." Polite and definitive, that voice.

He put both hands on the barrel's rim and remained facedown. So, this was how he would meet Miss

MacDonald, head down, arse first, and his pocket journal crammed with outrageous notes about her. Nothing to connect him to Bow Street thankfully. With any luck, they'd ignore the journal and call for the Night Watch.

"Jenny, his coat," the lady said.

Footsteps pattered and excellent Northumberland wool brushed the barrel beside him.

"Lud. He's got a little book"—a pause was followed by incriminating page-riffling—"and there's lots written about you, miss."

"Give it to me."

Body sagging, he tossed his they'll-ignore-the-journal plan and formed another one. Swan Lane was in Dowgate, Sir William Calvert the alderman. A coin in the warder's palm would see a message delivered to the alderman: *Please alert Bow Street that Mr. Alexander Sloane is in prison.* By morning, Fielding would arrange his release and acknowledge the folly of tasking the duke's numbers man to a thief taker's job. It would only cost him his pride and a cold night in prison.

This would be a story to share with his brother over a pint, something to laugh about . . . someday.

"Tie him up, Jenny."

"No need for ropes." His voice echoed in the barrel. "I am unarmed and I mean you no harm."

"You are armed with pencil and paper, sir. That is lethal enough for me."

An interesting response. He would've ruminated on it, but a hand grabbed his arm and guided him upright. Pressure waned between his ears, the blood draining fast, leaving him light-headed. He leaned against the barrel to steady himself and discovered the hand guiding him belonged to Jenny.

She glared at him, a rag-curled Medusa. "Don't try anything. I've got a knife."

"I won't. You have my word."

To which Jenny grumbled a salty curse and jerked his hands behind his back.

Eyes stretching wide, he found Miss MacDonald in the courtyard, fog curling around her bare feet. She battled autumn's bite in a white shift, a flimsy untied night-robe of the same fabric, and a skein of unbound hair. Her rigid nipples and a door lamp illuminating her shivering body told him she was cold.

His gaze drifted lower.

A flaming bolt seared him.

Did he see a shadowed wedge . . . *there*?

His thoughts went up in smoke. Hot lust shuddered his loins, hungry and persuasive, a reminder that he was flesh and blood, a man who could be lured, a man in danger of losing his mortal soul to the goddess of Swan Lane despite the fact she pointed a biting glare and polished pistol at him.

The Scotswoman had a fierce, take-no-prisoners look about her.

Just how fierce, his wanton self would gladly explore. His eyes boldly pursued a jeopardous triangle—a carnal line drawn leisurely from breast to breast to the hint of gold curls between her legs. Legs that were shaking.

"You're cold. You should take my coat."

Gruff and sensual, he hardly recognized his voice.

Her blond-crowned head canted sideways as if this was a new development.

"Very gentlemanly of you. But my house is a few steps away."

Behind him, a wide slippery ribbon was looped around his wrists. A shiver wandered down his back. Miss MacDonald had ordered him bound by silk.

"All done, miss." Jenny gave the knot a final tug. "Want me to put him in the mews and tie his ankles?"

Little clouds puffed from the goddess of Swan Lane's lips. Her perusal wandered over him like a curious touch.

"No. Bring him to me."

Incendiary words. He should've argued for the mews, a plan his feet rejected. His body wanted to be closer to the Scotswoman and took him forward until he was an arm's length from her. A truce, of sorts. He studied the contours of her face, matching them to Fielding's ledger, while she studied his coat draped over the maid-cum-servant's arm.

Blond brows slashed a befuddled line. "Were you at White Cross Street today?"

He hesitated. *In for a penny, in for a pound.*

"I was."

A half smile formed on quivering lips. "And before you departed, did you . . . ?"

"Salute your cleavage? Yes. I did." Lust roughed his words.

That twitch of her lips did things to him.

"Quite an introduction, you and I."

"Memorable to say the least." Amusement grained his voice.

Night treated Miss MacDonald's creamy skin as kindly as daylight. Her confidence was equally appealing, something Bow Street's sketch couldn't

articulate. He'd happily debate which of her qualities—
self-assurance or attractiveness—was greater, but the
woman pointing a pistol at him was inclined to discuss *him*.

"And how do I know you are Mr. Alexander Sloane
of London?"

Her voice lilted mildly humored. Of all the questions to ask, it was oddly comforting and practical.

"In my right waistcoat pocket, you will find a Bank
of England cheque with my name preprinted on it."

Jenny's arm stretched to retrieve it. Miss MacDonald's gaze locked with his.

"No. I'll get it."

Lamplight frayed her hair's blond edges, spun
threads come to life. She took a half step closer, a soft
rosewater scent clouding him. Almost innocent and
gentle as the mist-dampened curl stuck to her cheek.
It wasn't the perfume of a sensual goddess.

His mind painted a dual portrait of her. By day,
a worldly young woman. By night, a village lass
trapped in London. When Miss MacDonald reached
into his pocket, she as good as reached into him. A
woman testing his mettle, curious for what she might
find. He stood rigid as a duke's man should, staring
above her head, absorbing the pleasurable shiver that
followed her fingers in his pocket.

She unfolded the cheque, the slip of paper proof
that he was a man of means, a responsible citizen,
and this was all a terrible misunderstanding. But
Miss MacDonald didn't take it that way. A quick
read and she stuffed the cheque back in his waistcoat
pocket, her eyes betraying nothing.

"Let's go inside, shall we?"

Miss MacDonald gathered flimsy white linen and

scurried to the door, the soles of her feet flashing
pink and white.

She wanted him in her home?

A man could easily wait inside or out for the Night
Watch to haul him away, but in the scant real estate
between where he stood and the door, a new plan
formed. Collect what was left of his brain and use it.
Gather whatever information he could on Miss Mac-
Donald and her maid-cum-servant, Jenny. And avoid
lust like the plague.

Chapter Four

*H*er house was small, four rooms in all if one didn't count the cramped scullery which Jenny had transformed into her own quarters. The whole of it was easy to navigate in the dark, and Mr. Sloane's agile movements all the more interesting. Warped steps groaned under the burden of his feet and hers with Mr. Sloane leading a reluctant charge upstairs.

"You could let me go. No harm was done," he said over his shoulder.

She nudged her pistol against the small of his back. "We'll see about that."

Mr. Sloane was in her house for one reason. An itch needed scratching—to see her gentleman hunter in full light. To know his intent. To know him. His startling forthrightness was a badge worth pinning on his coat the way soldiers wore medals. How intriguing, his lack of deflection. Equally intriguing was the back of him. Tight arse muscles bunching in black wool. Strong arms and shoulders, though not the heavy, meaty variety. Lean and taut, Mr. Sloane looked as if he was given to running or sprinting. Or a man who hunted on foot.

"Take the door to the left," she said when they crested the narrow stairs.

Mr. Sloane entered her bedchamber and stopped in the middle, a pink ribbon swaying from his bound wrists. She rubbed her arms for warmth while Mr. Sloane spun an easy circle to survey the room. The roaring fire and eight candles exposed clothes cluttering an open wardrobe and an unmade bed. Her mattress and counterpane were costly, snow-white clouds of comfort—ideal for baiting the curious man. Certainly better than holding up pretty stockings in a window.

Her bare toes pressed the floor. She wanted to see him in full light.

The inspection done, Mr. Sloane faced her. Fire's amber glow caressed firm lines and open features. By day, a man to take tea with your great-aunt; by night, a man to kiss and laugh with in bed. A refined gentleman far from her reach. There was pain in knowing that, as if she took a kick to her ribs. For too long she'd cavorted with men who straddled a world of right and wrong, but Mr. Sloane was not one of them.

His goodness singed her. This was a man who'd court a woman of excellent status, not the daughter of a Jacobite rebel.

"Mr. Sloane." His name slid off her tongue, warm and redolent.

"Miss MacDonald."

His bow was cordial, his voice sensual.

Beautiful, honest eyes stared at her, more bronze than brown. Crystalline and captivating. Life danced in them. Intelligence, however, was the greater light. It was his calling card and his weapon. She could fool herself and say Mr. Sloane was passably attractive, but her leaping pulse had a mind of its own. So did her nipples. *Pointy, treasonous things.*

This time Mr. Sloane looked into her eyes, not her nipples, unlike his ravenous consumption of her body outside.

"This is your bedchamber."

"As you would know, having watched it."

His smile was an affable crease used by all well-bred men. "Very ungentlemanly of me." Then, "How did you know?"

His first response was ingrained; the second was sincere. A man who wanted answers but wouldn't demand them. *A second son, perhaps? But not ennobled.* Arrogance sometimes dripped down on those who might inherit. None that she knew would even stoop to house a mistress here in Dowgate. She trusted Mr. Sloane, an instinct borne of years meeting men. Her hand already seemed to know, holding the pistol loosely at her side, the muzzle pointed at the floor as if it couldn't wait to be rid of the burden. Ironic how the body sensed right away what the mind took minutes, if not hours or days, to grasp.

"The cold air revealed you," she said. "You puffed like a dragon, and since I keep no animals, mythical or otherwise, I knew someone was standing in my mews."

His head dipped, trying to hide a boyish smile. Firelight caressed rich chestnut hair and a blunt-cut queue scraping pristine neckwear.

"I am an admirer, Miss MacDonald. Surely, you have had smitten men follow you."

A brittle smile spread. How disappointing, after having made such fine progress.

"I don't believe you."

"Which part?"

There was challenge in his voice, still smoky with lust. *Audacious man.* Definitely a second son. They had to work for everything, and Mr. Sloane eyed her as if he'd welcome a battle of wits. A third son would have rallied his charm.

"Your motives are suspect," she said at last and stretched her arm at two chairs by the fire. "Please do have a seat, Mr. Sloane."

With his hands tied, he stepped with care toward the tall-backed leather chair while she wetted a hand cloth at her washstand.

"That one is mine."

"My pardon." He swiveled in the confined space and dropped into the four-square wooden chair facing it. His arms flexed as if he was testing his bindings. "Has your maid gone for the Night Watch?"

She wrung the cloth. "The Night Watch won't be called."

"No?" A corner of his mouth curved politely.

A flutter tickled her belly. She did her best to quash it: men with polite smiles never affected her. Why did her body suddenly change its mind tonight? Damp linen in hand, she settled into her favorite chair. With the pistol and pocket journal nestled in her lap, she crossed one ankle over her knee and found his stare glued to her foot.

"Nasty business having to run barefoot outside," she said. "But shoes would have alerted you and I refuse to ruin my stockings."

"Yet, you won't call for the Night Watch?" He dragged his gaze upward. "I could be a terrible criminal."

"We both know you're not. A criminal wouldn't offer his coat, no matter how much I shivered. A true gentleman would."

"And you've come to this conclusion because you have ample experience finding men in your mews late at night?"

She scrubbed a stubborn smudge on her heel. *Interesting, his deflection.*

"Mr. Sloane, are you going to be that obvious? And here I had such hopes for a more invigorating conversation with you."

His mouth dented in the same guarded politeness he'd offered earlier. "I shall endeavor not to disappoint."

Her foot free of grit, she commenced cleaning her other foot, expecting more rebuttal. Instead, Mr. Sloane was like a hawk, staring at the cloth dancing over her arch and the bright pink balls of her toes.

"Your ankles, there's a shine to your skin," he said gruffly. "They are hairless."

"I wax my legs and rub oil over them when I'm done."

His glower sharpened. She raised her hem a few inches, giving a scandalous view of glossy, smooth-skinned calves.

"I am not calling for the Night Watch because it would be useless." She dropped her hem. "Sniffing my barrels is not a crime."

His hawklike stare shot up. "What if I sniffed elsewhere?"

Intensity melted into mischief. She sat up, washed by it.

"You cannot make free with my barrels, Mr. Sloane, or any other parts."

He sat back, a half smile forming.

"There aren't many like you," he said. "Pretty as you are, flattery won't work."

She, too, sat back and tossed the washcloth onto the hearth.

"Flattery, no."

The intimacy of wrongdoing stripped propriety off the bone. He'd been following her and had been caught skulking in her mews. Strangely, that helped them skirt the need for shallow conversation. Mr. Sloane looked ready to engage in in-depth conversation—and anything else that might happen.

"I know what works," he said.

Excitement sprinkled her skin.

"Whatever do you mean?"

"I mean, I know what stirs you, Miss MacDonald. You see, I've noticed you for . . ." He looked at the fire a moment, took a considered breath, and finished, his gaze direct, his voice even. "Well, for some time."

The dratted man hooked her fascination. The truth was she was known. She'd glimpsed it in his notebook. His revelations, his seeing her.

She crossed one side of her night-robe over the other. "Very well, Mr. Sloane. What *stirs* me?"

Eyes so beautiful, so penetrating, held her captive.

"Intelligence. Being an intelligent creature, you need a steady diet of it," he said. "To give and receive, I think, as iron sharpens iron. Men who can't see past your"—he offered a respectful nod to her body—"obvious appeal, don't see the real you."

Her knuckles whitened on her robe. Stillness expanded, punctuated by a dog barking from a distant house. One could almost hear the river's hush beyond her window, or the whispers of her soul laid bare. She did not trust herself to speak. A rush of denials would be too obvious, an acquiescence too mortifying.

"And you gleaned this in one day, have you?"

"Correction. Not one day. Several of them." Chin dropping, Mr. Sloane became deeply interested in the hem of her shift.

"What do you mean?"

His chair creaked. The glower returned, honesty's snare entrapping him.

"The thing is, I've noted your presence in . . . various places—"

"At Bow Street." She sat up triumphant. "That's where I've seen you."

She picked up his pocket journal and began thumbing the pages.

"I have been there of late," he admitted.

She eyed him over the book. "But you're not a thief taker."

"No. I serve the Duke of Newcastle."

"A Government position."

"I track financial records for His Grace," he said guardedly.

Calculation flared in her. The upper hand had been hers when she found Mr. Sloane arse up in a barrel. Now the tables were turning. Her hunter had been watching her for several days, he worked for the king's counselor, and he had no qualms about telling her.

"And today you decided to reveal yourself," she said.

"At White Cross Street, yes." He was earnest as a

suitor. "Today is the first and only day that I've followed you." Brows knitting, he cleared his throat.
"I am a gentleman, Miss MacDonald . . . not a—a . . ."

"Depraved man."

"No."

"I knew that in my courtyard, Mr. Sloane. Believe
me, I would not let a depraved man into my house."

"Your house, yes, but I am in your bedchamber."

His gaze cut, gentle yet precise.

"The fire is best and brightest in here. All the better
to read your notes."

She raised his notebook, his wry smile allowing
her deflection. A patient hunter, this Mr. Sloane, in
their unfolding game of cat and mouse.

"Let's see . . . You write that I possess small breasts
(as judged by my meager bodice) and I have lush
locks, and my hair is all my own (as judged by the
quantity falling about my shoulders). There are some
musings about my source of income and a hack doing my bidding. But this part . . ." Finger to the page,
she read directly from his notebook. "'Can Miss
MacDonald bend the will of men to her own? Evidence would prove that, yes, she can. I am a perfect
example (as judged by my freezing stones while I
stand in her mews without my greatcoat).'"

She lowered the notebook.

"Quite a lot of judgment," she said with mock disapproval.

Mr. Sloane grimaced.

"I was too free with my words."

"It's your journal, Mr. Sloane. Where else can a man
make free with his words?" She hesitated, a playful
grin forming. "Though I am very sorry about your
stones. I do hope they've warmed up."

His warm smile crinkled the corners of his eyes. "They have, thank you."

Excitement hummed in her limbs. She'd waxed her legs, read pages of notes, and captured an interesting man. All in all, a good night's work. Tomorrow the league would meet in her house. Their gathering would be a delight and a drudge as they would plow through several matters, some of which they might not find common ground. Anne had led by consensus; she would rather dictate.

One thing her late-night visitor had right was her need for intelligence. She devoured newspapers, pamphlets, and books. She listened and learned with the same skill she gave to flirting. Most times, hers was overt friendliness. True flirting, the sensual kind, like now, crackled dangerously. An odd response to a man she suspected trod the straight and narrow by habit and by choice.

Of course, a man like that would ask, "If the Night Watch isn't coming, what are your plans for me?"

"My plans . . ."

She tucked the notebook in her lap and drummed her fingers on it. This was her moment, take a grand risk or play it safe. Setting Mr. Sloane free would mean she'd have to be more careful watching her back. Hiring a dockside ruffler, perhaps, or a bare-knuckle brawler in need of extra coin.

Or she could take what she wanted.

She scooted forward, hair falling about her shoulders. Light glinted on Mr. Sloane's roguish whiskers. This close, fire revealed auburn and three shades of brown framing his mouth.

"I await your pleasure, Miss MacDonald." His words were smoke and silk and his eyes provocative.

She was tempted to drag a fingertip over Mr. Sloane's whiskers and see what happened. Her body certainly knew what it wanted. Another time, another night, she would've explored the polite dent of his mouth and the taste of mist on his skin. But this was clan business, and her life marched to its drum.

"One invaluable lesson has stayed with me over the years. It is that men always want something in return for services rendered, and this"—she held up the journal—"is evidence that you are investigating me. A task which you are ill-equipped to perform, if you'll forgive my bluntness."

Mr. Sloane's smile cooled. She studied him, choosing her words with care.

"I can't imagine the Duke of Newcastle worrying over a Scotswoman in Dowgate, and definitely not his brother, the Honorable Chancellor. Both men have more important things to do. Fielding, on the other hand, would." She tapped the notebook. "The man likes digging up dirt on hapless souls and putting it in his ledgers."

Mr. Sloane's face was a stiff, practiced mask.

Incredulous laughter huffed from her. "Does Fielding think I'm running a gang of cutthroats?"

"You hardly look the type."

"Small comfort." She studied her gentleman adversary, his careful wording leaving her with more questions than answers. "The magistrate has some leverage over you, doesn't he?"

Her arrow struck true. Mr. Sloane was positively arctic, trying to reveal nothing yet revealing everything.

"Your silence is rather telling." She sat back in her chair. "I have studied men far too long, Mr. Sloane."

"Perhaps if you used your intellect more, you wouldn't have to *study* men."

He could draw blood with his razor-sharp syllables. It had been forever since she gave a fig what people thought. No reason to awaken that unwelcome habit with Mr. Sloane, yet she heard her voice pitching defensibly.

"If I lived in your world of privilege and dominance, perhaps I might. But since this is the one I inhabit, I make do with what I have." Her Western Isles accent tripped off her tongue, the lax vowels and hint of Gaelic rising with her ire. "And since you are in my house, show a little respect. *Sir.*"

Mr. Sloane sat rigidly, his whiskered jaw working. His apology, if one could call it that, came as brief as his words.

"I might have been too forward."

She rested both elbows on her chair. Mr. Sloane would be a worthy adversary or an excellent ally. What he lacked in streetwise talent, he more than made up for with his intellect.

One entry in his notebook haunted her: *Miss MacDonald has no known source of income. How is she funded? This needs further investigation.*

The damage he could do.

"The hour is late," she said. "You're tired, I'm tired. All is forgiven."

"Does this mean you're letting me go?"

"Not yet."

"You intend to hold me here?"

Shock more than anger shaded his face and, on its heels, an alarming question sprang forward.

"Do you have someone waiting for you at home?" she asked.

An ache lit the back of his eyes.

"Home, at the moment, is an empty room at the White Hart off King Street."

"Not far from Bow Street."

"I assure you, I am not a thief taker. If I were, we both know I would be a very bad one."

To the contrary, Mr. Sloane would be the smartest man in service. A rapier among blunt instruments. She inched closer and touched one of his waistcoat's buttons, a warm-as-honey feeling gentling her voice.

"Fielding has some kind of hold over you, which means you need something from me. Information, perhaps? While I need help—shall we say—gaining entry to a certain place."

His chest expanded and contracted under her finger circling his button. If she ensorcelled men, this was how it was done. Faint touches, whispered words, intoxicating nearness. Flirtation was desire's lifeblood and touch the air it breathed.

His eyes slanted.

"You scratch my back and I'll scratch yours," he said tersely. "That's what you want."

Her finger stopped and she folded her hands in her lap.

"Aptly stated."

Mr. Sloane's lips parted like a man hungry for a kiss while anger burned in his eyes, a dangerous concoction of emotions and wants. Their knees bumped and their faces were lit by the fire's glow. Neither moved.

The hook was baited, and both wanted a bite.

"You have the night to think about it," she said.

His gaze scraped her like a blade.

"And where am I spending this valuable thinking time?"

Chapter Five

*W*here would you like to spend it, Mr. Sloane?"

He laughed, the low graveled sound of a tempted man. Miss MacDonald was a formidable adversary. Her talent in separating the wheat from the chaff in one's character was eye-opening and accurate. The possibilities she suggested? Endless. The Duke of Newcastle didn't expect him for a fortnight. Fielding didn't expect him for a week. He could spend seven unaccountable days and nights with the goddess of Swan Lane.

"A scintillating offer," he said in a husky voice. "But where I think about your proposition is a moot point."

"Which brings us to the matter at hand."

She stood, freeing their entangled knees. He missed them, which gave him pause. What kind of man missed a woman's knees? Or the pink parts of her toes?

"Are you willing to work with me?" she asked.

Blood throttled his veins. Amber light touched every curve and hollow behind her shift.

She might as well have said, *Are you willing to have me?*

His smoldering brain thought it. Carnal images lit the fuse with tangled limbs and sweet whispers. By force of will, his gaze climbed up the warp and weft of her shift, inch by inch. His prize was Miss Mac-Donald's radiant face free of cosmetics save carmine outlining her lower lip. A woman marked for life. It was good they weren't touching. One fraction of her flesh on his, and he would combust.

His voice was dry as dust when he said, "This place you want entry to . . . Where is it?"

She closed her night-robe and knotted the belt.

"A house on Bloomsbury Place."

"Sir Hans Sloane's house."

"Yes."

Sir Hans Sloane's house was the only house on Bloomsbury Place which the Government had a key to unlock. Or did Miss MacDonald think him a distant relation to the late physician?

"I am not related to him. By blood or by marriage."

"Which means you'll have to be creative."

Very brisk and businesslike her tone.

Looking nowhere else but her hazel eyes was a feat worthy of Atlas holding up the world.

"That's all you're going to tell me?"

"It is enough for now."

The Scotswoman was the queen of artful silence, giving him the opportunity to hedge his moral code. She ambled to her wardrobe and he watched, a parched man thirsty for a drink of her. She foraged through piled petticoats. Panniers and a pair of pink silk shoes fell carelessly to the floor. Shadows and the wardrobe door stole a better view of her.

His mind was a mass of unstable filaments. Might be good to piece them back together.

He shook his head as if that would unloose his sensual haze. He needed to think and collect information. To look carefully, everywhere. Little things spoke, such as DeFoe's pamphlet, *The Original Power of the Collective Body of the People of England*, lolling on the end of her luxurious bed. Its corners curled as if Miss MacDonald spent many a night reading the dead author. The walls were more talkative. Red and yellow posies had been painted in uneven rows.

"You've papered your walls in white and had them painted. A neat trick to evade the wallpaper tax," he said.

"At one pence per square yard of wallpaper, it is an outrageous tax. I painted them myself . . . hardly criminal."

"Like sniffing barrels?"

Her low laugh behind him was friendly. The rosewater scent that came with it was not.

She touched his shoulder. "Lean forward, Mr. Sloane."

Her voice was light and tender above his ear and he obeyed without question, a testament to their growing trust.

"I am not asking you to break any laws, merely open a door and walk away."

"The door at Bloomsbury Place."

Her warm hands grazed his. "Yes."

Cold metal slid between silk and his wrist.

"And I presume you will pass through it," he said.

"That's irrelevant."

A cool *snip, snip* and silk slid down his hands. He cuffed one wrist with his hand and rubbed ligature marks as pink as the silk ribbon Miss MacDonald tossed into the fire. She set her scissors on the mantel, the flames outlining her slender thigh. The display was not a carnal gambit, not with the serious line of her mouth.

"Why Bloomsbury Place?" he asked.

Miss MacDonald averted her gaze. "I am taking back something that was stolen from people I love."

"Then plead your case to the courts."

A soft noise of contempt passed her lips.

"I appreciate what you just shared," he said. "It's a daring revelation."

"But not enough to sway you," she said tartly.

He rose from his seat, flexing and rubbing his wrist. "In a single day, two people have asked me to skirt the law. I live for the law, Miss MacDonald, to see justice done."

"So do I, Mr. Sloane. In that, we are similar creatures."

A bark of laughter and, "I think not."

Hazel eyes narrowed. "Perhaps if you would suspend your judgment and look beneath the surface."

"Therein is my dilemma. My judgment. It is my most valued skill. When the Duke of Newcastle suspects a rat, I am the man His Grace calls to review fiscal reports."

Miss MacDonald was stiff and silent. He wanted to cosset the woman, a befuddling urge since minutes ago he would've gladly raised her shift and pounded himself to oblivion in the heaven between her legs.

"I am a barrister with a talent for numbers, Miss MacDonald, and one of the duke's most trusted men."

The grim salvo delivered, she clutched her nightrobe high on her chest.

"A barrister."

"His Grace has inferred that I am one assignment away from receiving letters patent."

She paled. "To be a judge, I collect."

"Baron of the Exchequer."

She searched the floor as one does when assimilating information.

"The financial courts . . . of course. That's what Fielding has over you." Miss MacDonald's guarded gaze met his. "Deliver damaging information on the Jacobite sympathizer, and he'll help you get what you want."

His grudging smile spread. Her intelligence *was* a sonata.

"Yes."

Bleached-white fingers squeezed her robe. "Yet, you've found nothing, save the fact that I might have dangerous ideas."

He softened. "Where else can a woman make free with her words but in her mind?"

A smile cracked her brittle facade.

"You see, Mr. Sloane, we are similar freedom-loving creatures."

The Scotswoman was everything he should avoid and everything that fascinated him. Smart, ready, fearless. Adventure with fair skin and lively eyes. A confident woman with boundaries, yet she wasn't afraid to break them if it was necessary.

She retrieved his pocket journal from her chair and handed it over. "I believe this is yours."

"You're giving it back to me?"

"I have no reason to keep it."

Words to cast a millstone around his heart, as if she'd said, *I have no reason to keep you.*

He reached out, two of his fingers deliberately grazing Miss MacDonald's hand under the notebook. Her eyes were liquid and dark. They stayed, fingers touching, a wish shared in their lingering contact until she let go.

Her cheek twitched and she cupped a hand over it. The worldly Scotswoman was not unaffected.

Her pistol remained carelessly on her chair, and for the first time that evening, he took a good look at what had been pointed at him. A French dragoon pistol, ornate silver butt cap, the metal trailing up the stock. *A. MacDonald* had been carved in the wood. He picked up the pistol and checked the frizzen and the pan. Both were shiny and clean. He sniffed the mechanism. It was absent of powder and shot's noxious aroma.

"Held at pistol point by an empty weapon," he mused. "This is a night of firsts."

He set the weapon on the mantel and found Miss MacDonald's eyes squishing sweetly.

"My ruse uncovered," she said.

"Why wasn't it loaded?"

"It never is. I get queasy at the sight of blood." She added a coy, "Perhaps you ought to put that in your notebook?"

He opened his mouth to ask about A. MacDonald, but her smile morphed to the pasted-on variety.

"Let me see to your coat."

The blonde nymph disappeared into the hallway. Her footfalls pattered the stairs, and he followed, slower this time. Miss MacDonald was waiting in the dark, his coat in hand.

"We seem to be missing your hat."

Her tone was sterile, and he ill-equipped to assuage it.

He took his coat, careful not to touch her. "My hat. It's still in your barrel."

"Let me take care of that."

She nipped off to the kitchen. "Jenny. Would you be so kind as to fetch Mr. Sloane's hat? He left it in the mews."

He tucked his journal into his coat pocket and waited in Miss MacDonald's hall, collecting his wits and shedding the last vestiges of lust and like, for he did like Miss MacDonald. He'd easily share a pint with her at a public house for the pleasure of talking with her. Nothing, however, could change bald facts. He was the Duke of Newcastle's man, a loyalty ingrained.

But other bothersome questions hung.

Who was A. MacDonald? And why did Miss MacDonald want entry to Bloomsbury Place? A name etched on an unused pistol was hardly germane to Fielding's request, yet the mystery burrowed like a pebble in his shoe.

Jenny came through the open doorway, hat in hand. He took it, not ready to say farewell. Miss MacDonald was a wraith at the foot of her stairs, a warning to his soul. The Scotswoman's familiar side smile had returned. Theirs had been a conversation laced with wicked lust and incriminating pleas, more than enough information for him to chase.

"Good night, Mr. Sloane."

"Good night, Miss MacDonald."

Jenny slipped around him to the door and opened it. "I can tell you where you can find a hack, sir."

"Very kind of you."

He stole one last look at the goddess of Swan Lane already vanishing upstairs.

Chilly night spilled through the front door. He stepped onto the narrow, cobbled lane outside. Candle lamps at Miss MacDonald's door and three others dotted a stygian path where mist and fog ate houses from the bottom up.

He turned and found Jenny in the doorway, a slit-eyed, rag-curled Medusa.

"You were going to tell me where I might find a hack?" he asked.

"There's no hack in Dowgate, not at this hour." She folded her arms over a sensible night-robe. "Miss MacDonald may get squeamish at the sight of blood, but I don't," the maid said. "I'll gut you like a fish if I catch you in the mews again." She raked him head to toe. "I'll gut you like a fish if I catch you at her front door too."

She shut the door. A hard *thunk* followed, the maid barring the door.

Protective fury rose inside him. To tell the loyal Jenny that he was the least of her worries. To demand she burn those Mermaid Brewery barrels. To warn her, horrible men would come and none of them polite. He stared at the barred door, anger rising. Jenny would fight for her mistress on that side.

Who would fight for Miss MacDonald on this side?

A worthy question.

He had a long foggy walk in which to consider it. He didn't don his tricorn, though. The brim was coated with flakes of lead. Or plumbago—the coveted ore the military used to make cannonballs. His fingers on one hand were shiny and gray. The same hand which had brushed the bottom of the Mermaid Brewery barrel.

Even small quantities of plumbago made a poor man—or woman—rich. Thieves transported it in all manner of ways, barrels with false bottoms being one, a smuggler's trick.

He studied the stone edifice, intrigued. The stone walls housed a pretty flirt, a fierce Scot, and a demirep who played with moral boundaries.

In short, the goddess of Swan Lane.

A woman who enthralled him, and a woman who owned pink silk shoes.

Chapter Six

He entered Westminster Hall, shaking off morning's fog. Probably the same one that had dogged him when he'd left Swan Lane. What a deucedly invigorating and frustrating night. His footsteps echoed, firm, steady, his hunt leading him upstairs. He pushed open the door of the Offices of the Exchequer and found the bespectacled Mr. Fernsby, the newest side clerk.

"Good morning, Mr. Sloane." The ruddy clerk juggled an armful of books. "Mr. Burton will be pleased you're here. He's wanted a word with you, sir."

"Excellent. I would like a word with him." He hung his greatcoat and hat on hooks near the door. "Immediately, if you please."

A wide table equipped with foolscap, quills, and ink sat in the middle of the room. He took a seat in one of the eight chairs surrounding the table and withdrew his pocket journal. Mr. Fernsby moved to the next shelf.

Alexander flipped open his notebook. "Perhaps I wasn't clear, Mr. Fernsby. I need you to find Mr. Burton."

The side clerk blinked at him, a book in hand angled on the shelf.

"Now?"

"*Now* and *immediately* are synonymous." He looked up from notes written at midnight. "Unless you have more pressing business?"

"Uh, no, sir. I shall find him right away." Fernsby dropped the books on the cart and scurried out of the room.

The Court of the Exchequer lived and breathed its hierarchy. Side clerks were new to the business of Westminster. To ascend the ranks, they had to study under a sworn clerk and be quick in matters of men and law. Sworn clerks were seasoned attorneys and had exclusive rights to search the records. Mr. Burton possessed the key to the Pell Office on the eastern side of Westminster Hall where all treasury transactions were stored. Paymaster rolls, crown expenses, money flowing in, money flowing out, including all the realm's taxes. Dusty business, the Pell Office, but in those ledgers, he would trace Miss MacDonald's life in London.

Money was history and character. Every shilling spent a story. He was about to learn hers.

On clean foolscap he wrote a list:

Bloomsbury Place
Hack, plate number 183
Fletcher's House of Corsets and Stays
Mermaid Brewery

> *Swan Lane (four windows)*
> *Miss Cecelia MacDonald. What taxes has*
> *she paid?*

He rolled the quill between thumb and forefinger. Taxes were unsentimental; nevertheless, a keen eye could read a tale in them. Not unlike a name carved on a pistol. He hesitated, pinching the quill.

Last night, her haunted eyes . . .

He'd stumbled on a wound, a chink in the lady's armor. Fielding would be the proverbial dog with a bone if he learned of it—unless Alexander discovered it first. Thus, he added *A. MacDonald* with a solemn flourish as the door swung open.

"Sloane, what brings you to Westminster at this ungodly hour?" Mr. Burton sauntered in with a jolly, "The duke's work, is it?"

"Bow Street. My latest assignment."

"Tracking the crown's funds. I heard." Burton yanked a chair from the table. "Sounds as thrilling as watching grass grow."

The coded Jacobite ledger came to mind which listed the mysterious Lady Pink, something his friend would never know about. Smiling blandly, Alexander dropped the quill.

"Some of us have to make sure the cogs of government run smoothly."

To which Burton hummed a bored noise. A rangy man, he sprawled in his seat, legs crossed at the ankles, hands linked at the back of his head. This time of day, Burton could, but in an hour, he'd be as somber as any senior clerk, and casual appellations like "Sloane" would become "Mr. Sloane."

"We missed you at the Five Bells last night," Burton said. "Quite a lively time, it was."

"I can hear it in your voice."

Burton laughed, a husky sound. "It's the cheroots, man. They'll be the death of me."

"If not them, your late nights and early hours certainly will."

"Not all of us can be as single-minded as you." Burton grinned. "There are women who need the pleasure of my company. They'd welcome yours should you come round."

As to that, only one woman interested him—and she'd pointed a pistol at him and shown him her door.

"At the moment, I prefer this." He touched a finger to the foolscap and dragged it across the polished table.

Burton picked it up and scanned the list.

"I want treasury records on these places of business and names," Alexander said. "Everything you can find. Taxes, custom records, places of residence . . . their grandmother's favorite color if you have it."

Burton rubbed his chin. "The hack, the shop, the brewery should be easy, but tracking individual names . . . That will take time."

"I don't have time," he said tersely. He had six days and counting.

Burton sat up, his black robe tenting over knobby knees. "You are quite serious about this."

The blessedness of friendship was how quickly one man understood another.

"I am. I need the information by noon."

"Noon?" Burton's baritone pitched incredulously. "I have three depositions this morning."

"You, of all men, can find a way."

Burton set down the paper. "Since this is the duke's business, I could schedule something tomorrow afternoon—"

"No. Today." He scooted closer and dropped his voice. "Your key, leave it with me."

Burton was elbow on the table, his cheek resting on two fingers. They could be university lads, plotting their way out of a scrape, except this was no frivolous escapade.

Thus, Burton's insightful, "This isn't the duke's business, is it?" rattled him.

Damp palms testified to how badly Alexander wanted this and how ill-equipped he was for subterfuge—even if all he planned was to read tax records.

"I know what I am asking of you."

"I don't think you do."

Keeper of the Pell Office key was the highest trust. Access to records old and new a solemn responsibility.

"Assign one clerk to bring the records," Alexander said quietly. "I'll research them."

The clatter of shops and stalls opening sounded belowstairs. Amiable chatter passed outside the chamber's closed door, clerks starting their day. Witnesses would soon arrive, and the chamber he occupied, in fact, might be scheduled for Burton's depositions.

Shifting in his seat, Alexander dropped his voice and made his final push. "The key, four hours . . . that's all I ask."

"You, rummaging around the Pell Office?"

"You know I'm trustworthy."

"Trust is not the issue."

Sacred rules were. The Pell Office had centuries of them. One could believe the entire kingdom hung on tradition and procedure and the inviolable privacy of its financial records.

"If I didn't know any better, I'd say this is about a woman." Burton uncoiled himself from his chair. "But we all know Serious Sloane doesn't waste time chasing petticoats."

Serious Sloane. The appellation belonged to his university days. He gladly owned it, then and now. Firm direction was a badge of honor. Women had been passing fancies, nothing he invested in. If a woman let him know they liked his face and manners, he was more than happy to accommodate. But chasing a woman? He never had the time.

Burton, who was presently rolling up the list, managed to have ample stores of time.

"I'll do this under one condition: the key is returned to me by the noon hour and not one minute later."

Alexander gusted his relief. "I owe you greatly."

"A debt I shall collect, my friend. Our club has a cricket match at the end of the month, and no one plays deep leg like you." Burton batted Alexander's shoulder with the rolled-up foolscap. "I expect you to be there."

"I haven't played all summer."

"A fact of which I am well aware."

Burton's smile brooked no argument. The man lived and breathed three things: women, the law, and cricket.

"One end of the season cricket match, it is," Alexander said.

"Excellent. I shall pass my key and your list into Fernsby's capable hands. He will be at your disposal for fetching and researching ledgers."

"The new clerk?"

"He's bloody good. Treat him well, he's our new bowler." Burton winked. "Don't let the spectacles fool you. He's a lion on the pitch."

He sat back in the chair, relieved.

"Thank you, my friend."

"My pleasure." Burton ambled to the door. "Anything else you need?"

He twirled the quill, an outrageous idea forming.

"Do you know of a good mantua maker?"

Chapter Seven

"The *sgian-dubh* might be in Chelsea," Cecelia announced.

"Chelsea? I thought we were here tae talk about Bloomsbury Place." Aunt Maude helped herself to another biscuit.

"Dr. Sloane had three homes—the two he connected in Bloomsbury Place and another in Chelsea—something I discovered last night while reading the inventory list."

She stifled a smile and kept last night's other discovery to herself. No need to stir the pot. Aunt Maude was already in fiery form.

"How much fiddle-faddle can a body collect? If you ask me, the doctor had more money than sense."

"Like most Englishmen," Mary said between sips of tea.

Titters cluttered the cramped salon. They were Scots in London, one-time rebels who'd grown comfortable living among the enemy. Cecelia turned her back on the window to her mews. She'd had her fill thinking about a certain tall, intelligent Englishman and his tight . . . queue.

"It may take months to organize a plan," she said. "Look at how long it took to find a portion of the gold."

Four years was writ grimly on their faces. That's how long it had taken them to find a fraction of the Jacobite treasure. They'd settled in London, found their bearings, and began their league's mission. Strangers in a strange land, honoring the vow given to their clan chief in Arisaig, but she refused to spend another four years hunting the blasted dagger. A cunning woman had replaced the fresh-faced village lass she once was. Being unwed and without family, she had to be. London devoured unattended young women and spit out their bones. Waves of them flocked to the City, and the brothels welcomed them with open arms and false promises.

Men might think they ruled the City but women were its undercurrent.

Thus, she was not surprised to hear a certain woman's name creep into the conversation when Aunt Flora set a copy of *The Public Advertiser* on the table.

"I read this yesterday." Aunt Flora's work-worn finger tapped the paper.

All heads tipped for a view of the article. Mary Fletcher angled her neck as she was seated on the lone wooden chair brought in from the kitchen. She read the upside-down script aloud.

"'The Marquess of Swynford and the British Museum Board of Trustees will host a costume ball on the twelfth of September at Swynford House in St. James Square with rooms dedicated to the display of the late Sir Hans Sloane's collection. Giant turtle shells, finger coral, and plant specimens are some of the featured items in the Natural Wonders of the World exhibit. Certain curiosities will be displayed for the first time since the late doctor added them to his collection: shoes from around the world, Persian amulets, and'"—her gray gaze pinned Cecelia—"'centuries-old ceremonial daggers.'"

"The *sgian-dubh* is sure tae be among them." Aunt Flora's voice rose excitedly.

Mary continued her reading.

"It says the cost of a ticket is"—she paused to feign choking—"*two . . . hundred . . . pounds . . . a person!*"

"Two hundred pounds? To dress up in fanciful clothes and stare at the dead doctor's *à bric et à brac*?" Aunt Maude snatched another biscuit. "The English have lost their minds."

Margaret scooted to the edge of her seat. "Even if we scratched up the funds for one of us to attend, we still don't have enough time to form a plan."

"Or to sew a costume," Aunt Flora said.

"Nor should we." Mary set the paper in her lap. "The Marquess of Swynford is the Countess of Denton's brother."

Aunt Flora waved off her argument. "It doesna mean she'll attend his entertainment."

All the same, the Countess of Denton's name cast a pall over the room. The woman wanted revenge on their league; even if she wasn't aware of all its members, the lady had felt their sting. Last month, the league had sneaked into her house and taken back Jacobite gold which the countess had stolen from the Highlands. In the aftermath, Lady Denton had fixated on Anne Neville and Will MacDonald to her detriment. With those two safely gone, the countess would cast her net wider and find out who else was involved in the theft.

The women gathered in Cecelia's salon needed someone to protect them. They needed a leader.

Cecelia planted herself in her favorite green damask chair and curled one foot under her rump.

"We focused so much on getting the gold that we missed a chance to plan for this." She grimaced and delivered a smooth lie. "Though it pains me, we may have to let this opportunity pass."

"Very reasonable of you," Mary said. *Anne would've done the same* was the message in her eyes.

Cecelia's gaze dropped to linked fingers in her lap. This was the tension she'd breathed since the four women in her salon had fled the City after the night they'd taken back the gold. She had stayed, spoiling for a fight. Pure recklessness. But she'd been on hand to help Anne and Will when they needed it to escape the countess—an accident of fate, which made her rebellious decision forgivable.

"First, we need to see to Neville House repairs and Anne's warehouse on Gun Wharf." She looked at Aunt Maude and Aunt Flora. "And you two need protection."

Worry dimmed Aunt Flora's blue eyes. "You think Lady Denton will come after the likes of us?"

"You live in Anne's old house. At best, she'll think you are harmless older kin. At worst . . ."

Cecelia swallowed the rest of her sentence. She didn't have the heart to share her thoughts or the unpalatable note which arrived this morning at breakfast. This was the scale she balanced: How much to reveal? Of all the women in their fledgling league, the old spinster sisters faced the greatest risk.

Aunt Maude's brow furrowed. "What about Mary and Margaret? They need protection."

"Mary and I are safe, dears. We weren't inside Lady Denton's house, unlike the rest of you the night of the theft. And the Night Watch and the ward beadle are a constant presence on White Cross Street." Tender-hearted Margaret was the youngest of their number at nineteen. She covered Aunt Maude's hand with her own and gave a reassuring squeeze. "With all those eyes watching our shop, I am not afraid. But I do worry about you in Southwark."

"I have a solution." Cecelia reached for a bite of cheese. "We hire a man to protect Aunt Maude and Aunt Flora. He will live at Neville House and while he's there he does the repairs."

Aunt Maude's lips pursed. "Sounds like another mouth to feed."

"Pray tell, who is this manly paragon?" Mary asked.

She braced herself. "Mr. Rory MacLeod."

Mary was aghast. "The Countess of Denton's private footman?"

"Former private footman. I have it on good authority he left her . . . *employ* a day or two after we stole the gold from her house."

"He didn't exactly help us that night," Mary said.

Cecelia held the cheese to her lips. "He didn't exactly stop us either."

"But he is a MacLeod," Aunt Maude grumbled.

"And we live among the English. Pick your poison, dears—a wrathful countess or a MacLeod." She popped the bite into her mouth while the others digested that.

The Western Isles had witnessed centuries of MacLeods and MacDonalds at each other's throats. The rebellion's devastating end forced a truce on the warring clans, and many a MacLeod fled Scotland alongside a MacDonald.

"Let us not forget," Cecelia said gently. "Mr. MacLeod is a Highlander."

The reminder mollified Aunt Maude, and a knock at the front door paused their conversations. They refreshed their tea and indulged in biscuits, slices of cheese, and fruits, careful not to talk league business while someone was at the door. Jenny emerged from the kitchen and stood in the salon doorway, wiping her hands on a checkered cloth tucked into her waist.

"Miss? Shall I answer it?"

"Please do." To the room, she said, "We'll talk about the most harmless of subjects—sheep." The third and final part of their mission was restoring Clanranald's herds.

They chattered on about sheep until Jenny reappeared in the salon, a pristine dress box balanced in her arms. The small hairs on Cecelia's arms raised. A silk bow draped over one side of the box, a glimmer of elegance and refinement.

"It's from Madame Laurent." Mary breathed the words more than she said them.

Aunt Flora scowled. "How can you know that by a box?"

"The lavender silk bow is her calling card," Margaret said. "Madame Laurent has *the most* fashionable rooms on Evans Row off Bond Street."

Mary craned her neck. "Her name is probably embossed on the top."

Jenny nudged the box inches higher. She knew about the league, but she also knew whom she served.

"Miss, shall I take this to your bedchamber?"

Cecelia waved her off. "Put it on my bed, Jenny. I'll open it later."

Mary eyed Cecelia. "Are you denying us the pleasure of seeing what you purchased from Madame Laurent?"

Cecelia felt her flat-lipped smile expand.

"I did not purchase anything from Madame Laurent."

Starched petticoat bottoms scooted to the edge of their seats. Aunt Maude's lips pursed while the rest of the women peered from the box to Cecelia.

"Then who did?"

Mary's artful tone was interference coated with honey and served with a slice of jealousy. Only beautiful Mary, who generally ignored men, would have the audacity to test her. The corset maker's question was a push to Cecelia's shove. Pasting on a daring smile, she put her plate on the table already burdened with a hodgepodge of dishes.

"Bring it here, Jenny."

She inched forward, and Jenny set the box on her knees. A stylish gold leaf *M* and *L* inside a garland of flowers had been stamped on the box. Cecelia untied the bow, the aroma of dried lavender wafting. The elegant Provence scent—another sign of Madame Laurent. She lifted the top, finding bits of the dried herb scattered on white tissue.

Aunt Maude eyed the box. "Have you a new admirer?"

"I don't know."

She brushed aside the dried herb and unfolded the tissue. Underneath was dull, brown wool, a hideous shade. Nestled in the wool was a note. The women in her salon leaned unabashedly forward. Mary, stretching, Margaret and Aunt Flora in danger of tipping over, and Aunt Maude, who stood up because she couldn't be bothered with the pretense of sitting.

Cecelia opened the note for a private reading, and Mr. Sloane's tenor reached her ears, polite, educated, and limned with humor.

Dear Miss MacDonald,

> *Please accept this gift as a token of my gratitude for a memorable evening.*

A coy smile came. *Memorable indeed.* She turned her attention back to the brief missive.

> *At the very least, it will keep you in good health should you stumble across a rogue late at night.*

> *Warmly yours,*
> *Mr. Alexander Sloane*

> *P.S. I want to renew last night's discussion. If you feel the same, meet me at the White Hart, tonight.*

Intrigue multiplied in every word. She held the paper in one hand, caressing it with the other. Mr.

Sloane painted enough of a word picture with his dangerous invitation. *Brazen man.* She tucked his note between the chair and her petticoats and neatly lifted the folded brown wool. The box tumbled off her knees, and lavender bits littered the floor.

Mr. Sloane had gifted her with an abominable night-robe lined with pea-green felt. An ardor-smashing garment, if ever she'd seen one.

She stifled a giggle.

Well done, Mr. Sloane. You have baited the hook.

She had received gifts from men before. From a baron and an earl who thought they could buy her body. From a ship's captain who thought he could buy her loyalty. And from a merchant who thought he could buy her silence. No man ever thought to pique her interest—until Mr. Sloane.

"Brilliant," she murmured joyously. Her arms and the robe fell to a heap in her lap.

"Ugly is more like it," Aunt Maude said loudly. "It's a monstrosity."

"Maude," Aunt Flora hissed. "It's a gift."

Aunt Maude's lips pursed. "If that's the work of London's best mantua maker, then London's best mantua maker could learn a thing or two from Mary and Margaret."

Cecelia stroked soft wool. Pink thread bound one seam, eye-glaring yellow bound another.

"It's a wonderful monstrosity. I love it."

"But hardly fashionable." Margaret was diplomatic, collecting tissue at her feet. "It doesn't seem like something you'd wear."

"It's not. But I shall wear it anyway." Her voice tripped with delight.

Mary was stern-eyed, reaching for the note. She

opened it, an utterly intrusive act, but Cecelia was too humored by the ugly gift to care.

"And who is Mr. Alexander Sloane?" Mary asked.

Cecelia held out the box for Jenny. "Someone I met."

"We found him arse up in a barrel last night." The maid took the box, her chin tipping mutinously. "Out in the mews, he was."

"Ho!" Aunt Flora chortled behind fanned fingers. "Deep in his cups, was he?"

Mary was not amused. She eyed the servant with a *hold nothing back* glare. "Please explain yourself. I fear Cecelia may edit this tale, and we want details."

Pandora's box was opened, and Jenny looked ready to tell all.

"She'll do nothing of the sort. If you want details, ask me." Cecelia plopped the night-robe on the box in Jenny's arms. "Don't you have something to do in the kitchen?"

"Yes, miss."

Jenny exited the salon, her hems swinging a defiant retreat. Cecelia smoothed her petticoats, lavender's aroma rising from the fabric and from the dried bits on the floor.

She snatched the note from Mary. "That belongs to me."

Mary was stiff-necked, her gray eyes a glitter of chaotic emotions. Cecelia paced all of three steps to her narrow window. Mary's challenge was fair. Last night's incident was a splash of cold water. The women of her league, her kinswomen, were her primary concern. Trouble for one meant trouble for all. But Fielding's investigation was of her alone. She folded the note in half, deciding on a modicum of truth.

"It's true. Mr. Sloane was in my mews last night, and he was quite sober."

"What was he doing in your mews?" Aunt Flora asked.

"Watching me."

Aunt Maude planted a fist on her thick waist. "Hard for a mon tae watch someone when he's arse up in a barrel."

Cecelia touched cool glass, biting back a smile.

"His hat fell into the barrel. He bent over to get it. That's how we found him. Then Jenny tied him up."

Aunt Flora squinted at her. "Then what'd you do with him, lass?"

Cecelia averted her eyes, otherwise the old spinster's kind blue eyes would see too much. From her window, she glimpsed the Thames, its gray skin rippling like a snake.

"I took him to my bedchamber to ask him a few questions."

Margaret's maidenly inhale stung.

"Which is not the same as taking him to my bed," Cecelia said crisply.

"Well, he's no' there now. No' if he's sending you ugly night-robes." The settee groaned under Aunt Maude finding her seat again. "Is there anything else you need tae tell us?"

There was the rub. Of the league's members, only Anne knew that she was a person of interest in Fielding's ledgers, and once a body caught the magistrate's eyes, one didn't simply break free. With his latest funds, law enforcement was transforming. Which begged the question: Who should she fear more? Fielding, a man empowered by ambition; the countess, a woman empowered by greed; or the Duke of Newcastle, a man empowered by the crown?

She toyed with the gold medallion stamped with the number nine. They all wore the same gold piece made from melted French livres, the King of France's final support, a treasure which had reached Clanranald's shores after the surrender only to be stolen soon after. The war had been over, but for the women gathered here, their struggle had just begun.

She stuffed the provocative note into her petticoat pocket and chose a careful, "Mr. Sloane serves the Duke of Newcastle, but before learning that I might have propositioned him."

"'Might have'?" Mary's voice pitched high at the same time as Margaret said, "The duke advises the king!"

Cecelia tried not to squirm.

Aunt Flora, however, took the news in stride. "What was the nature of your proposition, lass?"

As the league's mother hen, Aunt Flora was the first to fuss and the first to be practical. She never batted an eye at Cecelia's assignations with men, be they real or imagined.

"I asked for his help to gain entry to Bloomsbury Place, but I didn't tell him why. He doesn't know about the *sgian-dubh* or about Jacobite gold in London, and he certainly doesn't know about our league."

Yet.

The unspoken word was a Damocles sword over their heads. The harder they worked on their mission, the closer the blade came—the price of success. Their first four years in the City had yielded fruitless searches. They'd been six women recovering from the aftermath of the Uprising and doing their best to help their kinsmen. It took all their strength to gain a foothold here, but they did. This summer, their labor bore fruit. Now, thanks to Mr. Sloane's insightful observations, the Duke of Newcastle and Fielding would hound them, unless she persuaded Mr. Sloane to share his unimportant findings. Or share nothing at all.

His Grace could hardly feel threatened by a small-bosomed woman with skinny arms.

"What did Mr. Sloane want from you?" Aunt Maude pressed.

She looked to the river. "Information. Something to appease Bow Street. He's there on assignment to watch crown funds."

It was the truth scrubbed clean of certain details.

"Watching crown funds is quite different from trying to extract information from you," Mary said.

"I know," she said quietly.

Aunt Flora stood up, her knees cracking. "I trust you'll pick and choose what tae say . . . something tae divert the magistrate."

The room stirred behind Cecelia. Dishes were slowly gathered. Crumbs wiped away as if the mention of Bow Street had sucked the life out of each woman present. Fielding and his poisonous quill. As magistrate, he strived to do good in London, but it couldn't erase the slap-in-the-face his past vehement anti-Jacobite writings delivered. His strident words were a wound that refused to heal.

The spinsters and Margaret carried dishes and trays into the kitchen, while Mary stood by the room's tepid fire staring holes into Cecelia's back.

"Mr. Sloane . . . is he the man who followed you to my shop?"

"He is."

Their league was on a wild race, careening out of control. None could stop the momentum which began four years ago when they pledged an oath to Clanranald's chief. Find the gold, find the dagger, find the sheep. Their mission had been clear, the path to achieve it not so much.

Mary crossed the room and at her shoulder said, "You're going to meet him, aren't you?"

"Yes."

"Are you mad?"

She spun around. "He's a good man."

"And you know this because you took him to your bedchamber?" Mary whisper-hissed.

"Careful how you judge, Mary."

Mary hugged herself tightly. "This isn't judgment . . . it's—it's fear."

Pottery clattered in the kitchen. The others had already recovered from the mention of Bow Street. Aunt Maude and Jenny were swapping recipes while Margaret giggled over something Aunt Flora said. Their joy was the air Cecelia breathed. She would fight to keep it, especially with cool, proud Mary, her harshest critic.

Cecelia pinched the fraying edge of a silk bow on her stomacher. "You're right to be concerned. I received another note this morning."

Gray eyes sharpened. "From another man?"

"No. From a chambermaid I've bribed at Denton House." She glanced at the salon's open door and kept her voice quiet. "Do you want me to get it for you?"

"Just tell me the contents."

"The Countess of Denton hired someone to investigate me."

A terse line slanted above Mary's nose. "Because she saw you with Will and Anne the night we took the gold."

"But the countess doesn't know about you or your sister."

"Which doesn't make me feel better. You're still in danger," Mary said miserably. A patient exhale and she asked, "Is it someone from Bow Street?"

"The note didn't say."

"Then it could be this Mr. Sloane."

"Working for the Countess of Denton, Fielding, *and* the Duke of Newcastle? I doubt it."

Dread silence hoisted itself on them. Their work these four years was a tangled web, spinning faster and tighter.

"You'll have to trust me," Cecelia said.

"I do trust you. It's why I did not read aloud the part where Mr. Sloane asked to see you tonight." Mary's eyes were the haunted gray of a winter-bound loch. "Please don't make me regret it."

Chapter Eight

St. Paul's Church faced Covent Garden, where sin and sanctity met. King Street carved a broad path between them with the White Hart at the westward end. It was a public house striving to belong. The facade was old brick parapets on a street with newly plastered cornices. Sensible lodging for a barrister serving the realm's most powerful duke.

Inside the White Hart, one found paneled walls and serving maids with starched aprons. Food steamed deliciously from pewter plates, the patrons staged and boisterous. A tableau of wealth on the rise. More velvet coats than wool, more pretty paste shoe buckles than tarnished tin. Cecelia stopped a mobcapped maid to ask about Mr. Sloane.

She wasn't surprised when the young woman uttered a polite, "He's been expecting you, miss. Please follow me."

The White Hart would oblige anyone if the right amount of money and discretion changed hands.

The maid took her up three flights of stairs to the last door, curtseyed, and sped off. From this height, the public room below was a hub of tasteful noise and Mr. Sloane's room a quiet place. She knocked thrice, the gentle force nudging the already cracked door. Through the slit, she spied him by a leaping fire engrossed in a piece of paper.

For a few seconds, he was hers. Deep in thought, his elbow on the mantel, a finger touching his lower lip. His regal profile belonged on a coin. Like a Roman senator. Or a minor king. A man who used his formidable skills of persuasion artfully, beguilingly, sensually. A man who righted the wrongs of the world and managed courtly handsomeness while doing it.

She was a tiny bit breathless, anticipating all his persuasive power directed at her.

Mr. Sloane's splendid bronze eyes found her, their light rising from the page.

"Miss MacDonald. I was afraid you wouldn't come."

She entered his receiving room and shut the door. Saint or sinner, she'd make this meeting hers.

"And miss the chance to thank you in person for your lovely gift? I think not."

Mr. Sloane advanced, his heel strikes slow.

"I thought you would find humor in it. I spent a good portion of my time and money hunting for the perfect night-robe."

"As well as you hunted me?" She removed her gloves, her pulse jumping.

"We both know I am not well-practiced in subterfuge."

Mr. Sloane stopped in the middle of the room. He stuffed the paper in his pocket, his gaze ranging over her from hem to head while she slipped free of her cloak. Anticipating his nearness made her breath heavier, her skin tighter.

"Yet you managed to filch the ugliest night-robe in London. A poor grandmotherly soul will have to wait until Madame Laurent's seamstresses can craft another one."

"Did my gift make you smile?"

She touched a hand over her heart. "I giggled like a twelve-year-old girl, Mr. Sloane."

He beamed. "Then it was worth every shilling."

Silly hominess strummed her senses when she hung her cloak on the hook beside his greatcoat. She smoothed damp palms down modest panniers and faced him. Their evening together felt inevitable, the outcome not. Mr. Sloane waited, his left hand gripping the opening of his coat. A habit, she supposed. She'd seen other barristers do the same.

"We are beyond the formal bow and curtsey, aren't we, Miss MacDonald?"

"Indeed, we are."

Light sparked in his eyes, an invitation to explore new boundaries, and not all of them polite. Her pulse nipped faster.

The league's business . . . she was here for the league's business.

The possibility of fun—or whatever might happen— had never hampered her spirit. Why start now? With the door closed, it was just the two of them. Control could go either way, and she preferred it be hers, though it was obvious Mr. Sloane wanted the same. His smile was a dangerous slash of white in a dark room, which, if she was not mistaken, was intentionally unlit. The door to a small bedchamber was open.

The bed was made, the window's curtains open, and light from outside flushed the counterpane with a decent glow. It would be exciting to do indecent things on it.

A rush of feminine power flooded her. Mr. Sloane had invited her here: it didn't mean she had to concede all authority.

She took languorous, hip-swaying strides forward. In the rough-scrabble world of London, confidence was her greatest asset. Better than beauty, more solid than transient money. Self-assurance was the gift she gave herself. Armed with it, she sauntered up to Mr. Sloane and drew a slow circle around a mother-of-pearl waistcoat button on his chest.

"Your note mentioned that you have something for me?"

A brow arched. "You do get right to the point, don't you?"

"We could waste time on the preliminaries, Mr. Sloane, but I've found directness a more delightful alternative."

Darkness carved hollows in his face.

"Candor, Miss MacDonald. A fine quality," he said smooth and low. "Are there other aspects you'd like to mention?"

Tightness twisted in her chest. "My qualities?"

"Anything to do with . . . business?"

She stopped her bold circle on his button.

That slight pause in his question—he *knew* something.

The clever barrister had done some digging. His eyes searched her as if he wanted her to spill everything. Her secrets, her past, her plans for the future.

Her heart thumped with new speed. It was the same rapid beat which throbbed in her when she stood on a ledge above the loch at home, the day she'd learned to swim. There was no safe wading in from the shore. The dare to jump and the fear that came with it was as sharp and invigorating then as now.

She willed strength into her voice. "I believe I demonstrated astonishing candor last night."

"You did—to a point."

"It would be unwise for me to reveal all, sir." She pushed his button, a tender warning. "As a barrister, you should understand that."

"I can only be of service when I know all the facts."

She huffed softly, her hand falling to her side. He smelled of soap and seduction and of skin that wanted touching. Even his ears were kissable and attractive.

"Then let's begin with this: my terms have changed."

He grunted. "Have they?"

She breathed the ease at having trumped him. He gestured to the high-back settle tucked next to the fire.

"Perhaps we should discuss these new terms of yours more comfortably."

She ambled past him and took a seat in the plain, slatted chair.

"Would you like a drink?" he asked. "I have wine, sherry—"

"Port suits me, if you have it."

He walked to a cabinet in the corner. Beside it was the door to his bedchamber.

"Port. A masculine drink."

"Does my choice surprise you?"

"Everything about you surprises me. In the best way."

His back was to her, rust velvet stretching across wide shoulders, the coat narrowing to his waist, the frock hem ending on his thighs. They'd both dressed well for this meeting, with enough formality and a trim of desire. Firelight touched Mr. Sloane's sinewed calves twitching under silk stockings. He was coiled energy. A man who knew what he wanted and would use rigorous strategy to get it.

Desire skittered delicately down her back. This would be their language for the night—a dialect for secrets, another for lust. Conversation would twine like a rope tightly twisted until one of them relented.

It wouldn't be her.

Mr. Sloane walked to the table, two tin cups clutched by their handles in one hand, a dark-glassed bottle of port in the other. He set them down and poured, tawny port streaming seductively from the bottle's mouth.

"I decided this was an evening for the entire bottle." Raggedness edged his voice.

She drank his port, its addictive slide coating her throat. "A tawny port. It matches your eyes."

Mr. Sloane took a seat on the pine settle nailed to the wall. "I am more interested in *your* eyes, Miss MacDonald. In everything about you."

The world became the small table. Their island. Anything could happen. Mr. Sloane took a long fortifying drink and set the nearly empty tin cup on the table.

"Thirsty business, is it? Having to talk with me," she said.

"In my short but esteemed turn as barrister, I learned it is the tendency of criminals to confess what is untrue. Imagine how astonishing it has been for me to cross paths with a reprobate—a pretty reprobate—who speaks the truth."

"This sounds like the beginning of a confession."

"In a way, it is."

She crossed one leg over the other and leaned in. "Are you sure you want to pour out your soul to a reprobate?"

He sucked in a quick breath as if she'd asked, *Do you want a quick tup? Or a slow one?*

His eyes pooled liquid and black, the fire a metallic orange-bronze flame dancing in the center.

"You are the most fascinating woman I have ever had the privilege to meet. I would be lying if I said I didn't want to taste you, but it is in our best interest to"—he hesitated, intent on his thumb stroking his cup—"to keep our arrangement strictly business."

"Because you never mix business and pleasure."

His tortured gaze met hers. "Because sexual congress taints clear thinking."

"The act does no harm, Mr. Sloane." She leaned closer, her voice whisper-soft. "Emotions do."

He breathed that in, a desperate man who found himself in an unknown land. If lust and secrets were dialects on their little island, their currency was honesty and truth. Strange coin shared between two people planning to skirt the law. But this was what she'd learned watching Fielding and his courtroom dramas. To parse words down to the filament. To play on facts and feelings with equal aplomb. In her brief exposure to Mr. Sloane, she'd learned he lived for the letter of the law, while she paid homage to its spirit.

Poor Mr. Sloane. Desire was ripping him to shreds.

"Let me make this easy for you. Rather than an open door at Bloomsbury Place, I want this instead." From her petticoat pocket, she pulled a torn piece of paper, *The Public Advertiser*'s announcement, and set it on the table. "A ticket to the Marquess of Swynford's ball. All perfectly legal," she added.

"But you plan to do something illegal."

Her shrug would've made a Frenchwoman proud. If this were a chess match, they were evenly played. Careful but not overly cautious.

He spun the paper around and read it. "This is Wednesday next."

"It is."

"At two hundred pounds a ticket, no less."

"It is. But I would think the Duke of Newcastle's man could get a ticket."

His laugh was low and quiet. "You've grossly misjudged my place in the hierarchy of His Grace's office. I am the undersecretary to the undersecretary."

"You are also a brilliant man."

Mr. Sloane's head dipped, a heart-swooning grin creasing his face. It was the kind of smile that made her want to climb over the table and kiss him. She resisted doing so and the urge to reveal how his insightful notebook illuminated his mental acuity.

"You honor me with your praise, Miss MacDonald, but this is beyond my reach, especially in so short a time."

"Is Baron of the Exchequer worth it?"

Mr. Sloane's grin died slowly. Her crossed leg

ticked back and forth under the table, steady as a clock. A new turn in their game of cat and mouse was afoot.

"Come now, we both know you didn't ask me here to flirt, Mr. Sloane."

"Because man cannot live by flirtation alone." He swallowed more of his port.

"This is business. You want the judge's seat badly enough to toss your fine morals aside and barter with a woman of dubious character."

He studied the fire, his fingers drumming the table while the cogs and wheels of his mind cranked. "*If* I managed to obtain two tickets—and that is a considerable *if*—what do I get in return?"

"I don't need two tickets. Only one."

"I shall escort you. Hence, two tickets."

"I don't need you to dance attendance on me."

"Nevertheless, I shall." He folded both arms on the table and leaned closer. "A nonnegotiable point, I'm afraid. Take it or leave it."

Mr. Sloane was a rampart that wouldn't budge. She studied his even features with new eyes. *Had the Countess of Denton hired him?* Why else would he mandate going with her to Swynford House?

Truly, these were the moments that tried her, the razor's edge of decisions she'd have to live with, whatever the outcome.

"It would be much easier for you to give me a ticket and walk away."

"I don't want easy, Miss MacDonald. I want you," he said in a velvet-smooth voice.

Molten lust flared in his eyes. Mr. Sloane wanted her, the Jacobite.

Her knees jellied. He wanted her and she wanted

him, but there was no competing with the magnitude of his ambition. Or hers.

What a tangle this was. A mere three months ago, the bloodthirsty Government had hanged Dr. Cameron, a high-ranking rebel who had the misfortune of being caught in Scotland seven years after the surrender. What would happen to a Jacobite woman living under their nose in London?

She couldn't help a belligerent, "You'll do anything to get your judge's seat."

He winced as if the words struck a tender nerve.

"I will need something to divert Fielding," he said. "Something big."

"Because he wants information on the horrid Jacobite woman. Just what does Fielding think I am?"

"I'm not privy to his inner thoughts."

His gaze honed on the tiny rosette pinned to her bodice—a piece of her father's Clanranald MacDonald kilt worn in his memory. She'd donned her most sedate gown to this meeting, the green velvet so dark it was almost black. Black lace flared from her elbows and trimmed her bodice, the rosette nestled underneath it. Of all the places he could look, his eyes found it.

"But we both know Fielding's opinions on the Uprising." He looked pointedly at the rosette. "Shows of Jacobite loyalty like that don't help."

"My rosette does not break any laws." She swallowed more port and added a mocking, "The Dress Act is safe to continue its insulting limits on kilts and bagpipes."

His mouth firmed.

"Wearing it is provocative. Good men died to preserve the Union."

She thumped her tin cup hard on the table.

"And good men died trying to end it."

Furious heat rose in her cheeks. Did Mr. Sloane fear she was about violent insurrection? Was that at the heart of his hesitation? She'd already confessed her queasiness at the mere sight of blood, and he knew very well she'd pointed an empty pistol at him.

"What I am about has nothing to do with . . . with bloodshed of any kind."

He reached for her. "Then tell me what you *are* about."

She jumped up and stalked to the window. His touch was suddenly unconscionable, as if it might set her afire and not the delectable kind a woman enjoyed. The *sgian-dubh* was so, so close. Her fingers curled, anticipating the hilt in her grasp. A simple dagger, ripe for the plucking, much easier than taking back Jacobite gold, and this man wanted her to—what? Bare her soul to get it?

It was laughable. Mr. Sloane wanted more than she could give to him or any other man.

He followed her all the same as if testy women were a matter of course. Perhaps that's how it was in the world of law and order. One had to wade through messy parts to find a satisfactory end. If so, she supposed Mr. Sloane was a master at it, cordial smiles and all.

"It strikes me that you and I are at an impasse."

"You think so?" she said with false brightness.

Being here was madness, the undercurrent of attraction as treacherous as striking a bargain with a barrister who served the crown. Mr. Sloane rubbed a finger across his cheek, which, she noticed, shined from a recent shave.

"I have my limits, Mr. Sloane. If you want this meeting to continue, you will have to breathe life into it."

His lips twitched. "You're not going to make this easy for me, are you?"

"No," she said stoutly.

Beautiful eyes, so breathtaking and direct, pinned her.

"We both want something and underneath that is something else we both want. Badly."

Her mouth dried. South of that aridness, her heart ticked with maddening speed while she listened to Mr. Sloane's genteel voice.

"Before anything else can happen," he said. "You and I need to build trust."

"How do we do that?"

She waited for the usual, disappointing male solution. A quick coupling. Salacious gropes. Anything to take the edge off their lust in order to get on with the important business of her getting the *sgian-dubh* and him one step closer to his letters patent.

Instead, Mr. Sloane's diabolical mouth opened with "I propose that you ask me whatever you want and I will answer truthfully. I, in turn, will do the same with you, expecting you to answer honestly."

She recoiled. "Anything? That is too much, sir."

He raised a pacifying hand. "You have the right to pass, once."

"I left those sorts of games behind when I was a girl of twelve, Mr. Sloane," she said, trying hard to maintain her resistance.

"Why twelve?"

"Because that is when I had to grow up rather quickly."

She wished Mr. Sloane had been the typical boor who wanted a tup. A man like that could easily be managed. But his stillness wooed her. Peaceful, alluring, shadows and light carving his face enticingly.

"My mother left my father and me to wed another man," she said grudgingly.

His eyes rounded. "Your mother was a bigamist?"

"Oh, wouldn't that be perfect? You could add 'daughter of a bigamist' to your journal."

Mr. Sloane was patient. She crossed her arms as if to stem a tide of words, but it didn't work.

"My mother was my father's housekeeper. They never wed." She paused a heartbeat to let that shocking news sink in. "You see, Mr. Sloane, bastard daughters of freethinking surgeons don't become fast friends with proper girls who play proper games. I didn't have time for them anyway. I had my father's household to run."

The fire crackled conspicuously in the corner. On the street below, a mother and father herded two children into a waiting carriage. She watched them under her lashes. She'd seen the family eating their dinner upon entering the White Hart. Cheerful, they were, chattering away. Outside, the father scooped up the boy and deposited him in the carriage. The sweetness hit a raw place. Mr. Sloane watched the tableau with her until the door was shut and the coachman snapped the reins.

"You see?" He leaned casually against the window frame. "That wasn't so bad, was it?"

What? Watching the happy family or admitting she didn't come from one? Mr. Sloane distilled the air. So calm, so comforting, the sting of her admission evaporating.

"You're trying to take the starch out of me, aren't you?"

"I'd settle for building a bridge of trust, Miss Mac-Donald, which is the only way we'll both get what we want." He paused. "As long as this isn't about anyone getting hurt."

She tried to absorb this new turn. To make sense of why he wanted her trust. This was what happened to women who lived in the shadows. Honest light was uncomfortably foreign.

"I'm only taking back what was stolen from people I love. Something that was sold to Sir Hans Sloane."

She looked out the window, a lost soul. In the distance, embers burst in the night sky like gold foil blown apart.

"Vauxhall fireworks," she murmured. "The last night of the pleasure garden's season."

Vauxhall usually ended in August, but the fine end of summer pushed the season another few weeks. More fireworks sparkled over Vauxhall's Italianate colonnades, offering a glimpse of the garden's splendor. London was a smelly, vicious, noisy place full of corruption and hypocrisy of all stripes. Despite it, the old bawd of a City had sunk her claws into her—in the best and worst way. The war was her past, not as ardent a cause as it was for Anne and certainly not in the same measure for Mary, which left her adrift. Tethered to a city she shouldn't love (and sometimes didn't), yet far from the home she once knew.

"Your point about trust is well taken, Mr. Sloane. I dally with men, but I don't trust them."

His left hand held on to his coat over the button-holes near his heart. He'd be resplendent in court robes, the austere black on a moral man. As judge or barrister, he'd balance ethos, pathos, and logos with a deft hand. She could at least offer the same to him.

"Very well, Mr. Sloane. You have until the last Vauxhall firework burns. Ask what you will and keep your free pass." Her chin nudged higher. "I don't need it."

"I can ask anything, and you will be truthful?" His voice dripped with disbelief.

Chapter Nine

"Yes. Anything," she said.

The mood shifted after Miss MacDonald tendered her offer. Naked honesty with a woman was sultry, as tempting as a kiss. As a barrister, he'd sifted lies from truth on a daily basis, seeing affidavit-men loitering outside the Inns of Court with straw in their buckles, the sign they'd lie for a price—and the wealthy families who paid for their lies. For the duke, he read financial reports, searching for dishonest numbers. Now Miss MacDonald promised him bald truth—a woman London's leading magistrate deemed worthy of a page in one of his ledgers.

If her honesty was glaring, her silence was too.

Miss MacDonald had said nothing about his requirement: two tickets to Swynford House with him at her side.

Moonlight showed her hazel eyes as glittering gems. A wise strategy, holding her tongue.

He ventured a smile. "You aren't planning on using your charms on me, are you?"

"I won't. As long as you don't use your legal wits on me."

"Hardly a fair fight. I'd lose, you know."

Her answering smile was a rapier blade's warning. "Do not test my tolerance, Mr. Sloane."

He let go of his coat. This was irritating. Why stoop to a boyish contrivance? All in the name of knowing a confounding woman who didn't fit in one of society's neat stratums. The Scotswoman defied them. A diamond-bright creature with eye-catching facets each time he looked at her. Two of them, in particular, could not be ignored—Jacobite sympathizer and canny woman.

He wanted more of the goddess of Swan Lane, her striking nature and bold familiarity, a woman at home in her own skin. The fair sex was complex, and Miss MacDonald was no exception. One part of her revealed would be like pulling a string in an intricate web. Pull one part, and the rest moved, except with Miss MacDonald, the rest of her would shimmer.

"I am very serious, Mr. Sloane. One coy play on words and I am gone."

Feet shifting, he didn't think, he didn't strategize. The first words out of his mouth came from sheer curiosity.

"What do you want to steal from the Marquess of Swynford's home?"

Her brow arched. They were on the edge of something new.

"A dagger, and it's not stealing, it's taking back what was stolen from my clan. Cumberland's men took it when they ransacked Arisaig." She added, "After the surrender," with blood-letting severity.

Miss MacDonald was too direct for the admission to be a lie, and he was too shocked not to believe her.

"All this maneuvering? For a dagger?"

"A very old, very sentimental dagger." Her throat worked a delicate swallow. "The *sgian-dubh* is ceremonial. Having it back means a great deal to our clan chief."

Well, that took the rug out from under his feet.

"Your actions are motivated by emotion and not financial gain."

The air softened around them. When Miss MacDonald raised her lashes, artless honesty shined back at him.

"When the Uprising started, Clanranald MacDonald's chief did not support the rebellion."

"What about you? Did you support it?"

Her hesitation was measured by her fingers worrying a bow on her stomacher. "I wanted what my father wanted." She looked out the window, her voice lacking conviction. "Our clan chief was good to me. I would like to bring him some happiness since he lost so much. The *sgian-dubh* will do that."

"Unfortunately, he eventually cast his lot with the rebels. Shifting his loyalty, a costly decision, I'm afraid."

His rueful judgment held no sting. War was a monster gobbling anything in its path, something Miss MacDonald understood by her quiet nod.

"Our chief would rather have his son and heir back in Scotland, which I cannot give him."

No one could give that, not even the king, should his heart thaw. The rebellion was a wound barely scabbed over. The return of high-ranking rebel sons this soon would rip it off. Because the son and heir to Clanranald MacDonald had fought in the Uprising, both father and son paid the price with the heir's exile to France. A boon, really, since many high-ranking rebels paid with their lives. But the clans had suffered. Herds destroyed. Villages burned. The Highlands decimated. Serving the Duke of Newcastle, he'd read the reports. More than fifty estates confiscated, thirteen of them catching the king's consideration. The spoils of war.

Like Cumberland's men taking an old dagger and burning homes in Arisaig.

Victory was easy this far from the battlefield. Until pained fury in a Scotswoman's eyes etched him.

Hers was a woman's view, the one left behind to clean up afterward. War was dirty, ugly grappling. Loyalties changing. One force pitted against another and victory an exhausting glory. There was no tidy end.

But this was different, the proud agony in her voice a weight on his back.

He would not rub salt in what was, in the end, a mutual wound. Both England and Scotland had suffered.

"You should have it," he said at last.

Her eyes widened in disbelief. "You agree?"

"Agree?" he scoffed. "No. But I can offer you my deepest compassion for your clan's plight."

"That sounds like something a solicitor would say before politely turning me away." She eyed his mouth. "And your bland smile is the stiff, well-bred variety. A token expression to go with token words."

"Seven years ago, we *were* enemies."

It was an arrogant brick in their bridge of trust. He couldn't regret saying it. They needed absolute truth, though his reward was her frosty demeanor.

A gusting sigh and, "I am trying, Miss MacDonald."

She looked out the window, her neck a pale kissable column.

"I suppose complete understanding is too much to ask."

The smallest crack broke her words. Her need stripped bare. A gratifying swell spread inside him, warm as a summer breeze. The goddess of Swan Lane had visited him for more than entry to the Marquess of Swynford's house.

"I didn't know you wanted my understanding."

Her mouth twisted bitterly. "Of course I don't want your understanding."

"You have my support to take the dagger." It was a guarded offering, a beginning.

"Very magnanimous of you."

Miss MacDonald's gaze consumed a distant place outside. She was probably counting the minutes until Vauxhall Garden's fireworks burned their last dazzling light. Then she'd be done with this torturous meeting. He half expected the interview to end with insincere apologies, and their bargain to remain undone.

She was still staring at the world outside when she said, "Take off your queue."

"What?"

Miss MacDonald was sylphlike and fair, her diamond-white-paste earbobs catching streetlights. The art of distraction. Keep him focused on a shiny piece to throw him off balance. Fielding would do the same.

"You heard me." Her earbobs twinkled prettily. "Take it off. I want to see you with your hair untied."

"That's hardly a question."

Her feline gaze met his. "Would you untie your queue for me?"

The carefully worded dare snaked through him. A choice to swim above her challenge or sink into soft, deft provocation came with it. *Ask anything* had been the nature of the game, its scope unsketched. His hands knew the answer. They rose slowly to his nape while she watched. Arousal made his arms cumbersome and his fingers clumsy. He untied the black silk ribbon mooring his queue. Blunt-cut hair fell forward and brushed his jaw.

Appreciation glinted in hazel eyes. "That's better."

Her voice caressed him and a shudder followed. The black silk was lustrous and slippery between his fingers, like sex.

"Do you want to tie me up again?"

"Is that your question?" Her smile slid sideways. "It is your turn."

For a heart-thudding moment, he considered it. Blood coursed his veins, honeyed and thick. *Caution, man, caution.*

He heeded the warning in his head and stuffed the ribbon, half in, half out of his outer coat pocket.

"You would be a formidable barrister in court."

"Well, we both know that will never happen."

Miss MacDonald took an unashamed survey of his hair, his jaw, his mouth, her gaze tormenting him wherever she looked. Pretty red lips parted, a bold slash of sin in moonlight. He could almost taste her almond face powder on his tongue.

"Is tying up men a preference of yours?" Nostrils flaring, he had to know.

"Is that your question?"

"It is."

"And you want to know if this is a peccadillo of mine?"

"Now who is playing coy with words?"

An elegant nod and, "Not a preference, but I'm not above trying it."

He shuddered again, an image teasing him: Miss MacDonald's manicured fingernails grazing his chest and his ballocks while his hands were tied. To receive pleasure from the alluring woman while restrained from touching her? Exquisite torture.

"I sense that might be an interest of yours." Miss MacDonald wetted her lips with the tip of her tongue. "Though perhaps not something you've tried."

The invisible barrier between them was collapsing until she murmured a treacherous question.

"Why are you living in the White Hart, Mr. Sloane?"

He balked.

She reminded him, "It is my turn to ask."

Two chests of clothes, three portmanteaus, and a cricketer's willow wood bat by the wall near the bed gave him away. A man on the run.

"The answer is long and complex."

"Then use your considerable skills with language to craft something simple and succinct."

When he didn't rush to respond, Miss MacDonald's arms folded under her scant cleavage.

"The fireworks appear to be waning, Mr. Sloane. If you wish to ask anything else of me, you had better be quick."

A glance in a southwesterly direction confirmed Vauxhall's end-of-season fireworks were spangling their last.

"I preferred your previous line of questions."

"It was fun. But my question stands and I will have my due, sir."

She possessed a siren's power to drive a man to madness, a woman as exacting as she was exciting. A deucedly swiveable mix. And, if he wasn't mistaken, she wanted a painful slice of his recent history.

She studied the years-old bat. "You play cricket apparently."

"Not much of late. I played voraciously at university. It was my one enjoyment."

"I attend practice matches as much for the sport as the fun of watching people," she said.

"You do?"

"Most Saturdays, yes." Her feline smile was a trap. "Now that wasn't so bad, was it?"

Her eyes suggested he move from the cricket bat to the chests holding all his worldly goods. Fingers digging into the velvet edge of his coat, he chose his words with care.

"I left my family home to keep the peace."

Feminine eyebrows arched, cool and expectant.

"You want more?" he asked.

"Fair is fair, Mr. Sloane."

Molars grinding, he wasn't going to split the vein of intimacy and bleed family trials at her feet. His worldly goods lined up along the wall already battered him and his choices.

"I have been saving to purchase a home of my own. During the summer season certain . . . events hastened those plans."

"You'll have to do better than that," she said.

Eyes on the floor, he scrambled to appease his inquisitor and found nothing. Floor planks were dark, his mind empty at how to explain a lifetime struggle—not life-ending woe, but the skirmish which had threaded his life for as long as he could remember.

"Have you a brother or a sister, Miss MacDonald?"

"None."

"Then, when I say you wouldn't understand, please know that I am saying that with as much forthrightness as I can muster. My brother is my closest friend and ally, but it was for the best that I take up residence here," he said in clipped tones.

He turned to the dying fireworks. Words couldn't cleanse him. Miss MacDonald must've grasped this and wisely held her tongue. Her velvet petticoats whispered against his calves, the tenderest part of their bridge.

Of all the directions this night could've gone . . .

He'd expected a self-serving turn—the Scotswoman advancing her purpose. Instead, Miss MacDonald wanted his hair unmoored and the reason behind his transitory state. Hardly the queries of a Jacobite rebel bent on destruction.

What was he to make of her?

"Look," she said softly, her elegant fingers touching the glass. "The fireworks are still burning, which means you have the final question."

Smoke clung to the sky above Vauxhall. Within the fading cloud, embers sparked, little stars flickering their last. Her offer was an act of kindness so their meeting wouldn't end on rocky notes. Her gaze sought his. She was a true artisan in the craft of humanity. Her flirtations, her laugh, her smiles were all part of a woman of incredible depth.

"You tempt me in the best and worst of ways, Miss MacDonald."

Of all the women to crave, he'd chosen her—a seductive Jacobite with a worthy heart.

"The fireworks," she whispered. "Their light is fading."

He consumed the shadow between her small breasts. Asking to see them wouldn't do, not with the considerable respect his soul was building for this woman. But he wanted—needed—something to sate his carnal nature.

His gaze ascended to her silken collarbone and the pale skin covering it.

"Your shoulder," he demanded gruffly. "I want to see it."

Knowing glittered in hazel eyes.

"Ask for it."

Jagged air left his lungs. Power was hers and he ceded all of it.

"Would you . . . please . . . uncover your shoulder?"

The corners of her mouth curled up.

"Uncover it yourself."

What a seductive taunt. She could drive a man to his knees.

His laugh was rough and primitive. "You multiply my pleasure."

Casual onlookers on the other side of King Street might see a man and a woman framed by a window. Sharper eyes would say seduction was afoot, but the keen observer would see the truth—a man surrendering to a woman.

He touched the tiny well at the bottom of her neck. So light, so bare, two reverent fingers, exploring.

Miss MacDonald inhaled fast.

The wispy sound struck sparks inside him. At least he wasn't alone in his arousal.

Moonlight splashed her breastbone, a fascinating stretch between neck and bodice. Potent. Enamoring. He dragged his fingers down her chest, and she kindly let him have his misdirection.

He was sinking deeper and deeper, consumed.

Almond-scented warmth rose from her skin. Many women wore the same scented powder, yet on the Scotswoman, the aroma was sweet and sinful. Not a combination one might attribute to Miss MacDonald, but there was the rub. Her complexity.

Perhaps his touch had conjured the goddess of Swan Lane.

He skimmed two fingers over her collarbone. "You fascinate me."

Miss MacDonald's lashes dipped.

"And you, sir, make me wet."

Deep inner muscles tensed. The goddess of Swan Lane was torturing him.

"Have a care, Miss MacDonald." His voice stretched tautly.

"Your mandate not to mix business and pleasure— it is a wise but difficult one to follow," she whispered.

Desire sawed his resistance. Vauxhall fireworks might've blinked their last. He didn't care. The Scotswoman had given him leave to undress her shoulder, and he would take his time doing it. He hooked his fingers in velvet and dragged the rich cloth until her shoulder was bare. Moonlight kissed it first. He was jealous, bending to kiss her shoulder second.

His lips brushed soft, soft skin so heavenly he had to close his eyes.

Miss MacDonald gasped. This was tender, carnal. More explosive than he expected. His hand on her sleeve was shaking. *He* was shaking, savoring her smooth round shoulder with his mouth.

She tasted like life.

Petticoats shushed. Her body slanted to his, a hint of what could be. Miss MacDonald was seduction in its purest form. Her skin, aglow. Her collarbone, fragile. Her blond curls snagged in velvet. If he tunneled his fingers in those curls his need for her would swallow him whole.

Could a man drown in three inches of a woman's unmoored sleeve?

Kissing the Scotswoman's body wasn't supposed to happen. Wanting her voraciously wasn't supposed to happen. With each passing heartbeat, his resolve was crumbling. He leaned in, needing her, his forehead touching her shoulder. Warm skin and her scent tempted him. He brushed his lips over the arc of her shoulder, and he tasted her again and found rightness and perfection.

He looked down. Velvet was crushed and twisted in his grip. How far astray they'd gone. He let go and took a punishing step back.

"Our time is done," he said in a ragged voice.

Miss MacDonald was heavy-lidded, her paste earbobs splintered pieces of light. Tonight, they had fallen prey to the art of distraction. He stood in the dark, while she was bathed in moonlight, her mouth a vermillion O.

"Give me information to satisfy Fielding," he said. "And I will move heaven and earth to get those tickets to Swynford House."

He would. Whatever it took to get her into the marquess's home, though he wasn't ready to spill how true his desire to get her there. Not like this with his cock heavy and his heart heavier. Miss MacDonald wanted a sentimental relic to soothe a brokenhearted old man. What he did to advance his ambitions, she did to heal her clan.

Their motives couldn't be more different or more damning.

She was a sensual woman with a heart of gold, while his was stark and flinty. To the outside observer, everything he stood for was right and everything she did was wrong. What a muddled world they inhabited.

Miss MacDonald's stupor melted by degrees. She set trembling hands on her stomacher and left her sleeve drooping.

"I accept your offer."

A jerky nod and, "Now it's time for you to go."

She walked across his room, her petticoats a sweet hush. She folded her cloak over her arm and opened the door, brightness flooding her. The goddess of Swan Lane turned the air to spun gold, so penetrating and beautiful it hurt to look at her.

"Meet me at Gun Wharf, one o'clock tomorrow," she said. "I have something you can give to Fielding."

"Gun Wharf, in Southwark?"

"Yes."

"How will I find you?"

A glow kissed her bare shoulder. "Don't worry, Mr. Sloane. We'll find each other."

Miss MacDonald closed the door, taking the light with her.

Chapter Ten

*W*hen the noon hour came, he took a hack to the mouth of London Bridge. From there, he went on foot. Carriages, carts, and drays moved at a snail's pace. Tempers spiked, flies bothered. Storied wattle and daub buildings crowded out the sun and his good mood. Crossing over to the borough of Southwark was akin to passing into another principality. Narrow streets, rough commerce, the buildings sagging under the weight of time and neglect. He wore his boots because he was certain he'd step in shite today, both real and metaphorical.

Last night, in striking their bargain, Miss MacDonald had shined a light on her honorable motive, while his scampered like a rancid beast needing to hide in the dark.

How ironic to see the last stop on London Bridge was a scale shop, the sign above the door reading JUSTICE AND SCALES. The leather-aproned proprietor was bidding good day to a man on foot when Alexander approached.

"Sir, would you kindly tell me how to find Gun Wharf?"

The scale maker eyed him through spectacles perched on the end of his nose. "Follow the noise, you're sure to find it."

"The noise?"

Between foot traffic, conveyances, and the river's rush, the din was chaotic. His vague smile must have won the scale maker's sympathy.

The older man chuckled. "Living on the bridge, a man forgets how loud it gets. Come. I'll show you." The scale maker led him to a narrow passage where London Bridge and land joined and stretched his arm at a throng in the distance. "See there? That's Gun Wharf. Finish line for the boat race."

"There is a boat race today?" he asked.

"Indeed. Southwark's annual Gun Wharf Sprint. Isn't that what you're looking for?"

"I was not aware of any race."

"It's the poor man's Doggett Coat and Badge race." Sun shined on the scale maker's bald pate. "Six wherries row from the Custom House to Gun Wharf."

Indeed, six wherries sliced the river like red splinters. Londoners had hacks to navigate the city's roads, and wherries to navigate the river.

The scale maker tipped his head at an ancient stone church near the bridge. "Cut through the churchyard to Coxes Wharf. Gun Wharf is next. Jog fast and I collect you'll make it in time to place a wager."

Alexander touched his hat. "My thanks for your help, sir."

He was trotting toward the church when the scale maker called, "Smart money is on Mr. Henry Baines."

Alexander whipped off his hat, the soles of his

boots punching dirt in the churchyard. At Timber Yard, he picked up the pace, dodging piles of wood. Men stacking lumber blurred on his right. The Thames blurred on his left.

His heart banged his chest. The youthful urge to run, to be there, to find Miss MacDonald and cheer with her. Glad he was for his old hunting boots, worn soft from tromping through fields. Breathing hard, he rounded a warehouse and ran into a deafening roar.

Sweat nicked skin under his cravat. He tugged at his neckcloth, sun-bleached wood quaking underfoot. Gun Wharf. He combed the crowd at three hundred strong, all facing the river, kerchiefs and hats striking the air.

He was supposed to find Miss MacDonald in this?

Chest billowing, he spied an older boy atop a barrel. A row of them lined a warehouse wall. The lad waved his Dutch cap like a pennant.

"Give 'em hell, Mr. Baines!"

Alexander grinned as he stepped nimbly onto a crate and leapt onto a barrel. He got his bearings and searched the bobbing heads. Salty warehousemen, thrum-capped sailors, and harlots with bright stays and not a glimpse of Miss MacDonald anywhere.

He checked his pocket watch. A few minutes past one o'clock.

This assignation belonged to the wayward Scotswoman, his respect did too. She'd won it last night. An adventuress, playing his game and making it her own. This meeting, at a Southwark boat race, was a point being made. He hungered to know it. Spine against the warehouse, he'd watch the race and wait. When it came to the gentler sex, sometimes waiting was all a man could do.

The lad beside him screamed at the top of his lungs, "Scull harder! Scull harder!"

Two wherries closed in on the finish line, which was a rope stretched across the mouth of Gun Wharf's U-shaped inlet. Bellows and shrieks pitched. The wharf shook. His barrel thumped the warehouse wall.

One wherry nosed ahead.

A small man at the stern, his face to the finish line, yelled to his crew and rowed with all his might. Three rowers, broad-backed men by the look, hunkered down and heaved with all their might. The wherry burst forward, spurting water off the bow.

The first rower reached high for the finish line rope and grabbed it.

The crowd roared their glee. Faces were cheerful, backs slapped, palms out for wagers to be paid. The last of the racing wherries slid into the inlet. The lad next to him hopped spryly off the barrel and tipped his wharf-grimed face toward him.

"Did ye wager on this race, sir?"

"Of a sort." Alexander scanned the crowd.

The Scotswoman was disappointingly nowhere. His companion on the barrels was a thin, straight-arrow youth of twelve or thirteen years.

"I hope you won something," the lad said. "I did. Everyone knows smart money's on Mr. Baines."

"So I've heard," he said distractedly.

The boy's chest puffed. "Next year, it'll be me sitting stern instead of Miss MacDonald."

"Did you say *Miss MacDonald*?"

"I did. Rowed, three years now for Mr. Baines in the Gun Wharf Sprint." The lad sniffed and offered grudging respect. "She's not bad, scrawny arms and all."

Scrawny arms indeed. He let this stunning revelation settle as if he'd learned Newton's apple fell up, not down, and pigs would soon fly over London.

"She's the only woman who rows," the lad said.

"A veritable repertoire of talents," he drawled.

The lad's brow clouded with suspicion. "If rep-er-twah means she can do things, then yes. Miss Mac-Donald's got skills. Do you know her?"

"She asked me to meet her here."

Tension faded from boyish shoulders. His admission that Miss MacDonald asked him to join her must've appeased the lad's concerns. The bristly protectiveness for the Scotswoman was gratifying. Miss MacDonald must be more to him than a legendary rower.

The lad grinned up at him like a conspirator.

"She's a different bird, that one . . . if you catch my meanin', sir."

Youthful eyes lit with a man-to-man warning: *tread with care.*

He tipped his head respectfully. "Thank you for the advice."

But Alexander's caution was drifting out to sea. The Scotswoman stirred his blood. Tasting her was the same as tasting recklessness. He had to have more.

The crowd was thinning, and six wherries floated like children's toys in Gun Wharf's inlet. Oars were stowed and rowers extended arms in congratulations. He locked on the Scotswoman, a compass arrow finding true north. Exhilarated, she doffed her tricorn, a blond braid tumbling free. Miss Mac-Donald shaded her eyes and scanned the crowd. He lolled against the warehouse, waiting to be found.

His erratic pulse mocked him. His casualness, an act worthy of Drury Lane. Her gaze reached above the crowd and found him.

Lightning might've struck, the bolt as kind as a sultry summer storm.

Her hand went over her heart as if to say, *You came.*

Of course he did. She'd won this day, same as she won both nights he'd spent with her.

A woman like that deserved honor.

Slowly, he lifted his hand and touched his hat, a respectful salute.

To which she unleashed a peal of laughter. Sweet, sweet music, it was. His ear caught and memorized the notes above the chatter. Miss MacDonald was just as enthralled, her vermillion smile shining for him alone.

He jumped off the barrel, spry as a lad. Oarsmen clambered up rope ladders tied to the pilings. Brawny young men and a half dozen older, salty sailors and rivermen. Calls were lobbed to meet at a tavern, while he waited hands on hips for Miss MacDonald. Her blond crown popped up between two pilings. Dressed in breeches, she ascended the rope ladder and hoisted herself onto the wharf. The goddess of Swan Lane, stealer of men's hearts. Half-mermaid and all woman, he was sure. Definitely a mythical creature. This woman with an untamed spirit and her grand smile was the reason he'd sprinted from London Bridge.

He didn't need a fortune-teller to augur what was plain as day—the Scotswoman would be his undoing. However, the lad beside him said it best.

"There's none like Miss MacDonald, sir. None a'tall."

Chapter Eleven

"Why, Mr. Sloane, how fitting that I, once again, find you on a barrel," Miss MacDonald said.

"Thankfully, I was on top of this one."

She laughed, music he wanted to hear over and over again.

The Dutch-capped lad eyed him oddly. "Is it bad, being on a barrel?"

"Never mind, Peter. Mr. Baines told me you're minding the wherry." Miss MacDonald dug inside a pocket and tossed a shiny coin into the air. "Something for your trouble."

Peter caught it in his open palm. "A half guinea. Thank you, miss."

"Consider it advance payment for the work you'll do tomorrow. Mr. Baines will need help cleaning the hull." She eyed him sternly. "Be a good lad and give that coin I just gave you to your mam." When a frown clouded the young man's face, she added, "Don't worry. More work is coming, and that will be coin you can keep for yourself like the wager you placed with Mr. Tuttle."

The lad was sheepish, slipping the half guinea into his shoe. "Didn't think you knew about that, miss."

"Oh, Peter . . ."

Hers was a gentle scold set to squawking seagulls, circling and landing. Though she spoke to young Peter, her eyes sparkled for Alexander. He basked in their warmth, deciphering what he could from their unusual rendezvous. Sun-grayed docks perfumed with eau-de-Thames, not the stuff of romance. The Scotswoman shined prettily, but on closer inspection, a man would find grit on her palms and strength in her frame, scrawny arms and all.

"Promise me you won't conveniently forget that the coin in your shoe is for your mam," she said.

Peter's chin dipped. "I won't, miss. You have my word."

"Good lad," she said with a wink. "Off with you now."

Peter strode toward the inlet. Alexander watched him disappear below the dock and reappear, hopping nimbly from wherry to wherry until he landed in what must've been Mr. Baines's vessel.

His gaze arrowed to the Scotswoman. "Half a guinea . . . generous of you."

Miss MacDonald's shoulder twitched vaguely. A breeze knocked a curl across her cheek which she wordlessly brushed back.

Was she a tad reticent?

Feminine lips softened. He tried to read their subtle shift. Every woman's body spoke a language all her own for the man who cared to watch. A deep study of the Scotswoman was in order. An evening worshipping her, perhaps. They were alone, save seagulls roosting on pilings, and a warehouseman padlocking a door on the west side of the wharf. Though it was half past one o'clock, the workday in this part of Southwark was done, while Alexander's had just begun. His labor wouldn't be tedious. With Miss MacDonald bedecked in men's garb, how could it?

He ambled closer. "Do you conduct all business assignations like this?"

She pointed her right toe and swept a courtly bow. "Whether business or pleasure, I aim to please."

Her braid swung forward, a rope of cream and gold. Windblown wisps rebelled and stuck to her damp cheeks. Her plain black frock coat and fitted breeches dressed her staidly until he looked lower.

"The color on your legs . . ."

"Robin's egg blue."

The stockings gleamed on shapely calves. He was riveted.

"Silk?"

"As one does for a boat race." The merest pause and she added, "I donned them for you."

Words to tickle his ballocks. His gaze narrowed.

"Are those the same stockings you held up to the window in the shop at White Cross Street?"

"The very same." Her eyes sparkled with sensual hints.

His navel clenched. He couldn't take any more of her seductive, verbal punches. A breeze carried a rusty laugh—his, of course. Baited and hooked, he was, and grateful for it.

Miss MacDonald set her tricorn on her head, the front point long. *A hunter's hat, the minx.* He couldn't stop his grin from drifting sideways.

She linked arms with him and offered a saucy, "Did I tell you that I purchased stays to match?"

His cock and balls twitched under a bombardment of images. Silk stockings and their slow slide down her legs. Robin's egg blue stays loosened, a nipple peeking, blond hair draped everywhere.

"Your stays should not be a point of discussion."

"They could be."

Words delivered with the softest tease.

"Miss MacDonald, this is business." His voice was a low warning.

She laughed, not chastened at all. "Oh, I know. But you must admit, what has passed between us goes beyond polite discourse."

Could he make it to Swynford House, Wednesday next, without seeing more of her flesh? Probably not. The irony of his circumstances was that he wanted to know *her* with equal ferocity. From the mundane: *How do you take your tea?* To the political: *What is your opinion of Lord Hardwicke's Marriage Act?*

"I should plead Parliament to pass a law requiring all hems must end at the knees," he said.

"The knees? Why stop there?"

To which he laughed and it felt good to walk with a woman he could be amused with.

"You are a saucy one."

"You wouldn't be the first say so."

He steered their stroll across Gun Wharf, their hips bumping companionably, their strides languorous.

"I collect, you enjoy being wicked day or night."

Hazel eyes glinted mischievously under a black brim. "Day or night. Do you have a preference, Mr. Sloane?"

The boat race cast Miss MacDonald in a new light,

her flirtations and sense of fun a diversion from deeper parts. Something solid and serious, perhaps. Certainly complex.

"My preference," he said as drolly as he could, "is to think with the flesh between my ears and not the flesh between my legs."

"Ah, yes, your path to the Exchequer."

"And yours to a certain dagger."

What a surprising conversation to have on a busy Southwark road. A bowlegged costermonger waddled by, his back laden with vegetable-filled baskets. A pair of stray dogs, tongues lolling, sat on their haunches in an alley. Drays trundled by, the thoroughfare barely wide enough to accommodate them and pedestrians. Gun Wharf's race watchers had migrated here, clustering in the street and alleys, nursing pints, their cheeks aglow. He guided Miss MacDonald closer to his side and got a whiff of her rosewater scent.

"The tavern looks full." She tipped her head at a brick and flint stone wall. "Why don't we wait here?"

With nowhere to sit, they huddled close. Harlots and sailors crowded the benches by the Iron Bell's door. Tavern maids sped in and out from the open door, frothy mugs in their clutches.

"Aren't you thirsty?" he asked.

"I can wait."

A shaft of sunlight blessed a blond wisp snaking down her cheek. He traced that fragile line from cheek to jaw and tried to forget that he wanted to swive the daylights out of her.

She didn't stop him. "Did you get the tickets to Swynford House?"

"Not yet."

"Then why should I share what I know today? That was the purpose of our meeting, was it not?"

His exploratory finger stopped. "Our business arrangement."

"That is why we're here."

Was touching her part of their unwritten contract? It might've been false comfort to think they could easily pick up last night's thread. Hidden in his pocket was a list, the fruit of his labor from reading the Pell rolls at Westminster. His bridge of trust with Miss MacDonald might fold under the weight of what was on it.

His arm dropped to his side. "I was unfortunately detained."

Miss MacDonald's attention drifted to revelers in the street behind him. "Then I see no reason to continue this conversation."

She was dismissing him? Resolve steeled his voice.

"Of the two of us, you have more to lose."

Her gaze snapped back and nailed him.

"You think me weak, do you?"

"Not weak. Vulnerable."

"Because I am a woman?"

"Because you are in a less tenable position."

"Why is that?" she asked softly, menacingly. "Because I am the defeated Jacobite? Your one-time enemy?"

Red lips taut, she put him on edge. How had he missed the detail of an oarsman with a carmine painted mouth when he'd watched the race? Everything about the Scotswoman was in plain sight, yet one could easily overlook the obvious because she was a woman and a commoner of no particular status.

"We are partners of equal standing, Mr. Sloane, or we are not partners at all."

He smarted at subtle truth brought to light. He had assumed the lion's share of power—and protective responsibilities which came with it—but this was something Miss MacDonald would not tolerate.

"You don't want a man's protection . . . which begs the question, what do you want?"

Pretty lips parted, and her startled attention fell like a warm blanket on a cold day. Her face was a shifting tableau he happily studied. Wide-eyed bafflement faded to mild alarm as if her wants were unexplored waters.

"Stop it." Hers was a kindly voice.

"Stop what exactly?"

"Trying to look after me. I've lived too many years taking care of myself. No need to change that now."

The brick and flint stone wall was cold and hard. A woman denying his natural protective instincts—what was a gentleman to do?

"We're already on our way to a delightful friendship," she said. "Isn't that enough?"

It wasn't, but he was hard-pressed to put his finger on what would be enough. Friendship and partnership could be one and the same for her. A contract. For now, it would do.

"I am trying to divert Fielding's attention away from you."

Her gaze darted to the boisterous street. "I would be happy if you tore the pages about me from his book."

"Know about that, do you?" He toed a pebble on the ground. "I shouldn't be surprised."

"Not any more than I was surprised to find you

arse up in my mews." A tight smile played on her face. "Why else would Fielding send you after me, if not for me being in one of his ledgers?"

An unyielding nature was her sharp edge. A blonde temptress, slight of build, who would never ask for rescue. He was on the verge of suggesting they brave the crammed environs of the Iron Bell and find a seat when she pinched his waistcoat.

"We need to leave. Now," was her urgent hiss.

Miss MacDonald pulled her hat low and darted into Mill Lane's traffic. She didn't check to see if he followed. Confused by her sudden exit, he checked the milling crowd. Fifty or sixty lively sorts, voices raised, eyes glossy from drink, and none with a care in the world, save a taut-limbed man in black, his eyes darkly penetrating. Beside him, a henna-haired strumpet pushed up on her toes, her malevolent stare spearing Miss MacDonald's departing back.

Hat tugged low, he sped past a tinker with a cart boasting a rack of clanking pans. Miss MacDonald was ahead by a dozen paces, her blond braid snaking down her back. He didn't look back to see if the henna-haired woman watched him too.

When Miss MacDonald neared the end of Mill Lane, he trotted after her.

"What was that about?"

She spun around, her frock coat flaring. "Nothing you need to worry about."

Molars grinding, he caught up with the Scotswoman who'd spent too many years looking after herself.

"A little worry is good for the soul."

Sailors and marines strolled Tooley Street, a dozen harlots with them. The noise rivaled the Iron Bell's celebrations. He matched the Scotswoman's stride as they passed a patten maker's shop.

"Humor me, Miss MacDonald. Are you hounded by debt collectors?"

"No, and my humor, at the moment, has fled me."

With that setdown given, he chose silence. A man had to know which battles to fight and when. Miss MacDonald was on a mission, leading him past raucous public houses to King's Head Yard. Shops gave way to warehouses and an odd quiet. Ruined pamphlets scattered everywhere, pages riffling in the wind. A muddy mongrel rambled by. Broken barrels flowered, their iron bands twisted and rusty. A rat sniffed the air from an overturned bucket, but otherwise they were alone.

"Is your humor replenished enough to tell me where we're going?" he asked.

Her mouth quirked. "To the end of King's Head Yard."

Beyond the alley's gloom were open fields, orchards, a smattering of wattle and daub warehouses. Two were charred and roofless. One of them might've been a public house at one time, but he'd wager all the buildings had been abandoned.

Miss MacDonald opened a wrought-iron gate to a small, triangular orchard. Six apple trees had been planted in rows of three, two, and one. Industry and nature met in this part of Southwark. Vauxhall's pleasure gardens were far west. The king's orchards to the south, Tenter Ground for the poor and two hospitals which succored them in the same direction. But this little Garden of Eden was clean and quiet.

Miss MacDonald wandered through the humble orchard, checking leaves and touching apples.

"What are we doing here?" he asked.

She dipped under a tree. "Fulfilling my side of our partnership."

As he drew near, she poked out from a branch and lobbed fruit at him.

"Have an apple."

He caught it, the paper crinkling in his pocket. His list. Miss MacDonald was an entrancing sight, blue-stockinged calves and black breeches in view while she pushed up on her toes to plunder the tree.

She emerged from green foliage, lips glossy with juice.

"Tradition says Eve tempted Adam with an apple."

"So I've been told." He took a bite, the apple's sweet-ness bursting on his tongue.

"The truth is, we were never told what fruit she offered him." A nibble, quick chewing, and she swal-lowed. "Truth, like trust, comes in the details, Mr. Sloane. Things are not always what they seem."

"You brought me to one of the king's orchards to tell me this?"

A breeze batted her curly wisps. "Not the king's orchard. It belongs to a league of Scotswomen—a small league, mind you . . . women who vowed to restore their clan."

Hairs on his nape prickled. The coded Jacobite ledger flashed in his mind.

"A league?"

"We grow the apples and give them to Scots living in Tenter Ground by Snow's Fields. My four years in London, and that's one of the things we do." Eyes sage and sharp, she added, "Perhaps you can report *that* nefarious activity to Fielding."

He smarted, the root of guilt running deep. He, like

Fielding, had assumed the worst of her: a demirep who lived by her sensual nature on one hand, a Jacobite sympathizer possibly stirring up trouble on the other. Miss MacDonald wasn't fomenting rebellion; she was feeding homeless Scots.

Arguments rose and died in him: to say Fielding championed the poor, though the magistrate favored strict societal structure; to say Fielding wanted justice and order, though his quill had dripped poison when he wrote about Jacobites; or to say that he, Alexander Sloane, cared about all Londoners, though his conscience needled him that he conveniently stayed on the other side of the river. Thus, he kept his mouth shut when Miss MacDonald pointed southward with her apple-holding hand.

"See there? Those empty warehouses? Beyond them is Cross Keys Alley. There's an abandoned tannery"—she wrinkled her nose—"you'd know the place by the smell."

He took another bite and listened.

"The old tannery . . . it's one of the places Mr. John Berry and Mr. Stephen MacDaniel hide stolen goods."

He swallowed fast. "Two of Bow Street's thief takers." Two of the toughest and most successful thief takers, in fact.

"They recruit men, sometimes boys," she said, her syllables sharp. "To steal things. Pewter dishes, blacksmith tools . . . it doesn't matter. Then Mr. Berry and Mr. MacDaniel haul in the fools they duped into thievery and collect a reward from the crown."

"The same crimes Mr. Berry and Mr. MacDaniel were accused of in '47."

"Exactly. When all is quiet, they sell the goods."

She pointed southeastward. "Sometimes they take their goods to the shipyards, there."

"To smugglers?"

"I don't know." Arm dropping to her side, she squinted toward those distant shipyards. "What I do know is that Mr. MacDaniel and Mr. Berry have been sniffing around Tenter Ground of late."

His first month serving the Duke of Newcastle, Alexander had been tasked to organize old reports which had followed the June of '47 Act of Indemnity, the law that freed the last of the rebels. The bowels of prison hulks had been emptied of almost a thousand rebel Scots. Men with no prospects, and the rebellion too fresh for Londoners to welcome Highlanders with open arms. Few of them found employment. Fewer found a way out. Untold numbers died of neglect. Others took to a life of crime.

"If you take me to this abandoned tannery on Cross Keys Alley, will I find stolen goods inside?" he asked.

"Not now. Mr. Berry and Mr. MacDaniel are smart. They don't store their goods in the same place, and they spread out their crimes. Sometimes several months apart."

His apple eaten, he tossed the core. "I can't use it."

"Why not?"

"Because they were acquitted in '47. To accuse them of the same crime, I had better have iron-clad evidence."

She blinked at him, incredulous. "Does that mean you won't do anything?"

He was parsing the facts as one did in legal matters. Grub Street readers adored dramatic tales of crime and punishment. In stories, the scales of justice weighed right from wrong, but the courts weighed evidence. Without proof, his hands were tied.

"I can't. Not without solid evidence."

"You won't even investigate it?"

"I'm not a thief taker."

"But you could right this injustice. If ever there was a man in a position to—to—*do something*, it's you."

He sucked in a deep breath of forbearance. A millstone of expectation weighed on his back. Hers, in fact. Miss MacDonald's eyes glimmered with hope. She wanted him to save the day, and God help him, he wanted to be that man.

"You understand, to bring the same charges against Mr. Berry and Mr. MacDaniel, the evidence must be indisputable. Anything less would warn them off."

The brightness drained from her eyes.

"Of course."

He rushed on. "It would take time, months, perhaps."

Hairs on his nape bristled. Miss MacDonald's calmness brought to mind a viper a few harrowing seconds before it strikes.

"But this isn't something you'd tell Fielding straightaway."

"Speak against two of his most productive thief takers? Fielding would ask for evidence, and there's none to give. He'd dismiss the news as baseless accusations."

Her smile was bitter. "And that leaves you reporting on the scurrilous Jacobite woman. Because Fielding wants to hear that."

He drew in a long, weighty breath.

"I will do my damnedest to divert him from you

but you must give me something tangible. Evidence, you see?"

She didn't. Miss MacDonald tipped her face to the sun and shut her eyes. She'd left one war behind and found another here in London against a driven magistrate and two corrupt thief takers. Smart, fierce, resourceful, the Scotswoman had accomplished much. By bringing him to this apple orchard, she'd revealed a tenderness for the forgotten. The moment should be illuminating and joyous, a trust shared.

Why, then, was his heart collapsing?

Miss MacDonald opened her eyes and walked away. When she passed the open gate, he followed.

"Where are you going?"

Miss MacDonald took two more determined strides before she spun around. Her cold eyes froze him in his tracks.

"Our bargain is done, Mr. Sloane."

"You can't mean that."

"I do."

He watched her, icy pressure expanding in his chest. It made his skin cold and his feet stuck in place. Late-day sun haloed Miss MacDonald on her slow backward walk, her heels kicking up dust clouds on silk-covered shins as she went.

"You don't have tickets to Swynford House, yet I have given you information to deliver to Fielding. That, sir, leaves you with everything and me nothing."

A faint wobble edged her strong voice.

"A true friend would see my cares and consider them his. But you have done nothing of the sort."

Her anguish sliced him. She was right, and he, an artisan of words, had nothing to say. Miss MacDonald had asked for his protection, a form of it, and he'd denied her because the law required facts.

Emotions, he was learning, did not.

Miss MacDonald held his gaze. Her feet came nearly to a stop. He grabbed the gatepost and watched her, transfixed.

"Miss MacDonald . . . I . . ."

Afternoon sun shined but he felt no warmth. The Scotswoman's fair mouth flattened—her final judgment before she gave him her back. She was walking away, her stiff proud spine tearing him apart. She took a narrow southwesterly road. Where she headed wasn't clear. Her purpose was. Miss MacDonald and her league of Scotswomen worked to save their neglected kin, the Uprising's abandoned foot soldiers. Would Fielding scoff in disbelief when he shared this latest find? If he told the Duke of Newcastle, would His Grace be moved to care?

What were a few suffering Scots to them?

For the first time in his life, he glimpsed himself and the city through the lens of a Scotswoman's eyes.

The ugly truth—he didn't like what he saw.

Chapter Twelve

An orderly mob gathered at a corner of Snow's Fields where the pond and Tenter Ground joined. All yelled at the top of their lungs, among them Royal Marines and beefy naval men. A cockfight or a bare-knuckle bout most likely, a hastily organized event devised by bored men with something to prove, as was the nature of Tenter Ground entertainments. Plans didn't exist in this part of Southwark. *Nab your fun when you can* was the motto. Ha'pennies were a treasure, and smuggled brandy an elixir.

Rough and transient, the citizens wore dignity and humor in equal measure. Thieves, laborers, an outcast harlot or two . . . the souls of Tenter Ground. She was fiercely protective of them. Those corrupt thief takers, Mr. Berry and Mr. MacDaniel, coming round were trouble.

A certain barrister-cum-government-man was more troubling. *He* got her hackles up.

Her lips pressed grimly. *Mr. Sloane.* Why couldn't he try and look beyond the obvious evidence? Because the man lived too much by the letter of the law.

Her footfalls punched soft earth. *Let him find comfort in his facts.* He'd find no comfort with her.

She strode forward, hunting for another man. Rory MacLeod.

Instinct told her the Highlander was either in the mob or the center of it. She squeezed between bumping, elbowing bodies and found two shirtless behemoths battling.

Ferocious and bloodied, men circled each other. One of them, MacLeod.

He was a sight, sweat sluicing down great slabs of muscle. Buckskin-colored breeches soaked at the waist. Leg hairs glued like dark threads to his calves. The second fighter was equal in size, a sun-bronzed man a decade younger. Fists cocked high, both brawlers took vicious swipes.

Her gaze dropped to the ground. A fighter's feet told the truth. That's what her father had taught her. Not sweat nor blood nor size. How a man moved mattered, the true tell of strength and stamina.

The young brawler's shod feet dragged through grass.

Mr. MacLeod danced on the balls of his bare feet.

The banty-sized Irishman, Mr. O'Shea, adjudicated the bout, flapping his hat to keep the crowd at bay. Men jostled her, their seaworthy curses spraying the air. Genteel sport—horse races, boat races, and cricket—was more to her liking. No blood, no violence. Legs braced, she held her ground, while the man beside her struck the air. A Royal Marine by his red coat.

The young lieutenant yelled, "Bellows to mend, George! Bellows to mend!"

She grabbed his sleeve and shouted, "Sir! How long is this fight?"

The startled lieutenant stopped punching air. His mouth curving in a friendly smile, he bent his tanned face lower.

"What's that, miss?"

"I said, how long is this fight?"

Though they were close, they had to conduct their conversation at a near yell.

"One round. It's over when one bruiser is felled." He cocked his head at the ring. "My money's on George, a gunner on my ship. You'd best be quick if you want to wager on this one. The fight's gone nigh on half an hour."

She checked the makeshift ring, which was marked by a trench in grass and dirt (probably made by O'Shea's heel). Mr. MacLeod danced with masculine grace, his muscle and sinew straining under sweat-slick skin. Rib cage billowing, the Highlander's queue was a dark line in the furrow of his back. Not the appealing blunt-cut queue of a certain barrister-cum-government-man. She swallowed the unwelcome comparison and concentrated on the handsome lieutenant.

"I've already wagered on one gentleman today and I'm afraid he was a disappointment."

"A gentleman, was it? His misfortune is my good luck." He took in her breeches. "And you all dressed up and ready for fun."

Jaw freshly shaved, cravat hastily tied, gorget polished to a shine on his neck—she knew the look. This was a young Royal Marine returned from a voyage, hungry for bed sport. Probably his first day back in port. They were of the same age, yet years apart in experience. Months ago, she would've welcomed sharing a pint, and other adventures should they happen. Not today. Spending time with the lieutenant would be like wearing an ill-fitting shoe. It'd be all wrong.

"A handsome man like you will find plenty of good luck at the Iron Bell."

She winked, but her cheer was barely skin-deep.

He set his tricorn over his heart. "Might I appeal to your sense of—"

A roar erupted. The lieutenant bolted upright.

Mr. MacLeod's fists rammed the gunner's face. One punch—two, three, four. Smashing blows. Blood arced, a stream of red and sweat and spittle.

She had to shut her eyes. Full-throated cheers pitched feverishly until she heard a body fall with a meaty slap.

Revelers eased apart, their chatter rising. When she opened her eyes, Royal Marines and naval men surrounded their fallen friend. Rory MacLeod sauntered over to a pile of clothes beside weathered jackboots, his lungs working hard. The Scot swiped his chest with a shirt, half listening to Mr. O'Shea.

Arms folded, she waited. As bare-knuckle fights went, Snow's Field paid the worst. Any brawler worth his mettle fought on the other side of the river. Smart brawlers put some thought into it and printed sheets to advertise the fight. They hired lads to hawk the fight and paper every public house and gentleman's club with the news. Those were bouts one planned for. If she read this one right, the Royal Marines and the gunner flat on his back had left their ship in the King's Yard, hungry for fun. The draw of a large Scotsman and an aimless crowd must've looked like easy quid.

But this was Snow's Field. Easy quid was hard

to come by. The gunner and his friends would get nothing, and Mr. MacLeod would get little more than nothing. Mr. O'Shea was, in fact, dropping four shillings into the Highlander's open paw.

"That's all?" MacLeod's Western Isles brogue rose in disbelief.

"Well, if ye'd agreed to fight the other three men, ye might be lookin' at a dozen to fifteen shillin's."

"In Brighton, I was paid twenty shillings for one fight."

"It'll be different next time, now that I know ye have middling talent," the Irishman said.

MacLeod's eyes rounded when he was deemed a *middling talent*.

O'Shea slapped the Scot's arm good-naturedly. "I didna think a man o' yer years had it in ye."

"My years?" MacLeod dumped his coins into a paltry purse and knotted it.

"Ye've got a good ten to fifteen o' them on the lads comin' out o' the King's Yard."

"I'm thirty-one. Hardly long in the tooth."

"But yer not a young cock o' the walk either."

MacLeod dropped his coin purse, its scant jingle a sad reward for his toil. He tugged on his shirt, and when linen cleared his head, crystalline blue eyes met hers and lingered.

Mr. O'Shea fussed with his buttonless coat.

"If yer interested in something permanent, I could accommodate ye."

MacLeod adjusted his shirt. "Didna know you had to fit me into your schedule."

"I'm a busy man, I am. If we come to terms, I'll arrange a bout within the week. By the taverns near Marshalsea."

"The prison? No' much quid to be earned by a prison."

"Patience, me good man, patience."

She sauntered forward. "Mr. MacLeod, Mr. O'Shea. Good day to you, sirs."

MacLeod nodded a mute greeting, and O'Shea tucked his thumbs into his waistcoat pockets.

"Miss MacDonald, me dove, I was just transacting a wee bit of business with yer compatriot."

"It sounded more like highway robbery. Everyone knows the best fights are across the river and someone with Mr. MacLeod's skills can easily fetch twenty-five to thirty shillings a fight . . . *if* he has a proper business partner."

Mr. MacLeod began to tuck in his shirt. The Royal Marines and naval men had procured a bucket and were splashing their groggy friend. Smoke wafted by, the work of two older boys squatting around a fire, roasting unknown meat.

Mr. O'Shea scratched a sparsely whiskered jaw. "Workin' the other side of the river would take some doin' . . ."

"It's possible that you *could* be the man for the job," she said.

"Well, it sure as shite isn't you, me dove. Dressin' like a man doesn't make ye one, and bare-knuckle brawlin' is a man's business."

To which she laughed. O'Shea's ire was understandable. The Highlander could be his golden goose.

"As it happens, I need Mr. MacLeod's services."

MacLeod's shirt tucking stopped. "What kind of service?"

"Something less violent, I assure you."

"Have ye lost yer mind?" The Irishman paced

two, three agitated steps. "A woman flashes a pair of pretty legs and ye leave me offer danglin'?"

"Her legs are damned sight prettier than yours, and I havena said yes. To her or to you."

"Would a finder's fee appease you?" she asked O'Shea. "Because we both know Mr. MacLeod will say yes to me. I am equipped to offer him better terms."

"Equipped." O'Shea snorted. "I know what happens when ye come round here, Miss MacDonald. All and sundry jump to the snap of yer fingers."

The Irishman spun around and sped toward the beefy naval gunners.

"Wait . . . O'Shea," MacLeod called after him. "I want to fight."

O'Shea tossed back a surly, "Ye know where to find me."

MacLeod picked up his waistcoat. "Women," he said good-naturedly. "Always ruining my prospects."

"Then you will be delighted to hear that this job means spending time with not one but two women."

"Two, is it?" His blue eyes glinted with mischief. "You and your maid?"

"I'm afraid not."

MacLeod slid on his waistcoat. "I'm listening."

The Scot was thick muscles and rugged appeal. Rough around the edges, definitely. Faint lines flared from the outer corners of his eyes. Smile marks, perhaps. Soldiers who squinted in the sun had them too. Every man's face was a story, and MacLeod's a bonny tale. Yet she couldn't stir up an ounce of attraction. Not even an erratic pulse.

Oh, this was dreadful. Her body had mutinied.

It wanted more question-and-answer games in the

dark. More sleeves lowered naughty inches. More queues untied and silk-bound wrists.

Her nipples tingled. *Mr. Sloane and his enigmatic touches.*

She was in the vicinity of an appealing man and . . . nothing.

MacLeod donned his coat. "I need details, lass."

She blinked. Had she lost precious seconds thinking about Mr. Sloane? MacLeod's expectant gaze told her that, yes, she had. She shook her head as one might shake off an irritating insect buzzing close.

"I will pay you three shillings, two pence a month to protect Aunt Maude and Aunt Flora. They're not really my aunts, they are—"

"I know about the MacDonald spinsters," he said, gruff and abrupt.

Well, this was a surprise.

"And I know what you've been doing." He tipped his head at the field. "Helping the Scots and Irish stuck here."

Here was a disorganized hodgepodge of tents, makeshift structures, and random fire rings—an army sergeant's nightmare bivouac.

"But you've no' been handing out gold." MacLeod reached for his boots.

Alarm spiked her pulse. She glanced over her shoulder. No one was in earshot.

"Please. Can we not talk about *that* here?"

A fortnight ago, MacLeod had caught Anne and Will taking seventeen hundred livres—a fraction of the treasure—from the Countess of Denton's study. He didn't stop them, nor did he go out of his way to help them. It was never clear if MacLeod hunted the gold for himself, or if he hunted something else.

"I'm counting on your honor as a Highlander to help us," she said stiffly.

"Even though I am a MacLeod." His brogue dipped, smooth and humored. "Your spinster aunts might no' want a MacLeod protecting them."

She wanted to laugh. How absurd. Clan feuds in London? When they needed each other? At least he was amused and not affronted at the idea of living under the same roof as two MacDonald spinsters.

"They will love you, especially when you repair Neville House and Neville Warehouse. And trust me, they will love feeding you."

His mouth quirked. "That's a lot of work for three shillings, two pence a month. I'd have better luck with O'Shea . . . slippery mon that he is."

"Working for me, you will have a roof over your head with your own bedchamber, as much food as you can eat, and your clothes washed and mended. Can O'Shea give you that?"

When he didn't rush to say yes, she petted his unbuttoned waistcoat. The ridged parts of his flat belly were visible under his shirt's threadbare linen. Tall and dark-haired, he was appealing.

"Four months, that's all I need."

His blue-eyed stare latched on to her adventurous hand.

"Let's say I give you four months. What will you do for me?"

This was exactly what she needed, a salacious invitation to erase Mr. Sloane from her mind, her vocabulary, her body.

She held her breath, and . . . nothing.

No flutter in her chest, no flush on her skin, and

when she opened her mouth, her voice was decid-edly crisp and businesslike.

"Come the new year, I will introduce you to the right men."

"I'm no' sure that's enough."

MacLeod's gaze flitted to O'Shea, who engaged in lively discourse with the Royal Marines and naval gunners. She touched his navel. Under his shirt, muscles rippled, iron-hewn, like furrows they were.

"Men who can arrange fights in Moor Fields' fairs, Artillery Ground, the White Lamb . . . all the choice places where you can make a name for yourself. I can give that to you."

Chin tipped high, she exuded confidence.

MacLeod grunted. "Quite sure of yourself."

"Why shouldn't I be?" And because his insight goaded her and she was that much closer to prov-ing her grit to the Highlander, she added, "If the first part of my offer isn't enough, consider this: I will see to it that you get a position in one of London's finest sporting clubs for gentlemen."

"What kind of sporting clubs?"

"Gentleman John's on Duke Street. Where nobs with no sense and too much money pay ridiculous coin to learn how to fight."

"Fight school?" Head shaking, he laughed. "Nobs payin' to get their heads bashed? When do I start?"

"Your four months for me starts today."

Eyes rounding incredulously, the Highlander couldn't believe his luck. She, however, was thor-oughly dismayed. Somewhere in their conversation, she'd stopped petting him. The body always sensed what the mind took its sweet time to grasp.

She tried to erase all memory of Mr. Sloane and his hot kisses. She truly did, but her body betrayed her. Here was a braw, blue-eyed Highlander with a nice bulge in his breeches, and she couldn't rouse a single urge to flirt.

Not even one.

Chapter Thirteen

$\mathcal{A}$lexander slid onto the pine settle, confident the seat wouldn't give him splinters and the beer wouldn't ravage his bowels. Such was the Five Bells—a haven for Covent Garden's quieter, well-mannered nymphs and the men who wished to find them. Not that he wanted to engage in Cytherean rites. The goddess of Swan Lane had a firm, if unseen, claim on his placket and the flesh behind it. Only the hazel-eyed siren would unmoor those buttons.

Or he would, to assuage primal needs as men often did to take the edge off.

He sunk lower on the seat, visions of her dancing in his head. He held steady until a new image teased him—Miss MacDonald kneeling before him, her soft mouth closing around hard flesh freed from his placket and hazel eyes watching him watch her.

He gripped the cold pint with a shaky hand and gulped.

On the other side of the table, a voice came from behind a newspaper.

"That is the sound of a man with a tale to tell."

Alexander *thunked* the pint on the table. "I spent my afternoon with a woman in Southwark."

"A promising beginning but rather sparse."

He took a bolstering breath. "An alluring Scotswoman who gave me my comeuppance."

"That's better. The tale of Serious Sloane meeting his match." Burton peered over the top of his newspaper. "Has a ring to it, don't you think?"

He swallowed more beer. "Except she left me hanging, as it were, in Southwark."

Burton winced. "Hanging?"

"A request was made that I cannot fulfill and the lady was disappointed."

"Doesn't that mean you left *her* hanging?"

"I won't quibble over who left whom hanging. Suffice to say, the lady and I left our meeting unsatisfied."

Burton hummed thoughtfully. "So, you're here for consoling conversation. Or perhaps you seek companionship of a livelier nature?"

Silly, giggling Covent Garden nymphs had walked into the Five Bells and were settling in to a table in the heart of the public room. Some might call them fair. Pink lips, pink ribbons, pink silks. Young and fresh, their faces full of delight, but they blurred like a hackneyed reproduction of masterful artwork.

"Mmm . . . No."

"Are you sure?" Burton lowered the newspaper. "The blonde with the spectacular cleavage is giving you a come-hither look."

"Hefty cleavages are overrated."

"I see. A night of consoling conversation, it is." Burton folded his paper. "Have you eaten?"

"I'm not hungry."

"You do have it bad. At least you can enjoy your misery in quiet, the latest patrons notwithstanding. The room cleared about an hour ago . . . some grand entertainment at Covent Garden."

The Five Bells was sedate. Fernsby hunched over backgammon at another pine settle with Mr. St. John, a ginger-haired sworn clerk. Four older gentlemen owned the Five Bells' dartboard. Near the fireplace, the clerks Mr. Basil-Smith and Mr. Patton battled stoically over a chessboard, their arms folded on the table. Tavern maids meandered the floor, plates of cottage pie and pints in their clutches.

Alexander stared into his beer. "I'm here because I need your help."

"Twice in one week. I'm honored."

"I need two tickets to the Marquess of Swynford's event, Wednesday next."

Burton stopped a passing tavern maid.

"Another small beer, Polly." He checked Alexander. "A small beer for you? Or hemlock?" The tavern maid giggled and Burton raised two fingers. "Make that two small beers—hold the hemlock."

Polly went to fetch their beer as four foppish lordlings with cheek patches and redolent strides invaded the room. Like sharks on the hunt, they claimed a table next to the Covent Garden nymphs.

"Tell me again about this outrageous request of yours," Burton said.

"Two tickets to Swynford for the British Museum's fundraising event."

"Why? Is your mother desperate to go?"

"Not my mother. The alluring Scotswoman."

"The one who rejected you today? You're courting her with a fundraising dinner?"

Was he courting Miss MacDonald?

"Yes."

Burton laughed. "Good Lord, man, if that's your idea of pleasing a lady—"

"She *wants* to go. And it is a costume ball," he added, as if that increased the excitement.

Burton's arms spread with faux delight. "Well, why didn't you say it was a costume ball?" His arms dropped. "Because it doesn't matter how you dress up those events. There's a reason the museum governors have had a hard time raising money."

"Could it be the corruption in their lottery?"

"Don't be factual. I'm trying to help you, man. Their events are dull, dull, dull. The lot of them take warm milk at nine o'clock."

More women with generous cleavages entered the Five Bells. They joined the Covent Garden nymphs laughing at a lordling's quip. The youthful gentlemen had to be freshly done with university with years of flirtation ahead.

Had it ever been that easy? Or had he simply not cared?

Burton cleared his throat. "Is it possible you misread the lady's intent?" A pause was filled by raucous laughter and, "I could tutor you on the art of courtship."

Alexander rocked his empty tankard. "My courting skills are fine, thank you."

Brave words, but they weren't entirely true. Miss MacDonald's anguished eyes haunted him.

"What kind of woman craves an evening with do-gooders high in the instep? Is your Scotswoman of the morally upright variety?"

Polly plunked down two frothy pints of small beer and cleared the empty tankards. He poured the cool drink down his throat, glad for the diversion. Miss MacDonald's character was an intricate map and he the intrepid explorer discovering her.

Burton slurped froth off his beer. "There's a correlation to London's morally upright ladies and sexual congress . . . or the lack of it."

"And this is important because . . . ?"

"Because up here"—Burton raised a flattened hand at eye level—"you have the sainted raise-money-for-foundling-homes women. They won't lift their skirts for any man but a husband, and few of them do even that." He lowered his hand two inches. "Here are the sainted raise-money-for-hospitals women who might let you grope them on a dark garden path." Burton lowered his hand another two inches. "And here we have the nearly sainted civically aware women, which includes museum enthusiasts. Women so tedious you don't want to grope them in the dark."

A moon-kissed shoulder came to mind. Miss MacDonald was splendidly carnal and complex, the most grope-worthy woman to walk the earth.

"The woman in question is committed to helping the lost souls in Southwark's Tenter Ground."

Burton moaned. "That's as bad as the shrill raise-money-for-foundling-homes women."

"Miss MacDonald is in a class all her own."

He defended her ardently, but Burton eyed him keenly, a hunting dog on the scent.

"Did you say MacDonald?"

"Yes."

"Isn't that the surname Fernsby researched? The one you had him digging through the Pell rolls for?"

Sometimes the sworn clerk was too smart for his own good. Alexander eyed him with cool equanimity.

"Can we stick to the matter at hand? Two tickets to Swynford House. Are you able to do it or not?"

Burton drummed fingers on the table. "Swynford House, Swynford House." Head canting, the sworn clerk was likely collating names and circumstances in the vast file of information between his ears. "As it happens, I know a viscount who just learned his heir is up to his chin in gambling debts. The viscount's name was in the paper, one of Swynford's guests. He could be persuaded to sell his tickets"—the drumming fingers stopped—"for a price."

"How much?"

"Five hundred pounds."

Alexander balked. "The tickets are two hundred pounds each."

"The extra hundred will help."

"That's highway robbery."

Burton rolled his shoulder. "It's your quid."

Alexander hadn't counted the cost of entry to Swynford House. His first effort had been through the duke's office to no avail. At the White Hart this morning, he'd dashed off a letter to the Marquess of Swynford's secretary, using His Grace's stationery. His letter had inferred the request pertained to crown business. It wasn't enough. If anything the stationery garnered a quick reply. A firm no, as it were. The marquess's secretary, Mr. Higginbottom, apologized profusely. If His Grace were to attend, that would be a different matter. But an undersecretary to an undersecretary? A polite no. Mr. Higginbottom waxed on about the harrowing task of transforming Swynford House rooms into an exhibit for the ages. The marquess's home was already bursting at the seams.

He squeezed the tankard. The cost of one night with Miss MacDonald equaled his annual income. His savings would be drained.

"Do it. Ask your viscount."

"Consider it done. You can deliver your cheque tomorrow at Artillery Ground."

"The viscount will be at Artillery Ground?"

"No, but you will. At half past one o'clock." Burton smiled smartly. "For a practice cricket match."

"I have other things I need to attend to."

"Such as chasing Scottish petticoats?" Burton rested a casual elbow on the table. "The first rule in wooing a woman is to make her pine for you."

Except Miss MacDonald enjoyed Saturday's Artillery Ground's practice matches. Showing up tomorrow would be a toss of the dice. He couldn't say which version of her he'd find under the tents surrounding the pitch.

The flirtatious Scotswoman? The fierce-eyed goddess of Swan Lane? Or the woman in breeches who gave him her back?

Buying the tickets was a gamble. The amount he would part with choke-worthy. But he'd hurt her, his high-minded Jacobite with pretty eyes and tempting lips.

He poured more small beer down his throat, but nothing drowned the ache of disappointing her. Somewhere between his fourth or fifth pint, wisdom whispered in his ear. This wasn't about flirtation or ambition, the crown or Bow Street. Nor was this about justice as he'd learned today. He was engaged in life's deepest, costliest endeavor—the game of love.

A subject he knew nothing about.

Chapter Fourteen

*F*un was the sole purpose of Saturdays at Artillery Ground. Practice cricket matches were casual, the crowds small, and no wagering was the general rule. Men still preened and women still watched, as one does when the sun shines and flirtation flows. Cecelia, however, was unapologetically mercenary, for today she sought entrance to Swynford House by way of the Marquess of Swynford's mistress, Miss Elspeth Cooper-Brooke.

Sharing the outing was Miss Hannah Burke, her mahogany eyes capturing deeper currents in the day's conversational waters. Secrets and lies bound their friendship. Elspeth was really Elspeth Nutt from West Midlands, the product of an unmarried laundress and a textile laborer. Miss Hannah Burke was Hannah Bettleheim, born and bred in Bethnal Green.

Both women lived their fiction. Cecelia tucked a curl behind her ear, content with hers.

"Why aren't you attending the marquess's costume

ball?" She plucked a red apple from a brass bowl and took a bite.

"Swynford rarely mixes business with pleasure." Wind teased Elspeth's impeccable strawberry blond curls. "Besides, his fundraising entertainments are boring, like the marquess himself." Elspeth wrinkled her nose. "Did I tell you? He still insists I call him *my lord* when we're in bed."

Sweet juices flooded Cecelia's tongue, a reminder of the apple she ate with Mr. Sloane. Once he became Baron of the Exchequer, would he insist on formality in bed?

"Men," Hannah said between sips of wine. "Odd creatures, yet they're all the same when they grunt and grind over a woman."

Their laughter chimed prettily.

"No man is my better when he's sweating for his pleasure." Elspeth nibbled a lavender-infused macaroon. "And we all know the marquess doesn't sweat for mine."

This was the nature of their Saturday outings. Gossip, advice, whispered confidences. Nothing was off-limits. One Saturday might be devoted to fashion, the next to sexual congress. They traded tricks such as how to wax ecstatic with a dull bed partner, how to bring a man to ecstasy in three minutes or less, and the best roads for maximizing pleasure during carriage frolics.

Today, however, a cloud settled over their table. Elspeth polished off a plate's worth of lemon and lavender macaroons all by herself.

Cecelia eyed yellow and purple crumbs. "I'll have to bring more next week."

"Please don't," Elspeth groaned. "Or my girth will outpace my corsets."

Hannah's smoky alto imparted distressing news. "Elspeth neglected to mention that she is on uncertain ground with the marquess."

"What's this?"

A crestfallen Elspeth dabbed a serviette to her lips.

"It's true. Swynford hasn't visited me in more than a fortnight. I fear he may cancel our contract."

"Which is why you need to listen to Cecelia when it comes to matters of contracts and money," Hannah said.

Wind batted the purple-dyed pheasant feathers in Hannah's hair. Fashionable choices were *de rigueur*. To see and be seen—as one does for cricket matches. They loved pretty gowns, but they were birds, snaring men. Men needed to believe they chased the fairest, most sought-after creatures. Hannah and Elspeth played the game, dressing for it, flirting for it, while Cecelia played a longer game. For her clan and for herself. Never had she sold her body to a man, and never would she.

Her heart ached for Elspeth, who believed the game of protector and courtesan would go on forever.

Nothing lasted. Love and fidelity were fairy tales. Her father had taught her that the summer he'd caught her kissing a visiting clan chief's son. She was thirteen then, her knees quaking the entire silent carriage ride home.

Would he give her the switch? Lock her in her room with bread and milk?

Clanranald MacDonald's good folk already gossiped about her father, the surgeon who'd planted his seed in his housekeeper's belly and refused to marry her. A frivolous, saucy-piece of a daughter was the fruit of their illicit union. It was to be expected with a child born on the wrong side of the blanket. Her actions shouldn't have been so shocking.

But that day was different. Her father had marched her upstairs and thrust a silver hand mirror at her.

"Tell me what you see."

She took the hand mirror, the metal cold in her slick palm. Fear glued her tongue to the roof of her mouth.

Her father towered over her. "Go on."

Her gaze darted from her father to her reflection. She swallowed hard. "I—I s-see blond hair. H-hazel brown eyes . . . like yours."

The weak reminder that she was his get didn't soften his ire.

"What else?" he snapped.

"My nose, my cheeks."

"Do you know what I see? A bored and foolish girl who thinks she can live by her appearance alone." Daylight from the window lit him sternly. "A girl who kisses lads without a thought to her future."

She squeezed etched silver 'til it hurt. She ached to say she kissed lads because they paid attention to her. No one else did in their cold house, especially with her mother gone. The deeper, sharper pain had been overhearing her mother say she needed to sever past mistakes—her daughter included.

The world threatened to spin, but her father's voice called her.

"Starting tomorrow, I will teach you to manage my medicinal elixirs."

"Your elixirs?"

"Do the job well, and I'll teach you to manage the rest of my affairs."

"But I already keep the household ledger."

Disdain twisted his mouth. "Which is good enough if marriage is your sole aspiration, but you need to learn the value of commerce."

The mirror hung limply from her hand. She turned to him, questions flooding her brain, too many to neatly organize for so startling a conversation.

"Why?"

His stern gaze cut. "Because a woman with money lives by her own rules. Remember that."

Freedom loving and fiercely different, he taught her how to multiply profits and avoid the marriage trap. Invaluable lessons which stayed with her. Hannah, who was nearing her thirtieth birthday for the second time, knew the tale. She reached across the table, pleading with Elspeth.

"Listen to Cecelia. She has the Midas touch."

"I don't know what a Midas is," Elspeth said. "Or why I should care about it."

Hannah glanced worryingly at Cecelia. "You've not heard of Midas? The fabled Greek king? Everything he touched turned to gold."

A lackluster shrug and, "His story might be in one of the books Swynford has gifted to me."

"Start reading them."

Elspeth's head cocked like a costly exotic bird. "I'd rather have gifts of jewelry. Gemstones last longer."

"Not when you sell them to cover your gambling debts," Cecelia said gently. "Wisdom and knowledge last longer, qualities which do more for women in . . . our circumstances."

Our circumstances.

This was the vague air they breathed. Young, independent women with no family, and beauty and friendliness their calling card. The uncertain future was a monster lurking around the corner, a truth Hannah grasped with clarity.

"Cecelia is kindly telling you that beauty fades and thighs thicken. Think of your future, Elspeth, and the day when no man will keep you."

Elspeth's chin tilted stubbornly. "My near future is my first concern."

Cecelia ate more of her apple, a rouged lip imprint encircling her bite. Youth and beauty were formidable cards. The folly in holding them was one's belief that they lasted forever, but time was a cruel bawd. She diverted herself by watching the open-air tent on the south end, the one where families gathered. Delight lit their faces, their joy catching.

Two new clubs strode past the family tent. They took the pitch, the crack of the bat and ball and laughing male voices rising. Smiling, amiable men in their prime. Men with ambitions—like her.

"Why not sneak into Swynford's fundraising event?" she asked. "He wouldn't turn you away."

"Stodgy men with fat coffers will be there. You should consider it." Hannah twisted around for a better view of the pitch.

Elspeth touched the brim of her straw hat as if the breeze might steal it. "This second match. What clubs are playing?"

So that's how it would be, Elspeth glossing over a prickly topic.

"A newly formed St. James Club," Hannah said. "Second and third sons, I think."

"Which means they're fun but have no money." Elspeth sipped her wine. "And the other club?"

"The Westminster Club."

"Barristers and clerks." Elspeth's nose wrinkled prettily. "Not the high-income sort."

"Not exactly low income either." Hannah's smoky alto dropped suggestively. "And they do give stimulating *conversation.*"

Cecelia had gone weak-kneed over Mr. Sloane's stunning honesty and velvety conversation. Both nights, theirs had been a fair give and take. Daylight was their problem.

Hannah turned back to the table.

"Prepare yourself, ladies. A Westminster man is coming our way." Her mahogany gaze pinned Cecelia. "And if I'm not mistaken, he's coming to see you."

Cecelia nearly dropped her apple. Speak of the devil.

Sun showered Mr. Sloane, a god of sport and manliness. His stride redolent and smile half-cocked, he slung his cricket bat over his shoulder. The hot, sweet memory of his lips on her shoulder shot through her chest . . . and other places. He might be coming for friendly conversation, as one did at practice matches. But his piercing, intelligent eyes owned her.

Her hunter returned.

"Cecelia, are you ill?" Elspeth asked. "You've paled under your powder."

Cecelia shot upright, her apple and serviette tumbling from her lap to the ground.

"I'm thirsty."

Ignoring the wine on the table, she snatched her shawl off the back of the chair and darted off like a rabbit to the next tent.

A local tavern had set planks of wood across barrels for a makeshift bar. She threaded between patrons with pints clustered in the tent, awkwardness flushing her. Voices and laughter hummed loudly. She charged onward, wrapping her red silk shawl around her shoulders as if it could ward off an unwanted man. The oak plank bar stopped her, otherwise she might've kept going. Isn't that what she'd done yesterday? Her dismissal at the orchard was borne of something she'd rather not name.

Mr. Sloane's plaguing effect.

His fingertip on her cheek outside the Iron Bell.

His delight when she swept a bow in men's garb.

His attention when she spoke as if he hung on her every word.

What man did that?

Her hands curled on rough wood. A man like him, respecting a woman like her, was dangerous. Even worse, she craved more. What good would that do? She would always be the scrawny Highlands girl who made reckless choices. Not the sort of woman a man introduced to his mother.

She needed a drink.

The tavern keep bellied up to the other side of the plank. "What'll it be, miss?"

She looked up from her clenched hands. "Do you have something to knock reason into a frivolous woman?"

The tavern keep chuckled. "A drink that strong can't be served here." He winked and cocked his head at the southern tents. "Families, you know."

Of course. Families. Salt in the wound.

A familiar brand was on a barrel above the man's head. "I'll have a Mermaid Brewery beer."

"It's a stout, miss."

"A pint, if you please."

"Make that two pints."

Mr. Sloane's tenor washed through her. He propped his bat against a barrel holding up the makeshift bar and rested both arms on the plank's edge. His rolled-up sleeve brushed the lace at her elbow, and she stared forward, absurdly giddy. He'd chased her. She shouldn't revel in that. Hadn't she spent the last hour convincing Elspeth to be an independent woman?

Haven't you spent these years since the war being one?

The barkeep set two frothing pints before them. Mr. Sloane kindly paid while she snatched her mug and drank deeply. The stout's foam slid down her throat, light and persuasive. She hoped it would push her heart back down where it belonged in her chest.

Mr. Sloane stared forward, his hand gripping his tankard. The same hand which had saluted her, twice, and the same hand which had written scurrilous information about her in his journal.

"Mr. Sloane," she said coolly.

"Miss MacDonald." He took a drink and added, "I, for one, would never think you a frivolous sort." Humor tinged his voice.

Irritating, that. So he heard her.

She nursed her tankard with both hands and stared at the barrels. Flies were buzzing a lazy trail, one barrel spout to another, while the barkeep swatted them with a rag. She hoped Mr. Sloane would leave; she hoped with equal force that he would stay.

"A fine day for cricket," Mr. Sloane said. "If I knew there was such excellent scenery, I wouldn't have missed this summer season."

She hummed dismissively and took a sip. If she tipped her head just so, the brim of her bergère hat blocked most of him from view.

"Tell me, is this a new mode of flirtation? Our speaking in profile?" he asked.

"Why do you care? Flirtation does nothing to advance your ambitions."

"Ah, you wound me."

To which she snorted indelicately.

Mr. Sloane's low laugh stroked her skin and his elbow bumped hers. How companionable they were: her staring straight ahead, slinging weak insults, and Mr. Sloane deflecting them as if this were a delectable game. She traced the rim of her mug, aware that he held all the metaphorical cards, while she held none.

"You might be pleased to know that I had an enchanting time with a woman yesterday," he said. "Exemplary flirtation was involved."

"'Exemplary'? Are you seeking high marks?"

"I strive to."

"And how does a man of your intellectual stature go about doing that?"

"With a boat race followed by a promenade through unsavory alleys crammed with litter, all to take in Southwark's derelict warehouses." He shrugged. "You know, all the entertainments women dream about."

She giggle-snorted and dipped her head. Her bergère hat was an elegant shield.

"I'm sure you swept her off her feet."

"Except I didn't."

The tenor of his voice dipped, quiet and sincere.

"I believe I hurt the gentlewoman in question and for that . . ." he said. "For that, I am gravely disappointed."

"Disappointed, Mr. Sloane?"

His feet shifted. "I am deeply saddened to have caused her pain when all I want to do is make her happy."

A pang bloomed in her chest. *Why did he say that?* Men didn't try to make her happy. Most wanted under her skirts, a smaller number wanted genuine commerce with her, but none ever concerned themselves with her happiness.

Until now.

Lashes low, she tried so very hard not to care.

"I am sure the gentlewoman in question will forgive you."

His elbow rubbed hers. "Does she?"

She tipped her face to his. Bronze eyes, tender and penetrating, held her in place. She couldn't run if she tried.

"She does," she said, her voice barely above a whisper.

His boyish grin was glorious. "I am gratified to hear it. Because I was hoping you could help me."

"How could I help a gentleman who has everything?"

"You could educate me. Let's say, how I might go about winning a particular woman's affections."

Hazy sensations fluttered up and down her limbs, sweet little butterflies of happiness. Oh, this was no good, this joy bursting like spring inside her.

"Her affections?" She took a sip.

"I've tried gifts, I should say *a* gift. Purely to appeal to her sense of humor and wit."

She fought a smile and lost. "A good start, certainly."

He hummed thoughtfully. "In reading the signs—"

"Mr. Sloane, women are not maps," she said with

mock disapproval. "Nor do we post road signs on how to win our hearts."

"Which is why I'm here . . . with you."

She sucked in a deep breath afraid something awful might happen—like a kiss. She desperately wanted to know the taste and feel of his lips on hers. She had wanted to know since the moment he'd saluted her cleavage.

"You are following a woman who gave you her back. Twice, in two days. A clear message to leave her alone."

The purr in her voice said anything but.

His laugh scraped seductively. "You see? This is why I could learn a great deal under your tutelage."

"I agree. You could learn a great deal . . . *under me.*"

Lust pooled darkly in Mr. Sloane's eyes. They were intimate, a breeze wrapping her hems around his leg, despite a lively crowd imbibing under the same tent and more liveliness on the grounds beyond.

"I thought you giving me your back was one of our unconventional greetings," he said gruffly. "We excel at those, you and I."

Her laugh was soft and her legs puddling wax. His wit gentled her better than summer sunshine. But why was he trying again? They were a mistake. A truth her tingling skin didn't question. Her rampant pulse didn't. For a woman fluent in flirtation, she was deplorably set back.

Mr. Sloane was not a man to be managed. He was too smart for that. But she did love the barrister's slightly stodgy patina, which made her fascination with him so flummoxing. They were ill-suited, and there was the fact that he'd come up short in getting her into Swynford House. The man couldn't advance her cause. As undersecretary to the undersecretary to the Duke of Newcastle, he wasn't well-funded, though silly considerations like money and position did not enter their equation. Therein was the crux.

What was the nature of their equation?

A yell came from the pitch: "Sloane! Come toss around the ball."

Mr. Sloane looked to his caller, a hand up to keep the caller at bay.

"My friend Burton," he explained quietly. "The man lives and breathes cricket."

Cecelia rested an elbow on the bar, a blatant attempt at nonchalance which had fled her. "Fortunately for you, Mr. Sloane, I have a soft spot for clever men with fine eyes and fine arses."

His mouth dented sideways.

She laughed. "You're actually blushing. I didn't think there was a male over twelve years of age left in London who could."

"You own the skill to make me do that . . . and other reactions."

His mouth was close. Not kissably close, but near enough to tempt. Near enough to see the fine grain of his skin, to touch the shape of his lips, and brush her fingers over day-old whiskers framing his mouth. A kind breeze stirred the black silk binding his queue. Revelers drifted from the tent, clearing a wide sight-line for Mr. Sloane's friend. Tall and rangy, his sleeves rolled up, Mr. Burton tossed a red ball up and down.

"Your friend is watching you," she said.

"No, he is watching you, as am I."

Her heart commenced its climb back into her throat. Especially when Mr. Sloane planted his elbow on the bar, his eyes intense, his smell masculine and clean.

"There is one thing I must know," he said.

"What?"

"If I couldn't get tickets to Swynford House, would you still enjoy the pleasure of my company?"

His question slammed her.

"As in, choosing me," he added with emphasis.

The world spun oddly. She was glad for the plank's solid support.

"I—I cannot let entanglements distract me."

His eyes narrowed a fraction. "Interesting. You bear a striking resemblance to a woman who told me entanglements don't get in the way. Emotions do."

She raised her tankard in salute. "If we were playing chess, I'd say check."

"Not checkmate?"

"No."

Arguments about the wrongness of them together bubbled up. She'd already told him too much. Her hunter needed a gentle setdown, one she'd give except a man in black positioned himself at the end of the bar.

His dark holes-for-eyes watched her.

Mr. Wortley! The Countess of Denton's chief cut-throat.

Icy sweat pricked her skin. She was in Southwark the first time she laid eyes on him. She'd hid in an alley after hearing him ask about Anne and Will. Warehousemen later told her Wortley and his men had meticulously searched the partially burnt Neville Warehouse with Lady Denton.

And here he was under the same tent.

She stared, unable to look away.

Wortley touched the brim of his tricorn, a cold smile cracking his visage. Revulsion swamped her, the sensation akin to being trapped in a room rapidly filling with water.

Mr. Sloane's back was to the man, his attention on something behind her. Hands jittery, she turned. *How to get away?* The countess's rabid dog had to know where she lived. He was here to scare her. It worked. She squeezed her tankard until her knuckles whitened.

Wortley wouldn't try anything, not midday at Artillery Ground.

But, he would come nightfall.

She swallowed hard. An appeal to Mr. Sloane was on the tip of her tongue, except a peculiar expression was on his face. Shock, disbelief, dismay. A Mermaid Brewery barrel was stacked high on another. Daylight showed a brand on the barrel's belly.

Mr. Sloane squinted at it. "The mermaid on that barrel . . . is that . . . you?"

Chapter Fifteen

*M*iss MacDonald was a vision in turquoise, the bodice dipping low. Between a heart-shaped patch on rouged cheeks and red-paste earbobs dangling from lobes he'd like to suckle, there was much to distract. All a fair excuse for missing the obvious.

The mythical woman branded on Mermaid Brewery barrels bore a striking resemblance to the goddess of Swan Lane.

The same flowing locks he'd seen when her hair was down. The same side smirk, wide eyes, and pert nose. The only feature he couldn't definitively match was her bosom. The mermaid burned into the barrel boasted two small breasts. Crescents with a dot above them.

His gaze dipped from the mermaid to Miss MacDonald's bodice and back to the mermaid. *Bloody hell!* Her breasts were on display for everyone.

"I am a partner in the brewery," was her blunt explanation.

Anger, hot and thick, flooded him.

Miss MacDonald's blinking gaze shifted to the end

of the bar. "It was a chance to put my stamp on the business."

"Doesn't every woman of business do the same?"

His tone drew blood. Miss MacDonald paled, her rouge bright red spots on colorless cheeks, but her hazel eyes were fierce and unapologetic.

"It was a youthful indiscretion. Have you ever indulged in one of those?"

A fly buzzed by his ear and he swatted it.

Her laugh was brittle. "I think not."

"My mistakes are not branded on wood for all the world to see."

"Therein is the difference between us, Mr. Sloane. I don't hide my mistakes. I own them."

"On barrels carted all over London."

His anger was illogical. Still, he was tauter than a bow string and thrown sideways—the goddess of Swan Lane's effect. Like a physics theorem or new-found law of nature. He was acutely aware of the flame of upset flaring inside him, and the fact that he was not entitled to it. Miss MacDonald was an independent woman of sound mind who could and would do as she pleased.

"I did it for love, or what I thought was love." She stood tall, her gaze flitting elsewhere. "Surely you've invested your heart in the emotion."

Heat simmered in his belly. Another man, loving her. It made sense, a woman who reveled in life would have past loves. He had only come close once—a pallid, colorless experience compared to the Scotswoman.

"Miss MacDonald . . ." He was fighting to understand.

She touched his sleeve. "Mr. Sloane, there is something I—"

"Sloane!" Burton called impatiently from the edge of the tent.

"It's a practice match," he said tersely.

Burton stopped tossing the red ball. The barkeep and two patrons walking into the tent stilled.

"A match which is about to begin," Burton said in clipped tones. "Since we're short two men, your presence on the pitch would be greatly appreciated. Miss . . ." Burton bowed to Miss MacDonald and sped off.

Tension twisted between Alexander's shoulder blades. "Now I've vexed two friends."

"You count me a friend?"

"I do."

"Then be a true friend, and accept me as I am, not as who you want me to be."

Miss MacDonald walked partway around him, her silk petticoats a hush against his thigh. Head turning, he locked on her the way moths follow light. A breeze soughed the tent's trim, and as a parting gift, the air carried her rosewater perfume to him.

"I don't know what bothers you more," she said. "That I've chosen my lovers instead of waiting for them to choose me. Or that I refuse to hide my sensual nature."

He curled his hand into a tight, frustrated ball. He'd give Miss MacDonald the sun, the moon, and the stars, but a deeper yearning lurked, as if his heart had told her, *Talk to me*, and when she did, Miss MacDonald met with judgment.

Bats and balls cracked on the pitch. Amiable conversation carried from tents rimming the field. A St. James cricketer sprinted to the wicket, laughing as he tagged it. Artillery Ground was awash in sport of all kinds, and he, Alexander Sloane, excelled at only one of them.

Miss MacDonald offered a quiet, "Go play your games, Mr. Sloane, as I must play mine."

Chapter Sixteen

*T*he Scotwoman's dismissal plagued him. He took to the pitch, his bat in hand. Burton threw the ball to him, and he caught it one-handed. Miss MacDonald was at the edge of the tent, a double-fisted grip on the shawl draping her shoulders. She deserved his full attention—instead he let a mermaid brand on a barrel flummox him.

He tossed up the ball and gave it a one-handed *whack* with his bat. The ball arced beautifully across the pitch.

Something was off. Her white-knuckled clutch on her shawl, her face going pale . . . and he forgot to tell her about the tickets to the Swynford House ball.

He turned to her.

Miss MacDonald was twenty paces away, head ducked as she was speeding off, her skirts a blue shimmer.

"Miss MacDon—"

"Sloane!" Burton yelled.

A *smack* vibrated in his skull. Pained fireworks exploded behind his eyes as a red ball dropped to his feet. He fell to his knees, cradling his skull. Anger spiked, then crawled away as happened with a strike to the head. Slick warmth oozed onto his palms. He checked his hands. They were coated with blood. On instinct, he covered his forehead and eyes, blocking the sun.

Footsteps pounded the grass. Shade covered him from a surrounding crowd.

"Mr. Sloane." Miss MacDonald's voice was at his ear, her hand the light touch on his back. "Tell me what you're feeling?"

"Only the pain of my diminished dignity, which seems to be a habit with you."

Miss MacDonald gently dabbed his forehead with a cloth. "I look forward to your third act. Hopefully *sans* blood." There was more tender dabbing. "You know I can't bear the sight of it."

"I am grateful that you and your senses are making an exception today."

Her breath feathered his ear. "You are my exception. For everything."

He basked in the moment. A breakthrough, he believed.

"Thank you."

She shivered against him, adding in a near whisper, "I must get away from here. Come with me . . . *please.*"

"Of course," he murmured. He wouldn't let her down again.

"If I cover the blood dripping down your forehead, I'll see less of the odious stuff and I can get through this."

He opened his eyes. Red silk danced over them. Beyond the fabric, he could see the blur of a gathering crowd. Miss MacDonald was on her knees beside him, her body gloriously close and her rosewater scent divine.

"Good to hear you talking, Sloane. For a second there, I thought you might be knocked out cold." That was the ginger-haired Viscount Felton, a St. James man.

"Too thick-skulled apparently," he jested.

Male laughs rippled through the dozen gathered around him. He winced behind red silk curtaining his face. Miss MacDonald was parting his hair close to the wound. The sting was ferocious.

"Everyone, back away. Give him some air." Burton knelt beside him. "He's still bleeding."

"There's always profuse bleeding with head wounds." Miss MacDonald's light fingers tested the gash in his hairline. "More so than other parts of the body."

"And how do you come by this knowledge?" Burton asked.

"My father was a surgeon for the Jacobite army."

Ardent words said while her fingers sifted through his hair. Mutters circled through the small crowd but Miss MacDonald didn't care. She applied pressure to the wound and addressed Burton and the circle of men as a nanny might instruct unruly boys.

"There are four common types of bleeding injuries: abrasions, lacerations, punctures, and avulsions. Mr. Sloane has a laceration." The evaluation of his scalp done, she stanched the cut with one hand while the other rested on his shoulder. To Burton, she said, "You may want to check your ball. I suspect a tear in the leather caused the cut when it hit his head."

"Or his hard head ruined a perfectly good cricket ball," Burton muttered.

Pride swelled in Alexander. Such cool authority in her voice and she was on her knees with him, her petticoats a blue cloud enveloping his right hand. A subtle twist of his arm, and his hand was on her thigh. Layers of silk and linen separated his hand from her leg, but he gave her thigh a reassuring, covert squeeze.

"A fine physic," sniffed a lordling. "Jacobite or not, I might need some tending after today's match. You can be sure I have the coin to pay for it."

Alexander swiped the silk shawl from his face.

"Keep talking like that and I'll jam my bat up your arse. Miss MacDonald is a gentlewoman and should be addressed accordingly."

He glared at the lordling from the ground, blood dripping over one eye. Not an enviable position, but the St. James cricketer slinked away from the circle.

She sat back on her heels. "Why, Mr. Sloane, defending my honor, are you?"

Burton scrambled to his feet. "Since your head is intact, can we get on with the match?"

Miss MacDonald was cleaning her fingers on her ruined shawl.

"Oh, I'm afraid he won't play, Mr. . . . ?" She rose elegantly from the ground.

Alexander reached for his bat, a throb building behind his eyes. "Miss MacDonald, allow me to introduce my friend and an esteemed man of the law, Mr. Peter Burton. Burton, this is Miss MacDonald, an accomplished woman of business and, today, my physic."

Her curtsey was quick.

"A pleasure, sir." Her mouth was a moue of distaste

while she examined her ruined shawl. "As I said, Mr. Sloane won't be able to play."

"I'm sure he can decide that for himself," Burton said.

"A head wound is very serious. He should rest and abstain from all excitement."

Burton bent over and picked up the cricket ball. "This isn't the first time Sloane's been knocked on the head. He'll get over it."

"A knot is forming."

"Which will remind him to keep his eye on the ball. We're already two men short. We cannot afford to lose him."

"So you said at the tent." Red silk bunched in Miss MacDonald's fist. "However, the facts are, a bump is forming and he needs to rest."

Using his bat, Alexander pushed himself upright. Burton and Miss MacDonald were squaring off like two dogs over a bone. He'd been bloodied and bruised in sport more times than he could count, and it never stopped his play, but there was a man in black watching from the tent. Cold and sinister that man. An unwelcome addition to the day and likely the cause of Miss MacDonald's upset.

Alexander tucked his bat under his arm and rubbed thickened blood off his eyebrow.

"What Burton means is he'd rather me bleed to death than lose to a cricket club with more arrogance than skill."

The bickering stopped.

Burton sighed, turning the ball over in his hand. A tear was in the leather. "If you must go, so be it. I suppose you'll need someone to look after you, though I don't know where your home is these days—"

"I know where he lives." Sun glittered on red-paste earbobs and a persuasive smile. "I can look after him." Miss MacDonald touched Alexander's sleeve. "Gather your things and come find me by the robin's egg blue carriage."

The Scotswoman sped off to the east end of Artillery Ground where carriages waited. Cricketers politely halted their batting in deference to a woman crossing the pitch. Her stride was brisk . . . almost urgent.

Together, he and Burton walked to a pile of coats and hats near the southern tent.

On the way, Burton tossed the ruined ball up and down. "Whisked away by a woman in a robin's egg blue carriage."

Alexander grinned. "Shouldn't every man?"

"*She* is why you sought tickets to Swynford House."

"She is."

Burton gave him the gimlet eye. "And you let me go on about shrill, upright women."

Alexander collected his hat and coat, a trickle of blood sliding down his forehead. The cut, he guessed, was the size of a thumbprint. It was best he go and not just because of his head. The St. James Club took the pitch, ready for their practice match to begin. Burton, however, lingered, his eye on Miss MacDonald already seated in the carriage.

"A woman like that at a boring entertainment." Burton scrubbed his jaw. "It begs the question . . . Why?"

Miss MacDonald poked her head out the window. "Mr. Sloane. We shouldn't dally."

He waved to her and set his hat on his head at a careful angle.

"Looks like it's off to bed for you," Burton said. "And a losing match for me."

He was going somewhere with the puzzling Scotswoman in a carriage he was sure didn't belong to her. He eyed the tavern tent. The man in black lingered where sun and shade met, his attention honed on the robin's egg blue carriage as if memorizing it.

Alexander waited for the shift in posture, for the moment the man in black would know Alexander watched him.

A lethal stare met his, palpable despite the distance. Miss MacDonald was the quarry and Alexander stood between them. The woman was mystery in petticoats. Her league, the *sgian-dubh*, her cold watcher. He'd barely scratched the surface of the woman he'd been tasked to follow. Primitive sharpness spurred him. The need to protect.

He would defend Miss MacDonald—with his life.

Sun blasting his face, he touched the brim of his hat. A nod, and the man in black touched his tricorn in return.

Another game was afoot.

Chapter Seventeen

*H*e was quiet the entire carriage ride. He didn't question the Scotswoman telling the coachman to deposit them at Covent Garden. He didn't question her when she darted along Henrietta Street and cut through St. Paul's churchyard before speeding off to the White Hart. He didn't question Miss MacDonald dashing off a quick note and paying a street lad the princely sum of three shillings to deliver it. He didn't question her telling the boy to exit through the White Hart's back door.

Once in his rooms, Miss MacDonald barred the door and rushed to the open window. She was careful to stand in the shadows while studying the street below.

"Are you going to tell me what this is about?" He took a seat on the pine settle armed with clean linens and a pitcher of water. "Because we both know this isn't about my head."

Miss MacDonald untied the ribbon securing her straw hat.

"You have been the soul of patience. I would've

dug in my heels and refused to go unless you told me what we were about."

He dropped a linen in the pitcher. "Therein is the difference. I trust you."

Miss MacDonald's face was a pale oval. A beautiful, lost soul stripped of artifice and lies. Her mouth quirked weakly as if it lacked the conviction to form her usual smirk. She was a cornered creature, bracing for destruction. The dismal light in her eyes hit him squarely in the chest. He'd seen more hope in bare-knuckle brawlers at the last minutes of a losing fight.

"Trusting the horrid Jacobite woman . . . What would Fielding think if he heard you say that?"

He wrung the soaked cloth, disappointed at her deflection.

"Tell me about the man in black."

"What man in black?"

Miss MacDonald turned to the window, giving him a view of his bloody handprint on her petticoat. Like an ancient tribal claim, that stain. His mark. Baser wants were not their problem; the necessary high-minded wants were. To be with Miss MacDonald meant they had to meet openly on both planes. The Scotswoman's mind was too agile an instrument to be ignored, and her heart and soul too important.

He patiently unwound wrinkled linen. "He was under the tavern tent. About my height, dark hair, military bearing with a calm I'll-rip-your-throat-to-pieces demeanor."

Miss MacDonald's hair was a frazzled halo, her clothes rumpled. Noise from late-afternoon traffic floated through the open window. Jingling harnesses, rattling carriages, hooves *clip-clop, clip-clop, clip.* All the sounds of life while in his room, something threatened to burst.

"I don't know what you want from me," she said.

"Let's start with the truth."

Her haunted eyes speared him.

"Otherwise I can't help you," he said.

"You want to help the dreaded woman who ensorcells men."

"A tired argument, quite beneath you. Even the devil himself pleads his case. Why can't you tell me yours?"

"Equal to the devil, am I?" Her tone met his, jab for jab.

"What I meant—"

"I understand your intent." She advanced on him, a cool blonde Fury. A woman who wasn't going down without a fight, which proved how frightened she was. "What I cannot fathom is why you want my secrets."

She stood before him, nostrils flaring and eyes blazing. He leapt to his feet, but Miss MacDonald's wrath sparked, a firework gone awry.

"You follow me home, write whatever tripe strikes your fancy, and you think you have the right to question me?"

"You asked for my help."

"I didn't ask for your help." Words so sharp she nearly hissed them.

"Then what was that pretty plea I heard at Artillery Ground?"

Her hems covered his shoes. Heat bounced between them. His, hers. Emotions boiling. Miss MacDonald looked as if she'd come fresh from a tussle, cosmetics smudging smoky lines around her eyes, and her lips faded carmine. A proud, glorious, passionate mess. A woman who didn't like needing a man.

Her brows pinched, the fight fading from her eyes. "I . . ."

He waited, but whatever needed out wouldn't come easily.

"Let me refresh your memory. You said, 'Come with me, please.' I detected a note of desperation in your voice. A woman who didn't want to be alone." A pause and, "Or are you about to tell me how mistaken I am?"

Composure rippled through her. She stood tall yet older as if the day had aged her.

"You're right. I don't want to be alone."

Her voice was loneliness and a whiff of despair, the sound reaching into his heart.

Honest hazel eyes met his. "When I'm with you, I feel . . . safe."

"You're not alone. With me, you never have to be."

Her eyelids quivered shut as if he'd delivered a healing elixir and she the dying woman who needed it. Blue shimmered seductively on her shoulder. A gap showed between skin and silk, a fragile shadow. An opening. He touched it and won her sharp inhale. Miss MacDonald trembled when he slid the fabric off her shoulder. The hat she held slipped to the floor.

His gaze dipped, fascinated by two hard nubs straining against silk.

He dragged both sleeves down her arms. This was heady, the sight of her skin intoxicating. Miss MacDonald wavered, a flush spreading up her chest and neck. She gripped his waistcoat, twisting the cloth.

Mere inches separated them when she said a resentful, "I don't want to want you like this."

He crushed her sleeves in both hands.

"You mean the unceasing need to breathe the same air as mine, to hear my voice as I crave yours, the anticipation, hanging on what you might say or do next because you are the most irritatingly captivating creature?" He exhaled long, his breath stirring her hair. "That kind of not wanting to want someone?"

Her lust-black gaze enthralled him.

"Yes."

"Now you know how badly I want you." His voice was hoarse, primitive.

Her mouth was inches under his. "Why?"

Desire unspooled, maddening carnal layers of it. He slid both hands into her hair. Bright red earbobs slanted on his wrists and hairpins clattered to the floor. His fevered hands roamed over her neck, her shoulders, and her hair.

Her grip on his waistcoat was unyielding.

"Why, Mr. Sloane? Why me?"

His mind raced with garbled nonsense. To say he'd slay dragons for her if the mythical beasts still roamed the Highlands? Or that he'd happily lay her clan's dagger at her feet? Most startling of all was his wish to give his name, his heart, and anything else the Scotswoman wanted. If he said that, his hazel-eyed cat would unsheathe her claws and race for the door. Thus, he let the next thing tumble out of his mouth.

"Because you are the goddess of Swan Lane."

Lips parting, she was stunned.

He took advantage of the moment and kissed her hotly on the neck. He found the low spot behind her ear. Her tiny hairs brushed his mouth. He kissed, he nibbled, tasting the sweet salt of her skin.

She arched her neck and whispered, "The goddess of Swan Lane . . . it's poetic."

Silk wrinkled and bunched in his hands. Cloth ripped and she groaned.

"Poetry. Not a skill I claim, but"—he interrupted himself to suckle her neck—"don't expect more . . ."

He couldn't finish. Two pink crescents peeked above her bodice. With her bodice askew and her sleeve torn, Miss MacDonald's fevered enthusiasm threatened to unveil her charms before he did. Her shaky hands flew over his waistcoat buttons.

"Don't stop!"

Chaotic heat ricocheted in his limbs. Don't stop kissing her? Staring at her nipples? Running his hands through—

He groaned, a deep, guttural rumble.

Her lusty hand sliding over his placket shocked him nicely.

"You're long and hard," she purred.

The goddess of Swan Lane bit his earlobe. Searing pleasure shot from where her teeth marked him to his ballocks. His laugh was a husky foreign sound.

"So, that's how it is when you don't want to want someone."

She rubbed the length of his phallus, a wicked gleam in her eyes.

"Imagine what'll happen when I decide I do want you."

Air hissed between his clenched teeth. He slid his hand into her bodice. Soft flesh warmed the backs of his fingers. One tug and dress pins popped off, and her stomacher was a nipple-freeing three inches lower. Breasts like crumpets, the bottom curve a finger's width thick.

Exquisite.

Her sacque gown gave way, sliding lower. He jammed it down to her elbows, trapping her. A half smile forming, she warmed to his game. The Scotswoman arched her back and thrust her breasts at him.

She was breathing as if she'd finished a sprint.

"Kiss me."

His gaze tripped over the sensual delights of a half-undressed Miss MacDonald in the afternoon. Sunlight streamed through the window, catching the gold crowning her head and a wash of darker strands like rich threads. She was life. Tender, teasing, smart. A woman to wrest his soul from its colorless existence.

"Where to kiss first . . . Here?" He touched her mouth, her breath steamy. He dragged his finger gently down her lips, her chin, to skim her breastbone and the scant valley between her breasts. "Or here?"

Her skin pebbled. Anticipation stretched, a new torture. Lust and affection shined in the deep pool of her eyes. She was learning—he would give as good as he got.

MR. SLOANE'S EYES flared darkly. Her proper barrister-cum-government-man was everything dangerous. Queue mussed, a gash on his forehead, the seductively masculine dent of his mouth. He fisted her hair and gently lifted it off her neck, glorying in the color and texture of her hair.

"You would tempt a monk."

"A man should know his options."

"You are my only one."

She gasped when their bodies pressed together. His mouth on hers, a passionate connection, as alarming as it was melting. He massaged the back of her head, her nape. A thousand tingling sensations washed her spine. Mr. Sloane was well-practiced in the art of making her want more. She wound her arms around his neck, her body arching against him as if it knew. *This is home. He is home.*

His lips moved over hers. Lush and hungry, sending joyous messages up and down her limbs. She kissed him back with a fervor she hadn't felt in a long, long time. Concentrated and hot as if to make up for not kissing him the night they met. It wasn't tender and sweet, but desperate and primal and knee-weakening.

He broke their kiss but held her, his magical hands drugging her with sensual touches.

"Mr. Sloane . . ." She was breathing hard, her words drifting.

"Call me Alexander."

The gift of his Christian name imparted, she dragged her mouth across his cheek, slow and hot. Alexander shivered against her. She couldn't remember what she had wanted to say; she craved his mouth like a famished woman. Their lips met. Her fingernails dug into the fabric of his waistcoat. King Street's noise—laughter, voices, carriages rumbling—drifted through the open window. Being in his arms, danger was a whisper gone.

She was safe.

When was the last time she felt like *this*? As if she could indulge in hours of bed sport and sleep for days, contented.

She suckled his lower lip, moaning when he expertly soothed a sore spot on her shoulder.

"Keep doing that and I shall never leave your side," she said against his mouth.

"I should be so fortunate."

His lips were sensual lines. With her fingers, she traced the outline of that soft tempting flesh.

"Tell me, do you want a quick tup? Or a—"

A knock at the door and a voice called from the other side.

"Alexander. It's me, Gideon."

Alexander groaned. "Bloody hell. My brother."

"And this was such a promising assignation."

"We're not done," he growled.

His warm, lean body slipped away from hers. She touched her hair and tried for the practiced mien of an experienced woman, but her hand was shaky. His calm hands started the work of righting his clothes. How demoralizing. Her cricket-playing barrister recovered quickly from his seduction while she trembled like a leaf.

"I deeply regret this interruption." His tenor scraped low notes.

She was hot and breathless, blinking at hairpins on the floor.

"Miss MacDonald?" He cosseted her shoulder.

She tipped her face to him. Of course he knew her Christian name, but like a proper gentleman, he would wait for her leave to use it. But she was too muddled to say her own name.

Three rapid knocks came again. "Alexander?"

"A moment, if you please," he called out.

Sensuality's ephemeral glow was evaporating.

"My hairpins . . ."

She knelt down, collecting those fallen hairpins. Her hair would be an easy fix. Not so with her clothes—or her soul. His kisses rattled her. She'd need the day to recover.

What would happen if she gave her body to this man?

Anticipation shot warm honey through her veins. The pins for her sacque gown shined between floor planks. There was no rescuing them. She was on her knees, jamming hairpins in place, when she spied her hat and a footprint on crushed straw.

Alexander dropped to one knee, his grin denting sideways. He drew a tender circle around her exposed left breast.

"Though it pains me, you ought to put away your lovely breasts."

Her skin tingled.

"A shame," he said. "Since I worked so hard to free them and didn't get to explore them."

"You are incorrigible." She hiked up her stays, mildly drunk on his touch.

He cupped her face and kissed her soundly.

"I am anything you want me to be."

She struggled with her slumping stomacher. "Can you save my wretched reputation?"

"There is nothing wretched about you."

"I'm afraid my gown says otherwise. Just look at me." Her voice was a tiny bit frantic.

Surprise lit his features a split second as if her dismay was unexpected. They were on his floor, their voices hushed to hide the obvious—an assignation interrupted. He tipped back, assessing her rumpled sacque gown. A sleeve was torn, embroidery frayed at the bodice, and her lightly boned stomacher bent.

Slivers of metal glinted from unreachable places. "Most of the pins for my gown have fallen between the planks. I have nothing to put myself back together."

The door latch rattled. "Alexander!"

"A moment, brother."

"My wrap. Please fetch it." She plumped her panniers, skittish as a cat. "I'll tuck myself away in your bedchamber and try to right myself."

Mr. Sloane grabbed the red shawl from the middle of the floor. He walked briskly back to her and gently wrapped ruined red silk around her shoulders. Kind, burning eyes looked into hers. Her future was in them, a frightening feeling as vast as the ocean. Tenderness soaked her when he joined their hands together, closing the shawl's end over her fast-beating heart.

The door thudded on its hinges. "Alexander! What is happening? Why aren't you letting me in?"

"Now we're just being rude." She pushed up on her toes and kissed him. He tarried, but she patted his chest and tipped her head at the bedchamber door. "Go on. I'll be right in there."

"You and your pretty crumpets-for-breasts."

Her breasts were more biscuits than crumpets, but if he wanted to think they were more sizable, who was she to correct him?

She slipped away and closed the door to reconsider the folly of seducing a morally upright government man.

Or had the government man almost seduced her?

Chapter Eighteen

*A*lexander opened the door with the smile of a kiss-sotted man, which his brother was too busy glaring to notice.

"What the devil is wrong with you?" Square-jawed Gideon pushed through the door and stopped in his tracks. "What happened to your head?"

He touched his head, the minor wound all but forgotten. Such was the goddess of Swan Lane's effect.

"A cricket ball gone awry."

"You? Serious Sloane missing a cricket ball? That hasn't happened since you were thirteen."

"I remember. The ball you lobbed at my head because I had vexed you."

Gideon's mouth curled in a victor's grin. "As younger brothers do."

The grin stayed until Gideon's gaze shot like an arrow true to the bedchamber door and the sound of muffled footsteps behind it.

"Welcome to my humble abode." Alexander couldn't help the triumphant note in his voice.

Gideon removed his hat and set it on a hook. "You were detained by a woman, I collect."

"An entrancing woman." His chest might've expanded, which drew attention to the button he'd skipped while hastily buttoning his waistcoat.

Gideon eyed the incriminating button with arched brows and innuendo.

There were a lot of questions in that expression, as only brothers could convey. Questions of birth and breeding, status, and similar items of note would top his older brother's list.

"Your new life must be exhausting," Gideon said.

"I work long hours to earn my keep."

Gideon smoothed his gray velvet coat. "Are you going to introduce me to your guest? Or do you plan to keep her hidden away?"

"Another day, perhaps."

Alexander crossed the room and touched a taper to smoldering embers in the fireplace. As he lit the sconces, an alluring rose scent lingered. Gideon had to smell the same gentle perfume. He was curious how Miss MacDonald would see his brother. It was possible she was peeking through the keyhole. They shared the same height, though Gideon carried a stone more muscle and was meticulous about his hair and his place in the family hierarchy. It might be the two sausage curls above his ears, an affectation which had consumed his brother since he'd discovered their father's pomade. Alexander rarely touched the stuff, a divergence there. An appreciation for a woman with a mind of her own was another. Gideon preferred the gentler sex in tidy categories: doting mothers, sainted virgins, and wicked women one engaged for entertainment purposes only.

Thus, it was no surprise when Gideon lowered his voice to ask, "Have you hired a Covent Garden doxy?"

"Who says I hired a doxy? Perhaps the lady hired me?"

Gideon's jaw unhinged and there was a muffled laugh behind the bedchamber door. Alexander couldn't say what possessed him to suggest such a thing. The goddess of Swan Lane's influence? Or the residue of her sensual kisses?

He tossed the taper into the fire and settled for vague truth.

"She propositioned me a few nights ago," he said. "A business arrangement, as it were."

Gideon's eyes rounded. "A woman *hired* you—for sexual congress?"

Alexander cracked a laugh. "No, I mean the lady is here to discuss something of a delicate nature. I do hope I can count on your discretion."

"Of course."

A solicitor to the marrow of his bone, Gideon grasped nuance. London's good folk parted with hefty sums to buy his discretion and his shrewdness.

Alexander took pity on him. "Have a seat. Should I call down for tea? Or do you prefer something stronger?"

Gideon planted himself in the chair like a new sailor thankful for terra firma.

"Nothing for me, thank you."

Alexander took a spot on the pine settle as laughter from the street drifted through the open window. "You see, brother, I have a few secrets of my own."

He might've been playing deep but he had nothing to lose. Gideon had stolen one woman from him.

Instinct told him never in a million years could Gideon steal the goddess of Swan Lane. She was a gift—her laugh, her scent, her soul. The lady might be tucked behind a door, but her radiance touched him. And he needed to be worthy of her. A humbling prospect. A drink, he decided, was a good idea after all. He rose from the bench and splashed port into a cup. The chair creaked behind him. Gideon was restless too. When Alexander turned around, his brother was by the fireplace, his well-shod toe toying with a pebble-sized lump of coal.

"Something bothering you?" Alexander asked.

Gideon reached into his pocket. "I am here to deliver this."

Foolscap, the paper folded appropriately, was in Gideon's hand. A stylized *S* stamped in white wax showed—the color for private festivities, especially weddings. The invitation a token of greater things. His brother's eyes glowed with the peculiar awe of a man in love.

Alexander was measured, crossing the room.

"Felicitations to you and Phoebe." His voice was rusted. "I am happy for you, truly."

"Thank you. It means a great deal to hear you say that."

Emotions tumbling thickly, Alexander deposited the invitation on the mantel beside the list of names and businesses from his visit to Westminster. Evidence concerning Miss MacDonald on one paper; evidence concerning another woman on the other. When he looked up, his brother's face was inscrutable above his perfect cravat. It was Gideon's solicitor's mien when treading lightly.

"You will be there . . . won't you?" Fire caught the sheen in Gideon's eyes.

"Of course."

Alexander's heart swelled from the deepest brotherly bond. He slapped Gideon's shoulder good-naturedly, and they chuckled. A redolent sound. Brotherly competition drifted away with it. Affection and boyhood scrapes knit them together, more than blood and bone. Their unspoken ties would remain just so until their dying day.

"I am pleased to hear it," Gideon said. "I did wonder . . ."

"That was last year. We've all moved on."

"You especially."

Chests crammed with Alexanders books and clothes with his cricket bat on top punctuated Gideon's point. He'd left the family home to make his own way in the world, but the pile looked more forlorn than that of a settled gentleman.

Gideon coughed into the ball of his fist. "And you're not the least bit upset?"

Was he? The fire warmed his legs, bringing memories with it. Had it been a year since he last found Miss Phoebe Kent sharing passionate kisses by a fireplace with his brother? Yes, it had. A very busy year in which he buried himself in his work for the duke and forgot the woman he once had a *tendre* for. How easy it was to forgive and forget.

"Phoebe will always be dear to me," Alexander said. "But I meant it. I *am* happy for you."

"Thank you. The banns have been read . . . I can scarce believe I will soon be a married man."

"It will be good to see the family again."

"Yes, Mother especially misses you."

Alexander stared into the cheery fire. He missed his family. The dinners and jovial debates. The quick-witted Miss MacDonald would enjoy them too. A pang bloomed in his chest at the tender picture of her joining the Sloane family dinner table.

"Well, I must be off," Gideon said. "Phoebe's expecting me."

"Never leave a beautiful woman waiting."

Gideon winked and checked the bedchamber door. "Agreed."

"Let me see you out."

They crossed the room, late-day sun streaming through the window. Gideon retrieved his hat and turned it over, twice.

"Is it too much to hope that you'll reconsider the working arrangement we once enjoyed?" Gideon asked.

"The family business. The other reason for your visit, I collect."

"Our custom dropped after you left."

"And Father wants me to return to the fold."

"He doesn't know that I'm asking." Gideon fussed with his hat. As the prideful eldest son, the admission cost him dearly.

Theirs had been a neat legal arrangement. Father and eldest son, gentlemen solicitors, and the youngest son, a cunning barrister for criminal cases. Anyone in legal trouble paid a solicitor a princely sum to find a barrister to take their case. As the legal hierarchy went, solicitors were considered gentlemen, while barristers were tainted by the unsavory task of defending the accused. Dirty business, but Alexander did it.

"Thank you, but no. I'll stick to my plans."

"Baron of the Exchequer. You're aiming high," Gideon said not unkindly.

"Your confidence in me is overwhelming, brother," he said dryly.

"We all know you're the brilliant one, but be reasonable. I'll be king of England before you get your letters patent."

Alexander stood rigid as a duke's man. "You have your path, and I have mine."

Cautious eyes, so like his own, stared back. Gideon had taken on the dual errand of delivering the wedding invitation *and* to implore the errant son to return. A daunting task. Alexander would wholeheartedly embrace his family, but not the family business.

Gideon opened the door, gracious in defeat.

"Walk with me to the street, will you? I want to bend your ear while I wait for a hack."

"Of course." Alexander glanced at the bedchamber door.

A few minutes more . . .

He went downstairs with Gideon, and they dissected a legal matter concerning a London bank until a hack materialized. He waved farewell to his brother, dearly tempted to fall back into his old life. His black robes and barrister's peruke were a familiar path. But a more intriguing adventure called— a certain fair Scotswoman waiting for him in his bedchamber.

He waded through the busy public room, beefsteak and fresh baked bread teasing his nose. A fine dinner to share with Miss MacDonald. They should eat before indulging their *other* appetite. Smiling, he bounded up three flights of stairs, hoping Miss Mac-

Donald was already naked. Instead, he found his door wide open. The bedchamber door was open as well. He sped across the room.

The bedchamber was empty. The window at the same angle, candles flickering over the mysterious Jacobite ledger open on his bedside table.

A chill scratched his nape.

"Miss MacDonald?"

Calling for her was foolish. She was gone.

The man in black.

His mouth went dry. He'd promised to keep her safe.

The possibilities of what happened shot at him like canons unleashing hell. He tamped down fear's rush and strode to his chest. He searched for his pistol and pouches of ball and shot. Calmly, methodically, he poured the powder, visions of a frightened Miss MacDonald haunting him.

He would grind the cutthroat under his heel.

Who was that man?

A criminal out for the *sgian-dubh*?

Firm and precise, he rammed the ball home.

Blood pulsing coldly, he wiped his pistol clean. Another dangerous fact—the coded Jacobite ledger was left open, but not taken. *Why?* His brain set that neatly aside. Miss MacDonald was in danger; he knew it as sure as he breathed.

He donned coat and hat, hellish questions pressing in. Had the man in black followed them, biding his time in the public room, waiting for the right moment to grab Miss MacDonald? But how could a man take a woman against her will through a crowded room?

Chapter Nineteen

*B*y day, London Bridge was choked with commerce. By night, it was the crossroads for drunkards, fools, and thieves. Its narrow road was hardly sufficient, yet the Government dragged its feet on what to do with the dying bridge.

Lady Denton sipped her ale and waited by a stingy-sized casement window overlooking the river. The view was impressive and worth the shilling she paid to secure her seat. The water's rush was another benefit—it muffled conversations.

Ships listed and wherries darted, the lightermen's candle lanterns chips of aged gold in the night. Frigates caught her interest, one in particular with a cruel captain who had a love for money. Most men could be bought. The valiant few who couldn't were a passing interest, save one Scotsman who had branded her heart. Will MacDonald.

Blasted Highlander. She took a long draught of ale, waiting for another Highlander.

"Careful, milady. Mr. Wortley's no' here to see you safely home. An' I didna see any of his men outside."

Rory MacLeod dropped his tricorn on the table and slid onto the seat opposite her.

"My carriage is at the end of the bridge. No one knows I'm meeting you, and I want to keep it that way." She smiled from the shadow of her hood. "Servants like to talk."

"I wouldna know about that."

She brushed back one side of her hood for a better view of him. Scarred at his eyebrow and chin, his features rugged, a maroon bruise bloomed on his face.

"How did you manage that?"

He touched his cheek as if remembering the bruise.

"A quick bout at Snow's Field."

Scrabbling for farthings from Southwark's tight-fisted folk. Not a smart decision. At their first meeting in Brighton, she'd sized him up, a bare-knuckle brawler of middling talent. After he lost a bout, she'd hired him to entertain her for a time. Vivid blue eyes and flashes of charm saved MacLeod from being just another ruffian.

"You are something of a mystery. A man adrift?"

"Do you really care, milady?"

His voice was graveled and deep. A pleasure to hear in the dark, tangled in silk sheets, until he'd sauntered off, leaving her cold.

She sighed and let go of her hood. Shadows were better.

"No. I want information."

MacLeod generally rubbed her the wrong way. Her bed was the only place he rubbed her the right way. Otherwise he was a brute with no finesse. Will, at least, had a tender gentlemanly side. He had wanted to learn, and she had been thrilled to offer her tutelage. But those days were gone. Will Mac-Donald and a sorry band of Jacobites had taken her gold. Jacobite women, in fact, if the whispers were true.

No one messed with her money.

Sitting in the high-back settle, a small table between them should've been cozy. MacLeod, however, waved off the tavern maid as if he couldn't spare more than a few minutes of his time. He planted an elbow on the table, mild tolerance painting his face.

"There's no' much to say, milady."

"Didn't Cecelia MacDonald hire you?"

Crystalline blue eyes narrowed. "She did. Yesterday."

"You don't look happy that I know that."

The Scot needed a good reminder. She had eyes everywhere.

"Why hire me, if you doona trust me?"

"I don't trust anyone, Mr. MacLeod."

His mouth was a grim line.

"I agreed to keep an eye on Cecelia MacDonald and two harmless old Scotswomen for you, and that's what I'm doing."

"No, you agreed to do my bidding because of the stunning amount of gold I promised you." She jabbed an emphatic finger on the table. "You are not *keeping an eye* on children. These women stole from me."

"You *think* they stole from you. As I recall, Cecelia MacDonald was in your salon all night when the theft happened. She couldna have been the one to empty your safe."

Except the safe wasn't emptied. Certain documents had been tucked away with the gold.

If anyone read them . . . .

She turned the ring on her finger, refusing to argue the finer points of thievery with him. Mr. Wortley had tracked down rumors of a league of Scotswomen. Part rabid dog and part bloodhound, he had gone over the guest list from the night her gold was stolen. Wortley had honed in on Anne Neville, Will Mac-Donald, and one Cecelia MacDonald because the blond Scotswoman was seen with Anne. But there had to be more. Scots always banded together.

Hiring MacLeod to investigate Cecelia MacDonald and her compatriots was a gamble. He'd been in her employ less than a month when she approached him with the proposition, but he was a Highlander, which made him a risk as much as it made him her perfect spy. The Scotswomen wouldn't suspect him.

He was supposed to stay in Southwark and report to her who came and went from Neville House. Miss MacDonald hiring him to repair Neville House was an unexpected boon.

"Have you learned anything about the Jacobite league?" she asked.

"What league?" He leaned forward, his big hands linked on the table. "You really think Jacobites would be fool enough to form a league? In London?"

"Anything is possible."

He scoffed. "Get in your fancy carriage and take a trip through Tenter Ground by Snow's Field, milady. That's where you'll find your Jacobite league."

"What are you talking about?"

"I'm talking about women who help Scots at Tenter Ground. Food mostly. Some with employment. Others, they pay their passage home or to the colonies. That's your league, right there," he said, jutting his chin at her. "A league of ordinary charitable women."

"And how do they finance their good deeds?"

He looked at her as if she was soft in the head.

"Helping people find work isna expensive." He frowned. "Look, all I know is they were four women, milady, now it's three. Miss MacDonald and two elderly clan aunts."

"There must be more," she said stubbornly.

"There's no'," he said, just as stubborn.

Four men ambled into the quiet tavern, dockside rufflers. Their coats ragged and smelling of pitch, their hair lanky and unkempt. Their bloodshot eyes roved over the ruby ring she twisted on her finger and her black taffeta cloak, her plainest, though it was too fine for this establishment. A Queen Anne pistol sat in her petticoat pocket, small but convincing. She'd have one shot should the oafs try anything.

The newcomers huddled around a table, calling for ale. One of them scratched his whiskers and sized up MacLeod.

"I need details," she said quietly.

"Like what?"

"Like what they think they know about me."

Men could be deplorably inept. Mr. Wortley was a pleasant surprise, his grasp of life's little details enlightening. She parroted his wisdom.

"Much can be gleaned from habits, visitors, correspondence, and such," she said.

MacLeod's grin was a crooked mess. "You want me to report to you when they take their tea and biscuits? I can do that."

Irritation flared hotly. A man mocking her—she hated it.

"You do that, Mr. MacLeod. As long as it doesn't tax the resources between your ears."

His grin froze. "Insults, milady, are one thing I doona miss."

She massaged her forehead. A *mal de tête* was forming. What did she expect? A list of names and future plans? MacLeod had been in their midst for one day. Even the uniquely skilled Mr. Wortley wasn't that good. Her gaze drifted to the frigate in the heart of the river. Miss MacDonald's fate was sealed. But first, there was the matter of the *other* contents in her safe.

"Just keep your ears open to any gossip about what else was in my safe."

"I thought all the gold was taken."

"It was," she said sharply. "I—I need to know if they read anything."

He snorted in disbelief. "What thief stops to read a book when they're stealing?"

She held her tongue. Being vulnerable rankled her, and she'd said too much already.

MacLeod picked up his hat. "If there's nothing else, milady . . ."

She checked the four ruffians working on their second round of ale. This night was terribly un-fruitful.

"I'll go with you."

The Highlander escorted her across a floor sticky with spilled beer. Gold jingled softly in her other petticoat pocket. Ten half guineas. A healthy sum for her unlikely spy, the first of his payments.

Outside, the cold air was damp and mildewed, and light scarce. Two Night Watchmen wandered into Nonsuch House, the garish Dutch building. MacLeod was a hulking form, scanning the empty bridge road. A nearby waterwheel sloshed loudly underneath.

"Are you sure there's nothing else?" She had to raise her voice to be heard.

MacLeod's breath billowed small frosty clouds. "You set me to watch over two old Scotswomen. Their lives are cooking, mending, and giving aid to Scots and Irish in Tenter Ground. Their biggest excitement is talking about Miss MacDonald attending a costume ball Wednesday next."

"Where is this costume ball?"

"Some nob's home. Swynford House, I think."

Her fist clenched in victory within her cloak. Miss MacDonald in a crowded entertainment at her brother's house—priceless news indeed.

"That is exactly the kind of information I need."

She dug in her petticoat pocket and retrieved the purse of half guineas. His first payment.

"Keep your money, milady."

"You don't want it?"

His eyes were an unnatural blue in the dark. "Save it for later but insult me again and I canna guarantee the quality of my information."

This was an unwelcome development. She returned the purse to her pocket.

"Respect above gold," she said carefully. "What a surprise you are, Mr. MacLeod."

"I know what I want and I'm no' fool enough to let you know what it is. Godspeed, milady." He took three, four strides down London Bridge when he pivoted sharply. "One more thing, milady."

Night blurred his form, but his stance was soldierly.

"You willna touch one hair on Miss MacDonald or the two elder ladies' heads."

"I mean them no harm. I only want information."

The silky lie assuaged the Highland brute. The

meeting was fruitful, though she lacked her usual finesse, talking about the contents of her safe. Very unwise of her. Some secrets were too terrible to see the light of day.

MacLeod headed down London Bridge to Southwark, seemingly content with his false control. Men. They lived too much by the force of their hand. MacLeod's information was the gold she sought. His act of rebellion troubling. Thus, she pulled out her Queen Anne pistol and shot him dead in the back.

Some plans, unfortunately, got a little messy.

Chapter Twenty

Later that same night . . .

𝓕letcher's House of Corsets and Stays was dark, not a soul in sight. Cecelia ceased knocking on the door and pressed her nose to the window, cupping her hands on both sides of her face to block the street-light. All was blessedly in order. Floors swept clean, flattened corsets propped on shelves, an empty vase awaiting fresh flowers come morning. All so neat and orderly, and her inches from ruining it. The news she brought would destroy their peace.

They were losing, badly.

Outgunned, outmanned, and outwitted by the countess. Her lips twisted bitterly. *Blasted woman!*

She balled her fist and pounded on the door until candlelight flickered through wavy-paned glass. The door swung wide. Mary gawked.

"Cecelia, what are you doing here at this hour?"

"A friendly visit."

"This is your day for cricket and your courtesan friends."

She swept in, head high, her courage a thin veneer. "I was at Artillery Ground earlier today."

Mary closed and barred the door. She was dressed for comfort in her favorite rose-hued robe volante. A neat braid snaked over one shoulder, and she smelled like cloves, custard, and comfort. Mary moved her brass candleholder, assessing inches to the right and to the left.

"Is that a bloody handprint on your petticoat?"

"Yes, one of the cricketers received a small head wound. He bled profusely and I stanched it."

Mary's lips twitched. "Received it, did he?"

"I didn't hit him on the head, if that's what you're thinking."

Candlelight splashed Cecelia as if she were a specimen observed. The glow stalled on her slanted stomacher, one corner bent and poking unnaturally against the shawl. No amount of red silk could hide the passion-ruined piece or hide her carmine-smudged mouth.

"Must've been quite a cricket match," Mary said.

"I'll tell you all about it in your fitting room." She eyed the ceiling where Margaret's footsteps pattered across the floor above. "Keep your sister away."

Mary's amusement faded. "It's that kind of friendly visit. Very well. Go to the fitting room and I'll bid Margaret to give us some privacy."

Mary handed her the candleholder and Cecelia rushed through the unlit shop. In the fitting room, she lit sconces and set the brass candleholder on the table. The fitting room held two benches and a bedside-table-cum-writing-desk. In one drawer was foolscap and pencils. She took one of each and quickly sketched a costume.

The shawl slipping from her shoulders, she leaned over the little table like a tortured student. Her skin was fevered, her stomach roiling. She'd fled the White Hart chased by a ferocious idea. Now it stared boldly at her from the page.

Slippered footsteps crossed the narrow fitting room. Mary plopped down on the bench facing her.

"Margaret is doing the dishes. You will come up, of course, before you go home."

"I'm not going home. It's not safe."

"What about Jenny?"

She glanced up from putting finishing touches on the sketch. "I sent a note warning her to stay away. I suspect she went to her sister's house."

"What is this all about?" Mary scooted to the edge of her seat. "And, Cecelia, you had better tell me everything."

She put the pencil down. Fear was beginning to consume Mary. It was understandable. Fear made a person demand full knowledge as if control came with it. It didn't—a truth Cecelia grasped. On her long walk, she'd weighed the facts and cleared her mind—all the better to set her startling plan in motion.

"It's the countess. The vile woman is ten steps ahead of us. Her man, Mr. Wortley, showed up at Artillery Ground today."

Cheeks blanching, Mary touched her lips. "We're not as clever and secretive as we thought, are we?"

"I'm afraid not. The countess is toying with us—with me." She took a deep breath. "Mary, Mr. Wortley *wanted* me to know he was watching me."

"The man the countess has following you."

The note from Denton House's spy.

"He must be." She sagged in the seat, worn out.

"But you escaped him."

"Escaped him? No. He let me go. I left Artillery Ground with Mr. Sloane, the wounded cricketer. I took refuge in his room at the White Hart."

"The same Mr. Sloane who followed you to my shop and gifted you with an ugly night-robe."

"The very same."

Mary's rueful gaze skimmed her mussed hair. "And you managed to tend his wound rather passionately."

"This"—she waved both hands over her dishabille—"wasn't supposed to happen. I was watching the street below his window. We started arguing and then suddenly we were kissing."

"As one does."

Mary was amused, crossing one leg over the other and smoothing wool over her knee.

Cecelia bristled. "I have no emotions about the man."

The lie sank like a millstone in her chest.

"No feelings at all?"

"None save minor frustration and the minutest flare of attraction. He is a means to an end. At least he was," she said miserably. "I left a note telling him I must never see him again."

Repeating the lie that Mr. Alexander Sloane was of no consequence would make it true. Wouldn't it? The dismal lump camped on her heart said differently.

"If I didn't know any better, I'd say you were more upset about severing your connection with Mr. Sloane than Mr. Wortley following you."

She rested an elbow on the table as if the thing would hold her up. Four years of the league's business and her dual life had exhausted her. The rose-scented shop had become a second home, and the league her family. But Mr. Sloane with his perceptive eyes and wickedly kissable mouth was a luxury she couldn't indulge.

"There's more, isn't there?" Mary was the soul of gentleness, watching her.

Perhaps she, too, felt the strain of their four-year hunt.

"Mr. Sloane's brother came to the White Hart for a surprise visit. He knocked on the door when we were in the throes of this . . ."

She waved a hand over her ruined stomacher.

Mary's lips twitched. "When you were tending Mr. Sloane's wound."

Cecelia's mouth curved slightly.

"I couldn't meet his brother in a state of dishabille, so I hid in his bedchamber and put my ear to the door."

"And what did you learn when you eavesdropped?"

"That Mr. Alexander Sloane," she said slowly, "is a good moral man."

A man who deserved a woman of sterling character, not a demirep tainted with Jacobite sympathies.

Misery pressed down on her, nearly eight years' worth. The Uprising and its aftermath, her home burned, her father on a prison hulk. Within each heartache were secrets upon secrets. She'd never meant to be part of this league. Anne had asked, and she'd refused. Her resolve changed the day two of Cumberland's men dragged her behind her half-burned house. They'd clawed at her gown, their breath stinking, their laughter cruel. She'd kicked and screamed as they tried to do their worst. Anne had saved her, pistol-whipping one man, knifing the other.

She'd clambered to her feet that day, a different woman. Barely nineteen yet aged by war and sorrow. There, standing beside two dead good-for-nothing soldiers, Anne had asked her again to join the league.

Her fate had been sealed then, as it was now.

"I didn't come here to discuss Mr. Sloane." Cecelia passed the drawing to Mary.

"You're still going after the *sgian-dubh*?"

"Yes. To do it, I'll need that costume by Wednesday."

Mary studied the page. "This isn't a costume."

"It's a maid's costume. I'm attending Swynford's ball as Betty Burke."

Mary's inhale was sharp and scandalized. Betty Burke was Charles Stuart's fictious name when he dressed up like an Irish maid and escaped Scotland after Culloden.

Mary examined the drawing more closely. "Cecelia, the petticoat, is it—"

"Clanranald MacDonald's plaid? Yes, but it must be painted silk."

"By Wednesday? There's not enough time."

"Surely you know someone in Spitalfields who can do it."

"Of course I do, but the cost would be exorbitant."

"I'll pay it."

Color drained from Mary's cheeks, her voice a thin wisp. "As you shall pay a price for wearing this. They'll throw you in prison."

"It's not a kilt."

"But it *is* an act of rebellion." Mary scowled ferociously. "I fear the English will not see the humor in you dressing like this."

"I'm not doing it to humor them."

"Why do it?" Mary's gaze nailed her. "Is this some foolish idea to honor your father? It's not your fault he died in a prison hulk. He made his choices."

"As I have made mine."

Her heart was a tight ball in her chest. Torment wanted to eat her alive, resolve its counterbalance. The emotions had been her companion since fleeing Mr. Sloane's room, and the decision which followed, freeing. She didn't know how she'd gain entry to Swynford House, but enter it she would.

"After I left the White Hart," she said, "it was all I could think about."

Indeed, the multitude of steps from the White Hart to White Cross Street firmed the plan in her mind.

"I know that look, Cecelia. You're planning something reckless." Mary shook the paper. "And this proves it."

"It doesn't matter."

"Of course it does. Do you think this will be a grand comeuppance to the crown?" Mary snorted indelicately. "The king won't care one whit. No one will know. You'll be smacked down like a fly—one less Jacobite."

"I am resolved."

"I beg you, wear something else and we can all

carry on with our lives, but this . . ." Mary was at the edge of her seat, her voice shrill. "This is reckless."

"But that's just it. We *don't* carry on with our lives. We're still cleaning up the aftermath of war."

"And flouting Clanranald MacDonald colors is . . . what? Falling on your sword in the name of clan pride?"

Beyond the fitting room, she could hear the goings-on in the street. A pedestrian whistling an aimless tune. Carriages rolling by. Life. The past, the present, a fine web connecting in this moment. Yes, her father had made his decisions, and she was gladly running headlong into hers. If she didn't shed the past, it would devour her future.

"My oath was to return the *sgian-dubh*. Wednesday next, I shall fulfill it." Steel threaded her words. "Do you remember where the marquess's house is?"

Mary set aside the paper, her shoulders slumped in defeat.

"It is at the corner of St. James Square and Charles Street."

"There's a window in the ladies' retiring room that opens onto Charles Street. It's near the back of the house with an elm tree in front of it. Wear men's clothing and wait for me there. At ten o'clock I'll pass the *sgian-dubh* to you through that window."

Mary reached for her. "Why don't you climb through it and leave with me?"

She patted Mary's hand. The plea was sweet.

"Charles Street is too busy. A woman in a ball gown crawling through a window would definitely draw attention."

Sadness and confusion clouded Mary's eyes. "What you're doing doesn't make sense."

It did to her. Perfect sense—a vow fulfilled and she would be free.

"I'll wear an apron pinned to my gown. It will cover my plaid-painted stomacher and petticoat. Once you have the *sgian-dubh*, I'll remove the apron in the women's retiring room. That should create a diversion."

"Ensuring that I get away."

She took a deep breath. "And in a way, so will I."

"That makes no sense."

She began folding her ruined shawl, an emblem of a cataclysmic day. "The rebellion has been our constant companion. Isn't it time we let go of a war we lost?"

Eyes wide, Mary fell back against the wall. "You're—you're leaving us."

"The league, yes."

"I cannot believe it."

"We will always be friends. That will not end."

Stained silk was on her lap, the shawl ruined like her. She'd long ago made her peace with that scrawny Highlands girl. That girl became a woman who fought hard to honor a father who'd died in a prison hulk and to honor a clan chief who'd given her a home when Cumberland's men had burned hers to the ground. She'd fought hard against the memory of two dead soldiers who'd tried to violate her, and she'd fought very hard against one living, greedy countess. But the time had come to let go— the league, her past, and her present delight, Mr. Sloane. She was poison to him.

Every choice had a price; Mr. Alexander Sloane was hers.

Lashes heavy, she fingered damaged silk. He was the first man to truly see her, his eyes kind and intelligent. Her eyes burned, their sting dripping salt to her mouth.

Her new freedom tasted bittersweet.

Chapter Twenty-One

*S*unday morning in Dowgate was an obvious mix of those who churched and those who didn't. Clean-cheeked families migrating to St. Michael's Lane, hair combed and breeches pressed, were the former. Solitary males slinking along, hats pulled low and cravats askew, were the latter. Men who'd sold their souls. Like him. He'd come to take it back. A respectable place, Dowgate was. Dyers, fishmongers, clerks lived here.

And one slippery Scotswoman.

He knocked on her door and waited as a gentleman does when returning a woman's hat, except Miss MacDonald wasn't inside. She was turning onto Swan Lane, her blue petticoats shimmering. Footsteps clicking fast, she mulled the ground on her quick journey home.

When she was closer, he called to her, "Is this a new fashion? Greeting guests outside the front door?"

She stopped short, startled.

"Mr. Sloane. What are you doing here?"

Her morning alto was sensual to his ears. Her hair,

he noticed, was more down than up, a just-tumbled-from-bed look while she stood an aching six paces away, staring at him sadly.

"I found this in my room"—he held up her hat—"red ribbons, not quite my shade."

A reluctant smile bowed her mouth. Promising, that. But she was quiet, almost awkward with morning sun shining on her.

"I recall the hat belonged to a headstrong seductress who visited my room at the White Hart. Twice, in fact," he said. "She bore a striking resemblance to the goddess of Swan Lane."

"A goddess? In Dowgate?" Her head cocked. "I don't believe I've heard of her."

This was the opening he needed.

"A pretty blonde . . ." He held his hand just below shoulder level. "About this tall. Flirty thing with a clever, clever mind, though her fierce heart is . . ."

Words dried in his throat. Miss MacDonald's grip on her shawl whitened. Her hazel gaze wouldn't let him go.

"Is what?" she asked softly.

His mouth quirked. He would tell her what she deserved to hear.

"Her heart is her true beauty. She's certainly won mine." He cleared his throat. "My heart, that is. Which is why I thought it best to return her hat to her."

The benefit of talking to a woman standing in the sun was witnessing her lashes flutter and her delicate swallow—small tells to bolster a man declaring himself. His admission, however, poured more misery on her.

"Oh, Mr. Sloane, this—us . . . it cannot be."

Her formality jabbed him. He was Mr. Sloane again.

"Why not?" he asked patiently.

"Because you shouldn't be seen with me." She rushed forward. "Didn't you get my note?"

"Are you referring to the unsigned note left on my mantel?"

"Yes." Miss MacDonald fished for a key in her petticoat pocket, her rose scent heavenly. Birds chirped, and a door creaked open down the lane. Someone doused a flowerpot on their doorstep.

"I found it after I loaded my pistol."

She paled. He wanted to succor her, but there were consequences to a woman running away and truths that needed to be told.

"The woman who kissed me passionately yesterday couldn't have written it. That woman would tell a man face-to-face she didn't want to see him."

She fit an iron key in the lock, her profile lifeless.

"Please. It's . . . better that I not see you again."

"I don't want better. I want you."

They were so, so close yet not touching. Her hand trembled, the tiny movement quaking him to the marrow of his bones. Miss MacDonald was a woman to change the shape of a man's soul, yet he floundered in reaching hers. She was cloaked in secrets and purpose, her history devastating but her heart braver despite it.

He touched her hand gently and breathed in her rosewater perfume. Her resolve was fracturing; he could feel it.

"I thought the worst when you weren't in my room.

I ran downstairs half out of my mind, thinking the man in black at Artillery Ground had something to do with your sudden disappearance. Except when I ran downstairs to search for you, one of the serving maids said you left the public room, alone. It made no sense." He quieted his voice. "Even after discovering your note. It seemed . . . cowardly."

Her profile pinched in pain.

"Therefore, I concluded a stranger scorched a path out the back door of the White Hart yesterday, not the Scotswoman I've come to know."

Her forehead touched the door. "Mr. Sloane, I am poison to you."

"I will be the judge of that."

"What a fool you are." She looked at him, agony haunting her eyes. "Continuing our connection puts you in peril."

"Why? Does Jenny mean to gut me?"

His jest fell flat.

"She's not here. I sent a note warning her off." She turned the key. "Jenny had the good sense to listen to me."

The door gave way and he followed her inside. Plain white paper covered the entry walls except for a garden tableau at the center. Vibrant blue birds matched a chipped Bristol blue vase on a table beneath it. He put his tricorn and her straw hat beside it.

"Are you going to tell me about the man in black?"

Miss MacDonald barred the door. "His name is Mr. Wortley, a cutthroat for hire."

"Who hired him?"

Light wavered in her eyes. As a barrister, he'd seen the same expression on the faces of those he defended—people deciding how much to tell. The irony branded him. Truth was light and freeing, while lies and half-truths crushed one's soul. The once vibrant goddess of Swan Lane was painfully subdued.

Whatever raged inside the Scotswoman was tearing her apart.

"Come with me," she said at last.

They took the stairs to her bedchamber. The room was chilly, the mood distant. They both could use some warming up. He knelt before the fireplace, finding stacked coals on the grate. He concentrated on striking firesteel to flint, choosing not to press her for information about Wortley. Miss MacDonald was moving about, opening and shutting her wardrobe.

"I came to London four years ago as part of a covert league of Scotswomen. Our mission was varied. Mine was to get Clanranald's *sgian-dubh*."

"So you've told me." He struck the flint, sparks flaring, but not catching fire.

"We helped Highlanders."

He focused on the unlit coals.

Miss MacDonald was a sylph in his side vision. Water splashing, cloth rustling.

"Most of all we came to take back Jacobite treasure."

Hairs raised on his arms. *The coded Jacobite ledger.*

"The Lost Treasure of Arkaig," he said.

Miss MacDonald was by the window, pouring water into a porcelain bowl.

"Yes. The Countess of Denton stole some of it."

Little embers sparked the tinder. He nursed the flame, letting her talk.

"Not all of it, mind you," she said. "We learned the countess was hiding seventeen hundred livres in her Grosvenor Square home."

He stilled. "Did you say seventeen hundred livres of gold?"

The pieces of a complex puzzle were falling into place, and he the unwitting witness. Miss MacDonald had surely read the coded Jacobite ledger in his rooms at the White Hart.

The more difficult question: Was she in it?

Daylight behind her was so bright his eyes hurt looking at her. A cake of soap sat on a small stack of linens. She was preparing for ablutions. With him in the room?

Breath caught in his lungs. It would be heaven to see her bare skin.

"Thank you for starting the fire." Her voice was sweet and smoky.

He pushed himself off the floor and dusted off his hands and his lustful thoughts. This was sobering business.

"Forgive me, but you've just accused a high-ranking woman of a serious crime."

It was a safe place to start.

She set the pitcher on the floor. "The Countess of Denton is a dangerous and terrible woman."

"And running off yesterday . . . That was out of some misguided effort to protect me?"

A woman looking after him? It should've nicked his pride, but he fancied a partnership was forming. Two people on equal standing. The Scotswoman, he imagined, wouldn't have it any other way.

At the moment, she was touching the curtain and checking outside. Pearled light splashed her despite wool-thick clouds smudging the sky. She was beautiful and contemplative in the same gown she wore yesterday. Had she slept in it? More importantly, where had she slept? Frustration nipped him. The mystery of her, her secrets and stunning revelations. He couldn't rush this or she'd shy away for good. But one fact was clear: the more he talked to Miss Mac-Donald, the less he knew of the complex woman.

He crossed the room to her bedpost. "I can't help you if you withhold information."

"I don't want your help." She let the curtain drop and faced him. "As it is, you've been unable to fulfill my one request."

"Ah, the costume ball at Swynford House."

She was adorably surly. "I've carried on well enough without a man's help. I'm sure I can muddle through where the costume ball is concerned."

"No doubt your fortitude is iron-clad, but it is the nature of human beings to need each other—regardless of their sex."

She unpinned a red earbob and dropped it on the washstand. "As only a man would say."

"There is no battle between us. I freely admit I need you."

Her hand reaching for the second earbob froze. Sadness etched her features.

"Don't—don't say things like that."

He was mercenary, dipping his hand into his coat pocket to withdraw two tickets. "If you don't need me, perhaps I should toss these into the fire?"

"You got the tickets to Swynford House?"

"I did." He fanned the tickets.

She reached for them, but he jerked his hand back.

"I want to hear you say that we make a fair partnership."

Her eyes narrowed, catlike and vexed. "A fair partnership?"

He raised his arm. "On second thought, an excellent partnership. The two of us . . . together."

"It's a costume ball. One night, Mr. Sloane."

"Alexander," he corrected.

Her lips curled inwardly. Anger was her shield against the intimacy growing between them and the demands of her league. She stood on her toes, reaching for the tickets, bumping into him.

He stretched his arm above his head and wound the other around her waist. "You and I are more than one night. And you know it."

A prism of emotions flared behind wisps of hair falling across her face. Affection and heart-aching sadness shined brightest. She was warm and right, her body slanted against his, silk rubbing wool, the hush intoxicating. He desired her body, but the deeper craving, the better one, was wanting her mind, her wit, her spirit joined with his.

Eyes locked and bodies touching, he lowered his arm and offered the tickets.

"We can get on well by our own faculties," he said as one heartbeat passed onto another. "But how much better would our lives be if we were together?"

Her lips softened. He *was* breaking down unseen barriers the secretive woman had erected. First with honest words, then with tickets delivered as promised (more words, he supposed, but a gentleman was defined by his words). He clasped her hand and turned it palm up. Pink and white flesh, life lines, love lines, her flesh. He kissed her palm and set the tickets on top of his kiss.

"You have earned my trust and my utmost respect," he said. "I hope to someday earn yours."

Her eyes pinched sadly.

She folded her fingers over the tickets. "Everyone has a tale. Some complex. Others dirty. Mine is both." Her voice was fragile. "I am not yet twenty-five but I've already lived two lifetimes. And I am so, so tired. My burdens are too great and too messy to put on someone else."

"Try me."

Her mouth twisted a wobbled line. She was graceful, slipping away and tucking the tickets in her wardrobe. She shut the wardrobe door and leaned back, tucking her hands behind her.

"You ask too much."

Her voice was the distant sound of a lost soul.

"And you give too little. We both know I could marshal the crown's considerable resources and hunt down whatever else you're not telling me—about you and your league."

"You won't do that," she said quietly.

"Because I'd rather hear it from you. As is customary when two people care about each other."

Her eyes were luminous.

"You presume much."

She walked to her washstand, every swish of silk ruining him. Everything faded in the wake of this woman. Fielding . . . the Jacobite ledger . . . the judge's seat as Baron of the Exchequer.

Cecelia pulled a pin from her hair, and his breath caught. A lock tumbled across her shoulder. The one he'd kissed. She was a portrait of debauchery, petticoats wrinkled, her hands rummaging through her curls. *I could do that for you* was on the tip of his tongue, but temptation was the Scotswoman's currency.

Who would they be if they couldn't get past this?
Thus, he glued his spine to her bedpost and endured
the torture of her undressing.

Lithe arms raised, she removed hairpins and
dropped them in a small bowl on a bedside table.

"For what it's worth, I do trust you. More than
you'll ever know."

Aching words that tore him. There was distance
in them. He was a government man, secretly tasked
to follow her, to dig up dirt. Perhaps he wanted too
much, too soon. Their bridge of trust had begun the
moment the Scotswoman pointed her pistol at him.
Control was of the essence—mostly hers. The facts
sketched her in one light, yet being with her sketched
her differently. Innocent and saucy, clever and strong.
An admitted thief with a tender heart. What was he
to make of her?

He was surprised when she removed her stomacher
and began an astonishing tale. She told him of her
home burned to the ground, of two English soldiers
who'd tried to violate her, and their quick demise. Of
coming to London and starting a new life. The league,
each woman in it, and the Jacobite gold they searched
for. She shared future plans to smuggle sheep—
sheep!—of all things back to the Highlands. An entire
herd, minus paying the excise man because you can't
build a herd with one ram and one ewe. And she re-
peated the most stunning news: until last month, the
Countess of Denton had hidden a portion of the lost
treasure of Arkaig in her house.

Cecelia was half-dressed, her back proud.

Every word by turns scandalous, dangerous, and
treasonous.

Men met their end on Tiburn Tree for much less.

She ended her tale with an elegant flourish of her hand. "Last month, our league took back the treasure and returned it to our clan." Chin tipped, she added, "And I refuse to say we stole it since by rights, it's ours."

"Is that all?" He wouldn't quibble over the crown's claim to the gold.

"Don't you think that's quite enough?"

How alluring she was in her loose gown and angelic white stays. Her shift bunched above her stays as if she'd cinched herself in a hurry. A woman hastily armed for the day. Faint shadows darkened skin under her eyes. His fierce Scotswoman, her armor was breaking.

And there was no mention of a larger group beyond her humble league of Scotswomen.

"What I meant is, have you told me everything?" he asked pointedly.

She examined her torn sleeve. "Yes."

He quashed his disappointment. Moments ago, she had poured out shocking revelations, each word a brushstroke. The public and private portrait of Cecelia MacDonald. He'd add another—the secret woman. The one whose heart was hidden. Had she buried it in Scotland? Not out of love, but for protection?

Was Miss MacDonald a scared Highland lass, putting on a brave face?

She took threats in stride. A cutthroat dressed in black, her newest frightening dilemma.

Alexander reached into his pocket. Could be she still viewed him as another dilemma to be dealt with—a government man, a barrister, Fielding's covert investigator. The odds of her trusting him were not favorable, and the paper in hand damning evidence. He held it up. She eyed the paper wearily and began to stretch free of her *robe à la française.*

"What is that?"

Chapter Twenty-Two

*I*t is evidence that your father, a dead Jacobite rebel, has been paying your taxes."

She stopped undressing. Time stalled as Alexander unfolded the paper, its webbed creases proof he'd carried the note for several days. In less than a week, the cunning man had done what Bow Street's best couldn't. He'd followed the money.

She wore her best pasted-on smile.

"You produce the most astonishing things from your pocket."

His features were cool with a touch of menace. "This is a serious matter."

"I can tell." Silk, warm from her body, slid down her arms. "That, I presume, is your barrister's face."

His kissable mouth firmed. He wore his triumph poorly. Terse eyes, brown scruff on his jaw, his breeches wrinkled as if he'd fallen asleep in them. The foolscap in his hand was his trump card and his torment, she supposed.

"Well, are you going to read the charges against me?"

His menace deepened. "These are facts, not charges."

"Your manner tells me otherwise." She tossed the silken mass of her gown aside.

His stare never wavered. "Is your father still alive? He is A. MacDonald, I collect."

What a nice mess this was, and she, three days from taking the *sgian-dubh*. Between flirtation and kisses, it was easy to forget Alexander Sloane was not an ally and not quite an enemy. He could do damage with the contents of his list—to her and others. She dropped a folded linen square into the bowl of water and reached behind to untie her petticoat. A thin layer of grime coated her, as if she'd worn the gown and her secrets for ages. Despite the brusque barrister-cum-government-man staring at her, it felt good to shed them. She would let go of every little thing, but there was a point here. Her secrets were hers to keep and hers to share. A taste of her ire would make him think twice about digging up hers.

"A. MacDonald was my father's name. Alistair MacDonald, if you must know."

Her fingers made quick work of the tapes. Blue silk slithered to the floor. Alexander's razor-sharp stare bounced between the bowl of water and the petticoat puddling at her feet.

"Are you—"

"Washing myself? Yes. I feel . . . *dirty*," she said with relish while untying her underpetticoat. "Don't worry. I'll keep my shift on. It is the same one I wore your first night here. We muddled through then, didn't we?"

"We did." But his voiced was gruff and unconvinced.

A lock of hair slipped from his queue, and the air in her bedchamber shifted to something primitive. He watched the underpetticoat drop to her ankles like a wolf about to pounce on its prey. She stepped out of the undergarment, and his eyes narrowed, lust and caution warring in them. Perhaps the barrister had spent too much time around liars and thieves. She might be a thief, but she was no liar.

The man and his bridge of trust.

"You are distressed," he said.

"You think so? We made an agreement at the White Hart, the direction of which was quite clear."

"I delivered the tickets, as promised."

"While investigating me at the same time." A heartbeat of silence passed. "You and your *decent partnership.*"

To which his mouth pinched. So, her handsome hunter grasped that he couldn't have it both ways. *Nor can you* was the whisper in her head. Disappointment burrowed deep inside: Alexander had said nothing about ending his investigation or what he'd say to Fielding in his report Wednesday next, but she'd bite her tongue before saying more about that.

"Make up your mind, sir. Work with me or don't. Straddling both sides is hazardous to one's health."

She gave him her back and bumped the water bowl. Alexander's presence burned her. She wanted him to stay and she wanted him to go. Her conundrum was made worse by the lump in her chest rising to her throat . . . as if she might cry.

How infuriating!

Fast fingers flew over the pink ribbon binding her stays. What a ridiculous sight she must be with her panniers and pockets still on. Draped in silk, a pretty silhouette. Stripped down, it was silly. Structured cane hips, no linen covering them since these were her summer panniers, and the pockets sad little sacks patched in two places. Not the ideal tableau for giving a man a tongue lashing.

Except Alexander's footsteps came quietly behind her. Warm hands skimmed her shoulders.

"Why do we make this hard?" he asked.

A shard of tension slipped off her back.

"Because you shouldn't be here."

"Why?"

He drew fragile lines on her skin. A tingle flowed everywhere he touched.

"We . . . are wrong for each other." Her voice was a ragged wisp.

Declarations of her scandalous reputation and his moral uprightness melted when Alexander lifted her hair off her neck and kissed her nape. Tender, magical lightness tripped down her spine.

"I see nothing wrong here." He rained sweet kisses on her shoulder. "No dragoness scales. Only the soft flesh of a woman."

Skin pebbled wherever his mouth touched. The feel of his lips was light and delicious. She stretched like a cat, grabbing handfuls of her shift.

"I didn't know dragonesses existed."

"Of course they do. Otherwise we wouldn't have little dragons."

She smiled despite her wish to stay vexed with him.

"What a colorful mind you have."

"Oh, you have no idea." His voice was rife with innuendo.

Pleasure flowed wherever his mouth touched.

Tender kisses and sultry words, both felt good on her skin.

"It's possible you're the dragon," she murmured.

A dreamy sensual haze infused her bones. A cascade of seduction and awareness. Of cool brass buttons pressing her shoulder and strong hands on her stays. His palms massaged her ribs, the sound of it whisper-soft.

"Only one way to be sure," he said.

"You'll undress for me?"

His laugh was wicked and low. "Strip me and see for yourself." His persuasive hands rose to her shoulders. "Arms up."

She complied, twining her arms above her head. Alexander slid loosened silk stays up her body and over her head. Hair fell over her face, the curling tips feathering her skin. She rested her cheek against the cool wall as gentle hands worked the panniers' tapes behind her.

"Panniers. A medieval contraption if I've ever seen one. Puts women at a distance from the men who want under their petticoats." His grumble was velvet against her ear. "You're knotted."

"The hazard of dressing oneself."

"Where did you go last night?"

"To my friend Mary."

He kissed the knobs of her spine. "You could've stayed with me."

Eyelids drooping, she gave in to the luxury of his attention. Him undressing her was a delight. His warm smell, his sleeves brushing her skin. Panniers creaked and the undergarment dropped. Firm hands cupped the indent of her waist before traveling down her shift-covered hips and thighs like a sculptor adding artful finishing touches. He raised her hem discreet inches, untied her garters, and nudged her stockings lower.

Warm breath teased her thigh, and he kissed the back of her knee.

"Definitely no dragoness scales here."

She whimpered. His sweet seduction would be her undoing.

Alexander was on his knees. She'd soon be on hers. Expert hands skimmed her legs and his thumb drew a line in the crease where her bottom and thigh met.

"No scales here either." Lust grained his words.

"You are quite thorough."

Her body was swimming in a pool of delight. He caressed her ankle, a mute command to step free of her pannier. She glimpsed what a future with Alexander would look like. He would be a thoughtful, loving companion, a man to show gentle care—with her or any child he fathered.

She squeezed her eyes shut. Tears wanted out. Why torment herself with what she couldn't have? The crown gave letters patent to men of the highest moral fiber. Alexander would have to marry an upstanding woman, not a tainted daughter of a Jacobite rebel.

"Alexander . . ."

Air cooled behind her.

"You could call me Alex . . . if you prefer." He stood up and swept her hair over her shoulder.

"Alexander."

She cleared her throat, trying to sound like a woman with her wits about her, but his mouth was hot and insistent. His kisses would leave scorch marks on her shift.

"I like hearing you say all the syllables of my name," he whispered between kisses.

Warm hands held her captive, rubbing and sliding over her ribs. She writhed against the wall, her hips knowing what she wanted. The world could disappear. The French could invade. She didn't care. She wasn't going anywhere.

Until a cold damp cloth touched her nape.

Air hissed between her lips. Water dribbled down her back. The chill shocked, erotically so, the teasing wet trails slipping down her torso. Practiced fingers dragged her shift down to her waist.

"You mean to bathe me," she said huskily.

"I mean to take care of you."

His words tugged at her heart. Hadn't he already twined a rope around the organ? Her heart leapt at the sound of his voice and throbbed at the feel of his touch. And he was just as thorough, shattering her defenses with each swipe of the cloth.

"Turn around."

His voice beguiled her to unpeel herself from the wall. She turned and faced him, her narrow chest expanding and contracting as if her lungs could barely keep up. His eyes seared a leisurely path from her eyes to her mouth to her breasts. A masculine brow arced as if querying, *Aren't you going to cover them?*

Her chin tilted a mutinous denial.

A gruff laugh and his mouth dented sideways. "You are one pleasant surprise after another."

"No need for false modesty. There is a reason why I'm half-naked," she said with equal smokiness.

His eyes smoldered darkly.

"Then I should do something about that."

He dipped the cloth in water, wrung it out, and

dragged it from her neck to her right nipple. Exquisite icy heat sparked that nib of flesh. She melted against the wall as he stroked the damp cloth in sluggish swirls over her breastbone, the furrows of her ribs, and around her navel. She did a fine job maintaining her composure. She couldn't be with Alexander, but nothing would stop this dalliance. She'd seize the luxury of being with him—until she couldn't.

Goose bumps flared across cool, damp skin. The tingle was a reminder that she was alive. So was the joy in watching him, brows slashed in concentration, a lock of hair brushing his whiskers, and his mouth sensual and studied. Only Alexander could manage that heart-bending combination. She tucked the lock behind his ear, but his focus burned intensely on her body like a master of music cultivating his next sonata.

How perfect to be his chosen instrument.

He drenched the cloth again. Soap might've been involved. It was slippery and fine on her arms and torso. Her maestro seemed especially fond of worshipping her breasts, eliciting sweet cries from her. Careful fingers spun erotic circles on the tips of her nipples.

Her blood ran thick as honey.

"You are, if anything, attentive." Her voice was pleasure-drenched.

"To your breasts, yes."

Her husky laugh followed. "My biscuits."

"Crumpets," he corrected, his eyes pinning her. "My favorite." Artful fingers traced barely-there curves. "You are the pinnacle of loveliness. Not all men crave bountiful bosoms."

Well!

Who was she to argue with a man who loved small breasts? Hers, especially.

She braced both hands on the wall to keep from falling down, such was the state of her jellied knees. At her feet was the list. Another truth out. Businesses she'd supported. Scots whose taxes she'd paid in her father's name. Not quite underhanded, but suspicious all the same.

Alexander possessed her secrets and he possessed her. She almost didn't care. She was floating in bliss, a testament to his thorough seduction. And her traitorous heart wasn't in the mood to give up the sensual government man making studious love to her nipples, one swirl at a time.

Chapter Twenty-Three

$\mathcal{C}$ecelia folded her hand over his. When he looked up, sunlight glinted on blond hair falling in wavy threads over her face.

"You do remember why you're here, don't you?" she asked.

"I am looking at her."

Her thighs shifted seductively against his as if her body mutinied against the words of reason coming out of her mouth.

"What about your bridge of trust?" she asked.

"You mean *our* bridge of trust?"

Pretty hazel eyes met his, the center a pool of black he could get lost in. This close he could see varying threads of blond in her hair: the shiny golds, buttery yellows, and a smattering of earthy browns.

He kissed the corner of her mouth. "Who needs bridges when we can swim in rivers of lust?"

She giggled against his mouth, the vibration sweet. The Scotswoman breathed life into him in more ways than he could count. Her wanting to share more of her heart and mind was a good thing—but right now?

He nuzzled her cheek. "I only wish to put the bloom back in your cheeks."

"Oh, you've put the bloom in my cheeks." Her eyes sparkled with erotic mischief. "If we keep this up, the bloom will be mutual."

Her hand stayed on his, as much an invitation to keep going as it was a reminder of his purpose. If they were to make progress, what they shared would have to be more than skin-deep. She had a point, though he didn't like it. From the moment Miss MacDonald had threatened to shoot him in the arse, sexual congress was inevitable. Incongruent logic, but there it was. The Scotswoman had a fascinating talent for bending the natural order. Who was he to argue? Anticipation was its own delight, and he was a very, very, very patient man.

He surrendered the cloth and tested the length of a curl falling over her nose.

"No woman has affected me quite like you."

His delectable, half-naked seductress smiled. "The passion between us will happen."

"Are you sure?" he asked rather grumpily.

"Absolutely." She scraped her fingernails across his jaw. "But we both crave a meeting of the minds. We need it, you and I."

His mouth twisted a testy line.

She raised her shift and slid one arm through the sleeve. "We can't be ruled by what's going on in your breeches."

"What about my breeches?"

"Your cock has turned your placket into an equilateral triangle."

There was no arguing the evidence. Brown wool stretched to a point, its profile a perfect triangle.

He scrubbed a hand over his mouth. "I may be a walking geometry lesson, but you're the one wearing one earbob."

To which she touched her ear and laughed. "A fine parry to my thrust, sir, but you will . . . recover?"

"Other than my ballocks in a knot, I'm fine." His voice was strained.

"Good. We have the rest of the day, but at the moment, another subject needs our attention first." Her gaze dropped to the floor and his followed to the much-traveled list.

"History."

He picked up the paper, her pink silk shoes a short distance away. Very sobering those shoes. The coded Jacobite ledger came to mind. He couldn't rule out the possibility that he was standing in Lady Pink's bedchamber. He was sorely tempted by Cecelia's scent, by red nipples poking her shift and velvet skin aching to be explored. There was wanting to be with a woman, and there was truly wanting her. To understand the woman, to know her heart, her mind, her past—all to fuel a future with her. Honest, weighty discussions were the only way it would happen.

But a patina of weariness crept back into her eyes.

Cecelia reached into her wardrobe and covered her loveliness with Madame Laurent's hideous brown creation.

"Shall we?" She stretched an elegant arm toward the tight seating arrangement by the fireplace.

They were about to plant themselves before the cozy fire he'd built when a pounding knock sounded below.

"Cecelia!" A frantic woman's cries followed a fist banging the front door. "Cecelia! Are you there?"

Chapter Twenty-Four

Cecelia rushed downstairs with Mr. Sloane behind her. She opened the door and found Mary Fletcher, her face waxen and her head bare of her mobcap.

"Cecelia!" Mary collapsed into her arms. "You are safe!"

"Of course I'm safe. Why wouldn't I be?"

Mary unfolded herself from a fierce hug. "Mr. Mac-Leod was shot late last night on London Bridge."

"Is he alive?"

"Barely. He was shot in the back after he left a tavern. At first, no one called for a doctor because the Night Watch thought him dead."

She clapped a hand over her mouth. "Oh no."

"He lay there for at least an hour while the Night Watch debated if they should take him to St. Magnus or St. Olave's—"

"How awful!"

St. Magnus and St. Olave's had grave pits for the poor. Her skin crawled at the notion of MacLeod barely alive while men discussed where to deposit his unwanted body. With rampant crime, the impoverished dead were more nuisance to the government than true concern.

"But he *is* alive?" she asked.

"Yes, yes. The Night Watch heard him groan. They called for a doctor and carried him to the Ram's Head."

She stiffened. "The Ram's Head . . . on London Bridge?"

Mary nodded emphatically and rushed on. "Mr. MacLeod is very lucky. The lead ball landed in the meat of his back."

"MacLeod certainly has a lot of that."

"The doctor said two inches to the left and it would have hit his spine. He'd be dead for sure."

"Come, have a seat in my salon."

"I can't stay long. I need to get back to Margaret." Mary began to walk the half dozen steps to the salon when she stopped short, her eyes rounding on Mr. Sloane at the foot of the stairs. "You're not alone."

"This is Mr. Sloane."

Formal introductions were made. Mary's gaze bounced from Mr. Sloane to Cecelia, her mind cyphering the calculus of a man with a woman in her night-robe.

"Apparently, I don't have to worry about your safety," Mary said diplomatically.

Cecelia could feel Mary's eyes land on the one earbob dangling from her earlobe. She really should've taken a moment to remove it, but sensual pursuits and all.

"Yes, well . . ." She waved off Mary's analytical stare and headed into her salon.

She curled up in her favorite chair, her mind racing. Mary took a spot on the settee while Mr. Sloane made quick work lighting a fire in the cold room. Mary stared at the floor, wisps of hair rioting around still pale cheeks.

"You look like you could use a drink, Mary," Cecelia said.

"Yes—yes, I think I could."

"Mr. Sloane, would you be so kind as to bring two cups from my kitchen—three, if you'd like a drink—and a bottle of brandy? You'll find them in the yellow cabinet."

Mr. Sloane stood upright, eyeing her as if she'd asked him to enter the maze of the Minotaur. It was an unusual request.

"Mine is a small house, it'll be easy to find it," she said.

His mouth dented a knowing grin, a man who grasped when two women needed some privacy.

"I'll do my best to navigate the wilds of your kitchen."

"Thank you."

She delighted in the muffled sounds of Mr. Sloane stirring about her kitchen; there was a hominess to it.

Mary scooted closer on the settee. "It looks like you and your hunter are getting on quite well. I can't think of a single man I know who would fetch spirits for a woman in an unknown kitchen."

The noises coming from her kitchen were a comforting sound.

"He's not like most men."

"And you trust him?" Mary's voice was barely above a whisper.

Cecelia plucked lint off her knee. She did, probably

more than she should. "Mr. MacLeod is our primary concern. Where is he now?"

"At Neville House. A coal boy making his rounds at dawn on London Bridge recognized him. Mr. MacLeod was loaded onto a dray and taken to Neville House. Aunt Maude sent word to me and I went immediately to Neville House."

"Did Mr. MacLeod say who shot him?"

"He's unconscious and feverish." Mary slumped back, rubbing her forehead. "He lost a lot of blood. I'm not sure that he'll live."

"Does the Night Watch know who shot him?"

"No one saw it happen. Witnesses at the Ram's Head say he was with a woman wearing a plain black cloak of a rich fabric and a red stone ring, but her hood was pulled forward such that no one saw her face."

A chill tripped down Cecelia's spine. "Why would she shoot him? A fortnight ago, he was in her bed."

No need to clarify the woman in question; there had only been one *she* who deserved their caution. The Countess of Denton.

Mary's tired gaze met hers. "We don't know it was her."

"I don't need facts to tell me the lady shot him."

"How can you be so sure?"

"Because that woman has a sentimentally twisted heart." At Mary's blank stare, she leaned closer, jabbing her finger in her chair's arm. "They met at the Ram's Head. The same tavern where Will was arrested for wearing his kilt."

Blood drained from Mary's face. The details of Will's arrest in August wouldn't be fresh on her mind, but they were in Cecelia's.

"But a woman of her position, skulking about late at night," Mary said doubtfully. "When she has cut-throats to do her dirty work?"

"And do you know what that tells me? The countess trusts no one."

"Do you think MacLeod was the one spying on us?"

"Very possible." Cecelia chewed her thumbnail. "Wortley wanted me to know I was being followed. But MacLeod spying on us is a disappointment."

Mary snorted indelicately. "The bugger. To think we brought him into Neville House."

"We need to give him a chance. If he recovers, we'll know the lay of his heart."

"You're more forgiving than I am. I'd give him the boot the moment his eyes open."

"He may be our best weapon . . . especially if the countess thinks him dead."

"*If* she shot him." Mary's stern visage was a fair counterpoint.

"I believe she did. It's a sign the woman is getting desperate and I want to know why."

Chapter Twenty-Five

$\mathcal{A}$ man in her kitchen had to be an anomaly. He prowled the stone floor with the vague familiarity of someone comfortable laboring with his hands. After Miss Fletcher departed, he'd foraged for bread and butter. Cecelia had curled up in her chair, shocked at the bad news her friend had delivered. To soothe her, they talked of benign things. She shared glimpses of her childhood, and he had done the same. But as morning melted into midday, their stomachs rumbled, and he'd led Cecelia into the kitchen.

"I'm not sure what you expect of me," she'd said. "I can boil water, but that's it."

He was already rummaging for the beginnings of a proper meal.

"Have a seat. I'll take care of you."

When she witnessed him set a rasher of crisply cooked bacon on the table, her brows steepled a question.

"Where did you learn your kitchen skills?"

"Our family lodge in Cotswold." He was on one knee, stirring greens in a pan of sizzling bacon fat.

"Every year since I was a boy of eight, my father, brother, and I ensconced ourselves for a week of hunting, twice a year. Pheasant, partridge, roebuck, a little fishing when we could."

"A hunting lodge, that sounds wonderful."

"*Lodge* is a kind word for the primitive cottage we used. No servants attended us. We chopped our wood, cooked our food, and cleaned up after ourselves. A week to be wonderfully dirty, tromping around the countryside."

She was at the table, sipping tea he'd made for her. Looking after the independent Scotswoman was a badge of honor. The woman was changing the shape of his soul, one smile, one word, one kiss at a time.

He heaped cooked greens on his plate and hers. Bacon, bread, and greens—a feast. He pulled the tax list from his pocket and set that down as well. They would be done with this.

She tipped her chin at the paper. "I see you're serving up my past."

He set the fat-glistened pan on the table.

"Stunning finds, don't you agree?"

"Taxes are never stunning," she said dryly. "But I salute your excellent powers of investigation. You unearthed what I thought would never see the light of day."

Did nothing surprise the Scotswoman? Possibly not. Her breasts, after all, had been immortalized on barrels of beer all over London. A woman that audacious would hardly raise an eyebrow at fiduciary findings. More interesting was the distant storm in her eyes. From Miss Fletcher's distressing news? Possibly. But a niggling voice in his brain challenged the convenient explanation. The same voice prodded him to share the storm brewing inside him—Cecelia and the Jacobite ledger.

But first things first.

He took a seat on the bench facing her and draped the serviette across his lap. "Why transact business in your father's name?"

She poked the greens with her fork.

"I did it, in part, to protect the league. But mostly to honor my father and Jacobites thriving in London . . . a jab at the crown, if you will."

"Oh, now you've really poked ole King George in the eye, paying your taxes."

Her giggle-snort was sweet music. She gave up on her vegetables and planted both elbows on the table. She smiled widely, the skin squishing the outer corners of her eyes.

"I love that about you. Your humor. No man makes me laugh so easily as you do."

He sat taller under her praise.

"I would do much more for you."

"I—I'm not sure that is wise. Not for a man of your ambitions. Our connection is already precarious."

"But not impossible." He let the moment breathe, then asked, "Are you still a staunch Jacobite?"

She tore off a bite of bread and stared at the fire's cheery glow. "I grew up in a staunchly Jacobite home, yet I am . . . less ardent."

"Making money in the heart of enemy territory can do that."

Daylight caught dust motes in the kitchen. Cecelia was quiet, her eyes hazing as if she was retracing history.

"My first time in London was '47. To collect my father after the Act of Indemnity freed the rebels, but the sergeant at arms turned me away. My father, a surgeon and a property owner, was considered a rebel of rank. Never mind that the English burned his house to the ground. I returned in '48 and waited again at Tilbury Fort, quiet as a church mouse, if you can believe that. This time, a new sergeant at arms turned me away. In '49, I received word the last of the prisoners were to be released." She shivered, her fingers pinching her bread. "The sky was pissing rain that day. I could see the *Jane of Alloway* anchored in the river, a sorry excuse of a ship. The stench from it was awful. I waited until the sergeant at arms informed me that my father had died the day before I arrived."

"I'm sorry."

His words were inadequate. Guilt was a peculiar pitchfork, heaping recriminations and *what ifs* on her. It would do no good to remind Cecelia that her rebel father had made his decision; it would do no good because his daughter paid a price as one does in rebellion, and by the torment in her eyes, her debt was far from over. She had been a young woman visiting the City with no other family to speak of, and she'd been, what? All of nineteen then?

"There was the league, of course," she went on. "At first, I didn't want to be part of it. I was quite done with war and rebellion."

Hers was a life built in two parts: the foundation laid in Scotland with a love for the Highlands and an unusual father, and the rest found in London. A young woman, making her own way in the world. She had claimed her father a freethinking Jacobite. How ironic, his daughter finding her liberty in the heart of the beast, as it were.

"I did what I could to honor my father. I found Mr. Munro, who took care of him on the prison hulk."

"Mr. Munro . . . the hack driver."

She nodded. "I paid the Commissioners of Scotland Yard on his behalf for his hackney license and I bought his horses. He found an abandoned carriage in a warehouse in Southwark. Mr. Munro had been Arisaig's wheelwright before the war, so he was quite skilled in repairing it. And, like me, he had nothing left in Arisaig."

"You are his business partner. The same for each person on the list."

"I am."

He was humbled by her story. She had every right to be indignant with him. Cecelia MacDonald was nothing more than a woman of business with a good heart.

He scraped his fork through his vegetables. "How did you get the funds to start these businesses?"

"Gambling." Daylight shined on her bitter smile. "I came to London with the clothes on my back and the lessons in commerce my father taught me. I used my paltry winnings to help Mr. Munro. In return, he pays me a portion of the profits once a month and—"

"He drives you around London."

"—free of charge." She smiled angelically. "The benefit of commerce and friendship. Eventually, my portion grew such that I could start other ventures."

"What about the ostentatious robin's egg blue carriage?"

"That is Miss Elspeth Cooper-Brooke's folly. She rents the carriage, the horses, the coachman, and an attendant to me when her passion for *vingt-et-un* exceeds her monthly allowance."

"What an enterprising woman."

"Thank you." She nursed her tea with both hands and sipped.

He picked up the list. "What about the dyer?"

"That would be Morag, Jenny's sister. Her husband died on the *Jane of Alloway*. Morag lives here in Dowgate. She's very talented with dyes."

"I see you paid two pounds for her to join the Worshipful Company of Dyers."

"It gave her the start she needed as a young widow. In turn, Morag dyes cloth for Fletcher's House of Corsets and Stays at a favorable price." Her gaze pinned him kindly. "Her way of showing appreciation."

"You have your fingers in that pie too." He felt a grin of admiration growing. "The king should give you charge of the treasury. You'd make quick work of the realm's debt."

Miss MacDonald scoffed in good humor. She tipped forward to better read his list. "What else do you have?"

"The Mermaid Brewery."

"Ah, that would be David MacDougall, a young foot soldier who was also on the *Jane of Alloway*. Mr. Munro told me he helped my father. Helping MacDougall seemed the least that I could do." A corner of her mouth curled up. "While the business partnership continues, our *tendre* for each other was short-lived."

He put down the list and nudged it aside. Lovely and smart, the Scotswoman had lent a helping hand to those in need. Their common thread, a prison hulk. The more he dug into her past, the more humbled he was.

"What about the barrels out there?" He tipped his fork in the direction of her mews. "I found traces of plumbago. Are you a smuggler?"

She balked. "Have you thought ill of me all this time? Over that?"

"I need to know the truth."

"My business partner, Mr. MacDougall, bought the barrels in Battersea by way of Romney in Kent."

Battersea was a haven for smugglers.

"The false bottom in those barrels was discovered *after* a batch of ale was ruined."

"You're not a smuggler."

"I never have been, but I saved the barrels to figure out how the false bottoms were made." She smirked. "Knowledge like that is handy for a woman like me."

He swirled a forkful of greens. "Forgive me for assuming the worst."

Her shoulder rolled, expressive and Gallic.

"I am an honest woman of business with a talent for making money." Her chin rose a defiant *Take that!* inch. "You can put that in your report to Fielding."

Forks scraping, they ate in silence. Alexander had touched a nerve. He and Fielding had assumed the worst of her. Was that because their days revolved around criminals? Bow Street's magistrate dealt with the dregs of London, while he tracked financial miscreants for the crown.

He dragged the serviette across his mouth, not liking this turn. He'd not taken great risks while Cecelia had laid bare pained history in her cheery kitchen with its egg yolk yellow cupboard and lime white walls. Nor could he forget what she'd shared about the Countess of Denton and the stolen treasure of Loch Arkaig. Troubling facts. His head was swimming with them.

One being high treason.

He uncorked the brandy, his decision calmly made. It was time to right a terrible wrong. While amber spirits splashed in his cup, he prefaced a new proposition.

"His Grace would see me hanged, drawn, and quartered for what I am about to tell you."

Her brows steepled. "Then perhaps you shouldn't."

He ignored her chide as he ignored years of lectures in jurisprudence.

"When you were in my bedchamber at the White Hart, did you notice a ledger with torn pages?"

"The one filled with gibberish? Yes."

His hand was surprisingly steady as he set the bottle down. It was no small comfort to acknowledge the Scotswoman had more courage in her little finger than most men dreamed of having in their lifetime. In future, he would have a care with his thoughts and not judge so rashly. Miss Cecelia MacDonald was walking proof that assumptions were often lies in sheep's clothing.

He corked the bottle and tapped it snug with his palm. "That ledger contains coded records for a secret society. His Grace has tasked me with deciphering it . . . the financial columns in particular."

She saluted him with her dish of tea. "Godspeed to you."

He hesitated. "It came into our hands last month."

"And why does the Government care about this secret society?"

"Because they smuggled Charles Stuart into London three years ago."

Cecelia fumbled her dish, her tea splattering the table.

"He was here?" Her voice pitched high.

"Yes."

She set her dish down hard and dried her fingers. "I don't believe you. There was no hint from Clanranald about it."

Her shock and disbelief were understandable. Even better, her reaction confirmed that Cecelia MacDonald was not part of the secret society. But telling her about Charles Stuart had pushed them into new ground. He took a drink of brandy, needing its sharp bite. Treasonous words were out; there'd be no washing them back down.

"Those loyal to Stuart in Scotland did not know," he said. "Only a trusted number in London did."

Emotions assembled on the Scotswoman's face. He could only guess at them: dismay, disappointment, and stubborn disbelief. The fact of her *not* knowing Charles Stuart had been in London was final proof that she worked solely to restore her clan, and rebellion was not her aim. It was as much a comfort as a prod. Cecelia had done her part to build their bridge of trust. The time had come for him to do his.

He swigged brandy, adding to the fire in his belly.

"What I am about to tell you must stay within these four walls."

She reached for him with a sympathetic hand. "You don't have to tell me."

He scrubbed a hand over his face. Today was monumental for him—his trust and his morals and his measurement of justice.

Cecelia poured amber spirits in her cup and added more to his. "It looks like you and I need this."

Her hair was down and the ugly brown robe he'd given her was wrapped around her body. He could almost see their future together—if they survived what he was about to tell her.

He nudged his plate aside. "Tucked inside the Jacobite ledger was a thin file. It contained a rubbing of a token on foolscap and two letters, tracing Charles Stuart's journey from Antwerp on September twelfth to London September sixteenth in 1750. He departed London on the twenty-second of that month."

She gusted her disbelief. "He was here. For six days? I can't fathom it."

"Indeed, he was, dressed as a French clergyman. He wore an eye patch and he put boot black on his eyebrows to disguise himself. Before he arrived in London, someone commissioned a jeweler near Pall Mall to strike medal seals featuring his head. The tokens were given to those aiding Stuart. If a clandestine meeting was set, all parties had to show their token."

Arms folding under her bosom, she wasn't convinced.

"Jacobite trinkets . . . that doesn't mean anything. You've got to have better proof than that." She leaned in, her hazel eyes sharp. "*If* he was here, why didn't the English arrest him?"

"He had help from the inside. Soldiers were sent to County Stafford and to Suffolk. Both places, a wild-goose chase because Charles Stuart stayed in London. He admitted it in a letter that our spies intercepted while he was in Rome."

"The first letter in the file."

"Yes."

Cecelia absorbed this. From her quiet kitchen, the joyful noise of laughing children playing in the alley came from behind her mews.

"And you say this secret society brought him here?"

"That was the information passed on from Pickle, the code name of a former Jacobite," he said. "It was Pickle who first alerted His Majesty to Charles Stuart coming to London."

Her nose wrinkled. "There can be no more inglorious a name as Pickle."

"Inglorious or not, Pickle's information has proved inviolable. While the king no longer cares about Charles Stuart's coming and going, the Government does. Especially finding those in powerful places who aided him."

"You think he came to London to reignite rebellion? That would be foolishness. He would only risk his life for"—eyes wide, she gasped—"for money!"

"The Jacobite ledger is a money trail His Grace asked me to review."

She slapped the table, rattling dishes. "More treasure in London! I knew it!"

"The second letter in the file was an undated correspondence from the Cluny of MacPherson to Charles Stuart, claiming almost thirteen thousand French livres remain of the Loch Arkaig treasure."

"That miserable rat." Her lips curled against her teeth. "The Cluny told Anne he had only a few hundred French livres."

"The Government is aware of him," he said dryly. "Though we don't know his exact whereabouts."

"He's in a cave somewhere in western Scotland,

trying to foment another rebellion. Gone a little soft in the head, I think."

"But the treasure has the interest of many."

"Gold's fever."

"Even the king has it. That is why I have been tasked to study that ledger," he said. "I've tracked columns of dates and names, smudged and torn bank drafts. But one entry stood out. Payment to Lady Pink."

"A code name, I collect." She grimaced over her brandy. "Better than Pickle."

He drew a slow circle around a knot in the table's surface. The storm within was building.

"Lady Pink was compensated handsomely for shipping a French clergyman from *A* for Antwerp to *L* for London in September 1750. She also arranged for his departure six days later . . . each movement matching the information in Charles Stuart's letter."

"Intriguing, but I don't see why it matters to me."

He braced himself. "Payment for delivering Stuart was seventeen hundred French livres."

Cecelia stood up fast, her face blanching.

"To the Countess of Denton?"

"To Lady Pink," he corrected. "Notes in the margin said she would disguise herself with a pink mask and a pink powdered wig."

"It's unfathomable—Lady Pink is Lady Denton."

"Lady Pink was the only one paid in French livres . . . facts which are too damning to ignore."

Cecelia paced the kitchen like a caged cat. "Seventeen hundred French livres is the exact amount we found in her safe." She barked harsh laughter and gave him the gimlet eye. "But don't try to tell me she is a Jacobite. I won't believe you."

"If I were to hazard a guess, Lady Denton has adapted her ethics to her circumstances."

"Is that barrister-speak for vile, greedy, and cruel?" she snapped. "Because the woman has no ethics."

"She is a thief for a selfish cause. Herself."

"While I am a thief for an unselfish cause?" she said archly. "Were you going to say that next?"

Cecelia was restless and upset. He tried to interject calmness.

"I was going to suggest we prove she is Lady Pink."

"How?"

"Evidence, of course. We start by looking for ship's records."

She eyed him silently, warily.

"Think of it," he said. "Together, you and I possess unique and powerful knowledge."

"No one else knows about this?" she asked.

"Only the two of us."

Was Cecelia thinking of their conversation in her Southwark orchard? What a wicked week of truth and treason they'd shared. Sunlight poured around the Scotswoman wrapped in the unsightly brown robe. He'd followed her through this kitchen with his hands tied behind his back and she garbed in a flimsy shift and robe, the night his adventure began with the goddess of Swan Lane.

She stopped her pacing. "You said *we* prove Lady Denton is Lady Pink."

"I did."

"You want to work with me," she said carefully.

"I want to be with you in every sense of the word."

Undammed currents flowed hot and sweet. Theirs would be a partnership, a joining, an *us*. His vocabulary was already adapting, but there was no sense in spooking her. Fierce mystical creatures, he suspected, were cautious about matters of the heart.

Miss MacDonald clutched her night-robe as one does when riding a speeding carriage.

"Exactly what are you proposing?"

Chapter Twenty-Six

*T*wo river barges anchored the Southwark side, their torch flames slanting in the midnight wind. Mr. Baines's wherry scraped the wall near Arundel Stairs. Ink-black water slapped the narrow unlit boat while Mr. Sloane steadied his sea legs and reached for a dark timbered wall.

"The rope," he said.

Cecelia passed it to him, her stance less graceful. Mr. Sloane wound the rope around the piling while the boat wobbled under quickening currents. She hugged a piling and had her hat knocked off her head.

"Steady, Mr. Baines," she said. "I'm getting a mouthful of pitch."

"I'm doing the best I can, miss, but the river's churning something wicked." Mr. Baines fought to hold his wherry in place with a pike pole. "Storm's coming."

Nature was dropping billowing clouds and biting winds. Waves stirred. Thunder and lightning flashed in the distance, a gift coming from Brighton.

"The rope's secure." Mr. Sloane held on to his hat lest the wind take it away.

Cecelia let go of the piling and collected her tricorn off the wherry's floor. To Mr. Baines she said, "Give us half an hour."

"I'll be here." Pike pole in hand, he walked nimbly across two benches and hunkered down, pulling his greatcoat tightly about.

With no lamps, their journey from Swan Lane to Arundel Stairs was precarious and illegal, but it paled in comparison to what she and Mr. Sloane were about to do. The barrister-cum-government-man led the way, stepping over a bench to stand beside her. Night sketched his face above hers, hawkish yet refined. They'd dressed in black from head to toe save plain linen shirts but no cravats. With his shirt open at the neck, the exposed cloth fluttering, he could be a pirate or a smuggler on a midnight run. A black scarf hid her hair and coal dust smudged her cheeks.

Mr. Sloane touched her elbow. "We look for ship manifests from three years ago. That's all. We're in. We're out."

They'd already dissected which of the countess's warehouses would house shipping records and when and how to breach it.

His teeth slashed a wicked white crescent in darkness. "Before you know it, we'll be back in your bedchamber to finish the bath I started this morning."

"How can you think about sexual congress at a time like this?" She hoisted herself from the boat to Arundel Stairs, thrilled to her toes.

Sex and Sloane, there was a ring to it like excellent music waiting to be heard. He was right behind her, the wind carrying his low laugh. They scampered up the stairs to Arundel Street. Candle lamps dropped blurred splotches of light every ten paces. Cecelia plastered herself against a brick wall between the first and second halo. Her pistol bumped her spine, tucked in the back of her breeches. Alexander was similarly armed. No barrels or crates blocked their view from the river to the Strand.

"Why couldn't she have properly dingy warehouses?" she asked. "That's what we have in Southwark."

Alexander extracted a slim metal file from his coat pocket, followed by a second piece which looked suspiciously like a woman's hairpin. He squinted at the hairpin and ran his thumb over a hook at the end of it.

"Look at you, cavorting with a Jacobite woman *and* picking locks. What would His Grace say?"

Bronze eyes sparkled in the night.

"He'd take one look at you and congratulate me on my choice of companion." He closed his fist around the metal pieces. "Now let's see if I remember how to use these."

They trotted to a narrow side door on Arundel Street. Mr. Sloane dropped to one knee and went to work on the padlock which secured it. Cobwebbed mist fell on their heads. Excitement throbbed inside her. Danger came with a certain thrill, or it might've been Alexander. He was methodical to her daring. A precise balance. A perfect partnership.

She kept her back to the wall, watching his, checking from the riverside to the Strand.

"Strange, how empty it is."

Not a soul was in sight, not even a rat.

"The blessing of a coming storm," he said, concentrating on the padlock.

"Have you noticed, the outside of her ladyship's warehouse is terribly clean," she said. "No rotting cabbages. Bricks in perfect repair. It's unnatural."

Blowing wind soughed over them. Alexander concentrated on the lock, adjusting his tools by minute degrees.

"If I have to break into a warehouse, I much prefer a clean one," he said matter-of-factly.

The upright barrister had surprised her by taking her to his rooms at the White Hart. He'd jammed clothes into a portmanteau to ensconce himself in her home for a few days, because he'd meant what he'd said about not leaving her side. Then he'd shocked her when he added lock-picking tools to his portmanteau, a forgotten token from a merchant who had been on trial for fenced goods.

She hooked her heel on a brick behind her. "You never told me what happened to the gentleman who bequeathed these tools to you."

"Transported. Seven years."

"Oh. I thought there might be a happy ending."

"Not when you fence goods stolen from two members of Parliament. But considering they demanded a hanging, seven years' hard labor isn't so bad."

"Therein is the lesson," she mused. "Don't agitate the ennobled."

Metal clicked, and the padlock sprung open.

Mr. Sloane rose to his feet and winked. "We'll make an exception for the Countess of Denton."

To which she laughed quietly and unhooked a candle lamp off the brick wall. They entered the dark warehouse and walked into a wall of wool. Its oily earthy smell filled the warehouse.

"This way." She held up the lantern and they sidled through a narrow gap between two walls of wool twelve feet high.

Once through the gap, light splashed an organized cavern. An aisle wide enough for a drayage ran through the heart of the warehouse. More wool bales were stacked against the far wall. Crates marked Silk clustered next to crates marked Wallpaper which were next to more crates marked Dishes. A golden-eyed tabby cat looked down from its perch on one of those piles of crates.

Alexander touched her elbow and nudged his chin high. "The clerk's office must be up there."

She raised the lamp. "Up there" was a loft opened to the warehouse below. A crane stretched from the loft, heavy ropes dangling from it with an iron hook at the end. To reach the office, they took the stairs built against the wall.

The office was unlocked. Inside, a lone window looked out on the river. Through it, she could see a heftier crane reach over the quayside, the wind batting its rope like a toy. A slanted clerk's desk, a chair, a bookshelf crammed with ledgers, and a lone cot cramped the tiny room. A side door to the loft had been left open.

Alexander was already on his knees thumbing through a ledger.

"The light would help," he said.

She took the hint and crouched on the floor beside him. The shelf had been recently dusted.

"Even the ledgers are clean."

"A boon for us. No trace of our visit," he said.

She pulled a ledger off the shelf and began the in-elegant task of skimming the pages. Rebellion was a dull exercise. They riffled through one ledger after another, careful to return each one to its same spot on the shelf. Her current book listed food supplies and ammunition for a nine-hundred-ton East Indian ship, but the dates began to blur.

"I'm not finding anything." She yawned and checked her pocket watch. "Our half hour is nearly done."

"This is promising. A muster roll dated 1750."

She shelved the book. "What is a muster roll?"

"Something Parliament requires. Ships must file reports with the Seaman's Fund Receivers upon return." His gaze met hers above the book. "It's a list . . . ship's owners, sailors, and so forth. Sailors pay a tax of 6 d for each month they're out to sea. Been that way since '47."

"Taxes," she scoffed. "The Government gets you one way or another."

He studied the ledger, his mouth denting sideways. His adorable half smile was her undoing. It was hard to say if his mouth was more appealing in the shadows or in the light. He kissed equally well in both circumstances.

"Look at this." Alexander set the book on the floor.

Excitement flared in his eyes and she let herself simply feel. To hear the noise of howling wind and thrill at huddling close to him. Shadows drew Alexander with new symmetry, a different man than the one she'd found in her mews. He was truly a partner in this madness. She couldn't help but stare in wonder and give this new equation time to nestle in her heart.

Every part of her cried out, *Yes . . . him.*

"Look at this." He was tapping the page like an impatient tutor.

She looked down.

Sailor hired in Antwerp, Monsieur Abbé.
12 September 1750

Next to the entry, the column for his pay was blank.

"*Abbé,*" she huffed. French for abbot.

"It was clever to not pay him. This, I collect, is the only record of his journey."

The East Indiaman's details were at the top. The *Rebecca*, it was, and the Countess of Denton was one-third owner. Her brother and the Duchess of Ranleigh owned the remaining two-thirds.

Her pulse jumped. "Is this enough?"

He tore the page from the ledger. "It's a very good beginning. We follow the trail, we build a case."

"You're thinking like a barrister."

She closed the book and returned it to the shelf. They were still on their knees when Alexander folded the page in fourths and gave it to her.

"You should keep this," he said.

She stuffed the paper in her pocket and set her hand over her heart as if he'd given her a token of courtship.

"Thank you for this. For everything."

"You are the brave one," he said. "Enduring—"

She pressed her mouth to his, fast and startling, a bit ungraceful and flavored with coal dust. Their mouths weren't moving, though his hand crept up her arm. Solid, reassuring. It landed on the same shoulder he'd kissed with smoldering passion.

Desire ripped through her. But they were in a cold warehouse, and her kiss missed the mark.

They pulled apart, him blinking at her. She was clutching the open ends of his coat.

"You were right there . . ."

"I am."

"And I thought I should kiss you," she said a little breathless. "But I've shocked you, haven't I?"

"In a good way." His tenor was humored.

"The kiss . . . I can do much better."

His low laugh put butterflies in her stomach.

"I know you can." He traced her temple. "Why don't we go home, clean each other up, and find what else we're good at together?"

Excitement fluttered everywhere. This was gold, a man enamored with a woman even when she has a scarf on her head and coal dust on her face.

"Let's go home," she said.

Home. The word had slipped easily into their conversation. She would've basked in the cheer of it, except a door creaked open below.

Chapter Twenty-Seven

She froze, barely breathing, the air touching her insides before fleeing on a wispy exhale. Only once had she felt this way—the day two of Cumberland's men circled her, evil pooling in their eyes, when they'd caught her sifting through her charred home. The taste of charcoal on her lips didn't help.

Fear choked her, and still her ears sharpened to every noise.

"A game of dice wouldn't hurt ye. Your best of seven against mine," a booming voice said.

"Not for money," was the clipped reply. A cold, efficient voice, that one.

"Aw, Wortley, ye took my quid last night. Give me a chance to win some back."

Wortley! She mouthed the dreaded name to Alexander.

He touched a finger to his lips for quiet (as if she needed the reminder!) and he blew out the candle lamp. Howling wind and the rope whipping the wall outside disguised the lamp's squeaking glass door.

A rivulet of smoke twisted thinly, her hope going with it.

What were they going to do?

Her gaze cast wildly about. The window did not open. The side entry was not an option; they'd have to go down the stairs. That wouldn't work. Wooden stairs creaked, and Wortley would see them.

Alexander touched her arm and pointed at the door to the loft.

"No," she whispered in his ear. "They'll see us."

"It's too dark. We'll be safe if we stick to the wall."

She grabbed his coat. "What will we do after that?"

Her heart kicked faster than a running rabbit. Voices and movements from below reached her ears, almost painfully crisp. The soft pop of a jar uncorked, a squeaky hinge, male laughter over a shared jest. Alexander crooked a finger at her to follow. They both slinked along on the balls of their feet, careful not to touch the door.

Inside the loft was a treadwheel and a half dozen bales in haphazard order. A wooden deadeye, the tool used for tensioning ropes, sat on the floor. She stepped over its iron tail, sidling the wall in darkness with Alexander. He was leading them to the quay-side wall—to a padlocked door.

She gripped his sleeve, her fingernails scoring it.

"What will we do?" she whispered in his ear.

He pulled the file and hairpin from his pocket and held them inches from her nose.

"We go through this door and swing down the crane's rope to Mr. Baines's wherry." His grin dented sideways. "It will be an adventure."

An adventure? Swinging from a rope off the

Countess of Denton's warehouse did not qualify as fun, adventurous, or anything remotely exciting. Her eyes must've sparked with indignation. Alexander caressed her char-dusted cheek.

"Trust me."

After tonight, their bridge of trust would be iron-clad, if they managed to escape. His calm response soothed her. Her tense shell fractured enough for her to take a deep breath and give a jerky nod.

He removed her hat and kissed her scarf-covered ear. "Watch my back," was his whisper before he knelt to work the padlock. She pulled her pistol from the back of her breeches. The filigreed butt was cold in her clammy palm, a sense of power slowly coming with it. Irksome tremors faded. She listened to the rope knocking the warehouse wall outside and the two cutthroats below.

"Her ladyship wants to leave Friday next," Mr. Wortley said. "A quiet jaunt . . . you understand?"

A grunt and dice clattered on a wooden surface. "Bloody hell! Four again. May as well give next month's pay to ye."

A hand slapped the board. Dice jumped and rattled. One hit the floor.

"Get your head out of your arse and listen to what I'm telling you."

She took a cautious step forward. Two lamps lit their conversation, a tepid yellow. Wortley's hat was off and he leaned menacingly at a beefy, florid ginger twice his size. Fear rounded the bigger man's eyes.

"I'm listening."

Wortley eased back. Lean and wiry, he was garbed in his usual plain black wool.

"Prepare to be gone a month. Pack your pistols and

ammunition. We're taking her ladyship's unmarked carriage—"

"The black one?"

"Yes. Park it at dawn at the end of Upper Brook Street on Tiburn Lane. Lady Denton will meet us there."

The tabby cat rubbed Mr. Wortley's leg. The cutthroat reached down and petted it with gentle, unhurried strokes.

"Just the two of us with her ladyship?" the florid man asked. "What about her chests of clothes?"

"Don't worry about that. Your job is to prepare the carriage and drive it. For now, that's all you need to know." Thunder cracked overhead. "And, Gifford . . . not a word to anyone."

The barest scrape of metal on metal sounded. Her eyes had adjusted well enough to see Alexander's mouth set a grim line. The big quayside door was bound by a larger, heavier padlock which was not cooperating.

"It's not working," he said in the barest whisper.

Her thready pulse banged in her ears. Wind gusted and the crane's moorings whined beyond the quayside door. They'd been inside for at least an hour. And Mr. Baines? A loyal friend but the storm had to be doing its worst. His wherry in a storm such as this wasn't safe.

Below, Gifford asked, "Are you keeping watch tonight?"

A hollow laugh and, "You tossed the lowest number. This watch is yours."

Gifford grumbled, "That cot's not fit for a child. I'm better off sleeping on two wool sacks put together."

"Your choice. I'll check the Arundel Street door, then I'll be on my way."

She stiffened. The Arundel Street door was left open.

Wortley stopped petting the cat. "Did you hear that?"

Wind screeched like a banshee. Rain had begun to pound the roof. Thunder and lightning followed.

Gifford cocked an ear. "Aye, the storm."

Wortley's glare landed on the loft. His hard-as-musket-ball eyes were cold and soulless. Shadows masked her, and she was glad for her coal-smeared face. Had the cutthroat heard her feet shift? Gifford was oblivious, dropping the dice in his pocket and hefting a barrel lid off the bale of wool. He sauntered off mumbling about the storm.

The rope outside *thumped, thumped, thumped*.

Mr. Wortley picked up a candle lamp and held it high. He was squinting at the loft.

Her skin was terribly cold, her fingertips icy.

Alexander was at her side, two pistols in hand. "Cock your pistol at the next thunderclap."

His murmur was hair-raising. Cool and calculated, as if he'd weighed the cost and had already decided he'd shoot a man tonight. His lips brushed the shell of her scarf-covered ear.

"See the warped plank? Middle of the quayside door?"

She looked over her shoulder. Large planks for a large door. At the center, aged wood bowed, gaps bracketing it a finger's width. Rain dripped through those cracks.

She acknowledged him with a jerky nod, and his mouth moved against her ear.

"When you're ready, cover your face with your coat, and shoot that plank at close range. You and I will escape through the hole."

"One shot won't be enough." She glanced at his weapon-filled fists. "Two are better to blow apart that door."

Cool menace glimmered in his eyes. "I'm saving my ball and shot for the two men below."

Her heart sank. Her one shot wasn't enough to defend them. The loft morphed into a gloomy prison, and the two of them with nowhere to go and nowhere to hide. Her ears rang tinny. She was trapped, fear eating her alive.

"But outside?"

"We're jumping into the river next to the wherry," he said quietly. "We'll grab it and climb in . . . unless Mr. Baines isn't there"—a casual shrug and—"in which case, the current will take us."

"Jump into the river? Are you mad? There's a storm out there."

"Pick your poison. It's them shooting us or braving the river. If Mr. Baines is gone, don't fight the current. Go with it. Ride it to any of the London side stairs and hold on. I *will* find you."

Alexander's eyes glinted inches from hers, a vise grip of cool determination. She fed off it.

She'd rowed the river, never swam in it. She knew what to do if caught in a current. Wherrymen swapped stories on how to survive the Thames, good anecdotes best consumed with ale.

Alexander scowled. "You can swim, can't you?"

"Yes, b—"

"Good. The mother of my children should know

how to swim." He caressed her cheek. "We can do this."

The mother of his children?

Jaw-slackening words to be sure, except the stairs creaked. Goose bumps screamed up and down her torso. Wortley must be climbing the stairs in stealth. Gifford might be with him. Another ponderous creak and her heart climbed into her throat.

The Countess of Denton's cutthroats were coming.

Alexander pointed to his pistol. Together, they raised their weapons. Her gaze locked with his, the seconds counted by sweat pricking her hairline.

When thunder cracked, they cocked their pistols to its percussion.

A faint smile hooked the corner of her mouth. Anne had made her feel resolute, but the very English Mr. Alexander Sloane made her feel invincible.

She tiptoed to the quayside door and stopped three feet from it. She raised her arm for a one-handed shot. This close, she wouldn't miss. One last look at Alexander and she yanked the front panel of her coat over her face. Alexander was behind her, his back strong and true.

He'd had her back since the first night she brought him to her bedchamber. A man like that ought to experience a woman's full appreciation. She'd do her best by him. Tonight.

Arm steady, she shot the door.

Chapter Twenty-Eight

Who knew shooting a door could be so cleansing? The recoil knocked the fright out of her. Splinters big and small sprayed the air, showering her coat with wood fragments. Her ears were ringing and acrid smoke stung her nose. The shot was definitive. A gaping hole was in the quayside door.

It was a good hole, but not big enough.

Alexander pivoted off her back, and the world sped up. His booted foot smashed the planks.

Mr. Wortley and Mr. Gifford stampeded up the stairs.

Copper's tang flooded her tongue. If she survived this night, she would remember it for the rest of her life.

Alexander kicked the quayside door again and again, while the rumbling footsteps of running men kept coming. The wooden deadeye with its iron tail sat on the floor. She grabbed it as hulking forms crested the stairs. Fury lit their eyes. She slammed the loft's side door, blood pounding in her ears. She was quick, wrapping the deadeye's chain around the latch and jamming the deadeye's round head onto a hook in the wall.

"Open up!" Mr. Gifford bellowed.

The door rattled under a heavy fist. Fear squeezed her chest. The deadeye chain bought them a minute at the most. Footsteps scuttled, and a lead ball blasted a hole in the side door. A beefy arm punched through the hole and reached for the latch.

She drove her pistol butt down on thick fingers with all her might.

"Ahhhh!" A scream rent the air.

A hand grabbed her by the scruff of her coat. Alexander.

"Let's go!" he yelled and dragged her to the quayside door.

Rain spattered a jagged hole in that door. Outside, the crane jutted over sinister onyx water below.

"Climb out and jump!" Alexander cried. "They're coming!"

The will to live took over. She grabbed the splintered edge to steady herself and put one foot on the crane. At the end, twin ropes as thick as her wrist whipped the air. Behind her, Alexander gave a push.

"Go!" he yelled.

Her heart banged ferociously. She wasn't graceful, putting one foot in front of the other. Wind and rain stung her cheeks and dark fear almost swallowed her. A shot rang out and she jumped, hugging her knees to her chest. She dropped like a cannon ball into the stormy river, the watery slap shocking and cold.

Sinking yet weightless she opened her eyes. Tiny crystalline bubbles floated, mesmerizing in pitch-black.

The river entombed her, frigid and alive. Her body halted its descent and she floated in silence. Uncurling her limbs, she climbed to the surface. Her head popped above the river's choppy skin. A hissing inhale and she breathed.

Churning water swatted her face. She kicked to stay afloat. Mr. Baines and his wherry was a red sliver bobbing harshly. She thrashed wildly, calling his name. Alexander hung on the side of the wherry.

He was alive, his fierce eyes searching the water.

"Cecelia!" The wind carried Mr. Baines's voice.

Thunder and lightning blasted. The river lit up under the jagged bolt. Pistol shots rang out. Hot orange flared high above her head like Vauxhall fireworks. Mr. Wortley stood on the hole she'd made, the wind battering his coat. But he was a figure growing smaller by the second. The current was taking her away.

She kicked with all her might to keep her head above water and air in her lungs.

From rowing, she knew how to survive a current. Every wherryman lived by the creed of *Don't panic. Ride the current.* Common wisdom said to grab something solid and rest on it. Then scuttle ashore, hand over hand if possible. Good advice, but nothing prepared her for a storm-tossed river. She was gulping air and water. The river wanted to swallow her whole and take her out to sea.

"Miss MacDonald!"

Mr. Baines? Serrated waves slapped her face, but she could see the riverman. He fought to stand upright and drive his wherry with the long pike pole.

"Cecelia!" Alexander was half over the wherry, extending an oar.

He was her *something solid.*

She fought with all her might and reached. The angry Thames was sweeping them downriver with frightening speed. London Bridge loomed ahead. She kicked and kicked. Her fingertips grazed wood . . . and slipped.

Another stretch, another frantic thrashing of her legs. Her arms were a windmill against furious water, and she gripped the oar's paddle with icy, slippery hands.

"Hold on." Alexander's voice rose above the wind.

His face was jagged with fear. He was hauling her in by the oar, hand over hand.

"London Bridge is coming," Mr. Baines warned over the wind.

She dared not look. They might survive going under the bridge, but she wouldn't.

"Please," she whimpered but the wind ran off with her plea.

Her exhausted legs floated behind her. Rough, roiling water battered her. It was all she could do to hold on to the oar. The storm sapped her will, but Alexander's fierce visage was her lodestone.

"Hold fast," he commanded.

Her head fell back as strong hands seized her and yanked her up. The wherry teetered and swayed. She was half in, half out.

Mr. Baines, his hair plastered to his head, fought the river with his pike pole. "Swan Lane Stairs ahead. We can make it."

Alexander reached over the wherry and clamped her by the back of her breeches. She was hauled into the wherry like a drowned rag doll. Panting hard, she curled up in a ball against Alexander and glued her ear to his chest. His thudding heartbeat was the most comforting sound. Wonderful and heartbreaking. He wrapped his arms around her and shielded her from pelting rain.

"Thank God you're alive," he said against the crown of her head.

As long as she lived, she'd never forget his fierce eyes when he held out the oar like an angry demigod, forcing the river to give her back to him. She curled up tighter, his possession of her perfect. Wind whistled around them. The wherry jolted and slowed. Wood scraped a solid surface, stopping them.

"We're here," Alexander announced.

Here was safe harbor, ten feet of pilings, jutting into the river at the foot of the Old Swan Lane Inn. Mr. Baines quickly spun a rope around two pilings.

"Come on," Alexander said. "Let's get you home."

When she scrambled up, her hand which had been clutching him was sticky. She splayed her fingers and held them up to scant light. Blood coated her hand. Her stomach threatened mutiny, but sheets of rain were already washing the blood away.

"Alexander . . ." She touched his chest.

Lightning bolted across the sky, illuminating a deep gash in his arm. Flesh flopped like a half-peeled apple. Blood dribbled from it, pulsing in time with his heartbeat.

"Oh no," she moaned.

It was too much. The blood, the violence, the boat jostling underneath her. She leaned over and let the river take the contents of her stomach.

She cuffed her mouth with the back of her hand. "I'm so sorry. For everything."

He cupped her scarf-covered head, his voice grained

with exhaustion. "It will heal. First, you and I need a warm bed and a long night's sleep."

It was difficult to say who helped whom out of the wherry. Mr. Baines did his part to help them up Swan Lane Stairs, but the storm wasn't helping. Wind blew shop signs and rattled windows. A motley trio, they hobbled over to Swan Lane. A pebble gouged her foot. She looked down. Her shoes, her pistol, and her good sense had been swept away. Her home, at least, was twenty paces ahead.

She unlocked her door, and they stumbled inside. Alexander was leaning heavily on her, his face a dreadful waxen hue. She looked to the wherryman.

"Mr. Baines, please help me."

Mr. Baines took all of Alexander's weight. "Where do you want him?"

She stepped back. The meat of Alexander's arm glistened.

Her stomach spasmed. "Lay him down by the fireplace in my salon."

She ran to the kitchen, her feet slapping a soggy trail. Fists curling on the table, she braced herself. If it weren't for her, Alexander wouldn't be in this mess.

His blood was on her hands.

Why don't we go home, clean each other up, and find what else we're good at together?

His words throttled her.

Alexander could've died tonight.

She uncorked the brandy they'd left on the table and guzzled. The elixir seeped out the sides of her mouth. She swiped the dribbles, sniffling. Guilt was a carcass best picked over another time. A certain

Englishman needed her now. The bottle in hand, she snatched Aunt Flora's unguent from the pine cabinet, a stack of Jenny's clean checkered dishtowels, and her biggest knife.

In the salon, Mr. Sloane stretched out before the fire. She knelt beside him and set the blade on a flaring coal.

Mr. Baines was rubbing his hands for warmth. "I put extra coal on the fire."

"Smart of you. You need a good warming. We all do." Lips quivering, she removed Mr. Sloane's boots and stockings. To Mr. Baines, "Please help me get his clothes off. He'll catch his death in wet clothes."

Alexander pushed himself upright with his good arm, but when Mr. Baines tugged the coat, he stopped him.

"I can do it."

Pride blazed in bronze eyes at half-mast. They didn't have time for this. He was still bleeding, though less profusely. Alexander steepled a stubborn brow. Her gaze lifted from it to the wherryman.

"Would you be so kind and fetch some blankets, Mr. Baines? Do you remember where Jenny keeps them?"

"Yes, miss." He sped off.

She touched Alexander's chest. "This stubbornness of yours is ill-advised."

Wet hair hung ingloriously over his face.

"I am sitting on your floor like yesterday's fish. Let a gentleman have his pride."

He winced and removed his coat. She tossed the sodden thing aside, glimpsing his wound. Deep, but not to the bone. She squelched a heave that wanted up and concentrated on his waistcoat buttons. Keeping busy helped.

Alexander was chin to chest, watching her unbutton him.

"Is Mr. Baines another admirer?"

So that's what this is about. She scooted closer, their heads nearly touching.

"He's a friend."

"A braw friend. Isn't that what Scotswomen say about a man who catches their fancy?"

Wraiths of steam rose off soaked clothes like smoke as if they were in the midst of a trial by fire, but this ordeal was far from over.

"Scotswomen say a lot of things about men." She tugged off his waistcoat and tossed it aside.

"Such as?"

White linen clung to his chest, brown nipples poking the fabric. With his queue nearly undone, dark hair fell in disarray. The careful man of the law was gone, and in his place a heavy-lidded man with a savage edge. His spate of jealousy over Mr. Baines was surprising and ill-timed.

Her lips firmed. "We need to get your shirt off and stanch your wound."

Removing the shirt was a negotiation between his body and the wound. The linen was half over his head when he pressed his point, "What do *you* say about men?"

"I've said a lot of drivel over the years."

None of it had stuck. Nothing that mattered—until Mr. Alexander Sloane. Together, they were a beautiful mess. An all-consuming yearning that shouldn't be.

The shirt cleared Alexander's head and she added

it to the heap of clothes as Mr. Baines strode in with an armful of blankets.

"Will these do, miss?"

"Yes, thank you." She was grateful for the interruption. "Before you leave, Mr. Baines"—she motioned to the knife—"would you . . . ?"

She couldn't finish the sentence. Mr. Baines nodded and, gentle soul that he was, he dropped to one knee beside her.

"You'll want to lay on your side, sir."

An exhausted Alexander obliged, rolling with his right arm up. Amber light flared over his cricketer's body. Lithe, compact muscles, his breeches gapping at a lean waist. She'd been judicious, looking everywhere but the wound. Her barrister-cum-government-man would take a scar with him for the rest of his life. Not the best remembrance of her, but she'd make sure his arm didn't fester.

"The wound must be cleansed before closing it." She uncorked the brandy with a soft *pop*.

"Do you want me to do it, miss?" Mr. Baines asked.

This was a test, Alexander waiting and vulnerable, his sodden queue sticking to his muscled back.

"No." She leaned forward and touched his hip. "Brace yourself."

Sweat sprang up in her hairline. This would sting something awful. She tipped the bottle. A quick, good dousing and he cursed between clenched teeth. His breath was fast and shallow.

"I can think of a hundred better uses for that brandy," he said between gritted teeth.

"I can think of a few myself." She dabbed excess wetness off his arm and his back. "We'll compare notes another night."

Alexander's regal profile tilted toward her, firelight touching the red in his whiskers. There was a rugged, timeless quality about him. A wounded minor king in repose or the demigod who saved her life.

Mr. Baines pushed up on his knees and reached for the glowing knife.

She stopped him. "No, I'll do it."

"Are you sure? I'd prefer not to endure this twice should you err." Alexander's voice was gruff from pain.

"I will not err." To Mr. Baines, "Thank you. From the bottom of my heart. For everything."

Mr. Baines blushed.

"Please go home and get warm," she said. "I will take care of him."

Home, for the wherryman, was a short walk to Ebb Gate Lane. She saw him out and walked back to her salon, pulling the scarf from her head. Rain stamped her roof. The night was not fit for man nor beast and their venture a fool's errand. The page of evidence was a soggy lump in her pocket, and her father's pistol at the bottom of the Thames.

The night had been a disaster.

Alexander was half turned to her. "Ready to brand me?"

"Not really." She knelt behind him and tossed the wet paper they'd taken from the countess's warehouse into the fire. "I regret this night. I fear it cost us so much . . . and for what?"

Tired bronze eyes pinned her. "Never regret doing the right thing, even if you get the wrong outcome."

What about your blood on my hands?

Orange light danced on his chiseled torso. With glowing skin and a lean muscled form, the rest of

Alexander Sloane appeared hale and hearty and very touchable.

But his eyelids were heavy and his vitality draining fast.

"A blanket . . . please," he rasped.

"You don't want me to take off your wet breeches?"

"I don't want to move another inch. Besides, I could use a good steam," he jested sleepily. "It'll be like a Turkish bath."

She covered him with a blanket. His head was down and his breathing had slowed to normal, but another painful shock was coming. She reached for the knife and found the handle was warm and the blade hot and ready.

She touched his shoulder.

"Prepare yourself."

Eyes closed, he nodded.

Lips curling against her teeth, she gripped the knife and pressed.

Flesh sizzled. Mr. Sloane's agonized roar rang in her ears and her soul. Sinews stood out on his neck and sweat gleamed on his chest. Seconds passed, an eternity. She tossed the knife, mortified at the blistering flesh on his arm, but the wound was sealed. She slathered on the soothing unguent and wrapped a clean brown-and-white-checked kitchen towel around it. She tied the knot, and Alexander flopped on his back, pulling the blanket to his chest.

"Take heart, my Jacobite goddess. You were fierce and quick-thinking tonight. A brave, brave woman."

"But the muster roll was destroyed. We have no evidence."

"What we have is definitive information." He took her hand and kissed her knuckles. "Facts are like a bread crumb trail. You follow it until you have what you need to file charges."

She stripped off her coat in frustration.

"You don't seem bothered at all that we were shot at, and you wounded, and both of us almost swept out to sea." She lobbed her coat and attacked her stockings. "All that? For one bread crumb of information?"

Mr. Sloan's sleepy, grumbly voice slayed her.

"Only one thing angered me . . . you nearly drowning. I feared I'd lose you forever."

Chapter Twenty-Nine

Is this how you're taking luncheon now? Laid out on your salon floor?" The voice was Jenny's.

Cecelia cracked open a sleep-crusted eye. A blur of petticoats stood in the doorway.

"Jenny . . . Is that you?"

"I should hope so. Who else cooks your food?" A disgruntled pause and, "Though someone's been messing about my kitchen and left dirty dishes."

Alexander was adrift in sleep. Jenny stepped into the salon, a basket at her side. She was scowling like a disapproving nursemaid at piles of damp clothes exuding questionable odors, an open bottle of brandy, and her naked mistress stumbling from a makeshift bed on the floor. Cecelia slid from the warm cocoon and snatched another blanket to cover herself. Her salon was absurd theater. Dried blood spotted the floor and dirty footprints were hither and yon, along with a stack of brown-and-white-checked linens. And the knife.

Jenny toed the blade. "I won't ask what happened here."

"You are, as always, the soul of discretion."

The maid harrumphed. "This is more than your usual tricks, miss."

Cecelia sniffed the air teased by whiffs of fresh baked floury goodness.

"What do you have there?"

"Oh, nothing but some eggs and cream." Jenny was coy, lifting a corner of the towel on her basket. "And a dozen of Morag's crumpets. Made this morning."

"And her blackberry jam?"

"Of course, miss. Only a dunderhead would serve dry crumpets."

"Bless you." She scurried to her settee and patted the low table. "Bring them here."

"What? No plates? You haven't gone wild these past two days, have you?"

"She's a veritable Amazon." Alexander was awake, scrubbing a hand over his face.

Mouth puckering, Jenny planted a hand on her hip.

"I see you've returned. Lookin' worse for the wear with my kitchen towel on your arm."

He propped himself up on one elbow and managed a lazy morning smile. "I hope you're not planning to gut me. I am a wounded man."

"Wounded man." She sniffed.

"We could try again, couldn't we?" he offered.

Jenny's frown softened. "If Miss MacDonald likes you this much, I suppose we could. Let me put these things away and I'll have a light luncheon ready in a trice."

"With crumpets, I hope?" Cecelia asked.

"I know what puts a smile on your face, miss." Jenny's gimlet eye scanned the room. "And when you're done eating, I'll put things right in here."

Jenny sped to the kitchen, mumbling about two days gone and the house an exploded mess. The aroma of baked goods lingered, teasing Cecelia's growling stomach.

Alexander stood up, his movement rusty. "Did she say luncheon?"

"She did. We slept late." Cecelia curled bare legs under the blanket cloaking her.

Daylight bleared through the window, and they both squinted at the brass clock on the mantel ticking a quarter past noon. They'd slept that long, did they? The night's thrilling adventure had worn them out. Their hearts were a different story, the organ shy in daylight. Brown hair snagged Alexander's whiskers. His chest a natural cuirass, he was a Roman sculpture come to life. More philosopher than general, yet every bit a lost soul unsure of his surroundings. He was naught but dirty, wrinkled breeches and bare feet.

"Fire's nearly out." He squatted to nurse it with coal.

Sinew twitched on his back. Silken skin kissed by light, firm knots flexing underneath. He was careful, setting the black lumps in strategic spots. Tired and sore and stiff, he might be, but his feet told the truth. Alexander balanced on the balls of his feet.

Her father's voice rang in her head.

"Look at a man's feet. How a man moves . . . that's the true tell of strength and stamina."

She clutched the blanket under her chin. A man, fighting for her. For how long? In her almost a quarter century of life, men didn't stay. Not in the true sense of the word. They chased high-minded ideals or they chased the next woman.

Was the barrister-cum-government-man different? He had planted the sweetest seeds in zher heart.

His quiet this morning might be the weeds of regret.

Once the fire greedily devoured new coal, he stood up and swiped black dust across his breeches. His portmanteau was in her bedchamber, a nice place to escape and armor himself for the day. She had no idea how he planned to spend it. His ardent vow not to leave her side might be choking on those weeds of regret. The wound sealed with a burn and a vengeful countess were enough to make any man think twice about casting his lot with a Jacobite woman of no account.

From the kitchen, crockery clinked. A meal of sorts would come. Life was returning to normal, but Alexander's presence branded her soul.

She tucked the blanket over her toes. "I'm sure you'd like to clean yourself and dress, no?"

Her own hair was more rat's tail than braid. A hot bath would be divine.

"A good idea. Walking about in public like this"— he splayed a hand on his bare chest—"would see me hauled off to St. Luke's Hospital for Lunatics."

How he planned to spend his day was the unknown. It hung like a question mark between them. A day without him looked bleak and wrong. Her surroundings took on an uneasy gloom: the white papered walls with painted birds mocking her, the furniture a decade past their prime, and the mess on her floor a vague bother.

The world, it seemed, narrowed to the half-dressed Englishman in her salon.

Back straight, she heeded prideful whispers, refusing to ask his plans.

"Please avail yourself to my bedchamber."

He flashed a wicked smile.

"Save two crumpets for me, will you?"

He was on the stairs before she huffed a heart-warming laugh. The man was mad, but an idea took shape as Jenny bustled in, bearing a dish with velvety chocolate, blackberry jam, dice-sized chunks of ham, and crumpets glistening with butter. She set the tray with plates and utensils for two on the table.

Jenny's gaze latched on the pile of clothes. "What do you want me to do with Mr. Sloane's clothes?"

Cecelia sipped chocolate, ambrosia against the world's ills.

"See them laundered."

"That's new." Jenny was an obelisk of disapproval. "Men have tarried here, miss, and I never batted an eye. A day or two and they were gone. But doing a man's laundry is . . ." She hesitated. "Domestic."

The maid sliced that last word with holy fervor. A puzzling turn. Jenny had never shirked fun where males were concerned. Jenny was pretty with a mind of her own and Cecelia was aware of a butcher, a footman, and a sailor who shared a pint with her now and then. What she did with her free time belonged to her. But the maid worried a corner of the brown-and-white-checked towel tucked at her waist.

Cecelia set down her chocolate. "Jenny—"

"I know, miss. It's not my business. You've done a kindness by me and Morag, something I can never repay."

"Jenny—"

"And I shouldn't play the scold." The maid was busy, filling her arms with laundry. "It's—it's . . . I worry about you."

Jenny was an anxious face over a mass of laundry. There were troubles galore here. The maid might be fretting over Alexander's growing importance in their small home. Or the maid read events of late as a portent of disaster. Blood on the floor, a knife with it, and a gentleman caller staying long enough for his clothes to mingle with hers in the laundry. The scene in the salon could be a sign of more trouble ahead.

With MacLeod shot in the back and Alexander shot in the arm, things were getting desperate. Cecelia had to plan accordingly.

She hugged the blanket close. "Do you remember the documents I asked you to take to Morag's house?"

Jenny's eyes rounded. "Yes."

"Good. Why don't you take those smelly clothes to the laundress and spend the rest of the day with Morag? While you're visiting her, make sure you have those documents on hand."

"But I'd rather look after you, miss, and—and the house is a terrible mess . . . and what about the dishes?" the maid cried.

"It will all be here tomorrow. Unless I convince a certain gentleman to wash the dishes with me."

Jenny harrumphed. "You doing dishes? The world is coming to an end."

The jest erased the tension furrowing Jenny's brow. They'd named the papers hidden in Morag's home Cecelia's Doomsday Documents. Instructions and legal writs for her business partnerships—documents Jenny was to take to a solicitor on Little Ormond Street if anything happened to Cecelia. She'd had no cause to worry, not really. But she'd never worn Clanranald MacDonald plaid colors in London, or masqueraded as Betty Burke, or stolen a relic the

Government considered theirs. On Wednesday, she would do all those things.

But today was Monday.

Three days and two nights stretched before her. If the world was going to end, she knew exactly how she'd spend them.

Chapter Thirty

The door to her bedchamber was ajar. Light pinched through the opening. With the tray in her arms and the blanket a loose cloak, she bumped her bottom against the door and headed in, back first. It was a careful negotiation, her eye on the tray, and the blanket hiked indecently high.

She backed into the room. "After last night, I've come to the conclusion every woman should shoot something. It's very freeing."

She swung around and her command of the king's English stalled. Alexander stood in profile, a dark tuft of hair showing at the apex of his legs. Daylight limned his nakedness. As in, not a stitch of clothes covered him.

"What was that?" His smile dented.

Wicked, wicked man. He likes having the element of surprise.

And she liked the wonder of seeing him. Lean, marbled perfection. Her Roman senator philosopher at a standing bath. Dark hair loose, his jaw unshaved, a touch wild he was. Uninhibited, beautiful. Pale everywhere, save the ombre hue of his forearms and face. His confident, breast-saluting hand was dragging a washcloth over his chest.

What a crime to cover all that glorious male flesh with clothes.

Especially his penis stirring to life.

She watched it, the cogs and wheels of her mind cranking slowly.

"Well, good morning to me," she said.

His laugh was a delight.

"You like to watch, don't you?" His voice roughed with seduction.

"You . . . yes."

He turned and faced her, the wet cloth trailing this way and that on his torso. Her gaze tracked it like a cat following a toy dragged along on a string before pouncing. His roving hand washed the length of his penis. Eyelids drooped. His, hers—the pleasure was mutual, the air electric.

Honey ran thickly in her veins. Her limbs were heavy and warm, and the flesh between her legs swelling tenderly.

Alexander wetted the cloth. "Don't you want to put down your tray?"

"It is silly, me holding it."

She set the tray on her bed which earned her an arched brow. She simply smiled and slathered black-berry jam on a crumpet and took a bite. Tart, sweet preserve squished at one corner of her mouth. She walked to her high-back leather chair, the blanket falling off her back.

His laugh was the texture of sex. "Now we're getting down to business."

When she sat down and crossed her legs, leather groaned.

He swiped a long trail over his thighs. "I'm jealous of your chair. It gets to feel your bottom before I do."

"And I get to watch you."

Black hairs matted wetly on sinewed thighs. Droplets trickled over his knees, then his calves where muscle flared. The legs of a man given to running. Pure artistry.

"You missed a spot," she said.

He put cloth on his hip. "Here?"

She shook her head.

He washed his navel. "Here?"

"Lower."

He scrubbed his abdomen. "Here?"

"Lower."

Tension drew a line, his eyes to hers. Hot, combustible, charring the air. Her upright barrister moaned when he dragged the cloth over his dark nest of curls and cupped them.

And rubbed.

No finer torture existed than the agony of anticipation.

The muscles at his navel clenched. His nipples were points on his chest. His thighs taut as his toes turned white, pressing the floor. The linen cloth danced in his hand. Her handsome Englishman arced forward, a slave to it. Hanks of hair bracketed his face. Bronze eyes pooled, glossy and dark. The word *primitive* didn't do him justice. He was carnal passion stripped to the bone. Animal yet refined.

She gripped the armchair, the crumpet forgotten. "You would make a nun blush."

His eyes lit with fierce need. "I will have you."

"Or I shall have you."

It was a dangerous thing to say. Like red meat tossed to a hungry beast. His nostrils flared and his mouth stretched a furious line. When she uncrossed her legs, he looked every inch a fire-breathing dragon. Alexander dropped the cloth, his penis jutting.

Blood pulsed in her ears, louder than last night's thunder. There'd be no finessing this. No slow, tender joining. No quick insertion of a sponge preventative (the smart woman was vigilant about those things). Usually, she was. But she scooted forward, her bottom rubbing leather, her legs spread, lascivious and wide.

She ran her fingers through her cleft, wet *snicks* following each stroke.

Alexander stared at her slick pink flesh, a man enslaved.

The world was her bedchamber. Nothing else existed except him watching her.

He strode across the room, his cock stiff. "Is this new torture? Denying me?"

Blond wisps fell across her eyes. Her breath tripped louder, in and out. She was weak and she was strong. The erotic balance of a woman caught in the throes of self-indulged passion with the man she wanted watching her.

Alexander moved behind the chair and played with her nipples. Arousal arrowed hot and needy from his featherlight touch. The ache exquisite. Soft twirls, then cupping her breasts and teasing the barely-there curve at the bottom.

His talented hands coaxed sweet begging moans from her.

"Please—please . . ." Her bottom rode the edge of her seat. "Now. Please. Now!"

His husky laugh was diabolical. This was what happened to the woman who took an intelligent man to her bed. He took his time, learning her body. Alexander stroked her back while her fingers stroked her nub. He came around and cuffed her wrists with his hands. The denial shocked her.

Lust burned in his eyes. "Come with me."

His pressure was light and guiding, urging her up. When she did, her belly brushed his cock and the world exploded. He snatched her close and she grabbed him, careful with his bandaged arm. Their mouths met in a cataclysmic kiss, scorching and testy. As if enough was enough.

"Blackberry," he said against her mouth. "My favorite."

She cupped his face above hers. He was beautiful, shadows and light, regal and accomplished. She dragged her thumb across his sculpted mouth.

"Take me from behind and spill your seed on my back."

"I've a French card—"

"No. I want to feel *you* inside me."

Knowing flickered in his eyes.

"Nothing between us," he said.

"Nothing."

Their noses were inches apart, a secret world curtained by his hair. A new intimacy in their bridge of trust. She rubbed his jawline, his raspy whiskers tickling her palms.

"Can you manage it?"

She might as well have asked, *Can you manage what grows between us?*

Alexander's eyes softened.

"For you, I will."

Deep affection trimmed his voice. It should've frightened her, but he trailed fingertips down the sides of her breasts to the indent of her waist. A caress, a promise. The torture was split equally between them. She was asking for his self-control, a sacrifice for the pleasure of their skin touching in the most intimate way.

She reached for the empty pistol box on the mantel. It's height, width, and sturdiness would serve. She stepped on it and positioned her legs. Holding on to the mantel, she bent down and thrust her bottom up.

He hissed. "You're killing me."

Alexander touched one finger to her nape and began a dawdling trail down her spine. Obedient goose bumps followed. She watched him over her shoulder, lost in the moment. He looked like an ancient king of yore, toying with her. With his hair loose, the arm bandage, and the bruise at his hairline from the cricket ball, Alexander could be a warrior-king home from battle. A man enjoying his spoils.

He caressed her bottom, his touch barely there. Featherlight and gentle. His thumb drew a line through her cleft; his hands felt the shape of her thighs. She shuddered. The carnal anguish inside was brutal. She *had* to touch herself.

She burrowed one hand between her legs and groaned.

Relief was sweet. A quick peak, another building behind it.

Alexander grabbed her hips. "You'd better hold on."

The box scraped the floor. His cock pulsed against her. Rubbing, stroking, her wetness coating him. His penis was hard, teasing, teasing, couched between her thighs, sliding the length of her cleft. A new rhythm sprang, this one as tender as it was steamy. His body glued to her back, his kisses scorching her neck. Sweat sheened her arms. The fire was hot to her legs. She couldn't get any hotter.

Until his cock nudged her entrance.

"Ohhhh . . ." she moaned. "Please, you must . . ."

Her bottom twitched with pleasure.

"What must I do?" His voice was sensual and textured—a man who knew what he was about.

Smooth and round, his penis tantalized her. An inch, no more. Her balance faltered. She had to grip the mantel with both hands.

"Should I do this?" Hands on her hips slid to the front of her thighs. To her mons.

Fingers riffled through her damp curls. The nub between her legs ached fiercely. His fingertips flirted around it.

"Or should I touch here?" he whispered, drawing a faint line on the nub.

Delicate quivers rippled through her. Her legs were shaking and her emotions spun like windmills in a storm. Talking seemed impossible. She rocked with him, against him, striving. Words slurred to unfeminine grunts. When his intelligent, seeking fingers stroked her nub, she cried out and rammed her bottom against him.

Explosive lust charged her spine. He was seated deep inside her, the shock eye-opening. His exhale gusted her neck. Everything was heavier. The air heaving in and out of her lungs, the blood coursing her veins, her braid dangling like a rope. She was burning. Flesh slapped flesh. She was on her toes, straining, straining, finding a rhythm. One of his hands covered her breast. The other made messy circles on her sloppy wet nub. Pleasure licked her thighs. She closed her eyes, needing the privacy because a horrible truth consumed her. Alexander owned her.

She was utterly possessed by him. Body, heart, and soul.

An insatiable hunger came with his possession. A desperation which climbed brighter than the sun, hotter than fire, her emotions soaring with it. Theirs was a savage, wordless joining, but no less elevating. Alexander was holding her. She was safe.

His hardness moved inside her, a glorious grounding force until lights shattered behind her closed eyes. She cried out his name, the pleasure within stunning. The world was cataclysmic.

Bliss rippled everywhere.

Alexander's release came a second later, his body shuddering.

"Cecelia . . ."

His voice was a raw scrape, ruining her.

Panting hard, she looked down. She was on her toes like a seasoned bare-knuckle brawler. He was too, his body pressing hers from behind, his seed sticky on her bottom. His arm curved around her waist as if he'd never let go.

Drunk with intimacy and emotions, she wanted him in every sense of the word.

But instinct was her weathervane; it warned her, she and Mr. Alexander Sloane were in the fight of their lives.

Chapter Thirty-One

*C*ecelia was not entirely put back together. It had been hours since her interlude with Alexander, but her body still wasn't her own. Their connection was too raw and her nerves too sensitive. She stared out the hack's window, trying to get her bearings. Soul-quenching sexual congress was one thing. Every woman needed a good coupling now and then to set things right.

But the earthquake in her heart was quite unfair.

Her handsome barrister was rearranging her otherwise orderly existence. Light from passing street lamps slanted on his mouth soft with satisfaction. Alexander had been ardent about not leaving her side. Her silly wondering, would he stay or wouldn't he, had been a waste of time, especially when other worries encroached.

The *sgian-dubh*. The countess and Mr. Wortley and the Marquess of Swynford's costume ball.

She crammed them away and lived for Alexander's thumb caressing the back of her hand. They'd worn gloves but they both took one off to hold hands, skin to skin. She fed on his warmth. He was a good man, his sense of justice a beautiful revelation.

Where would their adventure take them?

For now, it led them to White Cross Street, the genesis of their cat and mouse game. The hack rolled to a stop and the door opened.

"Fletcher's House of Corsets and Stays, miss." Hat to his chest, a gray yarn wig capping his head, Mr. Munro was a kind thread. "Will ye need me to fetch you later?" he asked as she exited the hack.

She glanced at Alexander. The world tipped, uncertain. Planning more than an hour ahead with him was new territory.

"Would eight o'clock at the Silver Fox suffice?" Alexander spoke to Mr. Munro before he angled his face to her. "I hear they serve an excellent cottage pie on Mondays."

Mr. Munro grinned. He approved of a gentleman taking the lead.

"Eight o'clock, sir. I shall be there." He bowed smartly and climbed back on his perch. A snap of the reins, and the hack rambled onward.

Alexander was donning his leather glove, a tentative smile curving his mouth.

"I might've rushed that."

"You did, but I forgive you. This is new for both of us."

"I know. I heard Jenny earlier today. I collect she disapproves of me."

"Oh, Jenny has an opinion about everything," she said, batting the air.

"I can't say that I blame her. It is one thing to . . ." He paused in deference to passing pedestrians before lowering his voice. "To spend the night in your bed and quite another when laundry is involved."

"The laundry worries you?"

"Our clothes washed together *is* domestic."

She laughed and spoke to him in a scandalous whisper. "What about the *other* things we did together? Does yelling your name in the throes of passion count?"

A rakish smile chiseled his Roman senator's mouth. "You moaning my name, it's quite fascinating."

They were standing close, White Cross Street's late day shoppers passing by. She craved his humor, his voice, his intelligent conversation. Upright and strong, a man of the law, Alexander had bent his moral code for her. But how much longer would this last?

She touched his sleeve. "You know, you do not have to stay with me."

"It's not a matter of having to. I want to . . . as long as you'll have me."

A breeze riffled black silk securing his queue. He was stalwart and true, his jaw shaved, his cravat proper. A man on the verge of asking for more.

Hairs on her arms raised, the same as when she'd skimmed fingertips over a glass tube demonstrating electrical currents. Amber, sulfur, and glass rubbed together, producing a shock of light. Stunning to see, more stunning to touch.

Almost too much.

She caught sight of her face in the shop window. The luminous eyes of a startled doe looked back. A hunted woman snared by her choices. She was dressed in brown velvet, the hue similar to Alexander's wool coat as if they meant to be a matching pair. Beyond her reflection, somewhere in the shop, was her near future. Her costume and with it came a course of action. Taking the *sgian-dubh*. A pledge fulfilled.

The man beside her—a pledge waiting to happen.

"Cecelia?" His voice was a gentle prompt.

"We've nothing to worry about. We'll have fun, you and I." She was brittle and overbright, adding, "For as long as it lasts."

Hurt patinaed his eyes but he clasped both hands behind his back, morphing into the solid gentleman she knew him to be.

"Nothing to worry about? We were shot at."

She smiled and petted the front of his coat. "You know what I mean. Why don't you go to the haberdashers and purchase a new hat?"

Like her, he'd lost his tricorn in the river, but he wasn't budging.

"It will be a judicious use of our time. You at the haberdasher shop, while I see about my costume. Then we'll meet at the Silver Fox for some fine cottage pie."

He checked the bustling street. "That's not a good idea."

"Do you honestly think Mr. Wortley and his ilk are lurking in a corset shop?" She took one step toward the shop door and waved him off. "Go on. We'll test the absence-makes-the-heart-grow-fonder axiom."

"For a quarter of an hour?"

She opened the shop door. "How about half an hour? Enough time to buy your hat and finish a pint before I get there."

She let herself into Fletcher's House of Corsets and

Stays, but Alexander tarried outside, a breeze stirring the hem of his coat. His eyes burned a trail to her through the shop window. She blew a flirty kiss and her vigilant protector finally blended into the foot traffic on White Cross Street.

"Here to see your treasonous costume?" Mary was at her shoulder, smoothing red-and-white-striped petticoats.

"Straight to the point as always." Her gaze slid to serious gray eyes slanted to hers.

"Would you want me to be anything less?"

"Never."

"I'm pleased to hear it." Mary linked arms with her and they began walking slowly through the shop. "I'm quite pleased with how your costume turned out. I've added a mobcap to complete the effect."

"An ugly one, I hope."

"It's one of mine," Mary said dryly. "Is that ugly enough?"

They laughed and swapped news. Cecelia shared the disastrous visit to the Countess of Denton's warehouse, omitting Alexander's treasonous secret because she'd promised not to breathe a word of it. A hunt for the gold, she'd called it. Mary puzzled over that, but it wouldn't be the first time Cecelia had taken matters in hand without consulting the league.

Once they were in the fitting room, Mary drew the curtains shut and shared her latest news.

"Mr. MacLeod is alive." She pulled the treasonous costume from a cabinet, adding, "He woke up long enough to drink some water before falling back to sleep."

Light glimmered on splendid green silk. Within

the *robe à la française* gown was a painted petticoat. Cecelia stroked it, the cloth a perfect imitation of her clan's tartan.

"Your Spitalfields silk painter worked magic. Whatever she charged, it's worth it."

"I'll send you the bill when I have someone deliver the costume." Mary carefully put away the silk. "Would tomorrow suffice? Margaret's hemming the apron tonight."

"Tomorrow, yes."

She would add it to her schedule, in between kissing Alexander and an invigorating study of how to make him cry out her name in ecstasy—a trial-and-error approach she was sure he'd appreciate.

Mary hugged her and saw her out. Cecelia headed down White Cross Street, her mind a cozy ruin. Would Alexander curl up and read in bed with her? Or kiss her senseless? After she tended his arm, of course. A diverting picture, except a black-sleeved arm grabbed her.

She gasped. The rangy Mr. Wortley was beside her, his eyes burning with a careful-or-I'll-rip-your-throat-to-pieces message. His grip manacled her arm as they walked.

"Miss MacDonald. Doing some late-day shopping?"

Her mouth dried. All she could do was put one foot in front of the other.

Mr. Wortley chuckled. "What? You've nothing to say? I thought you were the mouthy one."

The Silver Fox sign hung ahead but they walked past it. She was cold and scared, forcing herself to look forward. Nothing to give away Alexander and the *tendre* she felt for him. The cutthroat might think the barrister was a passing flirtation. She'd had enough of them. She didn't fight Mr. Wortley when he steered her to the end of a dark alley. Crates and broken buckets littered the cobbles. Otherwise they were alone in the dark.

Mr. Wortley shoved her against the wall and touched his knife to her throat.

"You scream and I'll cut you. Understand?"

She nodded jerkily, her fingers icy though she wore gloves.

"Bad things happen to women all the time in the City. Especially the pretty ones," he said.

Wortley cut a vicious picture. Black hair loosely tied. Large nose and sun-grained skin, his vicious stare slanting viciously to and fro over her face.

"No one will shed a tear if one fair Jacobite goes missing."

"Is that why you've organized this little *tête-à-tête*? To tell me you'd weep for me?"

His mouth quirked. For a split second she flirted with kneeing his baubles until he collared her throat and jammed the back of her head against unforgiving brick.

She swallowed hard.

"Lady Denton has foul plans for you." His face pinched in mock pain. "I wouldn't wish them on a dog, miss. I've tried to sway her, but she is one determined woman."

Terror sunk its claws into her. Knees shaking, she feared collapsing. Mr. Wortley's hand was on her neck, the other with his knife at the ready in her side vision.

A thought punched through her fright.

This has nothing to do with the warehouse break-in. He doesn't know.

Carriages rumbled on White Cross Street and pedestrians had thinned. With the dreary light, anyone looking down the alley might think an assignation was in progress. Bodies pressing, faces close. Her mind raced. To scream? No. She wouldn't test the cutthroat. She couldn't. Alexander would charge in and he was unarmed. Her eyes shuttered.

Please don't come looking for me.

When she opened them, male appreciation glinted in Wortley's eyes. His hand on her neck slid higher, cupping her jaw. His face was close, fascinated.

"You're trying to scare me off," she rasped.

"I'm warning you off, compliments of Lady Denton. I convinced her you're not worth it." His mouth twisted a sneer. "I told her it was a waste of my time following a woman of no account."

"Because you have more important people to harass."

The quip drained her last ounce of courage, but she couldn't regret it. Hardness dropped like a portcullis over Mr. Wortley's features. His thumb smeared carmine off her lips and down her chin. Nostrils flaring, he dug brutal fingertips into her jaw.

"Go back to Scotland. Otherwise the countess will make sure you disappear."

Chapter Thirty-Two

Cecelia had walked into the Silver Fox a little . . . off. She was by turns cagey and quiet or bright and brittle, though he couldn't fathom why. Any queries to her welfare had been met with platitudes and excuses. Was he presuming too much by reading her mood? Their connection was too new for him to assume he could intrude, but a wall was firmly up.

Once their food had been served, she encouraged him to dig into his cottage pie while she poked at hers. Thanks to the punctual Mr. Munro, their ride home had been equally stiff. Their bridge of trust needed something intimate. When they arrived at the stone cottage, Jenny met them in the entry and took cloaks and hats.

"Will you want a restorative, miss?" She added a grudging, "Or you, sir?"

Cecelia stormed up the stairs. "Nothing for me."

Jenny's mouth puckered as if Cecelia's mood was his fault. He took it in stride, noting the pristine house.

"Thank you for tending my laundry and cleaning up the mess."

The maid picked lint off the cloak she was holding. "That's what I do, sir. I clean messes."

Jenny eyed him sharply, which he took as a warning not to get too comfortable playing house with her mistress. The maid slinked off, taking the candlelight with her. He wanted to tell the surly servant he'd gladly wed her mistress, but this was a night of uncertainty. Miss MacDonald's restless footsteps banged abovestairs. Sex soothed, certainly. But women were complex creatures. Their hearts and minds needed feeding first.

On a whim, he fetched a book from the salon.

When he strode into her bedchamber, the fire cast subtle amber light. Cecelia was bent over a water bowl, scrubbing her face. Her vigor was frightening, as if she was determined to erase herself.

He touched her shoulder. She was haunted eyes and cherried cheeks.

"Have a care," he said kindly. "I like your face as it is."

"What has my face done but gain unwanted male attention?"

"You have my attention."

"And if I looked like a gargoyle, would you be in my bedchamber?"

His surprise was reflected in her mirror, a man snared by her loveliness and charm.

"You are more than your face."

She averted her eyes. Yes, he loved her face, the slopes, the light, the pertness of her chin. Her face was her calling card, the doorway to her intelligence, her wit, her *joie de vivre*. But love, he was learning, was not about taking, but about giving.

What could he offer her right now?

Water dripped down her temples. She swiped it with the back of her hand. "I've been old since I was twelve. I knew then how to get what I wanted, if not my face my sauciness would . . ." She hesitated, the mood in her bedchamber sobering. "I've never been the most beautiful woman in a room, but I've always aimed to be the most interesting." Pained eyes speared him. "But what if who I am is not enough?"

"Enough for what?"

"Just . . . enough."

Her voice was a sad wisp. She was slipping into a fog of vagaries. He couldn't force her to crack them open, but he could lure her away from them with tantalizing bait. He'd held up a book, and she read aloud the title on the spine.

"*The Female Quixote or The Adventures of Arabella.* What do you want to do with that?" As soon as the words were out, a faint smile quirked. "Forgive my banal question. I know what to do with a book; I'm not sure your purpose in bringing it to my bedchamber."

"My purpose? To please you, of course."

Her brows shot to her hairline. "You don't want to engage in a more invigorating activity?"

He traced a wet tendril stuck to her cheek. "One come hither look from you, and I'm your partner for all manner of invigoration."

A tantalizing hook was dangled.

"But I don't think you need bed sport," he said quietly.

"And what do you think I need?"

"Book sport." He grinned at astonishment wiping her clean. "I think you need to recline in bed and be read to."

She touched her lips, huffing softly. The sparkle in her eyes was returning.

"Those are the most seductive words a man could say."

He drew a line on her collarbone, absurdly happy at hitting a bull's-eye with her. The Scotswoman's skin was like silk in the amber light. It was a joy being in the same room with her, clothed or not.

"The idea came from my first night here. I saw a pamphlet on your bed."

Amused suspicion clouded her features. "Did Jenny, perchance, help with your selection?"

"How could you think that? Your maid is barely civil with me."

She pulled a pin from her stomacher. "It just so happens that you have selected my favorite book."

"Did I?"

She hummed her "yes" while freeing another pin from her gown. He tucked the book to his side, deciding not to tell her Fielding applauded the book. The magistrate had written an article about it in the *Covent-Garden Journal*. But the outside world had no business here. The cozy bedchamber was their haven.

He was stepping over discarded stockings when she asked, "Why aren't you naked yet?"

Glee brightened her face. He tossed the book on her bed and rapid undressing commenced. Who was he to refuse naked bedtime reading? Shoes were kicked off, coat, waistcoat, and breeches dropped in a pile.

Petticoats and panniers topped the mess. A dash of laughter and bumping bodies went with it.

Together, they sank into the altar of her bed. Reading aloud to Cecelia was more intimate than sex. Snow-white linens warm from her body and their mingled scents wove into the fabric. His voice was the gentle intrusion. Holding her, his gift. She twined her legs with his, the goddess of Swan Lane at rest.

Her stone house was heaven on earth. He would gladly stay forever.

Each sentence he read was a question: *See what happens if you let me stay?*

The book unfolded a tale about a young woman raised by her widowed father in a distant castle. She spent her days reading novels of romance and adventure, believing the world was the same as in her books. When her father died, Arabella set her sights on London and Bath. There she found the world was not so kind. In her travails, Arabella threw herself into the Thames to escape a man who was chasing her.

As he read, Cecelia rested and her breath evened. This went on for at least two hours until the bedside candles had turned into flickering stumps and the sky filled with stars.

He tried to put the book down.

Cecelia scratched a soft line across his bare chest.

"Please, don't stop." Her muffled voice was over his heart.

He kissed the crown of her head and picked up where he left off: Arabella falling ill and a doctor treating her. But her true sickness was discontent—a woman battered by the world. The doctor set her right with a few words, as things happened in books, and young Arabella returned to her late father's castle where she soon wed a man, as things happened in romance.

The story done, he blew out the candles. The drowsy Scotswoman snuggled close, her rosewater scent writing itself on his heart. He stroked a lock of her hair and stared into the darkness. *The Adventures of Arabella* could be *The Adventures of Cecelia* except the hole in Miss MacDonald's heart would not heal from token words.

He held her, unsure what could.

Chapter Thirty-Three

*H*er rebellious body knew what it wanted. Her mind was the reasoned partner, reminding her of what could not be. Tomorrow was Wednesday, the day Mr. Sloane must report to Fielding. And when she thought of that meeting, he was Mr. Sloane to her, not Alexander.

Who knew what he'd say about her? No promises had been made. Theirs was a suspended state. Secrets and humor shared. Intimate bed sport, certainly. Last night was a shift. He'd held her, demanding nothing and reading to her. His tenor was tattooed on her skin, his scent stuck to her soul. No man had taken her to bed to read a book.

Utterly diabolical.

A man like that needed her appreciation.

She scraped the hair between his legs. Featherlight, crinkled curls, warmth rising to her hand. Morning slivered through a gap in her bed curtains. Dark lashes fanned Alexander's cheeks and whiskers etched his jaw. With one arm bent above his head, he was a dark-haired deity at rest in a sea of white.

Covers landed at his waist. Under them, her hand explored him.

If she could collect this moment in a bottle, she would.

How had they come to this, their beguiling intimacy? There was no undoing it. She'd have better luck unsetting the sun. Alexander was inevitable. More than a tumble but he couldn't be forever. Her heart twisted sadly, but she shoved that hurt aside. It was no use wasting precious time.

Nose to the counterpane, she breathed him in. His soap, his scent, was in the bed linens covering his stirring flesh. She kissed the magical rise.

"Kissed by a river nymph." The sleep-grogged voice of her handsome reader.

"I can't stop touching you."

"You don't have to."

"Except tomorrow is Wednesday," she said.

She was on her side, her head propped up by one hand while she stroked him lovingly with the other. His cock thickened, velvet on ivory. Her touch was indolent, his eyes languorous.

"Which means today is Tuesday," he said. "We have all day to ourselves."

She scratched soft lines over his abdomen. "To do anything?"

He grunted, his compact muscles tensing. His shirt rucked up higher while she traced taut lines on the flesh arrowing to the dark tuft between his legs. She combed the curly nest, her fingernails grazing his skin. He twitched and the bed ropes cricked. Linens shushed as she nudged them lower and exposed him from his navel to his thighs. She kissed the mysterious spot where hip and belly met, a taut muscled triangle sloping downward.

Alexander was the picture of male contentment.

"There is one thing I want." She kissed his hip. Muscles flexed against her mouth.

"Anything," he mumbled.

She kissed him again. "I want to know what happened between you and your brother."

The building eroticism stilled. His eyes opened. "My brother."

"A woman came between you, I collect."

"Of all things to ask me . . ." His words drifted tenderly. "Do you really want to talk about this *now*?"

"I do."

He affected a casual air, an arm over his head, the pillow comfortably dented, but he hiked the sheets strategic inches higher.

"I expected you to ask about my report to Fielding."

"Fielding is the least of my worries."

He cocked a brow, to which she grinned.

"It is Tuesday after all. The day I have you all to myself."

"To ask questions about another woman."

"Yes."

She caressed his ribs, which he apparently still trusted her with. His skin pebbled wherever she touched. Compared to yesterday's full nudity, it was a disappointment. She'd bled painful milestones for him. Was it too much to ask he do the same?

"Is this some kind of test?" Tetchiness crept into his voice.

She withdrew her hand, and his gaze followed its path to her hip. Calculation flashed in his eyes as if he did equations on how to get it back, but bleeding the truth was the only way he'd win.

"And in your telling, do not skirt facts, if you please."

She didn't know what drove her to prod him about another woman. She'd not been forthright about Mr. Wortley threatening her, but that was different. Wasn't it?

Alexander gusted a sigh. "Her name is Miss Phoebe Kent. Daughter to my father's childhood friend. She's six years younger than me, the sprite who tagged behind me and my brother."

"And?"

"And what?" His head shifted on the pillow. "Our parents would smile and hint at a union someday as parents do when they have hopes for their children."

She fell back on the mattress. "Not all mothers and fathers."

"No, I suppose not." He was quiet, bed ropes cricking again. "She is dark haired, symmetrical, and all that," he said, batting the air.

"Symmetrical?" She laughed.

"Like an hour glass was Phoebe."

"Oh, you are poetic."

His smile was lazy. "Doesn't warm a woman's heart, does it?"

"Not mine."

Quiet folded around them. Birds chirped outside her window. Children laughed in the alley behind her mews, signs of life while hers cocooned itself in her bed.

He turned to her. "What warms your heart?"

"You."

His lips parted. Unseen defenses shed themselves slowly. "As you do to mine."

She curled up beside him. "Then tell me what she did to your heart."

The soft entreaty covered them. Gentle and kind, her bed was a place to take a risk and heal wounds, together.

His chest rose and fell noticeably as words worked their way out. "She chose me first," he said pointedly. "But she eventually decided that I wasn't good enough."

Alexander's voice cooled on those last words, his pain bared at being deemed insufficient. Being chosen first by the symmetrical Miss Kent must have been important. Equally important was his omission: *I loved her and she loved me.*

"All my life, my brother has been the anointed one. We fish, and he catches more than me. We shoot, and he hits the target every time. In family matters, he is everything my father wants. A gentleman solicitor, not a barrister. Whereas I . . ." He waved his hand vaguely. "I have long wanted a different path."

"Which is not the anointed one."

"No. Baron of the Exchequer is a stretch."

"But you are daring enough to seek it."

"Yes." His mouth slid handsomely sideways. "You and I are alike in that. I respect you. The caliber of woman you are—your choices, even if I don't agree with them entirely. You are brave."

She caressed his ribs. "Thank you."

"Not quite poetry," he rasped.

"I don't want poetry. I want you."

He folded his hand around hers and brought it

to his lips. Intelligence was the backdrop to everything he did, his keen mind, his methodical drive, his undercurrent of daring. A man to lose himself in a task—and a woman—if he found her engaging.

He tucked his arm behind his head and stared at the canopy above. "She sought me, which was flattering."

Moments passed, measured by more chirping birds and more daylight breaking through their cocoon. A shadow washed his face. Distant pain, she imagined, and she wanted to wipe it away.

"In the end, my choices weren't good enough for her. *I* wasn't good enough." The corners of his mouth pinched white. "She wanted a secure path. It wasn't long after I was in His Grace's employ when her affections wandered."

"And your brother swooped in."

"Which hurt most of all."

"Not the loss of Miss Kent?"

"No." He stared at the canopy above. "She sought me; like a fool, I was flattered, assuming my plans would be hers."

She slid her hand up his shirt and found his heartbeat. The cadence was strong and true, like him.

"I'm sorry," she whispered.

Alexander wrapped his arm around her and pulled her close. "I'm not. If I would've yoked myself to her, then I couldn't be here with you."

"Then let's not waste another minute of our time together."

She chased away Miss Kent's shadow by planting passionate kisses on Alexander. To his chest, his neck, nipping here and there. They spent the day in bed, laughing and indulging sensual whims. Together, they were a well-matched pair in bed sport. And when he was flat on his back, she rode him. Her skin sheened and the bed shook, and when her handsome hunter found his pleasure, she did not withdraw from him.

Chapter Thirty-Four

*H*e studied the world beyond Fielding's office window. Twilight and fat clouds charcoaled Bow Street's rooftops while London's good citizens were clutching their coats against trailing winds on the streets below. The very same street Miss Cecelia MacDonald had donned her gloves, flirting, as it were with gentlemen dancing attendance on her, while he'd watched.

Never had he imagined the Scotswoman would sharpen his mind. Or steal his heart. She'd used the tenderest weapons—wit and kisses and motives so pure they glimmered.

A mere seven days and he was a profoundly different man.

Fissures breached his soul the way sunshine fractured a frozen lake come spring. Cecelia MacDonald was all that was good and beautiful in a dull world. London didn't deserve her. He didn't deserve her.

But he'd fight for her all the same, starting with his report to Fielding.

The old crow was presently reading five pages

of carefully crafted lists and dates and places. The foolscap scraped as the magistrate slid one page behind the other in his slow perusal. Snorts of derision punctuated the silent read. Fielding's phlegmy coughs did too.

"You expect me to believe Miss MacDonald is a paragon of virtue?" Fielding asked.

"I expect you to believe the truth."

The chair creaked. "I wanted a report of the woman's whereabouts. Not this drivel."

Alexander turned around. Fielding was standing with the aid of a cane. His peruke framed a haggard face made pale above his black robe. Watery, bloodshot eyes peered at Alexander.

"You wanted evidence," Alexander said. "And I gave it to you."

Fielding ambled around his desk, his cane thumping the floor. "Feeding apples and bread to the Scots in Tenter Ground has to be a ploy. I can't believe that's all she does."

"It isn't. She also feeds the Irish. It's in my report."

Fielding's eyes slanted slightly. "Don't be coy with me."

He steeled himself. He *was* toying with Fielding, a man who aspired to rid the streets of crime and make London a safer place. Some respect was due. But Fielding could never rid their fair city of corruption. For that he'd have to crack open high places full of rot. He'd also have to look within his own thief takers.

Alexander was surprisingly comfortable, his arms loosely crossed and a finger tapping his lips.

"Did you read section three of my report?" he asked. "The other goings-on in Southwark?"

"About Mr. Berry and Mr. MacDaniel? Unsubstantiated rumors. I won't countenance them."

"Yet, you'll countenance unsubstantiated rumors about Miss MacDonald. Why? Is it too hard to believe a Jacobite sympathizer can do good for others?"

Fielding's eyes narrowed. "You're under her spell."

Spell was inadequate for the prism of emotions he felt. Fascinated? Enthralled? Beguiled? None did justice to what flourished inside him.

"She is a treasure."

Fielding wiped a handkerchief across his nose. "I'll give you another chance to get this right, Mr. Sloane. You have one week to dig up dirt on Miss MacDonald."

"And if I don't?" Alexander stood tall as a duke's man should.

"I will make certain you never get the letters patent."

Fielding's threat had lost its sting. Alexander walked solemnly to the door, and reached for his hat on a hook. He had important work to do, namely escorting Cecelia to a costume ball and seeing her safely gone from it with her clan's *sgian-dubh* in hand.

"Mr. Sloane, where are you going?"

Alexander smiled. A small stone cottage in Dowgate came to mind.

"I'm going home," he said, putting his newly purchased tricorn on his head. His old hunter's hat, like his ambitions, had been swept out to sea.

"I'm not done with you."

"But I am done with you, sir. I will not spy on an innocent woman."

Fielding hacked a wretched cough and pinned

sickly eyes on Alexander. "What about Baron of the Exchequer?"

"I don't want it."

To which Fielding's jaw dropped.

"His Grace knows," Alexander said. "I informed the duke that I can no longer fulfill my duties for the crown." He glanced at the window where light rain sprinkled the glass. "Another duty calls."

Excitement hummed in his veins. He was free, and he had the lovely Scotswoman to thank for it. Because of her, invigorating changes were afoot.

He opened the door and swung it wide, voices spilling past him. Clerks and witnesses milled about. The magistrate would be at his bench until midnight because criminals thrived in the dark.

"There's corruption in Bow Street," Alexander said. "You need to clean it up."

"Berry and MacDaniel."

Fielding eyed him shrewdly, patiently. It couldn't be easy to learn his most productive thief takers were rotten. It was equally possible Fielding suspected Berry and MacDaniel of misdeeds.

"You sent me out to learn the truth, and I did. The problem is, you don't like what I found."

The old crow leaned heavily on his cane. "Lady Justice has a mind of her own."

"On that, we can agree."

Alexander was ready to do some cleanup of his own. He touched his hat in salute and walked out into the night.

Chapter Thirty-Five

Swynford House sparkled as St. James houses do when polished for a ball. Gauze hung in the arches imbued with delicate papier-mâché birds and butter-flies to mimic the late Sir Hans Sloane's collection. Potted trees and plants added to the appeal. Cecelia strolled Flora and Fauna Hall with Alexander, who was entertaining her with a recounting of female prudery as per Mr. Burton.

Alexander raised his hand shoulder-high.

"According to Burton, the nearly sainted civically aware women are this level of prudishness. Which includes museum enthusiasts. Women who are so tedious a man wouldn't want to grope them in the dark."

She laughed and spoke intimately behind her fan. "We should find an alcove and test that theory."

"Shall we do that before or after you find the *sgian-dubh*?"

She snatched a glass of champagne from an obliging footman and sipped, the bubbles tickling her throat.

"I am at your disposal until half past nine, sir."

She and Alexander would separate half an hour before she took the knife. He would go abovestairs, giving him a plausible alibi in case anything went wrong. It was something she'd insisted. He knew her plan up until the plaid silk petticoat and stomacher. If all went well, the diversion wouldn't be necessary.

"You make a tempting chambermaid," he said.

"Thank you, sir."

Forest green silk shimmered in candlelight. A white apron pinned to her bodice covered her to her hem (hiding petticoats and stomacher painted a Clan-ranald MacDonald silk) with a mobcap finishing her costume.

"Your costume suits you," she said.

He dressed as a knight with breastplate armor complete with tunic, hose, and pointy-toed medieval boots.

"Last time I wore this"—he tapped his champagne flute to his metal chest—"I was at university."

"A sign you need to have more fun, play more cricket matches, and attend more parties, and the like."

They dipped into a library filled with fantastical items from nature. Treelike coral and giant turtle shells bigger than her bathtub were on tables. They stopped to admire a Guinea butterfly in Muscovy glass.

"Being with you is the most fun I've ever had."

As he gulped champagne, his declaration seeped into her. It was as tender as any declaration of love, said in Swynford House when she was less than an hour away from taking the *sgian-dubh*. Stress etched his face, and she wanted to smooth it away. There was something fragile about their days and nights together.

"I'm not expecting you to respond in kind," he said. "But, given the chance, I want to be the gentleman who makes you laugh and smile and pours all manner of happiness into your heart."

Her lips parted softly. This was as close to an ardent declaration as they'd come. She lost herself in the slow dent of his smile. Was a future with him possible? New revelers swarmed the table. A pirate with a paunch leaned in, bumping her. He set a glass eye ring to his eye for a better look. Everyone had donned a costume. Even the footmen played along, with butterflies and birds pinned to their coats and wigs.

Alexander cleared his throat, the spell broken. "We should view the old knives and amulets next."

"Looking for relics, are you?" The elderly pirate straightened. "Go to the library off the entry. Pink walls, a crescent-shaped bookcase. Can't miss it. The only room like it in the house."

"Thank you, sir," she said brightly.

They exited Flora and Fauna Hall, Alexander's gaze slanting on her.

"You already know where the relics are, don't you?"

"The *sgian-dubh* sits between sixth-century Persian amulets and a Roman gladius. Last table in the pink library."

Amusement rumbled in his chest. "When did you manage that?"

"When you were detained by a nymph at the refreshment table. A brunette with impressive symmetry."

He tipped his back and laughed heartily.

"Only one woman's symmetry fascinates me."

"So you say."

"You doubt me?"

They passed a drawing room, the decor lovely and the guests mildly sotted. A jester and a plague doctor hunched over backgammon. A foursome of two medieval wenches and two monks played whist. Joy was everywhere. If she had doubts, it was about her mission. Tonight wasn't the same as stealing gold in the dark. She would have to snatch the *sgian-dubh* with people filing in and out of the room. Taking the gold had been executed with the league, something planned months in advance with each woman looking after the other. None of them were here to watch her back.

Pressure amplified in her head. A warning voice came with it: *This is what happens when you act alone.*

Except Alexander was with her, his profile a regal line.

"I have no doubts about you," she murmured finally.

Kind burning eyes glanced at her. "I'm glad to hear it."

The clock was ticking to the inevitable hour. Her mind raced.

What if the night went terribly wrong, and she never saw him again?

What if the night went terribly right? There was a chance she'd still not see him again.

She stopped their promenade by the dining room. The grand room had been converted for dancing since the ballroom abovestairs displayed curiosities. Alexander waited, patient and thoughtful. To her left, across a sea of Italian marble, was the pink library where the *sgian-dubh* waited. Her reward for these four years in London.

What if another reward was unfolding?

Love with Mr. Sloane.

Was it possible to steal love and a relic in the same night?

She looked into the intelligent eyes of her knight in shining armor. Unbearable emotions played her, sweet and bracing and poignant. Like beautiful music that should never end. She knew differently. Everything did end eventually. A body's days were numbered and hearts had no guarantee. She slid a hand up his wine-red sleeve embroidered with gold. Under it, a bandage bumped her palm. She could have lost him, but this was not a night for loss. Victory was afoot.

In the next room, men and women in fanciful costumes were dancing an allemande, and she was Cecelia MacDonald, a woman who lived without regrets.

Her face tipped to his. "Dance with me."

Chapter Thirty-Six

Cecelia graced the night, eyes sparkling and her mouth painted an ungovernable carmine red. A woman who embodied life. When his Bow Street assignment had first begun, he'd watched her vividness from afar, drawn to her incandescence. The Scotswoman was a beautiful fighter. She had pushed through her painful history and still found reasons to dance.

Her request was an invitation. An opening, and he would seize it.

"Yes, I want to dance with you," he said.

He drew her as close as her panniers allowed and maneuvered them into the throng of dancers. A row of forty or fifty men bowed to a row of curtseying women. With a light handhold, they ventured into their first steps. Bodies pressed, the hot, noisy swarm expanding and contracting to violin music. Cecelia laughed joyously, her pointed toe kicking shimmering hems under a hundred blazing candles.

"Have you always been a flirt?" he asked.

Her hazel eyes sparkled. "I was born a flirt."

They linked arms for the first spin. Miss MacDonald was lost in the fluid freedom of dance.

"You should try it. Flirting more," she said.

Their hands switched for another rotation. Her silk hems brushed his calves, the whispery touch sending a thrum of pleasure up his limbs.

"I never acquired a taste for it . . . until you."

They parted, as befitted the dance. The Scotswoman's mouth curved a very pleased, very feline smile—the same artful look when she walked in on his standing bath. They turned, keeping time with dancers.

From her row, her gaze locked with his and her lips parted softly. Seconds passed, two measures of music, an eternity for him.

The rows came together. Their hands clasped, her touch exciting.

Her panniers brushed his hip, a small agony that.

She angled her face to him. "What else have you acquired a taste for?"

They were side by side, rotating, her rosewater scent soaking him.

"Since meeting you, I have acquired a taste for river swims, for reading in bed, and—"

They spun around and rejoined their hands.

"—I have a new appreciation for surly but loyal housemaids."

She giggled and he adored the sound of it.

"Is that all?" she asked.

"You want more, do you?"

"From you? Always."

A tender pang twisted his heart. How fast and hard could a man fall for a woman? He was in danger of sweeping Miss MacDonald into his arms and running off with her into the night. If he did, he'd never let her go.

They separated, the paces between them stretching his agony. Oh, he had it bad, a besotted man counting the seconds until he could touch her again. A hundred dancers' shoes clicked the wood floor. Sweet violin notes played, his heart dipping and swaying with them. They pranced to each other and linked arms. Cecelia's pretty nose tipped to his, her eyes expectant.

"I'm not poetic." His mouth dented sideways. "As you read in my pocket journal."

"Your words are poetry to me."

She was a little breathless, a vein ticking at the base of her throat. They slowed their rotation, and he was caught by the bright prettiness of her hazel eyes and her brown lashes framing them.

"Since meeting you I want to revel in the summer sun and play cricket again. I want to feel silk ribbons binding my hands, and spend the day in your bed talking—"

"Only talking?"

Her eyes were dark fireworks.

"For everything with you," he said possessively.

Her brow arched, coy and practiced. "You have an excellent faculty for words. I would like to hear them."

Their rotation slowing, he touched his chest.

"There's a fire deep in here that was dormant—my love for justice."

"And how is that fire now?"

"It burns brighter because of you. Everything does."

Cecelia stared in wonder, her hand gripping his tightly. Music played on. They were standing still, a sea of dancers spinning around them. His gaze, he knew, burned intensely. She was at his side, and he would fight mightily to keep her there.

"Life with you is an adventure," he said, his thumb stroking the back of her hand. "I never want it to end."

Her lips opened wider.

"What are you saying?"

Her slim cleavage pumped faster. A gold medallion nestled in it. The old coin hung on a black ribbon—the same one she wore when she flirted with him through the shop window on White Cross Street.

The same coin that bound her to a league of Jacobites, but a time for decisions was upon them.

Their dance was done. Laughter and conversation burst everywhere. Women fanned themselves. Couples bumped into them, calling for punch. Air in his chest was light and frothy like champagne bubbles going straight to his head.

He raised their joined hands to his lips and kissed her knuckles.

"Marry me."

Chapter Thirty-Seven

*Ch*andeliers gleamed on Alexander's breastplate. He was earnest, a true suitor—and she'd had a few, but none who had spent a whirlwind week investigating her, challenging her mind, cooking for her, picking locks, sharing treasonous secrets, shooting at cutthroats, and rescuing her from a stormy river only to bleed on her salon floor at midnight.

And his legs filled medieval hose rather nicely.

"Alexander . . . I—"

"I know," he said, caressing her hand. "This is poorly done, blurting my intentions like this." His mouth denting, he eyed a rambling man garbed as a satyr. "Suffice to say, you deserve something romantic and thoughtful. Not this."

Romantic and thoughtful was nice. His thumb stroking sensual sparks on the underside of her wrist was nicer. She wanted to go home and find out how smooth his tenor sounded when he read *Moll Flanders* or Lloyd's insurance records, last year's tax rolls, and Jenny's latest shopping list. Her favorite place was her head over his heart while he spoke. Romantic and thoughtful wasn't the problem.

Myriad responses wanted to come. Once organized, she would've shared them, except his mouth firmed and his caressing hand cuffed her wrist.

"Brace yourself."

She followed his sight line, a chill descending. She couldn't feel the floor for the numbness shooting up her legs. The Countess of Denton, costumed in a Grecian gown and a gold circlet crowning raven curls, approached.

"Miss MacDonald, what a surprise to see you here. Should I warn my brother to hide the family silver?"

Cecelia sketched a curtsey. "I know of only one thief in our midst, and she wouldn't bother with her brother's silver."

"What an impertinent creature. I should have you tossed from the premises."

Alexander bowed. "My lady."

The countess's sherry-colored eyes razored him. "We've met before, you and I."

"We have. When you visited the Duke of New-castle's office last spring."

His hand slid to Cecelia's elbow. Did he think she would pounce on the woman? In a ball of all places?

"Yes, I do recall." Lady Denton cocked her head, her pearl-drop earbobs dancing prettily.

Alexander kept a gentle touch on Cecelia's elbow while he and the countess engaged in topics of politics and commerce. It gave Cecelia a chance to thaw her glacial shock. What was the countess about? The lady walked safely in her world, commanding it, some might say, and she'd ordered her man, Mr.

Wortley, to warn her off. Yet this little ballroom meeting smacked of a cat batting a mouse before sinking its claws in deep.

Lady Denton pointed her closed fan like a scepter at Cecelia's hem.

"Are you wearing a clan tartan?"

Cecelia looked down. Her apron flapped over itself, revealing her petticoat. Dancing must've disturbed her costume.

She shook the apron back into place. "No. A tartan is wool, my lady. My costume is silk. An important difference."

The lady's suspicious gaze climbed up and down her. "What exactly is your costume?"

Alexander's grip firmed on her elbow. *Play nice with the greedy countess* was his message. He was cautious to the bone.

She was not.

"I am Betty Burke."

Seconds dripped, measured by Lady Denton's face, sharp and still as a viper before it strikes. Cecelia could've said she was a chambermaid but . . . temptation.

"Well," she said brightly. "If you'll excuse me, I'm off to find more curiosities."

She curtseyed. The countess snapped open her fan, her gaze on the black ribbon around Cecelia's neck.

Cecelia pushed through the ballroom's crush to find more crowds in the cavernous entry. The floor and walls were blinding white, the chandeliers a squint-worthy brightness. Tables of manuscripts and books had been set here. Swynford House was crammed to the gills and a clock above a man cos-

tumed in foreign robes said the time was quarter
to ten.

Heat pricked under her arms. Fifteen minutes to
snatch the *sgian-dubh*.

The always punctual Mary would already be waiting for her at the ladies' retiring room window.

Head high, she swept into the pink library. The
sign outside the door said RELICS OF MAGIC AND
WAR. Twenty to thirty merrymakers milled about
the room, footmen bearing champagne trays among
them. She took a glass and sipped. Champagne
burned her dry throat. Her feet sunk into plush
gray carpet as she walked. The end of the room was
quieter. Books lined circular shelves, their gold-
embossed spines glinting wealth.

The paunchy pirate, his glass eye ring pressed
close, bent over the last table.

"One man," she said under her breath.

She'd drop her glass, create a diversion, and slip
the *sgian-dubh* into her petticoat pocket. Before the
footman came to clean up the mess, she'd ask the
gentleman pirate about the Roman gladius which
supposedly had been cursed by a druid.

Ancient iron, glass, and stone pieces rested on
vermillion tablecloths. The starched red clashed with
the marquess's gentle pink walls. She checked a clock
on the wall behind the paunchy pirate. Ten minutes
to steal the *sgian-dubh*.

She swallowed sandy dryness in her mouth, careful
not to look too interested in the table.

"We meet again, sir," she said cheerfully.

The pirate blinked, his one eye owlish behind the
eyeglass ring.

"Yes, yes. We spoke at the Guinea butterfly." He

lowered the eyeglass ring. "Capital event, wouldn't you say?"

"Indeed, it is. The dancing, the curiosities . . . all wonderful and quite fascinating."

He smiled, displaying a gap between his front teeth. "Is this your first time in the Relic Room?"

His question was a lot like young swains asking, *Is this your first time in this pub?*

"It is." Her conscience niggled her over the lie. There was no need for it, yet the untruth just slipped out. Anything to put distance between her and the knife she was minutes from stealing.

"Is there a particular relic of interest? I'd be delighted to educate you." Her ruddy-cheeked gentleman pirate blinked solicitously before his gaze sunk to her bosom.

"Why don't you and I explore the table?" A tiny breath. "Together."

Her offer was red meat to a hound. His one eye gleaming, he picked up a Roman gladius and held it high.

"Meet the Roman gladius." He lunged forward, knees cracking as he jabbed air. "A good muscular weapon. One thrust to the liver and the enemy was felled."

"Oh my. Are we allowed to touch the relics?"

He straightened and sniffed, mildly affronted. "I am Viscount Redmont."

As if that explained everything.

"I am one of the board of governors for His Majesty's museum."

She touched her bodice. "My apologies, sir."

She glanced at the clock. Seven minutes left. Other than her jumping pulse, she was calm. Ready. Another distracting gladius demonstration and she'd stand hip to the table to slide the ceremonial knife into her pocket.

"I heard witches cast a spell on that particular Roman sword."

Woolly brows pinched in dismay. Viscount Redmont cleared his throat and raised an instructive finger.

"Correction. Witches are women, druids are men. And this"—he hefted the blade, candlelight a glare on old iron—"this is a gladius, not a sword. An important distinction."

"The same as a man casting a curse versus a woman." She added a sober, "The sex of the curse giver, it must be a grave matter."

He nodded vigorously. "Oh indeed."

The viscount launched into the history of the gladius. She checked the clock. Five minutes. A deep breath and she sidled up to the table. One side of her pannier bunched on the table. She touched the tablecloth, her hand searching for the *sgian-dubh*'s bone handle. Her gentleman pirate's enthusiastic lecture drew interest. A man costumed as a troubadour and another as a Greek warrior gathered close as the clock on the wall reached the tenth hour.

Her hand flattened on the table where the knife was supposed to be.

Nothing was there. She looked down.

The *sgian-dubh* was gone.

Chapter Thirty-Eight

*I*t's gone," she gasped.

The lecture halted, and Viscount Redmont squinted at her in dismay. "What's that, miss?"

"The *sgian-dubh*. It was here . . . and now it's gone."

She scanned the table. Amulets of stone and glass, a Viking sword, and another strangely curved blade, its metal time-blackened, lay on the table.

The ruddy-cheeked viscount set his eyeglass ring to his eye and searched the artifacts, dumbstruck. "It is missing. I saw it here before." A belly-deep grunt and, "Strangest thing."

The troubadour and Greek warrior started searching nearby tables, which drew the attention of a footman.

"Something amiss?" the servant asked.

The viscount scratched his ear. "It appears the *sgian-dubh*, a clan relic from the Highlands, has gone missing."

The footman set down his tray. "We should search under the table, sir. Could be it fell under there."

The footman went down on one knee, which drew

the attention of the rest of the room, as if Viscount Redmont's vigorous lecture on the tale of the Roman gladius wasn't enough to draw the eyes and ears of the room. She backed away, hoping the knife might've been hiding under the long red tablecloth.

Bristling hair on her nape informed her differently. The countess entered the pink library with two men in tow—Mr. Berry and Mr. MacDaniel, Fielding's corrupt thief takers. Lady Denton scanned the room, her eyes slanted to narrow bloodthirsty shards on Cecelia.

"There she is. Arrest her."

Blood congealed in Cecelia's veins. She touched her throat as if a rough hemp rope already coiled there. Heels sliding backward, she bumped a wall of books. Closed in by the crescent shelves, she had nowhere to run, nowhere to hide. Viscount Redmont and a footman blocked one exit. The advancing thief takers blocked the other.

"I don't understand," she cried.

The broad-faced MacDaniel manacled her wrist, his hooked nose and cudgel inches from her cheek. "We're arresting you. You understand that, don't you?"

"Why?"

The countess sauntered up to her. "For this."

Lady Denton grabbed the top of Cecelia's apron and yanked. Pins popped off. Silk ripped, and there for all to see was her stomacher and petticoat in brilliant Clanranald MacDonald colors. She lunged for the countess, but Mr. Berry caught her arm midair and pinned her wrist against the bookcase. Angry, infinite seconds ticked, marked by mumbles in the crowd.

Copper's tang spread over Cecelia's tongue. The same taste had coated her mouth when fleeing the countess's Arundel Street warehouse. But tonight, she was caught, and the *sgian-dubh* was nowhere to be found.

"Of course you know Clanranald MacDonald colors," she taunted. "The man who wore them couldn't bear the sight of you . . . the same as so many other men." She was vicious and desperate, a cornered creature going for the jugular. "Have you ever asked yourself why no man stays? I've heard they don't want to share the bed of a rancid viper—"

Slap!

Cecelia's head slammed hard to the right. Her left cheek stung fiercely. She laughed harshly.

"I see I've struck a nerve."

"You are a thief and a traitor to the crown." Lady Denton nearly spit the words.

Viscount Redmont elbowed forward. "Did I hear Clanranald MacDonald?"

"Yes." The countess glared ferociously at him.

His head swiveled fast from petticoat to table, his ruddy jowls jiggling. He pointed to the empty place on the table where the *sgian-dubh* once rested. "She was just asking about Clanranald MacDonald's ceremonial dagger. Now it's gone missing."

"I don't know where it is," Cecelia cried. To Viscount Redmont, "You and I talked the entire time I was here. I couldn't possibly have taken it."

"She's a known Jacobite, she is," Mr. Berry said. "She's in the magistrate's books."

"You know very well what I do in Tenter Grounds," she shot back. "Feeding hungry Scots is hardly a crime."

Glowering, doubtful faces closed in, their murmurs rising. The crowd was a costumed Greek chorus already condemning her.

The footman stepped forward. "Excuse me, my lady. But I saw her come in when the entertainment first started. Eyed the missing knife, she did. Lingered right here over it for a long while."

"You told me this was your first time visiting the Relic Room, miss." Viscount Redmont was a ramrod. "What have you to say about that?"

"I—I didn't take the *sgian-dubh*."

Viscount Redmont was hands-on-hips indignant. "Everything in this collection is the property of King George."

"But I didn't take it!"

MacDaniel jerked her like a rag doll. "You've broken the law on two counts. The Dress Act *and* thievery against the crown."

"You claim you didn't steal the *sgian-dubh*?" The countess leaned in, a malevolent gleam in her eyes. "There's only one way to know. Mr. MacDaniel and Mr. Berry will have to chain you to a wall and search you."

Breath sawed painfully in and out of Cecelia's lungs. The countess eyed her like a pitiful insect she was about to squash under her shoe. Cecelia blinked fast, a scream grabbing her throat. She searched the crowd frantically. Where was Alexander? But she already knew. He was abovestairs in the ballroom, waiting for her as they'd agreed.

Her heart plummeted to her knees.

Angry tears wet her eyes. "No! You can't do this."

The countess stepped aside. "Take her away."

MacDaniel and Berry hauled her off the bookshelf

so hard she stumbled. They held on to her, their hands vise grips on her arms. She'd have a bracelet of bruises to be sure. Terse voices rose in the crowd. Shock melted her joints. She could barely walk, which didn't bother MacDaniel and Berry. The men half marched, half dragged her to the entry where more revelers watched, talking excitedly behind fans, their eyes hotly accusing.

"Alexander!" She called for him, her cry lost in the noise of violins and the crowd.

Shame crushed her. The accusing stares grime on her skin. The thief takers marched onward, her own feet barely able to keep up. Past the front door, cool night shivered over her skin. Carriages waited. *Mary.* Was she in the crowd? She turned her head and searched but found only coachmen and footmen milling, their faces curious and no less charitable.

One figure dressed in black leaned against a tree lit with miniature candle lamps. His long blade whittled wood, the shavings falling around his feet. Mr. Wortley. His hard-as-musket-ball eyes held no pity as MacDaniel crammed her into a plain carriage that smelled of piss and vomit.

She pressed her nose against the window, ridiculously hoping Alexander would suddenly save her. He didn't. Only one man was watching her. Mr. Wortley. He shook his head and tossed the wood aside. Cold, numbing fear wanted to eat her alive. The cutthroat had warned her: *Go back to Scotland.*

Her chance to flee was gone. She couldn't save herself. No one could.

Chapter Thirty-Nine

Cecelia wasn't alone in her cell. A hardscrabble woman paced the cold confines, her yellow hems as dirty as her feet. Cecelia huddled on the floor, dank cold nipping the marrow of her bones. No matter how hard she hugged her knees to her chest, she couldn't get warm. Light rain spattered bent bars, the opening to the street below.

The restless yellow hems stopped. "Why'd they put the jewelry on you?"

Cecelia raised her head. "Jewelry?"

"The chains," the woman said as if any idiot would know. "You're a scrawny little thing. You couldn't hurt a fly."

"Flies, no. But a certain countess? I'd rip the hair off her head and scratch her eyes out if given the chance."

"That bad?" the woman cooed, stretching her arms through the bars. Rain dripped over her skin, and grime slicked her arms in various shades. "A prison bath. The only one you'll get."

"Where are we?"

"Gatehouse, and not the ecclesiastical side." The woman smirked while scrubbing her arms.

Gatehouse was a shoddy pile, once the church's prison. It had held famous men and women who ran afoul of the law. Newspapers reported stones falling on prisoners' heads, floors flooding in storms, and bars badly rusted. At the moment, Cecelia's bottom was planted next to a puddle on the floor. Citizens called for the ancient prison to be torn down, but crime outpaced good intentions, and Gatehouse was conveniently close to the Old Bailey.

"Got any family who'll bring you food?" the woman asked.

"No family," she said.

"Friends?"

Alexander came to mind. The league, certainly. But her heart and mind shoved the others aside to plant his adoring eyes and beautiful smile. Visions of Alexander asking her to marry him danced in her head. Her knight in shining armor. Why didn't she answer him right then? She loved him. Ferociously. Desperately.

A salty tear stung her eyes. She cuffed the wetness with the back of her hand.

"I have plenty of friends but none of them know I'm here."

"That's too bad. Food is scarce at Gatehouse." A clean *T*-brand scar showed through grime on the woman's thumb. Satisfied with her rudimentary bath, the woman in yellow flicked excess water off her fingers. "Name's Lilly, by the by."

"Cecelia MacDonald."

Lilly plopped onto the lone cot in the cell. "I heard MacDaniel and Berry working you over. Damn shame what they did to your gown."

Eyes shuttering, Cecelia tipped her head against the wall. Bile crawled up her throat. Not one hour ago, both men had pinned her to a wall. Their harsh hands scraped up and down her legs, ripping her stomacher and digging in her panniers for a knife that wasn't there. Cruelty had lit MacDaniel's and Berry's eyes. They'd mocked her and called her all manner of vile things.

She swallowed hard—this was only the beginning.

The cot squeaked. Bare feet slapped the watery floor, and a stench clouded the air. When Cecelia opened her eyes, Lilly stood in front of her, offering the cell's one blanket.

"Take it. It's only fair. I get the cot, you get the blanket, though be warned, its crawling with vermin."

She cringed. "You keep it."

Lilly tossed the blanket over her shoulder without a care to its inhabitants. "You know the day'll come when you won't be too proud to take it."

She shuddered at the grain of truth in Lilly's words.

Lilly squatted, her gaze on the earbobs. "Those are pretty. We could make a trade, you and I."

"They're paste."

"They're shiny and pretty, and I don't get a lot of pretty things, but you look like a woman who does."

Lilly smoothed ragged petticoats over her knees, her shrewd eyes scanning silk and torn bows. She was birdlike with a sharp nose and a small mouth, her dark tangled hair falling around pale cheeks as she fingered the silk petticoat.

"I heard MacDaniel talking." Lilly was wistful,

rubbing the painted lines. "This is why you're here. These clan colors on your petticoat."

"It's one of the reasons, yes."

"What's the other?"

"They think I stole a knife, but I didn't." A bark of laughter and, "I wanted to. I tried to, but someone else took it."

"Must've been some knife." Lilly dropped Cecelia's hem. "Are you a Jacobite?"

Cecelia's attention drifted to a corner of the unlit cell. Loyalty blurred in the dark. What time hadn't finished erasing, her current suffering soon would.

"My father was." And that was the heart of her loyalty. Admitting it freed her, which was ironic considering she was chained to a cell in Gatehouse.

"My Gemmy died at Culloden," Lilly said. "Fought for the Government, he did."

"Your husband?"

"We never married. He said we would after . . . but . . ." Head dipping, Lilly flashed a self-conscious smile. It said she really was a good girl despite ragged hems, a *T*-branded thumb, and following the drum to be with a man she'd never married.

"I'm sorry." Which was terribly inadequate.

"Why? You didn't drive a bayonet in my Gemmy's belly. Joining the army was his choice, like me joining a gang after he died was mine." Lilly stood up, yawning. "We all make our choices."

For that wisdom alone, Cecelia removed her paste earbobs. "I want you to have these."

"A trade?"

"A gift." Cecelia dropped them in Lilly's calloused palm.

Lilly petted the paste gems. "You need to be smarter,

miss. Giving gifts will leave you empty-handed, but trades . . . now that'll do you good. But I'll help you."

Lilly wandered back to her bed and settled down for the night. Cecelia hugged her legs for warmth and stared at a puddle on the floor. She might be defeated, but she wasn't crushed. Prison's quiet was giving her plenty of time to consider her choices, one by one.

Chapter Forty

London's prisoners thrived by the kindness of friends and family. One needed money to bribe warders and to pay off cutthroats who made a business selling their protection. Commerce was alive and well at Gatehouse. Cecelia counted herself fortunate to be incarcerated with Lilly, and the gift of sparkly paste earbobs a boon.

Lilly, as it turned out, belonged to the Royal Family gang. No one messed with them. Warders slunk by with mouths shut. Prisoners in other cells minded their own business. The gray morning found Lilly and Cecelia alone with the cold. Cecelia shivered in torn silks, eyeing the wool blanket Lilly wrapped around her own frame as she was sharing a tale of a brazen prison break in '49.

"This very window is where it happened." Lilly slapped the bent bars she'd stretched her arms through the night before. "Pried these bars off, they did, from the street below. Then they stormed Gatehouse, firing pistols, swinging cudgels and the like.

Two warders were nearly blinded by the powder and shot." She smirked. "That's why they leave ole Lilly alone."

As far as Cecelia could tell, those bars were the only part of Gatehouse Prison anyone had bothered to repair.

"A prison break . . ." she mused. "Will they try to free you?"

Hinges squeaked down the hall. Lilly was nose to the air like a hunting hound.

"Do you smell that?"

"Do you mean mildew and rust and the street below?"

Cecelia smelled Lilly also, but she was too polite to say so.

Lilly crossed their cell and jammed her face between bars. "No. I smell fresh bread."

One wall of their cell was bars bolted floor to ceiling. A lone torch lit the stone hallway, necessary even in the morning light. Male voices and footsteps echoed from down the hall. Cecelia sprang to her feet and ran to the bars, her ankle chains clanking.

"Alexander?"

A hulking Highlander came forward. "No, Rory MacLeod."

She grabbed the bars, hope trickling out of her. The bare-knuckle brawler's visit was unexpected. He looked worse for the wear, waxen faced with worrisome dark circles under his eyes and his brown wool coat sagged like old laundry. The broad-shouldered Highlander had to have lost at least a stone since she last saw him. Being shot and left for dead would do that to a man.

It was, she decided, the Countess of Denton's effect.

The woman was a spider stealing life from everyone who trespassed her web.

MacLeod took her shock in stride. "I brought some food for you."

He hefted a basket. Fresh-baked-bread's goodness wafted through cheesecloth covering it. The warder, a youth barely eighteen, stuck a key in the lock. Behind him, two older wary-eyed warders pointed pistols at Mr. MacLeod's back.

"Pass it through, nice and easy like," an older warder said.

Cecelia took the basket, and the young warder slammed the door and cranked the key. She hugged the basket, trying to read Mr. MacLeod's eyes.

Why was he the first man to visit her?

MacLeod looked over his shoulder at the men behind him. "I gave you a half guinea each."

The older, grizzled warder jerked his chin at the basket. "That was to deliver the food."

"And to visit my friend."

The second warder lowered his pistol. "Eh. What can he do? We searched 'im and we searched the basket. The lady's locked up, she is, and I need to take a piss."

"Go take your piss, Higgins." The grizzled warder kept his pistol on MacLeod. To the younger warder, "You, watch at the end of the hall. He so much as twitches wrong . . . come and get us."

"Aye, sir." The freckle-faced warder gave a wide berth to MacLeod. "Five minutes."

Lilly licked her lips. "I could hold the basket while you and the gentleman have a visit."

"The food should be enough to last a few days," MacLeod said.

Cecelia passed it to Lilly. "Go on. Take your fill."

Lilly scurried to her cot, hugging her prize. The mean-spirited warder slunk off, banging his cudgel on bars on other cells.

"Go on as you were. Nothin' to see here."

MacLeod touched a finger to his lips until the squeaky door at the end of the hall slammed shut. Cecelia gripped the bars and held her breath. He tipped back and checked the hall door.

"Looks like the young warder is doing his job from the other side of the door."

"He can dance a jig for all I care," she said overloud. "What news have you?"

He touched his finger to his mouth. "*Shhh.* Keep your voice down, lass. There are ears everywhere."

Knowing flashed in his eyes. No names would be said aloud.

"Is . . . everyone safe?" she asked.

He nodded. "We decided it was best I bring the food."

Her spirits sunk. She guessed the *we* he referred to was Aunt Maude, Aunt Flora, and Jenny, not Alexander. But a basket of food was a boon for which she should be grateful. Prisoners often went days without eating.

"Thank you for coming. Associating with me has become a risky proposition."

"And I have a hole in my back to prove it."

She winced. "You're looking hale and hearty for a man who was left for dead."

His smile was crooked. "I look like shite, lass, and we both know it."

Eyes closed, she touched her forehead to the iron bars. The league was so close to finishing their mission. Why, then, did they face such harsh set-backs?

"The countess shot me," MacLeod said.

She looked up fast. His bald words were delivered in a matter-of-fact tone.

"I informed the others in your league." MacLeod took extra care to lower his voice.

"I thought she was somehow involved. But why would she shoot you?"

MacLeod's face was inches from hers. "Lady Denton paid me to spy on Neville House. On all of you."

The iron bars she gripped were hard and cold, but weatherworn blue eyes staring back at her were harder and colder.

"It's the world we live in, lass."

What a stunning revelation. The Highlander wasn't going to beg for forgiveness. He was too practical for that.

"What a stony heart you have."

"I wouldna have let her hurt you or . . . the others. Nor will I."

"A vow of future protection? How comforting. Does your former employer know you're alive?"

The jibe rolled off MacLeod's back. He was a curtain wall of stone wrapped with a devil-take-you air.

"Have you gone to the magistrate?" she asked.

"I won't waste my way breath."

"Why not?"

He eyed her like a woman who'd gone soft in the head. "Because it's her word against mine. We both know all she has to do is snap her fingers and a dozen servants will claim she was home the night I was shot." His jaw worked menacingly. "There's only one way to get the woman—beat her at her own game."

"I tried that once," she said miserably. "And you see where that got me."

His gaze dropped to the chain, snaking out from under her hems.

The door at the end of the hall squeaked. "Sir, yer five minutes are done."

"Another minute. We hardly got our pleasantries out," MacLeod shot back, then said under his breath, "Half a guinea doesna buy what it used to."

The cell's cot cricked. Cecelia forgot about Lilly. She glanced over her shoulder and found Lilly sitting cross-legged on her cot, cheeks bulging as she munched bread. Hair tucked behind her ears, Lilly's earbobs spangled brightly in snarled locks as she ate.

MacLeod grabbed the bars and leaned in. "The countess is getting desperate, and I want to know why."

"What do you mean?" Cecelia pressed her cheeks against rusted iron.

"I keep going over our conversation the night she shot me, and the daftest thing stands out. She was angry about the stolen gold, but that's not what really vexed her." He scowled at the floor. "She asked if you and the others had information."

"About what?"

"The lady wouldn't say. She asked me to keep my ears open about what might've been read the night the gold was stolen."

Cecelia sagged against the bars, her vision hazing. Did Lady Denton keep treasonous documents in her Wilkes Lock safe? Papers which revealed the countess as Lady Pink and her connection to Charles Stuart? It defied logic. Why keep an incriminating file?

"Sir . . ." the warder's voice echoed.

MacLeod pointed at her. "Something in that safe has Lady Denton on edge, and I mean to find out what it is."

When night fell, Cecelia fell asleep tucked in a corner, her head and knees slumped against the wall. Hugging herself couldn't chase away the cold. Damp chill soaked her bottom and made sleep fitful until torchlight washed over her.

"Get up," a voice said.

She squinted at the intrusion, her limbs stiff and uncooperative.

A cudgel struck iron bars. *Bang, bang, bang!* She jolted off the wall. Lilly poked her head out from her blanket.

"Aw, 'iggins, whot's got yer smalls in a bunch," a voice groused.

"Let us sleep, man!" another yelled.

A voice in the darkness said, "I didn't pay you to awaken all of Gatehouse."

Fear crawled down Cecelia's spine. Lady Denton was here.

"Beggin' yer pardon, milady."

A metallic flavor splashed Cecelia's tongue. Fight and fright were a matched pair. They tasted the same as blasting a hole in a warehouse door and jumping into a stormy midnight river. She'd emerged from those events unscathed; she'd emerge from this one too. Cecelia brushed hair off her face and stared at the shadowed form by the torch.

"What brings you to Gatehouse at this hour? Looking at your future accommodations?"

Low laughter rolled from the countess. "You are a bold creature."

"Do I amuse you . . . Lady Pink?"

The jibe struck home. Taffeta swished and a black gloved hand grabbed the torch from the warder.

"Leave us."

The warder scurried down the hall and shut the door with a firm *thud*. Cecelia twirled a loose silk thread from a green bow dangling over her knee. *Lilly would fancy this bow.* The poor woman's eyes were frightened orbs peering out from the edge of her blanket. Cecelia was of a mind to rip each bow off and give them to Lilly as a remembrance of her.

"Are you going to come here?" the countess asked.

"Why should I when I'm trying hard to forget you exist."

"I am disappointed. Of the women in your league, I thought you possessed a fighting spirit."

She nailed the lady's gaze with hers and scrambled up ingloriously. She was alone, cornered, with nothing to lose. Fury boiled under the surface, the emotion fueling her to put one foot in front of the other. The chain dragged heavily. Hideous tremors quaked her knees, and torchlight assaulted her eyes. If this was a bare-knuckle brawl, Cecelia would be bruised and bloodied and the countess revoltingly fresh and ready for a fight.

"Here I am, *Lady Pink*."

Lady Denton nudged aside her hood. "Oh, you think you're the clever one, but you have no idea."

"You visited me to tell me that?"

"I'm here because I wanted to see your face when I told you your fate."

Cecelia yawned. "Then enlighten me or I shall go back to bed."

Lady Denton tipped the torch. Flames licked at rusted bars, their warmth touching Cecelia's face.

"Get used to your chains. There's a ship anchored in the Thames, *The Hannah James*. Tomorrow, you will be on it. I chose it for you because Captain Belmont takes his job transporting prisoners quite seriously. He will order his men to hold you down while they shave you bald." Her mouth twisted in distaste. "Vermin, you know. The good captain will take what's left of your ragged silks and sell them. You won't need them where you're going."

Cecelia clutched her stomacher. Behind it, bile churned hotly.

Eyes narrowing, the countess delivered her final blows. "Seven years transportation for violating the Dress Act. You'll spend each one of them on the king's sugar plantation . . . if you survive. Nasty place from what I hear."

"Seven years?"

Six months in prison was the usual sentence for the first time someone violated the Dress Act.

"Tomorrow you will be formally charged and, within a few days, taken to the Old Bailey." The countess smiled cruelly. "I dedicated my day to ensuring your sentencing."

"But my trial—"

"Is a mere formality. I've made sure of it. Justice, you know." Lady Denton brushed her hood forward. "Farewell, Miss MacDonald."

The countess walked away, taking dim light with her. Cecelia clung to iron bars, fighting to breathe. Darkness engulfed her. Outside Gatehouse, rain splintered the night. She listened to it, crushed. She could be standing on Tilbury Fort again, the day she learned her father was dead. Her dearest friends, the ladies of the league, had saved her then.

But this was different.

No one was coming to save her—not even Alexander.

Chapter Forty-One

*S*unshine beat her head, but she shivered. Higgins and the young warder led her from the bowels of Gatehouse and drove her through the streets in an open cart to the heart of Bow Street. Iron was cold on her skin and her choices. This time she was the entertainment, drawing merchants and matrons alike. They crammed the gallery, a blur of faces. Numbness was her cocoon, the only thing saving her from falling into a puddling mess.

Higgins deposited her on the bench for the accused. Five paces away was Fielding, shuffling papers on a plain table, a clerk at his ear. The clerk's whispers caused a frown to fall on the magistrate's face. She smirked. *Poor old crow, something upset his morning.*

Behind her, the gallery stirred and she braved a look. Would there be one or two encouraging faces among them? Most stared at her, their eyes sharp accusing slits. A few were Grub Street scribblers, but in the back, kind, encouraging smiles graced her. Mary, Margaret, Aunt Maude, and Aunt Flora sat in a row and Mr. MacLeod was with them. Of all the men to show today . . .

But Mr. Sloane was nowhere in sight.

She swallowed the hard lump of his absence. It was best to shore up her strength for her trial at the Old Bailey and the inevitable—seven years' transportation.

If she lasted that long.

But she would not bow her head in shame.

Fielding cleared his throat. "We are ready to begin. Miss MacDonald, come forward, if you please."

A hush descended. Her manacles clanked in time with her footsteps all of the few paces it took to stand before Fielding. Behind her, dozens of gawking stares landed heavily on her back. Fielding's linked hands rested on the table. A ledger with her sketched face was open beside him, a clerk's pencil-holding hand poised over it.

"I see your sketch artist captured my good side," she said.

The clerk chuckled.

"But it doesn't quite do me *justice*," she said. "Not a fair rendering, wouldn't you agree?"

"It's a beginning."

She raised her voice. "I'm nothing but a face and a few notes in your ledger, sir. Not even granted my two arms, two legs, two breasts . . ." She twisted around, smirking for the gallery. "Commonly known as the gentler sex."

The crowd tittered their amusement. A certain barrister-cum-government-man had relayed his private conversation with the magistrate. She smirked at Fielding. The old crow's eyes were fascinated. She was a shiny thing who would not go mutely to her fate.

Fielding offered a respectful nod. "I enjoy a good verbal sparring match as much as the next man, but this is a pretrial."

"I beg to differ, sir. I am an entry in one of your books. *That* is my pretrial."

"You object to my methods?"

"I do. Your motives for justice are worthy. Your methods, however, are ill-met."

His brows arched. "Indeed."

"The truth is in the details . . ." She nudged her chin at the open ledger. "But you have already painted me scurrilous. I doubt I will get a fair hearing."

Fielding balked, his chair creaking. A door slammed open, flooding the chamber with new light. All eyes turned to the two men racing inside. Burton was one, Alexander the other. He rushed in, black robes billowing and a sheaf of papers tucked under his arm. On his head was his barrister's peruke. The gallery erupted in loud chatter, and her knees jellied when he pushed through and stood shoulder-to-shoulder with her.

"You came," she whispered hoarsely, hoping he would hear her above the chaotic voices.

"Never doubt that I will be the man you need," he whispered back. "No matter the circumstances."

Her heart galloped fast and hard.

"These are trying circumstances." She swallowed the dry lump in her throat. "The countess visited me late last night."

Skin whitened around his mouth and he leaned over, speaking for her ears alone. "She also visited Whitehall yesterday."

Fielding pounded his table with an open palm. "Order! Order!" The chamber quieting, he eyed Mr.

Sloane. "This is a pretrial, Mr. Sloane. Your presence here is not necessary."

"I am here in the interest of justice, sir."

"Aren't we all?" Fielding was droll. He consulted papers in front of him and said louder, for the gallery, "Miss MacDonald, you have been brought here on two charges: theft and violation of the Dress Act. What say you?"

"I am innocent of both charges."

Fielding peered at her tattered gown. "A bold claim, considering you're wearing plaid petticoats."

"If it pleases the magistrate," Alexander began. "I would like to address Miss MacDonald's charges, beginning with the theft of the *sgian-dubh*."

Fielding sat back in his chair. "This should be interesting."

Alexander slapped a slim stack of papers on the table. "Here are sworn affidavits from Messrs. Berry and MacDaniel, vouching they did not find the missing knife anywhere on Miss MacDonald's person."

"Berry and MacDaniel. Do you accept the word of these two men?" Fielding asked slyly.

Alexander's jaw twitched. "They are in Bow Street's employ, are they not?"

"They are."

Alexander was formal, adding another paper to the pile. "This is an affidavit from Viscount Redmont, a man of sterling character. He testified that Miss MacDonald spoke of the *sgian-dubh* but he did not witness her stealing it."

Fielding scanned the affidavits. "Compelling evidence, but the knife has not been found."

"There were at least twenty people in the Marquess

of Swynford's library, sir. They would be just as culpable as Miss MacDonald. Some, in fact, were in the room longer than Miss MacDonald and therefore had more time to steal the *sgian-dubh*."

Alexander set another paper in front of the magistrate.

"A list of the people in the room. You'll want to question them first."

Fielding read the list aloud. "The Duke of Herndale, the Earl of Rothson, the Countess of Denton, Viscount Dern . . . Really, Mr. Sloane. This is a list of London's most esteemed citizens. You expect me to demand they come to Bow Street for questioning?"

"Does Lady Justice care about station?" Alexander raised his voice, pivoting to the gallery.

In the crowd, heads tipped one to another.

"Go on, Mr. Sloane."

"I should add, His Grace, the Duke of Herndale, lingered over the Viking sword and *sgian-dubh* the longest."

Alexander was almost innocent, imparting that news, and she loved him for it. Fielding passed the paper to his clerk as if the matter was done.

"Very well, Mr. Sloane, how do you address Miss MacDonald's blatant violation of the Dress Act?"

The magistrate was smug, folding his hands on the table. Mr. Sloane riffled through his papers.

"This is a waste of time and a gross miscarriage of justice. Miss MacDonald should never have been charged for a law that . . ." A heavy pause ensued in which the entire gallery tipped forward. "Never should've been written."

Shocked gasps filled the chamber. She turned to

Alexander, delighting in his Romanesque profile. He was a man for the ages. His mind knife-sharp, his tenor sonorous.

"It is a shameful law meant to grind a defeated people—our neighbors and kin to the north—under the Government's heel."

"Shameful or not, it *is* the law, Mr. Sloane."

The chamber was still as a tomb.

"Be that as it may, you cannot keep this woman in chains. She broke no law."

"Are you blind?" Fielding blustered. "I can see clear as day she has!"

"Parliament has a different view."

Shouts and cries erupted. Mr. Sloane raised a sheet of paper and began to read, which quieted the circus better than Fielding slamming his table for calm.

"The Dress Act states:

'That from and after the first day of August, one thousand seven hundred and forty-seven, no man or boy, within that part of Great Briton called Scotland, other than shall be employed as officers and soldiers in His Majesty's forces, shall, on any pretense whatsoever, wear or put on the clothes commonly called Highlands Clothes (that is to say) the plaid, philibeg, or little kilt, trowse, shoulder belts, or any part whatsoever of what peculiarly belongs to the Highlands garb; and that no tartan, or partly colored plaid or stuff, shall be used for greatcoats, or for upper coats.'"

Mr. Sloane stepped boldly to the table and slapped the paper on Fielding's ledger.

On the entry dedicated to her.

"The law expressly forbids men and boys wear the plaid, not women." He glanced at her, and said with the innocence of an altar boy, "We can all agree, Miss MacDonald is clearly a woman. A lovely one at that."

Cecelia's spirits lifted until Fielding's brow furrowed.

"How do you answer the law's mention of 'any such person . . .'? She is a *person* garbed in plaid."

"By definition, she is not."

"Not a person, Mr. Sloane? I'd like to hear you argue against that." Fielding chuckled and the gallery laughed with him.

"Indeed, she is a person, sir. But Miss MacDonald is not garbed in plaid."

Alexander flicked his fingers at the bench and Mr. Burton strode forward, a heavy tome in hand. The book was handed over, and Alexander flipped to a bookmarked page, and read the text aloud.

"According to the *Dictionary of Sir Thomas Elyot* a plaid is 'a garment consisting of a long piece of woolen cloth.' I also consulted the dictionaries of Messrs. Robert Cawdrey, Richard Mulcaster, and Edmund Coote and they concur with Sir Thomas Elyot. Highland plaid is wool. There is no mention of silk."

He set the dictionary on Fielding's table, while Grub Street's writers were scribbling in their pocket journals.

Alexander was solicitous. "I brought Cawdrey, Mulcaster, and Coote's dictionaries for evidence. Would you like me to read them as well?"

Fielding's glare would melt ice. "That won't be necessary." He closed the dictionary and shoved it aside. "Have you any other evidence you'd like to submit?"

"Yes, my final affidavit." Alexander set a sheet of paper in front of Fielding.

Cecelia touched her temple. *When would this charade be over?* She had never fainted in her life, but her limbs were weak and her pulse was racing. Events of the past few days were catching up with her—her life was catching up to her. There was an awful spinning in her head and her belly as if she was twirling faster and faster and might retch.

She was doomed. Fielding would never rule in her favor. But Alexander stood proudly beside her, looking at her, his kind, intelligent eyes shining with love. He was still in the fight.

"Miss MacDonald pleads the belly," he said.

"What?" She clutched Alexander's robe, her pulse weak. The world was going black, but his was the last voice she heard.

"I am the father of her child."

Chapter Forty-Two

*C*old water dripped down her temples and into her hair. She was weak as a lamb, stripped to her shift in a bed, decently soft, but not her own. She turned into a down-soft pillow, Alexander's scent in her nose. He was nearby. She could feel his presence, which was confirmed when the mattress dipped under his weight. How glorious was the feel of him, so close. She kept her eyes closed as he removed the cloth, refreshed it, and wrung it of excess water.

A kind hand wiped a cool cloth down her cheek.

"I can tell you're awake," he said.

She mumbled a groggy, "How can you know for sure?"

"I've watched you sleep."

"Well, if it's all the same, I'll keep my eyes closed. Interesting things happen when there's a washcloth in your hand."

His quiet laugh was diabolically seductive.

"I'm glad you're better. You had me and some very flustered Scottish women worried."

She cracked open her eyes. "I imagine they would be, finding that I am with child."

"There is that."

A boyish grin spread at being called out on that bald lie.

Every nerve in her body gloried in his nearness. She couldn't be angry with her brilliant knight in black-robed armor, though Alexander presently nursed her with his sleeves rolled up, his barrister's robe and peruke carelessly draped over a chair. His future, it seemed, was likewise carelessly tossed aside—for her.

She covered his hand on her face. "What were you thinking?"

"That I must save you, no matter the cost."

Her heart beat violently in her chest with need and love and deep, deep hurt. What an impossible combination to hold inside. They tumbled incongruently, her joy and her sadness. Any chance for letters patent had vanished the moment he signed the affidavit, claiming to be the father of an unwed Jacobite sympathizer's child. Never mind the charges leveled against her. And never mind that she was not with child.

"I'm a besmirched woman."

"And I love you just as you are. I love the way you curl your foot under your bottom when you sit in your favorite chair. I love your zeal for baked goods and overwrought romantic stories. I love your saucy tongue and your sharp wit and the way you look at me when either one of us says something clever. And I want us to never stop discovering each other . . . for as long as we live."

Happiness flooded her. The world was right even

though there was much that was wrong. Somehow the mess outside was bearable—because of him. She picked a loose thread on the sheet.

So, this was love, diving headlong into the unknown with a bridge of words under their feet.

"You'll never be Baron of the Exchequer." Her voice was barely above a whisper.

"Because I chose you instead."

She memorized him and this bittersweet moment. His blunt-cut queue and his need for order. His mouth, serious and sensual, the first part of his body to give his emotions away. And his intelligent eyes. They saw the world in a different, challenging way. He was a proper gentleman and a free thinker.

And he was hers. He'd certainly given up a great deal for their joining to happen.

No man had done that for her. Ever.

"This must be love, this wanting something so badly for you, yet it hurts, knowing you won't have it—because of me." She gulped and glossy tears watered her eyes.

"Don't cry. My life is with you." He dabbed hot tears rolling down her cheeks.

"But the work you could've done . . ."

"I will continue to do it. As a barrister. There's much injustice. You showed me that."

A wonderful glow spread down to her toes. This was new and exciting and hardly believable. Life with Alexander Sloane. She touched his knee as if her body needed reassurance for what her mind barely comprehended—life with him, forever.

"You were brilliant today."

"I had a lot to prove since you found me arse up in your mews."

She laughed softly, nervously. "I can hardly believe it. You and me . . ."

"Believe it." He rose from the bed. "I have something else you'll want to see."

She pushed up and flopped back against the pillows. Her body wouldn't let her budge an inch more. Sunlight filled the room as he walked, his bottom and thighs pleasant to watch. They were in the White Hart, noise of daily life muffled on the other side of the closed window. Alexander took a knife off the table and crouched on the floor. He slipped the blade between the planks and pried a piece of wood up.

"What are you doing?" she asked.

The wood squeaked as he worked. "Demonstrating my fealty to you, which is quite different than love, I think."

"Your fealty?" She giggled. "That sounds utterly medieval."

No man had said such things to her or fought so hard to keep her safe and protected. This would be a new, exciting path, a partnership with a man who saw her as his equal yet doted on her. Alexander kept levering the knife between two planks until one of them gave way. He reached into the hole in the floor and pulled out the *sgian-dubh*.

She gasped. "*You* took it?"

"I found it. After a short hunt."

He crossed the room and set the ancient knife in her hands. Time had polished the bone handle and dimmed the blade. Two small pieces of amber embedded the bone, but otherwise it was an unimpressive knife. She rolled it across her palm.

"So much ado . . . for this." Her gaze met his. "How did you get it?"

Alexander stretched out on the bed beside her and linked hands behind his head. "I waited for you in the ballroom as planned. Then I overheard guests gossiping about a ruckus in the marquess's library, and thief takers hauling away a woman accused of theft." He glanced at her. "I knew Lady Denton had struck."

"Vile woman."

"And careless. Before she left Swynford House, I overheard her tell a footman, 'Toss it in the river.' On any other night that would mean nothing to me, but I gathered that particular footman had the *sgian-dubh*. So, I kept an eye on him and waited. He went to the cellar and that's when I cornered him and demanded he give me the knife."

"And he just gave it to you?"

"With much encouragement from my pistol."

"Your pistol?"

"It was strapped to my thigh, hidden by my knight's tunic." His grin was positively rakish. "I've learned a thing or two defending criminals."

She laughed.

"The *sgian-dubh* was tucked in his coat," he said. "I encouraged him to leave London and find his fortune elsewhere."

She sunk deeper into the bed, her head on his chest. "I'm glad you're on my side. You would be a formidable enemy."

She twined her legs with his, fitting their bodies together. For a long time, they rested. His heartbeat was the music she needed. There was a steadiness being with him which fed her. The scent of his skin, the grain of his waistcoat against her cheek, his hand stroking her back. Alexander Sloane was her life. He would be her adventure, her future, and she would be his.

"What are we going to do about the countess?" she asked quietly.

"At the moment, nothing. She's on her way to Scotland secure in her false belief that she's eliminated you."

"I can accept that . . . for now."

He kissed the crown of her head. "Trust me."

"*Tha mo dhòchas seasmhach annad.*" The words poured from her heart. "My hope is constant in thee . . . Clanranald MacDonald's motto. I finally know what it means."

Sunlight glinted on the *sgian-dubh*. Her vow complete. She pushed up on one elbow and pressed her mouth to his. Alexander was sweet and salty with love and need. She drank from the well of his kiss, content.

"You are my hope, Alexander Sloane, and you will be for the rest of my life."

Epilogue

They were quiet as church mice, he and Cecelia. She was angelic in sunlight pouring through stained-glass windows. His family adored her, especially his mother. Her eyes had lit up when he whispered in her ear there'd be another wedding to plan. Very soon.

At the moment her motherly gaze was on Gideon and Phoebe exchanging their vows. All heads tipped for a view above rows of pretty bonnets, staid mob-caps, and men properly queued. His gaze, however, was on Cecelia.

"Stop it," she murmured. "Your focus should be on your brother and his bride."

"My focus should be on the object of my affection." He stroked his knuckles on the back of her hand.

They'd made a habit of removing one glove each in hacks, in churches, and in London's gardens and squares. Anything to savor each other, flesh to flesh. They'd put the bloom on each other's cheeks and a sparkle in each other's eyes. Jenny, of course, was slowly warming to his constant presence in the little house on Swan Lane. He kept his rooms at the White Hart like a proper gentleman, which barely appeased the maid.

When he and Cecelia bought a house on Evans Row, they informed Jenny she would be the stately home's new housekeeper should she accept.

Jenny had clapped her hands in glee. She'd hugged Cecelia, and she'd almost hugged him.

It was progress.

"That's so lovely." Cecelia's voice was dreamy.

She was watching Gideon and Phoebe staring into each other's eyes while the clergyman droned prosaic twaddle.

"I'd wager Gideon's not listening. Probably won't remember a thing."

Hazel eyes gleamed softly. "Will you remember our wedding day?"

He stroked her ring finger. "I'll remember you."

Was it possible love multiplied? Did it compound like interest, getting bigger and grander with time? He'd never contemplated the sheer joy of growing old with a woman. To see gray thread her hair and lines gently etch her face. With Cecelia he could. The notion settled on him like a warm blanket on a testy winter day.

It was possible love muddled his brain. He was becoming a terrible romantic. He'd purchased eight romantic novels to entice her to spend more time in bed. Yesterday, he'd spent an hour in Madame Laurent's shop designing a brown-and-pea-green shift to match Cecelia's ugly robe. The Frenchwoman had been incensed when he said the shift—preferably the ugliest shift she could make—would be a wedding gift for his wife.

Madame Laurent had grumbled about idiotic Englishmen.

But that was love. It made smart men soft in the head, and soft women smarter. It defied convention and it *was* convention. Centuries of tribes and nations attested to it. Lust might drive men and women, but love knit them, heart and soul.

Cecelia tipped her head, whispering quietly, "I was just wondering which of my friends will marry next."

"Because you're sold on the merits of wedded bliss?"

"Because I'm sold on you." She winked at him.

His mouth dented a grin, and he tried to be equally quiet. "My money's on Miss Fletcher."

"Margaret?"

He shook his head and said close to her ear, "Miss Mary Fletcher."

"Her? No. She'll never marry. Not for all the love of Scotland."

"Why? Is she too dedicated to the league?"

"More like too stubborn, too arctic, and too remote. She's a distant island. No man can reach her heart."

Their heads were bowed for a closing prayer. A quick blessing was given, an amen said, and the newly minted Mr. and Mrs. Gideon Sloane faced the congregation. Gideon shined like a man in love, and Alexander was truly happy for him because he understood.

Because his happiness—the clever blonde—was sitting beside him.

Acknowledgments

Thank you, Elle Keck, for your editorial vision with this series and your appreciation for saucy heroines like Cecelia and heroes who fall fast and hard like Alexander. Thank you, Christine, JA, and Brittani for your excellent attention to detail in copyedits. Thank you, Julie, Naureen, DJ, and Avon's cover art team for supporting my books and spreading the word about this series. You all are a talented, hard-working team, and I appreciate you!

The other half of my support team is my agent extraordinaire, Sarah Younger of NYLA. Signing with you was the best business decision. Ever. The same goes for Brian, my quiet alpha male hero. Your support ranges from doing laundry, to gentle encouragement, and telling me years ago, "You're a writer. I think you should write," when I was at a crossroads. Marrying you was the best decision. Ever.

Lastly, thank you readers. I love getting your emails and meeting you at book signings. You are why those of us listed here have these wonderful jobs. Long live books!

USA Today *bestselling author Gina Conkle*
returns to her Scottish Treasures series with

For a Scot's Heart Only

Where Mary Fletcher meets her
match in Thomas West

Fall 2022
From Avon Books

Give in to your Impulses!

These unforgettable stories only take a second to buy and give you hours of reading pleasure!

Go to *www.AvonImpulse.com* and see what we have to offer.
Available wherever e-books are sold.

AVONIMPULSE